Praise for Care & Custody

Care & Custody takes you very directly into the all-too-real world of children whose families are broken, and helps you understand the challenges and the heartbreak of trying to help and heal; this is a story for anyone who has ever wanted to help a child grow towards the light.

Perri Klass, MD
Professor of Journalism and Pediatrics
New York University

Just before I became a trial attorney, a senior Federal judge told me she uses *Law & Order* to teach her law students about criminal procedure: the original Jerry Orbach episodes were not just good drama but good law. So is *Care & Custody*. Bravo to Martha Gershun for getting it so right!

Steve Cohen
Partner
Pollock Cohen LLP

Every year, in the United States, there are over 3 million reports to Child Protective Services. This book shows what happens to kids after those calls are made. It is an inside view, written by a brilliantly creative writer who worked with kids in the foster care system for nearly 10 years. It is amazing that a book about such a troubling topic can be such a compelling read.

John D. Lantos, MD
Professor of Pediatrics
University of Missouri-Kansas City

Readers are encouraged to go to
www.MissionPointPress.com to contact
the author or to find information on
how to buy this book in bulk at a
discounted rate.

MISSION POINT PRESS

Published by Mission Point Press
2554 Chandler Rd.
Traverse City, MI 49686
(231) 421-9513
www.MissionPointPress.com

ISBN: 978-1-943995-64-6
LoC: 2018940471

Printed in the United States of America.

CARE & CUSTODY

A Novel of Three Children at Risk

Martha Gershun

Mission Point Press

Foreword

In many ways, foster care is an invisible system to most people. State and federal laws restrict the release of information about specific cases—an important way to protect the dignity and rights of the children and families involved. But the consequence is that few people understand the complexity and competing interests involved in resolving child protection cases.

At the same time, our laws enshrine important promises to children who need protection from abuse and neglect. It is a promise of safety, well-being, and a permanent, stable family. With state and federal governments spending billions of dollars a year to try to fulfill this promise, all of us need to understand how well we are doing.

But the public has little information on which to form this understanding. The news about foster care is typically negative. We read about cases where the system failed. Research studies point out that foster kids are at risk of negative life outcomes. All this is true. And all of it is incomplete.

Several years ago, during an interview on 20/20 for a piece about the over-medication of foster youth, Diane Sawyer asked me why—after so many years of legal reforms, studies conducted, and dollars spent—we still have such difficulties assuring the safety and well-being of foster youth. My answer was that we can pass all the laws we want, but change is all about what happens day after day, on the front lines where a large cast of characters work directly with and for the families and children. This work indeed is not rocket science; it is much more complicated, because it is about human nature and fundamental human rights.

I first met Martha Gershun early in her tenure as executive director of the CASA program in Jackson County, Missouri. What struck me the most was that here was someone who could take the myriad details of a complex system and extract the essential larger picture of what works and what doesn't in the lives of foster youth. Her "true fiction" approach takes you on a journey, along with the children whose lives are in the balance. It is a journey that dives deep into what can be a very dark experience. The invisible system of foster care will become very real as you read on.

What I expect you will find at the end of this journey is a realization that all children have dreams. They all have the right to expect adults to support them along that path to achieving those dreams.

It is my hope that this book will lift you up. As Martin Luther King, Jr., said "only in the darkness can you see the stars." I hope the journey ahead of you in this book inspires and motivates you to take action. Most of all, what you learn about foster care in this book will help you change the public view of foster kids. Too often, foster kids are pitied, stereotyped as hopelessly damaged. But foster youth are not problem kids. They are not statistics. They are real, valuable human beings with as much potential as any other group of youth. It just takes a few dedicated and caring people to let that potential flourish.

You could be one of those champions for foster youth. What could you do to help solve the very real system problems of foster care? Here's a start:

There are too few parents: As a result, many children are placed in group settings, even though a family setting would be more appropriate. It's an expensive expedient, costing more than seven times as much as family placement, and often not conducive to healthy child development.

> *What you can do:* Become a foster or adoptive parent. Contact your state child welfare agency to learn more.

Too many youth age out of foster care without a permanent family: Thousands of young people each year are sent directly out of foster care into the adult world, yet few are adequately prepared to make it on their own.

> *What you can do:* Mentor a former foster youth. The National Mentoring Partnership can help you find opportunities.

Foster youth often feel they have no voice in the system: Child welfare systems can be intimidating, and decisions about a child's future may be made without the child's knowledge, understanding, or involvement.

What you can do: Volunteer to advocate for and with foster youth. If you are a lawyer, you can provide pro bono legal counsel for them. You can also become a Court Appointed Special Advocate or a guardian ad litem. Even without a law degree, you can provide fact-based, common-sense advocacy for the well-being of foster youth.

Foster care systems do not always operate in ways that are conducive to healthy child development: There is sound scientific understanding of the key elements of a healthy childhood.

What you can do: In many states, reforms are underway to redesign child welfare systems based on healthy child development principles. You can urge your state policymakers to support such reforms.

But that is all ahead of you. Right now, feel free to sit back and begin your journey through *Care & Custody*. By the time you finish, you may find yourself on your feet, ready to get involved.

Michael Piraino
Co-Founder and Chief Reimagination Officer
Healing Learning, A Social Purpose Corporation
Retired CEO of the National CASA Association

Introduction

The inspiration for this novel was born during my eight years as Executive Director of Jackson County CASA in Jackson County, Missouri, where I had the honor and privilege of working on behalf of thousands of children like Tyrone, Alysha, and Hope, whose fictional stories I tell in *Care & Custody*.

First victimized by their parents or primary caregivers, these young people are forced into a child welfare system that is too burdened to function effectively and too often prioritizes the legal rights of adults over the desperate needs of damaged children. Some of these youngest victims are lucky enough to find safe, permanent homes. Some are lost forever.

More than 650,000 children are victims of abuse and neglect in the United States every year. Many of these children have been violently beaten, burned, and raped. Many more, like Tyrone, Alysha, and Hope, have been neglected by otherwise loving parents who themselves are drowning under the impact of domestic violence, substance abuse, and—most critically—the grinding effort of trying to survive in the face of daily poverty.

These children need everything. They need to be protected from violence and sexual molestation. They need food, clothing, and stable housing. They need beds. They need medical and dental care, mental health counseling, and behavioral therapy. They need school supplies and the opportunity to stop being moved from foster home to foster home, so they can finish the school year in the same classroom where they began.

But—more than anything else—they need a caring, consistent adult who commits to walking this path with them—who will do the hard work of understanding the details of their lives and their specific family circumstances, who will make informed recommendations about their needs, and who will advocate until they are blue in the face to see that those needs are met.

I retired from CASA in part because I wanted to seek a broader platform to bear witness to the journey these vulnerable children face and the heroic adults who struggle to help them find safety and happiness inside a terribly broken system.

I wrote *Care & Custody* as a "case file," so readers could experience one sibling group's story in the child welfare system as it unfolds in real time, day after day, month after month, year after year. These are the court reports, school essays, case notes, police reports, psychological evaluations, and other pieces of documentary evidence that reveal the heartbreaking trauma these children experience. This is also the story of the CASA volunteer who must question everything she knows as a successful upper-middle-class suburban professional when she comes face-to-face with the harsh realities of urban poverty and our broken child welfare system.

This book is fiction. But it is true.

We need to hear the stories of our country's abused and neglected children, in all their anguished detail, so that we are inspired to find better ways to strengthen families and provide consistent services and support to children in the system. We owe them that.

My own family and many dear friends and colleagues provided the encouragement, support, expertise, information, advice, and feedback to help convert the desire to tell these stories into a finished book.

Thanks are due:

> To my husband, Don Goldman, who left the corporate world to care for our children when they were young and later took up the mantle of nonprofit management to use his exceptional talents and significant energy to help those in need in our community. Your support gives me strength, your kindness keeps me sane, and your love brings me joy every single day.

> To our adult children, Nathan Goldman and Sarah Goldman, both extraordinary writers, who have shown me up close what true creative gifts look like.

> To Perri Klass, who gave unstintingly of her immeasurable talents as a writer, editor, pediatrician, and teacher and generously encouraged my fledgling writing efforts at every turn. I hit the jackpot when Harvard assigned us to be freshman roommates all those years ago.

To Gail Lozoff, who listened to this book evolve page by page on our Tuesday morning walks, and whose intuitive understanding of human nature has provided insightful perspective on anything and everything through more than 30 years of friendship and collaboration.

To Jim Abel, who offered counsel and encouragement on this project and every other important project in my life, as far back as I can remember. And who taught me that it didn't have to happen to be true.

To Carol Hallenbeck, my journalism teacher at Sunny Hills High School, who taught me how to write for clarity and impact and told us that real reporting begins when you leave your desk and venture out into the world.

To Doug Weaver, my editor at Mission Point Press, and the rest of the MPP team, who helped transform a rough manuscript into a real, live book.

To Gregg Lombardi, this book's first reader, who contributed ideas and encouragement, while doing his own important work to help the under-served in Kansas City.

To Rick Malsick, of blessed memory, a remarkable storyteller in his own right, who gave me books and read my poems and loved CASA with all his heart. I am profoundly sad that he died before he could read this book.

To the generous CASA staff and volunteers who shared their stories and expertise so I could more accurately reflect the reality faced by children in the system. Special thanks to Karrie Duke, Jessica Kerrigan, Laura Williams, Rachelle Kiesling, Robin Hansen, Hailey Holder, Michael Knabel, Michael Hunt, Beth Pierson, Amanda Privitera, Emma Bergin, Mercy Gbomina, Whitney Reed, Kathryn Hartzler, Lara Klover, Sheryl Kincheloe, Molly Eberle, Francie Mayer, Claire Terrebonne, Katie Wiehl, Lauren Langan, Judith Westmoreland, Anika Hickman, Megan Hover, Kate Nolen, Sandi Fried, Kelly Bergin, and Lois Rice. Your input and suggestions gave this story life and kept it real.

To Angie Blumel, Jackson County CASA's able new CEO, who graciously let me continue pestering the CASA staff with requests for help and advice, even after I retired from the agency. Under her thoughtful leadership, Jackson County CASA continues to flourish.

To Tara Perry, CEO of the National CASA Association, and the organization's generous, passionate board and staff, for welcoming me onto their team and expanding my view of the issues facing our nation's children beyond my local perspective.

To the many generous authors in the Kansas City community, including Sally Goldenbaum, Joel Goldman, Diane Salucci, and Barbara Bartocci, who kindly shared their own writing and publishing experiences and offered invaluable advice on how to proceed with this project.

And to my parents, Gloria P. Gershun and Theodore Leonard Gershun, of blessed memory, who raised their daughters to believe they could do anything they wanted to do. And we have!

Martha Gershun

Special thanks to the many people and organizations who gave permission for the use of their intellectual property in this book:

The National CASA Association
Jackson County CASA
Evinto Solutions, "The OPTIMA People"
The Kansas City Child Abuse Roundtable
Crosby Kemper III, Director of The Kansas City Public Library
Matthew Gould, Founder and President of The Giving Brick

Care & Custody
Part One

Mommy,
I'm sorry I told. We were hungry and Tyrone and me didn't know what to do. Hope was crying too. Don't be mad.

I love you.
Alysha

"Shhhhh . . . Hope . . . get up. It's time for school."

"Where's Mommy?"

"She's still asleep on the couch. Tyrone and I will get you on the bus."

"I don't know where my clothes are."

"Here are your pants and shirt from yesterday. Just put those on. Don't worry about panties. Can you find your shoes . . . maybe over there by the clothes on the floor?"

"Alysha, I'm hungry—can't we have Cheerios?"

"We finished them last night. And the milk's gone bad. But there will be something to eat at school. Let's just get there and you can share mine, too, if you're still hungry."

"Where's Tyrone?"

"He's getting ready, trying to be quiet. He doesn't want to wake Mommy. He'll walk us to the bus and then go across to his corner. Do you have your backpack?"

"I'm scared; I want Mommy to wake up."

"It's okay. Tyrone and I are here. We're always okay when we stick together."

From: Miriam Fine [mailto:miriamkfine@gmail.com]
Sent: Saturday, April 2, 2011 10:02 AM
To: hgoldstein@laramyjones.com
Subject: What's next

Good morning, Hazel—Shabbat shalom!

Remember those long years running up to our kids' Bar and Bat Mitzvahs, when we spent every Saturday morning at the synagogue? I have to admit, I miss it—not the part about listening to some nervous thirteen-year-old stumble through the prayers and offering their "wisdom" in the sermon. But the feeling of community among all those parents and all those kids going to worship at the same time for the same reason.

I even miss that mediocre tuna salad they always served at the Kiddush Lunch after services. I never understood why they used so much celery!

And I absolutely, positively miss seeing you every week. Who would have guessed that the best thing to come out of all that Jewish carpooling and all that Jewish parenting would be a friend as pure and irreverent as you?

I'm waxing nostalgic this morning. Or waxing something. It was a really hard week with mom. We had three doctor's appointments, one with her gastroenterologist and one with her allergist and one with her primary care physician. I swear, Hazel, she lies to them all! Not lying exactly . . . but she gets all dressed up for the appointments and puts on her very best "company" face. And then she charms them. You know how charming mom can be—all smiles and warm conversation—and by the time she gets around to her medical issues, she downplays all the symptoms that brought us there in the first place.

I feel like she treats her doctor's appointments like dates—her goal is to impress them with how smart and together she is for her age. Which might have been a good strategy in attracting Jonathan (what other mother finds a suitor at 80?!), but is not exactly the smartest strategy for getting the best medical care. It drives me nuts.

In the end, I'm not at all sure we are making any progress. The doctors think she is "marvelous for her age," and we leave with the same meds and the same encouragement. And then 24 hours later, she's calling me about an asthma attack or uncontrollable diarrhea. She's aging, Hazel. She can fool the docs, but she can't fool me.

I know this is one of the reasons I retired. Mom clearly needs more attention than I could provide while doing my bit as a corporate executive. (Isn't it funny that I never took time off to stay home with the kids, but now I'm taking time off to care for my mom?) But now that I'm in it, I have to admit—only to you—this is hard!!

I need a distraction. All recommendations welcome. And, no, I'm not going to have an affair.

Miri

_____

Miriam Fine
(913) 555-8436

"If I can't dance, I don't want to be part of your revolution." -- Emma Goldman

From: Hazel Goldstein [mailto:hgoldstein@laramyjones.com]
Sent: Saturday, April 2, 2011 3:38 PM
To: miriamkfine@gmail.com
Subject: Have I got an idea for you!

I'm sorry to hear things are tough with your mom. I remember that phase—when they still think keeping up appearances is more important than getting help. It's maddening. But that's who our mothers are/were, don't you think? Strong women who put the best face on every situation. And who want acknowledgment—especially from men in positions of power—above all else. It's their generation—they can't/couldn't help it. I miss my mom every day, but I haven't forgotten how hard it was at the end.

I can't help with your mother; I could barely help with my own. But I do have an idea for you (and, no, I'm not suggesting an affair—you and I both know who I'd suggest—and I know you'd never go for it—more's the pity . . .).

I think you should become a CASA Volunteer. Do you know what they do? They help kids in the child welfare system. I've run into them from time to time and just encountered them again through the firm's pro bono work; they're definitely the real deal.

They post on Facebook all the time looking for help. I just saw one a few days ago—when they post again, I'll tag you. You should do this. You'd be great. And it will absolutely, positively distract you from dealing with your mom. I promise.

Shabbat shalom—always,

Hazel

Hazel M. Goldstein
Laramy, Jones, & Haverford LLP
Direct Phone: (816) 555-3116 / Office Phone: (816) 555-3420 / Mobile Phone: (816) 555-3078
Fax: (816) 555-5298
Email: hgoldstein@laramyjones.com

Posts

Jackson County MO CASA
April 3 at 9:35 a.m.

April is National Child Abuse and Neglect Prevention Month. In Jackson County, we currently have 20 children and teens waiting for a CASA Volunteer to advocate for their best interests. To learn more about how to help, email Cherry Haines at volunteer@jacksoncountycasa-mo.org. You could save the life of a child.

From: Miriam Fine [mailto:miriamkfine@gmail.com]
Sent: Sunday, April 3, 2011 3:45 PM
To: hgoldstein@laramyjones.com
Subject: CASA

Hazel,

Well, aren't you the very best friend? Yes, of course you are—don't be smug.

I think CASA might be exactly what I'm looking for! We probably never talked about this (how is that even possible?), but I'm already connected to them. The Kappa Alpha Thetas adopted CASA as our national philanthropic partner about 25 years ago, so I hear about them in the alumnae newsletter. I never gave it much thought—too busy with Larry and the kids and Block—and it sounded like a big commitment.

And, to be honest, I've kind of kept my distance from all things KU after that bad night with Hal our senior year. But I must be getting old, because I don't really blame KU anymore—just that jerk. And it would be nice to do something good that ties back to my college days—which were mostly wonderful until they weren't.

And, second coincidence: Mom was involved in CASA! She was really active in the National Council of Jewish Women back in the eighties, when a bunch of early CASA programs were founded by either NCJW chapters or the Junior League (the irony . . . the Jews and the WASPs . . .). Anyway, Mom and her Jewish girlfriends took it on as their local project here, and they really went to town with it. She gave it up when we hit middle school, but I know it meant a lot to her back in the day.

It would make her really happy if I became a CASA Volunteer. And it would provide great cover when she wants me to do something I don't quite feel like doing. (No, no, I would never miss a doctor's appointment or, God forbid, a weekly hair appointment—but some of the other more "optional" requests—you know, a pop-up sale at Nordstrom's or a random visit to Target.)

So . . . you're a genius—maybe. We'll see where this goes!

Miri

Miriam Fine
(913) 555-8436

"If I can't dance, I don't want to be part of your revolution." -- Emma Goldman

"Come on, Hope, let's get your backpack off. There—we can look at your homework later. Look—Mommy must be home from work. There's Taco Joe's on the table. We can fix dinner later when Tyrone comes home."

"Maybe Mommy will eat, too?"

"Sure, maybe, sweetie. Let's see if she wakes up. We can save her some anyway. I'm going to read for my school book report. Can you play by yourself for a while? Quietly? Here's Mr. Snuggles."

"Can I watch TV?"

"Sure—if you keep it on really soft. And tonight we can wash out our clothes. I'll fill the bathtub, and we can pretend we're at the swimming pool. I know you like that."

From: Miriam Fine [mailto:miriamkfine@gmail.com]
Sent: Tuesday, April 5, 2011 8:04 AM
To: volunteer@jacksoncountycasa-mo.org
Subject: Becoming a CASA Volunteer

Dear Cherry,

I saw Jackson County CASA's post on Facebook looking for volunteers to help abused children. I have recently retired from my corporate career with H&R Block and would like to learn more about this volunteer opportunity. I am a Kappa Alpha Theta alum, so I know a little bit about CASA, but not much.

I don't have any experience with children, other than raising my own—a son and a daughter, both successfully launched. But I believe I am trainable.

Thank you for any information you can provide.

Miriam

_____

Miriam Fine
(913) 555-8436

"If I can't dance, I don't want to be part of your revolution." -- Emma Goldman

From: Cherry Haines [mailto:chaines@jacksoncountycasa-mo.org]
Sent: Tuesday, April 5, 2011 9:12 AM
To: miriamkfine@gmail.com
Subject: Your CASA Volunteer Inquiry

Dear Miriam,

Thank you so much for contacting us about becoming a CASA Volunteer.

A Court Appointed Special Advocate (CASA) is a trained community volunteer who advocates for the best interests of an abused and neglected child or sibling group in the Jackson County Family Court system. Our goal is to help each child find a safe, permanent home.

CASA Volunteers investigate the circumstances of their case and the situation of each child. They report to a CASA Case Supervisor and work with the child's Guardian ad Litem (in Jackson County this is a CASA Staff Attorney) to develop an action plan and recommendations for the Court.

Last year more than 250 CASA Volunteers advocated for 900 abused and neglected children in Jackson County. We still have many on a waiting list for our services.

Our next Volunteer Training Session begins April 11. Would you like to set up a time in the next few days to talk about how you can take the next step in becoming a CASA Volunteer?

Thank you for your interest in helping our community's most vulnerable children!

Cherry Haines
Director of Volunteer Programs
Jackson County CASA
www.jacksoncountycasa-mo.org
Direct: 816.555.8204

SAVE THE DATE for Jackson County CASA's 11th Annual **Light of Hope Breakfas**t on Thursday, April 14, at the Hyatt Regency Crown Center. Email LightofHope@jacksoncountycasa-mo.org to reserve your seat.

CASA
Court Appointed Special Advocates
FOR CHILDREN

Volunteer Application

Please complete this application in its entirety. All of the information is needed to process your application. Questions marked with an asterisk are required. Thank you!

Qualifications

Are you 21 years of age or older? *   ● YES   ○ NO

Personal Information

First Name *

Miriam

Middle Name *

Kay

Last Name *

Fine

Address *

5820 Lockridge Blvd.

City *

Leawood

State *

KS

Zip *

66209

Gender   ○ Male ● Female

Hispanic   ☐

Race *

Caucasian

Birthday *

11/8/1950

Home Email *

miriamkfine@gmail.com

Work Email

Home Phone *

(913) 555-9922

Cell Phone

(913) 555-8436

Marital Status	Married
Primary Language *	English
Additional Languages	some Spanish – not fluent	*
Education	BA, English, U. of Kansas
	MBA, Harvard Business School

Emergency Contacts

First Name	Lawrence (Larry)
Last Name	Kane
Phone	same
Phone 2	(913) 555-5524
Relationship	husband

Experience Please list any prior experience interacting with children.

Child Protective Agencies / Juvenile Court
If yes, Explanation: ○ YES   ● NO

Foster Care / Child Abuse or Neglect
If yes, Explanation: ○ YES   ● NO

Other Child Service Agencies
If yes, Explanation: ○ YES   ● NO

Domestic Violence   ● YES   ○ NO
If yes, Explanation:

> Raped by college boyfriend during senior year. Campus police and school administrators advised
> me not to file charges, since I had been drinking. I became a strong supporter of our local rape
> crisis center and domestic violence shelters based on this unfortunate early experience with the
> system.

Mental Illness / Mental Health Treatment   ○ YES   ● NO
If yes, Explanation:

How did you hear about our program?

I was a Kappa Alpha Theta at KU more than 40 years ago, so know about CASA from alumnae newsletters. Also, my mother was active in the Kansas City Chapter of the NCJW, so I have known about CASA for a long time. A lot of her friends (my friends now) were early CASA Volunteers in the 1980s. More recently, a friend who is a local attorney shared your post on Facebook looking for volunteers.

Volunteer Experience

Please list all current or former volunteer positions.

Organization Name | Planned Parenthood

Supervisor Name | Various

Service Dates | 11/1/2002 – 2/1/2010

Responsibilities | Escorted clinic patients, office work

Reason for Leaving | Too busy helping aging mother

Organization Name | Metro Org to Counter Sexual Assault (MOCSA)

Supervisor Name | Rachel Glickman, Volunteer Coordinator

Service Dates | 2/1/1995 - 2004

Responsibilities | Rape crisis hotline

Reason for Leaving | It just got too hard.

Organization Name | Congregation Shir Shalom

Supervisor Name | Rabbi Naomi Klein

Service Dates | 1/15/2000 - present

Responsibilities	Lay worship leader; Finance Committee

Reason for Leaving	ongoing

Employment

Please provide us with your current / most recent employment details.

Career Type	Marketing – Corporate Management

Status	Retired

Current Employer	H&R Block

Job Title	Director of Community Engagement

Address	1301 Main Street

City	Kansas City

State	MO

Zip Code	64105

Responsibilities	Assist tax offices w/ neighborhood outreach

Work Hours	None now!

Supervisor Name	No longer at company – he retired first

Contact Phone	n/a

Service Dates	12/1/1998 – 12/31/2010

Reason for Leaving	Retirement

Vehicle Information

Driver's License #

K94057365

State

Kansas

Exp. Date

11/8/14

Auto Insurance Co.

State Farm

Exp. Date

1/17/12

Background Information

Have you ever been substantiated as a perpetrator in any child abuse or neglect report made to the Missouri Department of Social Services or any other state?

○ YES   ◉ NO

If yes, Explanation:

Please describe any skills, strengths, or personal characteristics which you feel will enable you to be an effective CASA Volunteer?

I'm highly responsible, with a strong ability to set priorities, communicate goals, and work to accomplish objectives. I have a lot of experience working with others – as a leader, collaborator, and peer volunteer – and am generally well-regarded for accomplishing projects I undertake.

I'm something of a bulldog – I don't let go just because the going gets tough. I have a good sense of humor that gets me through unpleasant situations.

Do you have any personal experience with child abuse/neglect, substance abuse or domestic violence?

If yes, Explanation:

○ YES   ◉ NO

Have you ever been charged/plead guilty to or been convicted of any criminal act in the state or any state?

If yes, Explanation:

○ YES   ◉ NO

Release

By submitting this application I agree to give Jackson County CASA permission to contact any and all references I have listed. I also agree to allow Jackson County CASA to run Criminal and Child Abuse/Neglect background checks.

Initials

MKF

Date

4/6/11

Thank You

Thank you for your interest in advocating for abused and neglected children in Jackson County, Missouri.

From: Miriam Fine [mailto:miriamkfine@gmail.com]
Sent: Wednesday, April 6, 2011 9:15 PM
To: hgoldstein@laramyjones.com
Subject: Application Submitted!

Okay, Haze, I've gone and done it—submitted my application to become a CASA Volunteer. If this goes south, I won't forget it was your idea in the first place!

Their office is certainly lovely. It's the charming three-story brick house on Holmes, two doors down from that hulking Family Court building on the corner. I've probably driven past that thing a dozen times heading to Succotash for lunch—and truly never noticed it. How can anyone miss something that big?

I met with their Director of Volunteer Programs—a really nice gal named Cherry Haines. I feel like we've probably met her somewhere before—volunteering? PP support demonstration? Some community fundraiser? Does the name ring a bell? She's not Jewish, so it's not that . . . Anyway, she's really nice and smart, and she's been working there a long time.

The training sounds hard: five group classes . . . three hours each . . . Ugh! You know how much I like to sit still and listen. She promised it's interactive and engaging, so I have some hope. And I will definitely bring my knitting.

I feel silly saying this, but I'm kind of excited. I told Mom, and she was really supportive. She always is, of course—the perpetual cheerleader—but I think she really is very pleased to have me coming around to her community roots. She always wants me to be more engaged in Jewish stuff, and I think this counts. We'll see how it plays when I beg off a mother/daughter shopping trip to do something for CASA, but the set-up feels right. Volunteering trumps chauffeuring.

I think there will be other perks, too, adding a little meaning to "retirement" beyond just mom stuff and general leisure activities. You can only eat lunch with girlfriends so many times a week. And you can only work out so many hours to work off the lunches. I've already been to visit both Arielle and Isaac twice, and I think they are beginning to feel a little stalked. And Larry would definitely like to see me busier.

So—Larry and I have done a pretty good job raising up Arielle and Isaac. Let's see if all that parenting experience and that (ever-green) Harvard MBA can be put to good use! You get the credit if this works. Goals: Feel more purpose in my life / take legitimate breaks from helping mom / save a kid.

Your energized, terrified, never-bored/boring friend,

Miri

_____

Miriam Fine
(913) 555-8436

"If I can't dance, I don't want to be part of your revolution." -- Emma Goldman

From: Cherry Haines [mailto:chaines@jacksoncountycasa-mo.org]
Sent: Thursday, April 7, 2011 2:27 PM
To: miriamkfine@gmail.com
Subject: CASA Volunteer Training

Dear Miriam,

Thank you for submitting your Application to become a CASA Volunteer. I am pleased to inform you that you have been accepted for our next Volunteer Training that will begin on April 11th. We will distribute your Training Handbook at that session, which will include all of your course materials, as well as your homework assignments and guidance for independent study.

We will have snacks, soda, and coffee available at each session, and you are welcome to bring your own dinner or food to share with the group. We begin promptly, so we appreciate each student being in their seat and ready to engage at the start time for each session. In return, we promise to end on time.

Here is the full training schedule:

Monday	April 11	5:30 - 7:30 p.m.	CASA Training Room, 2544 Holmes, KC MO
Wednesday	April 13	5:30 - 7:30 p.m.	CASA Training Room, 2544 Holmes, KC MO
Saturday	April 16	8:30 - 11:30 a.m.	CASA Training Room, 2544 Holmes, KC MO
Monday	April 18	5:30 - 7:30 p.m.	CASA Training Room, 2544 Holmes, KC MO
Wednesday	April 20	5:30 - 7:30 p.m.	CASA Training Room, 2544 Holmes, KC MO
Saturday (make-up session)	April 23	8:30 - 11:30 a.m.	CASA Training Room, 2544 Holmes, KC MO
Court Observation	Scheduled individually		Meet at CASA to walk to Family Court

Once again, thank you so much for your commitment to becoming a CASA Volunteer and giving an abused and neglected child a voice. If you have any questions, don't hesitate to call or email me.

Cherry Haines
Director of Volunteer Programs
Jackson County CASA
www.jacksoncountycasa-mo.org
Direct: 816.555.8204

SAVE THE DATE for Jackson County CASA's 11th Annual **Light of Hope Breakfast** on Thursday, April 14, at the Hyatt Regency Crown Center. Email LightofHope@jacksoncountycasa-mo.org to reserve your seat.

From: Miriam Fine [mailto:miriamkfine@gmail.com]
Sent: Monday, April 11, 2011 10:15 PM
To: hgoldstein@laramyjones.com
Subject: Still Trainable

Okay, dear friend—I am not as old or inflexible as one might be led to believe—by my former employees or my children or my mother. Or even my beloved husband.

I loved training tonight!

My God, there's a lot to learn—about child abuse and neglect; about drug and alcohol abuse (did you know you can buy "clean" urine on the open market to scam a drug test??? If Larry ever loses his job or my retirement stocks plummet, I can always pay the bills selling pee); about the child welfare system (every state is unique—how is that right? Surely there are best practices, and everyone should use them!); about state family law (see previous editorial comment); and then how everything actually works here in Jackson County. Which, oddly enough, isn't like any other county in Missouri (or maybe the country)—don't ask me why. That's above my pay grade.

I took tons of notes—so much for my knitting plans.

Here's the most chilling thing: Last year there were more than 7,500 reports of child abuse and neglect in the metro area. Right here. Where we live. Where we raised our own kids. How is that even possible?

And there is a whole section in the annual government report that tracks child abuse titled "Child Fatalities." We define, count, and report the number of children who have been killed every year at the hands of their parents or caregivers. Can you imagine someone actually does that . . . kills their kids . . .? And then someone else tabulates the number and reports it . . .? My God!

On the sunnier side, the other students were all really nice. Some young-ish thirty-somethings (tattoos! piercings!). Two black men—a mid-level manager at Sprint and a retired paramedic. Their comments were really enlightening. Shame on me for my white, suburban privilege—this system looks very different if you're African-American.

The rest, not surprisingly, were women "of a certain age"—a lot like you and me. A few heavier, a few thinner, and one so strikingly gorgeous—in a tight, short skirt and stiletto heels—that I think I already hate her. Fortunately, there was a lot of emphasis on the fact that being a CASA Volunteer is an "individual endeavor." Lucky for her.

Too tired for more—and Larry has an early-morning breakfast tomorrow. You corporate lawyer types!

Lunch/drink/walk soon? Love you,
Miri

Miriam Fine
(913) 555-8436

"If I can't dance, I don't want to be part of your revolution." -- Emma Goldman

Child Abuse Facts for Kansas and Missouri

Brought to you by the Kansas City Child Abuse Roundtable

In 2010, there were 56,897 reports of child abuse made in Missouri. Of those reports, 7,676 were made for the Kansas City metro area. This was a 7% increase from the previous year. In Kansas, child abuse and neglect cases increased by 8%.

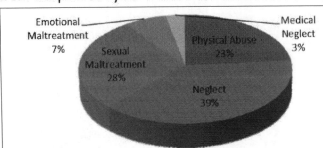

In the Kansas City metro, neglect is the most common form of abuse. This follows national trends where neglect accounts for 59% of reported abuse.

Child fatalities that have resulted from abuse or neglect have fluctuated over the last five years. These numbers only reflect the deaths that were reported.

Child Fatalities due to Abuse or Neglect, 2006-2010

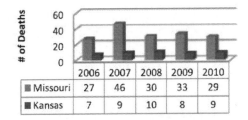

	2006	2007	2008	2009	2010
■ Missouri	27	46	30	33	29
■ Kansas	7	9	10	8	9

A child is abused or neglected every two hours in Missouri.

Children under the age of four years old are most likely to be victims of child abuse.

For more information on how you can prevent child abuse, please visit www.preventchildabusekc.org.

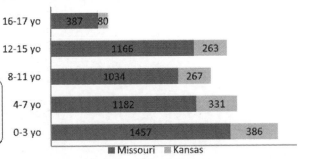

Abuse, Neglect and Exploitation Unit (ANE) Annual Report 2010-2011, http://ag.ks.gov/docs/documents/2010-2011-ane-annual-report.pdf.

Child Abuse in Kansas, https://www.kcsl.org/PDFs/29_November_2011_Child_Abuse_Statistics.pdf.

Child Maltreatment 2009, http://www.acf.hhs.gov/programs/cb/pubs/cm09/cm09.pdf.

Children's Defense Fund: Children in Missouri, http://www.childrensdefense.org/child-research-data-publications/data/state-data-repository/cits/2011/children-in-the-states-2011-missouri.pdf.

Kansas Service League Advocacy Fact Sheet, https://www.kcsl.org/Advocacy_Facts.aspx.

Missouri Child Abuse and Neglect Report for 2009, http://dss.mo.gov/re/pdf/can/cancy09.pdf.

Missouri Child Abuse and Neglect Report for 2010, http://dss.mo.gov/re/pdf/can/cancy10.pdf.

From: Miriam Fine [mailto:miriamkfine@gmail.com]
Sent: Thursday, April 21, 2011 10:09 PM
To: hgoldstein@laramyjones.com
Subject: I am trained

Haze, Haze, Haze . . . The best laid plans. It's been touch and go about whether I would actually get through my CASA training and be sworn in with my class.

Not surprisingly, Mom got hit with another gastro attack. It's so hard to predict what is going to bring this stuff on. I have a sneaking suspicion that she "forgot" to tell her dentist about the ever-lurking C. Diff bugs in her gut ("oh, honey—he doesn't need to know about my diarrhea—he's working on my mouth—it's a long way from there"), so he prescribed an antibiotic before her teeth cleaning (because, of course, she did remember to tell him about her hip surgery), and then the whole thing toppled. It is so counter-intuitive to me that antibiotics can bring this thing on—but that's the cruel irony of C. Diff.

I'm probably too harsh—maybe it was completely random—all I know is that we spent the better part of Monday night in the ER and then most of the next two days dealing with the hospital stay. Which is its own ridiculous statement, since the #1 place most older people get C. Diff is actually in the hospital.

I know you will tell me I have to take greater charge of mom's medical care—keep her from choosing vanity over providing accurate, vital info to her docs. You were such a good role model, Haze—no one could have been a better daughter than you were during your mom's last months. If I never said it before, I'm saying it now: You're a hero.

But, returning to me and my current whine: Sometimes mom doesn't even tell me she's doing this stuff—makes an appointment with the dentist, fills the antibiotic script (a CVS on every corner!), gets Jonathan to drive her to the appointment, and then, bam—C. Diff. She's at that terrifying intersection of Still-Too-With-It-To-Take-It-All-Away and No-Longer-Able-To-Get-It-Right.

But, yes, you're right—I need to do more. I will do more.

So in the end, sweet honorable generous Larry helped get Mom discharged late Wednesday, so I could get to my final CASA class. He's such a good sport—I'm not sure I'd have been up for staying with his mother in the hospital, especially if the dominant issue was diarrhea. But he loves her, and he loves me, and he's a good guy, and . . . in all honesty, she's a much better patient than his mother ever was.

So, I finished the class, mom went back home with all kinds of strict instructions that she may or may not follow, and I owe Larry big time. Nothing new about that.

Yours (always),

MKF

Miriam Fine
(913) 555-8436

"If I can't dance, I don't want to be part of your revolution." -- Emma Goldman

From: Miriam Fine [mailto:miriamkfine@gmail.com]
Sent: Sunday, April 24, 2011 9:22 PM
To: hgoldstein@laramyjones.com
Subject: Court observation - OMG

Haze—I'm almost done!

Friday I managed to fit in my two-hour Court Observation—which, probably no surprise to you, was really ninety minutes of sitting in the court waiting room and only thirty minutes of actual Court Observation.

Come to think of it, the waiting room part is probably the true rite of passage for this endeavor. I think they want to be sure you don't freak out going through the metal detector (it must be set tighter than the one at the airport, because it picked up the metal plate in my ankle) or walking up the gray, concrete staircase with the wide diagonal yellow stripes and coarse abrasive edging along every step. Honestly, I don't think they could make the place more institutional and foreboding in a Cold War nuclear-bomb-shelter sort of way if they tried.

The building sign outside aspirationally proclaims The Family Justice Center, which I can already see is tauntingly imprecise. Justice for whom? The kids? The mom? The dad? The foster parents? The grandparents? Society? I've already learned enough to know those interests are only occasionally aligned.

Anyway, the place totally creeped me out. And I'm a mature, educated, privileged (dare I say white?) woman who was visiting on a totally voluntary field trip. What must it feel like for a seven-year-old kid who's just been taken away from his mother? Or a fourteen-year-old girl who is about to go into court to face the man who raped her? Even thinking about Arielle or Isaac in a place like this makes me shudder. And they are educated and privileged (and dare I say, white).

After navigating the entrance process with Cherry as escort, we spent the next ninety minutes sitting on these curved orange and green pastel plastic chairs, which appear to be welded together. (Why are connected chairs always so close to each other?) The waiting room is cavernous, with bad institutional carpeting and packed with crying babies, scared-looking kids, sad women with bad teeth (moms?), angry men (dads?), and older black couples in hats and suits. There are also a million lawyers running around (you know this, I suppose). It's hard to tell if they are the helpers or the bad guys.

There are several men (no women) in security uniforms strategically positioned around the room. They seemed nicer than your run-of-the-mill Scary Guy in Uniform—one even smiled at me and nodded. I think they're used to CASA bringing over new volunteers and potential funders to see how the system works firsthand. I kept looking to see if they were carrying guns but saw no evidence. Cherry told me the only person who carries a gun in the Family Justice Center is the deputy in the judge's courtroom. She said he can also press a button that locks down that room in case of an "incident." Very comforting.

There are unmarked doors along all three sides of the waiting room, and each one seems to lead somewhere official. The big doors are for the actual courtrooms. There are four of those—three that look a lot like the oldest, wornest conference rooms back when I used to work at Sprint a million years ago—a big conference table in the middle, mismatched swivel chairs, and more chairs along the sides for "non-participating parties." Those courtrooms are for the three commissioners, and they each sit at the front, kind of high up on some platform thing, with a witness stand on one side and the court reporter on the other.

The judge gets the big, fancy courtroom that looks more like they do on TV (this is the one with the armed bailiff and the lock-down system)—it has tables for "opposing counsel" and an official three-foot-high carved wooden railing that separates the observers from the actual participants. Cherry told me that's the "bar," as in "pass the bar." Who knew . . . ?

I was told the other doors lead to back offices for the commissioners and the judge and other court personnel. And I think there are some conference rooms, too, for meetings with parents and families and mediators and all the other inner-workings of this absurdly complex system we call "child welfare."

But here's the really creepy part: Youth Detention is just past one of those doors! Yes, we were sitting, standing, talking, just down the hall from kids in jail. When Cherry told me that, I wanted to throw up. The messaging here astounds me: "It's okay, children, we're bringing you to this court building for your safety—you didn't do anything wrong—it's not your fault your mommy hurt you. Oh, the kids behind that door? Don't worry about them . . ."

And—did I mention—no windows anywhere! From the time you walk through the darkly tinted glass doors of The Family Justice Center, past the placards that tell you to stow your weapons and other contraband before entering the building (!), brave the metal detector, walk up the concrete designed-so-you-can't-slip-and-sue-us staircase, sit on the badly conforming plastic chairs, and wait for your name to be called to exit stage right to hear your fate in a wood-paneled room, there is not a single window.

It reminded me of a casino—and not in a good way. A place where you never know if it's dark or light outside—where the normal rules do not apply—where the regulars have adapted to some alternate reality, and you damn well better adapt, too.

These people need a marketing consultant!

The whole place made me think of a crowded inner-city train station in a Third World country, only instead of waiting to be called to board their train, everyone is waiting to be called to their courtroom. "Mitchell-Harris, Mitchell-Harris . . . all parties on the Mitchell-Harris Case, your train is now arriving in Courtroom #2 . . . Mitchell-Harris . . ."

It made me really sad. I don't think anyone expects those trains will take them somewhere good.

Do I sound cynical, my dear Friend Who Loves the Law? This is what happens when you force a grown woman through fifteen hours of training (plus one Court Observation), and then put her in a room without windows.

In any event . . . I am now ready to become an official, certified, real life Court Appointed Special Advocate. I will sally forth and save the world!

Yours (always),

MKF

Miriam Fine
(913) 555-8436

"If I can't dance, I don't want to be part of your revolution." -- Emma Goldman

From: shelling@courts.mo.gov
Sent: Wed, 11 May 2011 09:14:45
To: Camille.Harris@dss.mo.gov, Duncan.Walsh@dss.mo.gov, jriley@jacksoncountycasa-mo.gov,
hmiller@jacksoncountycasa-mo.org, Amartin@courts.mo.gov, mhosty@courts.mo.gov,
Mikaela.Johnson@courts.mo.gov, lraster@courts.mo.gov
Cc: Anorris@courts.mo.gov
Subject: *Confidential: Merritt - Washington

Names of children and parents on attachment below:

Tyrone Xavier Merritt	DOB 2/19/98
Alysha Marie Washington	DOB 4/7/03
Hope Sweet Washington	DOB 11/17/04

Parents with no apparent CASA, Children's Division or Abuse & Neglect Court history:

Joelle Jean Merritt   DOB 6/9/82

Marlin Thompson   DOB Unk.

Jerome Marcus Washington   DOB 10/24/87

Grandparents with no apparent CASA, Children's Division or Abuse & Neglect Court history:

| Mabel Merritt | DOB 8/28/49 |
| Roger Merritt | DOB 2/19/45 |

Initial Protective Custody Hearing will be Friday, May 13 at 2 p.m. in Division 40 in the Family Courthouse.

Can CASA take this case?

(See attached file: 5-11 – Referral to the Juvenile Officer: MERRITT-WASHINGTON.pdf)

Suzanne Helling
Director of the Office of the Guardian ad Litem
625 E. 26th Street
Kansas City, MO 64108
(816) 555-8083
(816) 555-4346 (fax)

Working with Families to Improve Our Future, One Child at a Time.
** Jackson County Family Court **

MISSOURI DEPARTMENT OF SOCIAL SERVICES
CHILDREN'S DIVISION
REFERRAL TO THE JUVENILE OFFICER

Date Submitted: 5/11/2011		Time Submitted: 8:00 a.m.			X	Initial Referral		
						Amended/Updated Information		

Child(ren)'s Name			DOB	Sex	Race		DCN
First	**Middle**	**Last**					
1 Tyrone	Xavier	Merritt	2/19/98	M	Bi-racial: Wh/AA		
2 Alysha	Marie	Washington	4/7/03	F	African-American		
3 Hope	Sweet	Washington	11/17/04	F	African-American		
4							

Address of Childr(ren) (Street, City, State, Zip Code)	Current Location/County of Child(ren)
4670 Olive St., KC MO 64127	Jackson County

Parent 1	Child 1		Address		Telephone
First	**Middle**	**Last**			
Joelle	Jean	Merritt	4670 Olive St., KC MO 64127		(816) 555-9384
Date of Birth: 6/9/82	Alias / Maiden:			Contact w/child(ren): Physical custody	

Parent 2	Child 1		Address		Telephone
First	**Middle**	**Last**			
Marlin	Unknown	Thompson	Unknown		Unknown
Date of Birth: Unknown	Alias / Maiden:			Contact w/child(ren): None	

Parent 1	Child 2		Address		Telephone
First	**Middle**	**Last**			
Joelle	Jean	Merritt	4670 Olive St., KC MO 64127		(816) 555-9384
Date of Birth: 6/9/82	Alias / Maiden:			Contact w/child(ren): Physical custody	

Parent 2	Child 2		Address		Telephone
First	**Middle**	**Last**			
Jerome	Marcus	Washington	Jackson County Detention Center - 1300 Cherry, KC MO 64106		Main Number: (816) 881-4200
Date of Birth: 10/24/87	Alias / Maiden:			Contact w/child(ren): Regular Visitation	

Parent 1	Child 3		Address		Telephone
First	**Middle**	**Last**			
Joelle	Jean	Merritt	4670 Olive St., KC MO 64127		(816) 555-9384
Date of Birth: 6/9/82	Alias / Maiden:			Contact w/child(ren): Physical custody	

Parent 2	Child 3		Address		Telephone
First	**Middle**	**Last**			
Jerome	Marcus	Washington	Jackson County Detention Center - 1300 Cherry, KC MO 64106		Main Number: (816) 881-4200
Date of Birth:	Alias / Maiden:			Contact w/child(ren): Regular Visitation	

Parent 1	Child 4		Address		Telephone
First	**Middle**	**Last**			
Date of Birth:	Alias / Maiden:			Contact w/child(ren):	

Parent 2	Child 4		Address		Telephone
First	**Middle**	**Last**			
Date of Birth:	Alias / Maiden:			Contact w/child(ren):	

CD-235 (REV 12/10)

The Children's Division, in submitting this **Referral to the Juvenile Officer**, requests and recommends:	

	protective custody as reasonable cause exists that the child/children is/are at risk of imminent danger of suffering serious physical harm, threat to life from child abuse or neglect, or been subjected to sexual abuse or is at risk of sexual abuse.

	Continued protective custody as protective custody was previously assumed by:
X	Law Enforcement Officer/Physician: KCPD at 3:45 - p.m. on 5/10/2011

X	the Juvenile Officer file a petition as reasonable cause exists to believe the child/children are without proper care, custody, and support and intervention is required to prevent personal harm to the child/children.

	the Juvenile Officer consider the information contained herein for informal services by the Juvenile Officer.

	the Juvenile Officer take no action as this matter has been referred to the Juvenile Officer as required by law, but the Children's Division does not believe any action by the Juvenile Office is necessary. [See additional explanation in Section 2(b).]

The basis for jurisdiction is:	

	The child is or children are from birth to but not including eighteen years of age; AND
	The child is or children are residents of __Jackson__ County, Missouri; OR
	The child is or children are found in _____ County, Missouri; AND
	Reasonable cause exists that the child is or the children are in need of care and treatment, in that:

1. The alleged conduct by parent, guardian, or custodian(s) has subjected the child/children to (check all that apply):	

	physical abuse
	sexual abuse
	emotional abuse
	no suitable caretaker due to arrest/incarceration
	dangerous environmental conditions in the family home
	exposure to illegal drugs at birth
X	lack of supervision by refusal to provide for or make appropriate arrangements for care of the child/children
	failure to obtain necessary medical or mental health services or education as required by law for the child/children
	the alleged perpetrator has access to the child/children
	Other:

2(a) The facts and circumstance of the alleged abuse and neglect are al follows: (Specifically describe the alleged abuse or neglect inclusive of all information in your possession as to the nature and severity of the circumstances, all relevant facts and evidence in your possession as to the allegation, the source of all information inclusive of the state the information was received, and the specific risk, safety concerns, and reasons supporting your request to the Juvenile Officer. Attach additional narrative as needed.) **** NOTE: If multiple children are included in the referral, please provide the specific facts and circumstances as to the risk to each child included in the referral.** Enter the Specific Details of alleged abuse/neglect.	

	Additional narrative is attached.

2(b) Explain the basis for the recommendation by the Children's Division that the Juvenile Officer take no action:	

X	Not Applicable

	Enter the specific reason(s) the Children's Division does not recommend the Juvenile Officer take any action in reference to this referal.

3. Substance use:	

	Not Applicable
	Unknown
	Describe known substance use history of concerns.
	Alcohol abuse by mother; alleged methamphetamine use by father of Alysha (Child 2) and Hope (Child 3)

	4. Prior history of abuse or neglect:
	Not Applicable
X	Unknown
	Enter prior history of child abuse or neglect:

	5. Criminal history of the parent(s), guardian, custodian of the child(ren):
	Not Applicable
	Unknown
	Enter criminal history available at the time of the referral:
	Father of Alysha (Child 2) and Hope (Child 3) currently incarcerated in Jackson County Detention Center for domestic assault against children's mother.

	6. Prior history of domestic violence: (List any incidents of domestic violence reported or reports indicating the same.)
	Not Applicable
	Unknown
	Enter Domestic Violence Information:
	12/14/2003 Domestic assault of Joelle by Jerome.
	9/30/2006 Domestic assault of Joelle by Jerome.
	2/9/2007 Domestic assault of Joelle by Jerome. Perpetrator arrested, convicted of domestic assault and parole violation, and sentenced to Jackson County Detention Center for 6 years.

7. Evidence and documentation:

(Identify all persons interviewed reports, photographs, and other information collected or relied upon in the course of the investigation and attach a copy of information relevant to or referenced in the referral to the Juvenile Officer.)

	Not Applicable
	Unknown

List the evidence and documentation information relied upon or collected in the investigation:

KCPD called when Joelle Merritt called 911 on 12/14/2003 to allege paramour Jerome Washington (then living in home) was hitting her. She declined to press charges on site and refused follow-up referals or assistance.

KCPD called when neighbors called 911 on 9/30/2006 to report fight, loud yelling next door. KCPD report indicates Joelle Merritt was bruised and crying when they arrived on scene. She said paramour Jerome Washington (then living in home) attacked her when she told him she was moving out. She declined to press charges on site and refused follow-up referals or assistance.

KCPD referred on 2/9/2007 when Jerome Washington was accused of domestic assault against Joelle Merritt in McDonald's parking lot (Jerome's place of employment). Jerome was arrested for domestic assault and parole violation. Joelle Merritt was taken to Truman Medical Center ER for injuries (broken jaw, cuts, bruises) incurred during assault.

Phone conversation with Mabel Merritt, mother of Joelle. Indicated that Joelle has physical custody of all three children. Jerome is father of Alysha and Hope and visited occassionally prior to his incarceration. Mabel also indicated that Tyrone's putative father, Marlin Thompson, has not been present since Joelle became pregnant while in high school (16) and never saw the child. His whereabouts are unknown.

Conversation with Tyrone and Alysha. Children indicate a history of domestic violence between Joelle and Jerome. Talk about activities that suggest Jerome was using meth while living with Joelle and later when visiting. Possible visits by drug dealer when Jerome was living in home.

Children indicate mother drinks alcohol in the home in front of the children and is often passed out in her bed or on the sofa, where they are unable to wake her.

Children indicate there is sometimes no food in the home. They rely on breakfast/lunch provided by the school and BackSnacks provided by school nurse for weekend food. Sometimes Joelle brings home food from work. Sometimes next-door neighbor gives them sandwiches.

Paternity:

Enter all information available as to the paternity of each child subject to the referral:

Paternity has been established on Jerome Washington for Alysha and Hope.
Paternity has been alleged on Marlin Thompson for Tyrone but has not been established.

	Reasonable Efforts and Services Provided:
X	The removal request is based on an emergency as this is the first contact with the family by the Children's Divison and the child/children could not safely remain in the family home even with reasonable services being provided to the family by the Children's Division therefore reasonable efforts were not possible.

The efforts by the Children's Division to prevent or eliminate the need for removal included (Describe all services provided including the data and service provider as may be applicable):

Case Management Services by the Children's Division: Date(s) case management services provided"

_____   _____

_____   _____

_____   _____

_____   _____

I, _____, as an authorized representative of the Missouri Children's Division, do state that basesed upon information I have obtained or which has been reported to me, I have reasonable cause to believe the facts and information contained herein support the recommendation of the Children's Division. The facts and information stated herein are true and correct to the best of my knowledge and belief. I am signing this affidavit understanding that knowingly making a false statement might subject me to the penalties for making a false affidavit.

* Further/updated information will be forwarded to the Juvenile Officer.

Camille Harris	Duncan Walsh	(816) 555-3850
CD Worker	Supervisor	Contact Information

Signed electronically in lieu of written signature.

Additional narrative as to the specific details of the alleged abuse/neglect:

On 5/9/11 Mrs. Ellen Grayson, 1st grade teacher at Whittier Elementary, became concerned that student Hope's (6) clothes were dirty on a regular basis and she kept falling asleep in class. Teacher also noticed Hope was very anxious about getting her school-provided breakfast and lunch. Cried one day when she missed picking up her BackSnack with food for the weekend. Mrs. Grayson took Hope aside on 5/9/11 and asked about her home situation. Child disclosed mother is always "asleep" and there is little food in home. She said her older brother Tyrone (13) and sister Alysha (8) feed her, wash her school clothes in sink, put her on school bus. Mother is "sick" and needs a lot of "cough medicine."

Per school policy, teacher reported to principal, Mr. Quintero. Together they spoke to Alysha (3rd grade), who initially said nothing is wrong at home. Then she breaks down, cries, and discloses mother is often drunk, children have little food and lack basic supervision. Says she and Tyrone are doing okay taking care of Hope. They don't want to tell on their mother because she needs them.

Mr. Quintero hotlines. Afternoon of 5/10/11 Camille Harris, CD worker, arrives at 4670 Olive St., KCMO, home address listed on children's school records, along with KCPD officer Ray Phoenix. Tyrone answers door and allows them entry. All three children are at home. Mother (Joelle) is heavily asleep on couch. Partially-empty cough syrup bottle and empty beer cans are on coffee table. Also partially-full container of Diphenhydramine capsules (Benadryl). Home is in disarray - clothes in piles on floor - dirty dishes in sink - cockroaches in kitchen. Children have one bedroom - all have beds with pillows and blankets.

Mother is awakened by police offier with some effort. She is disoriented, but starts to grasp situation. Cries and tells CD worker to call her mother, Mabel Merritt. Neighbor has Grandmother's number, and CD worker calls to ask if they can take children. Grandmother agrees, and children are taken into custody. CD worker delivers childrent to grandparents' home (5980 Quincy St., KCMO) and does walk through while CD office runs expedited Background Check on grandparents. Home approved for temporary placement until full Home Study is complete.

All three children are in school in the Kansas City Public School District. Tyrone is in the 7th grade (Central Middle School), Alysha is in the 3rd grade, and Hope is in the 1st grade (both Whittier Elementary). Children say they like school and their teachers. Alysha and Hope have not seen Jerome Washington since he was incarcerated for domestic assault against Joelle. Tyrone's biological father cannot be confirmed and alleged father cannot be located.

CD-235 (REV 12/10)

Photos – Washington Apartment, 4670 Olive St., KC MO

CASA Volunteer Training

Indicators of Child Abuse / Neglect

The indicators of child abuse and neglect vary widely. The behavior of an abused or neglected child and other family members may be sporadic and unpredictable, so these indicators should be used only as a general guide.

Child Physical Indicators of Abuse / Neglect

- Unexplained bruises, burns, broken bones, welts, or other unexplained injuries
- Consistent hunger
- Consistent poor hygiene; chronically dirty or unbathed
- Consistent lack of supervision, i.e., child participates in dangerous or inappropriate activities or is unsupervised for long periods of time
- Abandonment
- Often tired or listless
- Lack of adequate clothing or clothing not suited for weather
- Illnesses associated with excessive exposure and poor hygiene (home or personal), such as persistent scabies, ongoing bacterial infections, persistent head lice
- Child lacks needed medication (example: asthma medication)
- Persistent diaper rash or other skin disorders
- Sexually transmitted diseases
- Developmental delays
- Improper growth patterns, low weight, or weight loss

Behavioral Indicators in Child:

- Child begs or steals food, or exhibits other unusual eating behaviors such as hoarding food, eating others' food, eating from the trash
- Child assumes excessive responsibility for younger siblings
- Child relies excessively on older siblings or other children
- Child attends school irregularly or is excessively tardy
- Child regresses in potty training or exhibits unusual anxiety around toileting
- Child is fatigued or listless in school or falls asleep in class
- Child uses drugs or alcohol
- Child is delinquent or engages in status offender behavior such as truancy, running away from home, violating curfew, or general ungovernability
- Child is involved with Juvenile or other Law Enforcement authorities
- Extended stays in school (early arrival/late departure) or other places where care is provided
- Child states there is no caretaker
- Child unable to form appropriate relationships with peers and adults

Parent / Family Characteristics

- Highly stressful family situations, such as recent death, financial stress, parent incarcerated
- Single parent family
- Multiple children in home
- Recent marital / domestic relationship problems, including domestic violence
- Insufficient financial resources for housing, utilities, food, medical care, child care
- Mental retardation, character disorders, emotional illness of parent(s)
- Coldness, inability to empathize with child's needs
- Alcoholism, drug use
- Lack of support system; isolation and loneliness
- Poor self-esteem, immaturity, dependent, unable to carry continuing responsibility, poor or distorted judgment
- Depression or other mental illness
- Limited intellectual capacity, low IQ
- Parental history also reflects abuse or neglect
- Parents are emotionally detached from each other and/or the child(ren)
- Disorganized, inconsistent family life
- Parent unable to make decisions, passively accepts events, waits for others to solve problems/provide needs
- Parent unwilling to accept referrals for services or apply for public assistance
- Parent unable to give information on child's medical history, including immunizations, medications, allergies, injuries, and illnesses
- Parent unable to give information on childhood milestones, such as when potty-trained, first began talking, learned to walk
- Parent has serious illness or long-term chronic medical condition
- Custodial parent cannot be found
- Parent provides for self before providing for needs of child (examples: bed, clothing, coat, shoes)
- Parent is apathetic, feels nothing will change.

From: Jonathan Riley [mailto:jriley@jacksoncountycasa-mo.org]
Sent: Wednesday, May 11, 2011 1:13 PM
To: shelling@courts.mo.gov, Camille.Harris@dss.mo.gov, Duncan.Walsh@dss.mo.gov, hmiller@
jacksoncountycasa-mo.org, Amartin@courts.mo.gov, mhosty@courts.mo.gov, Mikaela.Johnson@
courts.mo.gov, lraster@courts.mo.gov
Cc: ablackstone@jacksoncountycasa-mo.gov
Subject: *Confidential: Merritt - Washington

CASA will take this case.

We're prepared to handle the 72-Hour Meeting and Protective Custody Hearing on Friday.

We have assigned CASA Staff Attorney Henrietta Miller as Guardian ad Litem, and Case Supervisor Anita Blackstone is assigning a CASA Volunteer, who will be present for the meeting and hearing.

Jonathan Riley
JACKSON COUNTY CASA
Director of Case Supervision
2544 Holmes
Kansas City, Missouri 64108
www.jacksoncountycasa-mo.org

Phone: 816.555.8218
Fax: 816.555.7788

SAVE THE DATE for Jackson County CASA's 7th Annual **Carnival for CASA** on Saturday, Sept 17, at Paradise Park in Lee's Summit. Email Carnival@jacksoncountycasa-mo.org to learn about Sponsorship opportunities and to purchase tickets for this family-friendly event.

From: Anita Blackstone [mailto:ablackstone@jacksoncountycasa-mo.org]
Sent: Wednesday, May 11, 2011 4:37 PM
To: miriamkfine@gmail.com
Cc: hmiller@jacksoncountycasa-mo.org
Subject: *Confidential: Merritt – Washington – meeting in advance of 72 hour

Hi Miriam,

It was great to "meet" you on the phone today. Thank you so much for agreeing to take this case.

As we discussed on the phone, we'll meet tomorrow at CASA at 10:30 a.m. I'll provide you with a copy of the Referral to the Juvenile Office that lays out the initial charges in this case, and we can talk about our strategy for the 72-hour meeting on Friday. As we discussed, we'll walk over to Court after the 72-hour for the Protective Custody hearing.

CASA Staff Attorney Henrietta Miller will be serving as the children's Guardian ad Litem (GAL), and I have copied her on this email. She is appointed as the children's lawyer, to represent their best interests before the Court throughout these proceedings. She'll rely on you for information about the children and family and your recommendations, but she's the one who will actually talk to the judge in Court and file any motions on their behalf.

I've set up a Case File for this case in OPTIMA, our case management system, and enabled your database rights as the CASA Volunteer on the case. The login and password you received during training will give you access. You can enter your volunteer notes after you meet the children and attend the hearing on Friday. Going forward, this will be your #1 way of communicating with us and providing your observations and recommendations for the Court. We all rely heavily on OPTIMA to keep track of how the kids are doing and what's going on at every stage of the case.

Let me know if you have any questions or concerns—now or at any time during the case. My cell is (816) 555-7943. I look forward to working with you!

Anita Blackstone
Case Supervisor
(816) 555-8236

SAVE THE DATE for Jackson County CASA's 7th Annual **Carnival for CASA** on Saturday, Sept 17, at Paradise Park in Lee's Summit. Email Carnival@jacksoncountycasa-mo.org to learn about Sponsorship opportunities and to purchase tickets for this family-friendly event.

From: Miriam Fine [mailto:miriamkfine@gmail.com]
Sent: Wednesday, May 11, 2011 8:15 PM
To: hgoldstein@laramyjones.com
Subject: I'm a real CASA now!

I've taken my first case! One of the CASA Case Supervisors just called. Her name is Anita Blackstone.

She sounds young—couldn't be much older than Arielle. But I think she knows what she's doing. (Mostly I think Arielle knows what she's doing, too, of course. Mostly. Don't tell her that her mother said that.) I'm going to CASA tomorrow to meet her and prepare for our first meeting with the kids on Friday.

I don't think I'm supposed to divulge case details—I signed a really official looking confidentiality document. I'm attaching it here. You're a lawyer—how much can I tell you? Can this fall under some attorney/client privilege? If I tell you, will I go to breach-of-contract hell?

For now, I'll keep it really general: three kids, all school age. This isn't one of those horrific stories you read about in the paper. No one was burned or raped or locked in a closet. At least not that I know of. I suppose it's my job to find out for sure. I think it's one of those "poverty" cases we learned about in training. Single mom, had her first kid in high school at 16 (remind me, please, to double my annual donation to Planned Parenthood!), dropped out, ended up in an abusive relationship. Mental illness and then alcohol abuse (or maybe the other way around?), and now she just can't take care of three kids.

Poor woman. I remember how hard it was to take care of TWO—and Larry is one of those great husbands who helped (a lot)! (Yours, too, I know that . . .) It was early in our careers, and we weren't rich, but we had a nice house, and there was always money to pay for food and clothes and babysitters when we just had to get a break. Not to mention my bi-weekly appointments with Carol. God, I miss Carol—how does anyone raise children without a good therapist?

So . . . my heart already goes out to this poor mom. Don't tell anyone at CASA—my job is always "best interests of the children." The adults' needs and desires aren't supposed to figure in. But you know what I mean—if we thought raising children was hard . . . imagine what it's like for her!

I don't know much more yet—and I probably couldn't tell you anyway. (Legal opinion on this— please??!! I don't see how I can do this if I can't tell you about it!) Anyway, for now—I'm really excited and really scared. I hope this young Anita can tell me what to do. I suddenly feel like the entire future of these three kids depends on me.

And everyone told me I'd be bored and irrelevant after I retired. Hah!

Your energized, terrified friend,

Miri

Miriam Fine
(913) 555-8436

"If I can't dance, I don't want to be part of your revolution." -- Emma Goldman

Volunteer
Confidentiality Agreement

- Volunteers must respect children's and families' rights to privacy in regard to personal information.

- Disclosure or verification of case information shall not be made to anyone who does not have a professional reason for receiving such information.

- No information shall be released to anyone not authorized to receive it, without the express written and dated consent of the party.

- Confidential information shall only be shared with professional staff at Jackson County CASA, Missouri Children's Division, and the Jackson County Family Court.

- Case records and notes, including all computer files, shall be secured and kept private and inaccessible to public view.

- Discussions of case related information are not to be held in public places.

- It is the CASA Volunteer's job to transmit the information s/he collects to the child's Guardian ad Litem and the Court. It is important to let all parties to a case know this at the beginning of a case.

- No one outside of CASA program personnel may have access to a CASA Volunteer's case record and activity reports without a court order.

- Any confidential materials received from another individual or agency may not be disclosed to anyone outside the CASA program's professional staff, except by court order or written consent of the party involved.

Duty to Disclose:

- CASA Volunteers are mandated reporters in the state of Missouri and have a duty to immediately disclose suspected child abuse or neglect to their CASA Case Supervisor.

- Volunteers have a duty to immediately disclose to their supervisor knowledge/ information that a party may harm himself/herself or others.

Any volunteer found to have violated these confidentiality requirements will be dismissed from service as a CASA Volunteer.

I understand and agree to adhere to the confidentiality policies outlined above.

Printed Name	Signature	Date

From: Hazel Goldstein [mailto:hgoldstein@laramyjones.com]
Sent: Friday, May 13, 2011 7:02 AM
To: miriamkfine@gmail.com
Subject: Good luck—you're doing a mitzvah!

So, today you get to walk into a courtroom in an official capacity—welcome to the world Larry and I inhabit on a regular basis! Not that Family Law is anything like commercial litigation or white collar criminal defense work—but you know what I mean. It makes me happy, in an odd sort of way—the Harvard MBA finally comes to her senses and pursues the law. It was clearly just a matter of time . . .

Okay, all kidding aside—good luck today. I know these children are amazingly lucky to have you on their side. It sounds like not much has gone right for them so far in life. No matter what happened in that home, getting yanked away from your mother by the cops and a state social worker has got to be traumatic. Maybe getting you as their CASA Volunteer is their turning point.

I'm really proud of you, Miri. You've always had a heart for good—and you're one of the smartest people I know. Not to mention your soft spot for kids. That's why John and I asked you and Larry to be the guardians for Joshua and David if anything ever happened to us all those years ago. I always knew you'd step up and do whatever had to be done for the children. And now you get to do it for kids who really, really need you.

So, dear friend, Godspeed today. I'll be eager to hear all about it. As my mom would have said: *"Gai gezunterhait!"*

Love you,

Hazel

P.S. I checked with the lawyer at the firm who handles our pro bono cases in Family Court. This isn't an official legal opinion, but he thought it would be fine if you told me about your case in very general terms. He said you shouldn't disclose identifying facts about the children or the family—no names, addresses, neighborhoods, schools, doctors, that sort of thing. He suggested referring to adults by their relationship to the kids (mom, grandma, asshole dad who beat the woman up, that sort of thing). You might check with your CASA supervisor, too, just to be sure.

Not your lawyer, just your friend,
HMG

Hazel M. Goldstein
Laramy, Jones, & Haverford LLP
Direct Phone: (816) 555-3116 / Office Phone: (816) 555-3420 / Mobile Phone: (816) 555-3078
Fax: (816) 555-5298
Email: hgoldstein@laramyjones.com

Staff
Dashboard

Volunteers
Dashboard

Volunteers

Lookup
Tables

Cases

User
Administration

Reports

Contact Log

Name	Fine, Miriam
Case Number	594
Activity Date	5/13/2011
Activity Type	Court Hearing
Subject	72 Hour Meeting / PC Hearing
Location	CASA / Court
Contact Type	Face-to-face
Hours	2.00

Notes:

Met all three children (Tyrone, Alysha, Hope) at CASA during 72-hour meeting in advance of the Protective Custody Hearing at Court at 2 p.m. Introduced myself as Ms. Fine -- their CASA -- which means I am there to help them. Said my job is to be sure they understand everything that is going on and also to tell the judge and other adults anything they want them to know. I said I am a volunteer -- no one is paying me to do this -- I'm here for you.

I don't know if they understood. They are still very much in shock from the initial removal two days ago. Mom entered the conference room and both girls ran over to hug her. Alysha kept repeating "I'm sorry, I'm sorry." She clearly feels guilty that she "told" on her mother. Mom seemed shaken, but composed. Hugged girls and gestured for Tyrone to come over, too. He seemed uncertain, but came over and hugged her.

Mom told them "Grandma and Grandpa will take good care of you. I'll see you a lot. This will be okay. We'll be together again soon." Grandmother came over and pried girls away. Hope sat on her lap and Alysha sat between mom and Tyrone.

Introduced myself to mom and told her I was her children's volunteer advocate. Said her lawyer could explain my role and how I would be helping her children. She nodded. Introduced myself to grandparents, who took my card. I think they want all the help they can get and will remember who I am. The children seem comfortable around them -- as if they know them well.

I took each child aside into the hallway and told them after the meeting everyone would take a short walk next door to meet the judge. I asked if there was anything they wanted me to tell him. Tyrone said: "Tell him we can go home. I can take care of my sisters." Alysha said: "Tell him I'm sorry I told about Mommy. We just want to go home." Hope just cried.

I sat between the children and Henrietta Miller, CASA Attorney, during the PC Hearing. Tyrone looked attentive but I don't think any of them understood the proceedings. It was all very official, with a lot of legalistic language and ritual. After the hearing we spoke briefly in the Waiting Room. I explained to the children that they would be going home with their grandparents for now, and the judge said they could see their mother very soon. I confirmed with grandmother that she was able to drive the children to their previous Middle and Elementary Schools, so there would be no disruption there. I asked if there was anything she needed, and she said no, that the children often visited and she had what they needed for now. She would go over to her daughter's house on the weekened and pick up clothes and toys and Tyrone's asthma medicine. I told grandmother I would call to find a time to visit next week. I told the children I would see them next week.

Children walked out with grandparents and mom and CD worker, so I did not see if departure was difficult.

IN THE CIRCUIT COURT OF JACKSON COUNTY, MISSOURI
FAMILY COURT DIVISION

IN THE INTEREST OF: **TYRONE MERRITT**
                      ALYSHA WASHINGTON
                      HOPE WASHINGTON

PETITION NO: **1416-JU0040987**
                    1416-JU0040988
                    1416-JU0040989

ORDER OF COURT UPON PROTECTIVE CUSTODY HEARING PURSUANT TO RULE 123.05

Now on <u>13 MAY 2011</u>, the following parties appear:

_X_ Juvenile:	**TYRONE MERRITT**	_X_ GAL for Juvenile:	**Henrietta Miller (CASA)**
_X_ Juvenile:	**ALYSHA WASHINGTON**		
_X_ Juvenile:	**HOPE WASHINGTON**		

_X_ Mother:	**JOELLE MERRITT**	____ Counsel for Mother:	_____
____ Father:	_____	____ Counsel for Father:	_____
____ Father:	_____	____ Counsel for Father:	_____
____ Father:	_____	____ Counsel for Father:	_____
____ Guardian:	_____	____ Other:	_____
____ CD Worker:	**CAMILLE HARRIS**	____ Counsel for JO:	**ABIGAIL NORRIS**

____ CD provided notification of this hearing to _____ , however _____ failed to appear.

The court takes judicial notice of the contents of its own file(s) and upon considering the information presented at this hearing finds:

_X_ It is necessary for the juvenile(s) to remain in protective custody.

____ It is not necessary for the juvenile to remain in protective custody and the child can be safely returned home immediately.

____ Children's Division made reasonable efforts to prevent or eliminate the need for removal of the juvenile from the home.

____ Children's Division did not make reasonable efforts to prevent or eliminate the need for removal of the juvenile from the home.

_X_ An emergency required the juvenile to be taken into judicial custody and, as a result, the Children's Division is deemed to have made reasonable efforts to prevent or eliminate the need for removal of the juvenile from the home.

_X_ Continuation of the juvenile in the home is contrary to the welfare of the juvenile.

____ The Children's Division has offered services to the juvenile's parents, guardian or custodian as follows:

_____

_____

_____

Accordingly the court enters the following findings and orders:

_X_   Until further order of the court, the juvenile is to remain in protective custody and in the temporary legal
        custody of:
                    _X_   Children's Division licensed placement:
                                CD may place with maternal grandparents if CASA/GAL agrees and mother does
                                not reside there (pending completion of approved Home Study).
                    ____   Other: _____, under the supervision of the Children's Division.

The court finds that the placement ordered is the most appropriate placement and is consistent with the best
interests and needs of the child(ren).
        ____   Capias shall be issued for the juvenile as the parent(s) have failed to produce the child for hearing.
        ____   The child is an Indian child as defined in 25 U.S.C. section 1903. Notification as required by ICWA
                    shall be made to the juvenile's tribe.
        ____   The child has special needs, _____. CD shall assess whether immediate services are required.

Visitation:
_X_   No contact with: ____ Mother   _X_ Father   ____ Other
_X_   Visitation with: _X_ Mother   ____ Father   ____ Other
        Visitation is to be supervised by <u>CD or parent aid or approved relative when appropriate</u>
        ____   Visitation with siblings shall occur as ordered: _____

Kinship Placement Options:
        ____   The Relative/Kinship Statement has been provided to _____
        ____   The Children's Division is ordered to investigate _____ as a possible relative/kinship
                    placement and shall present a home study to the court at the next hearing.

Paternity:
_X_   The court orders that the CD immediately begin proceedings to determine the paternity of <u>Tyrone</u>
        <u>Merritt.</u>
        ____   The court notes that paternity of this child has been established by court order in case number
        _____.
        ____   The mother is hereby ordered to disclose to the CD and the Juvenile Officer the name and current
                    address of all potential fathers of this child. Such disclosure shall be submitted in writing to the
                    CD and the Juvenile Officer with 10 days of this order.

Attorney Appointments:
_X_   Appointment of counsel for the mother
____   Appointment of GAL for the mother due to mental status or age
____   Appointment of counsel for the father
____   Appointment of GAL for the father due to mental status or age
____   Appointment of counsel for _____
____   Appointment of GAL for _____ due to mental status or age

PETITION NO: 1416-JU0040987 / 8 / 9

Voluntary Services:

The Children's Division is ordered to fund and provide the following services, which are voluntary unless otherwise ordered:

_X_ Psychological evaluation of: _X_ Mother ____ Father ____ Custodian _X_ Juvenile(s)

____ Psychiatric evaluation of: ____ Mother ____ Father ____ Custodian ____ Juvenile(s)

_X_ Substance abuse screening/evaluation of: _X_ Mother ____ Father ____ Custodian ____ Juvenile(s)

____ Individual therapy for: ____ Mother ____ Father ____ Custodian ____ Juvenile(s)

____ Developmental assessment of juvenile: _____

_X_ Parent Aide to supervise visitation for: _X_ Mother ____ Father ____ Custodian

____ Hair test for: ____ Mother ____ Father ____ Custodian ____ Juvenile(s)

_X_ Random drug testing for: _X_ Mother ____ Father ____ Custodian

NOTICE: Please be advised that failure to provide financial and other in-kind support for the child, while the child is out of your home, even if there is not an order for support, could be a ground for terminating your parental rights at a later date. You should maintain written evidence of any support provided.

The parents are required to cooperate with counsel and the court may permit counsel to withdraw from representation if the parties refuse or fail to cooperate.

Copies of this order were distributed to the parties at the hearing, if they appeared.

5-13-11   *Gerard E. Solomon*

_____

DATE   JUDGE/COMMISSIONER, FAMILY COURT DIVISION

IN THE CIRCUIT COURT OF JACKSON COUNTY, MISSOURI
FAMILY COURT DIVISION

APPLICATION FOR APPOINTMENT OF ATTORNEY TO REPRESENT ADULT

IN THE INTEREST OF:

JUVENILE NAME		BIRTHDATE	CASE NUMBER
Tyrone X. Merritt	(MALE) FEMALE	2/19/98	594
Alysha M. Washington	MALE (FEMALE)	4/7/03	594
Hope S. Washington	MALE (FEMALE)	11/17/04	594
	MALE/FEMALE		
	MALE/FEMALE		

This application is for an attorney for: ☒ Mother ☐ Father ☐ Custodian (If not parent) ☐ Guardian

VERIFICATION

I swear that I am the parent, guardian or custodian of the above-named child(ren) pursuant to 211.110 RSMo, that the following statement of income and assets are true and accurate to the best of my knowledge and belief and that I am without funds and property to enable me to employ counsel to represent me in this case. Specifically:

Are You Employed?
__X__ YES _____ NO   Where Taco Joe's

THE NEXT TWO STATEMENTS MUST BE COMPLETED TO DETERMINE ELIGIBILITY $1,130

My total monthly family income received by all members of my household is: $ ~~1,300~~ .
The number of persons residing in my household is: __4__ . (3 are children)

The following people contribute to the household income: _just me_ .

The total value of the automobiles I own is: $ 3,000 .

Do you own a home? _____ YES __X__ NO If yes, monthly mortgage payment is: $ _____ .

Please state the amount and type of any large debts you have. _NONE_

I hereby request that the court appoint an attorney to represent me in this case. If I have not yet been served, I waive service of summons for the limited purpose of permitting the court to appoint an attorney to represent me in this case. I otherwise do not waive my rights to notice of these proceedings.

Joelle J. Merritt	Joelle Merritt	419-48-8482
APPLICANT'S NAME (PRINT)	SIGNATURE	SOC. SEC. NUMBER
4670 Olive St.	Kansas City, MO 64127	(816) 555-9384
ADDRESS	CITY, STATE, ZIP CODE	PHONE NUMBER
		5/13/11
Email		DATE

TO THE APPLICANT: If your application is approved by the court, an attorney will be appointed for you in the next few days. You should contact the appointed attorney as soon as you receive notice of the appointment so that the attorney can assist in this case.

Rev. 9/03   For Court Use Only: Qualified? _____ YES _____ NO

From: Miriam Fine [mailto:miriamkfine@gmail.com]
Sent: Friday, May 13, 2011 9:42 PM
To: hgoldstein@laramyjones.com
Subject: Hard stuff

Oh, Haze—it was so hard. The kids were crying. The mom was crying. The teen-age boy was trying to hold it together, but he just looked ruined. I can't believe the best society can do is wait for a woman like this to get in so deep that all she can do is drink herself into oblivion on the couch and abandon her kids to their own devices. And then we step in? How does that make any sense?

Surely there are places she could have gone to get help? I know AA is free, but I think her problems were way bigger than that. Anita says there are a couple of free mental health clinics in the urban core, but they have really long waiting lists. And I'm not sure this mom had it together enough to seek out help—even free help. I know I'm supposed to be all about the kids, but I couldn't help feeling desperately sorry for her, too.

The good news is that the grandparents seem to be good people—he has a steady job as a school janitor, and she is a homemaker. I think they are deeply sad and embarrassed and angry that their daughter got into this much trouble and put her own kids at risk. They aren't ready to cut her off yet, but I can tell they will if they have to—they are all about the grandkids now.

Anyway . . . the kids are cute and sad. I don't think they understand who I am yet—I'm not sure they understand much of anything right now. The grandparents seem to have it together; I think the kids will be fine staying there while it all sorts out. I'm going early next week to check out the house and start "building a relationship," as Anita says.

Larry and I are going to the Tivoli tomorrow night to see The Girl with the Dragon Tattoo. Do you guys want to come? Mom is in a good place right now—planning to go to that musical at the JCC on Sunday with Jonathan. And I'm ready for some sex and intrigue to take my mind off the true horrors of the world. Come with us, won't you? Maybe even a stop for drinks at Kelly's Westsider after. . . ? Or at least popcorn during the show?

MKF

Miriam Fine
(913) 555-8436

"If I can't dance, I don't want to be part of your revolution." -- Emma Goldman

Staff   Volunteers   Volunteers   Lookup   Cases   User   Reports
Dashboard   Dashboard   Tables   Administration

Contact Log

Name	Fine, Miriam
Case Number	594
Activity Date	5/18/2011
Activity Type	Placement Visit
Subject	Child welfare
Location	Grandparents' Home
Contact Type	Face-to-face
Hours	1.00

Notes:

Went to visit children for the first itme in their grandparents' home after school, accompanied by Camille Harris, CD worker, and Anita Blackstone, CASA Case Supervisor. Anita suggested we all go at the same time, as Camille needed to visit that week anyway, and it would be less disruptive for the family.

The two-story single family house is small and showing some signs of age, located on a residential street that seems to be mostly occupied by African-American families. I saw a few other kids playing tag out front. Mabel greeted us at the door and seated us in the living room; said Roger was still at work. She seemed happy to have us, offered iced tea. The furniture is like the house - a little shabby, but functional. The house appears clean and cared for.

Mabel asked the kids to come sit with us, and I reminded them that I was their CASA Volunteer, and it was my job to be sure they were okay and look out for what they needed. I asked the girls to show me around the house. They share a bedroom, with bunk beds and cute "girly" sheets and comforters. Alysha told me they often spent the night with their grandparents before and this room had been "theirs" for a long time. There was a basket on the floor with books and video games, and a dresser for their clothes. Alysha told me they do their schoolwork at the kitchen table. She showed me the bathroom that all three children share - just off the hallway by the living room.

I asked Hope to go sit with her grandmother so I could talk to Alysha alone. She was quiet, but asked when she could see her mother. She said she wanted to tell her that she was sorry for telling and that she wanted them all to go back home. I told her that children should always tell the truth, and she did the right thing. I asked if she wanted to write a note to her mom. I said I could be sure that got delivered. I also told her Ms. Harris, who was in the living room with her grandmother, was setting up a time for them to see their mother very soon. She brightened at that, and then confided that she was a very good reader and had a lot of books at school.

She switched places with Hope, so we could talk alone. Hope seems very attached to her older siblings, and is very anxious when one of them isn't in the room with her. She said she "wanted mommy," and showed me her bunny, Mr. Snuggles, that her grandmother had brought back when she went to the house for their clothes.

I found Tyrone in his room playing a video game. His room is much smaller than the girls', but it has a bed and a dresser and a wooden desk he said his grandfather made for him. When I asked, he said he uses the family computer in the living room for a lot of his homework. Tyrone tried very hard to act grown-up and answer questions the way he thought an adult would. He provided information, but did not disclose any emotions. He said he hoped they could see their mother soon because his sisters "cry for her at night."

I rejoined Mabel and the others in the living room and confirmed that she had gotten the clothes and toys the children need from her daughter's home. She also picked up Tyrone's asthma medicine and emergency inhaler. I confirmed that the children are not on any other medications. I asked if she needed anything for the children, and she said it was hard to drive them to their two separate schools every morning. She asked if there was money to help her pay for gas. Camille said she would check with CD.

When we left Roger had come home from work and was in the kitcfhen putting a frozen pizza into the oven for dinner.

I agree with the CD decision to place the children in their grandparents' home and recommend this placement, pending the completed Home Study.

Activity Status	Approved

From: Miriam Fine [mailto:miriamkfine@gmail.com]
Sent: Wednesday, May 18, 2011 10:55 PM
To: ablackstone@jacksoncountycasa-mo.org
Subject: *Confidential: Merritt—Washington—questions after 5/18/11 home visit

Anita,

I'm so glad you were with me on my first visit to meet the kids today. I was nervous, and it really helped to have you there. I think I'll be good to go on my own the next time—Mabel and Roger seem very nice and not at all distressed about having strangers in their home. I think they know we really want to help.

Also, thank you for the advice about how much/little to disclose to friends and family when talking about my CASA work. It sounds like it's okay to talk in general about my case and what I'm doing: I'm going on a home visit this afternoon; I have Court today; I'm sad that the children miss their mom. What I can't do is reveal any specifics that would let anyone else identify these kids or this family: no names, no addresses, no schools, etc. Do I have that right? I don't want to break any rules or put CASA at risk in any way.

I went ahead and put the visit into an activity report in OPTIMA when I got home. Can you take a look and see if this is what you would expect from a Volunteer Activity Report? Is this appropriate to forward to the GAL and the Court as my recommendation for the children? I wasn't sure how much detail to put in—I can do more or less, and will be guided by your good counsel going forward.

I have three questions after today's visit:

I heard Mabel ask Camille if there was any way CD could help pay for the added expense of driving the kids to school, since they are now living outside the school bus boundaries. Camille said she'd "look into it." How does that work? What can I do to help with that?

Even to a layman, it's pretty clear that the kids are going to need counseling. Hope is melancholy and withdrawn; Alysha feels guilty; and Tyrone is basically suppressing all emotion and trying to act like an adult instead of a 13-year-old kid whose entire life has just been turned upside down. How do we make that happen? Camille didn't look like she was in any hurry to get a referral. I think the kids need to see someone ASAP. What can I do?

Alysha told me she really likes to read. I know we're not supposed to bring gifts or treats for the kids, but I wondered if books would be okay. I'd like to do something small to build a connection—and maybe just to make myself feel better.

Thanks for your help—I promise I'll get the hang of this soon and not bug you every single time!

Best,

Miram

Miriam Fine
(913) 555-8436

"If I can't dance, I don't want to be part of your revolution." -- Emma Goldman

From: Anita Blackstone [mailto:ablackstone@jacksoncountycasa-mo.org]
Sent: Thursday, May 19, 2011 11:12 AM
To: miriamkfine@gmail.com
Cc: hmiller@jacksoncountycasa-mo.org
Subject: RE: *Confidential: Merritt—Washington—questions after 5/18/11 home visit

Hi Miriam,

Thanks for your email. Don't worry about asking too many questions. That's what I'm here for!

First, I think you did a good job of re-stating our general view about CASA Volunteers discussing their cases with outside parties. Our job—and your job—is to absolutely protect the confidentiality of these children and families. On the other hand, we know this work is hard and often becomes an important part of our Volunteers' lives. We don't expect you to be completely silent about being a CASA Volunteer—we know everyone involved in this work needs an escape valve. Just use your best judgment and be sure that you always protect the children on your case.

To answer your questions:

1. I have rarely seen CD actually come up with the funds to pay for a family member to transport the children to school. It's a shame, because we want to do everything we possibly can to keep them with the same teachers and friends and not cause another disruption in their lives.

    Here's what I think we should do, if you agree: Since there are only seven school days left before the academic year is over, let's just leave it alone. If the children are still living with Mabel and Roger when the new school year starts in August, we'll push Camille to see if there really is any chance for CD assistance. She's a good worker—she'll help if she can. If CD can't help, we can use CASA Emergency Assistance funds to provide a monthly gas card for the grandparents. We can't do that forever, but it might be enough to get them through. Will you keep an eye on this and be sure to address it in August if it's still an issue?

2. I don't have good news on the counseling front. You'll recall that the Commissioner ordered a voluntary psych eval for all three kids at the PC hearing. But there's a long waiting list for child therapists that will take Medicaid in Jackson County, and I don't think Camille will be able to get that set up before the Adjudication Hearing in July. Let's ask again at the 30-Day Family Support Team (FST) meeting in June.

3. We could ask Henrietta to file a motion with the Commissioner if we believed that CD was willfully ignoring a Court order, but my bet is that Camille is working on this and we would just annoy CD if we took that step. Let's save our motions for bigger things, if needed, down the road.

4. Better news on the books. Cherry actually keeps a large stash of books for kids of all ages— from board books for babies up to young adult books for teens. Next time you're at CASA, why don't you go downstairs to her office and pick out books for all three of the kids on your case? You can bring them books as often as you want—it would make Cherry happy, too.

I hope all that is helpful, even if not wholly encouraging. This system is hard to get used to—things take a lot longer than you expect . . . or want. But hang tough, and you'll see that you're making a difference for these kids!

Best,

Anita

Anita Blackstone
Case Supervisor
(816) 555-8236

SAVE THE DATE for Jackson County CASA's 7th Annual **Carnival for CASA** on Saturday, Sept 17, at Paradise Park in Lee's Summit. Email Carnival@jacksoncountycasa-mo.org to learn about Sponsorship opportunities and to purchase tickets for this family-friendly event.

From: Miguel Quintero (mquintero@kcpublicschools.org)
Sent: Friday, May 20, 2011 4:45 PM
To: miriamkfine@gmail.com
Subject: RE: Hope and Alysha Washington - Confidential

Dear Ms. Fine,

Thank you for reaching out to inquire about two of our Whittier Elementary students, Hope and Alysha Washington. As noted in your correspondence, I was the person who called the Hotline after Hope's teacher, Mrs. Ellen Grayson, raised concerns about her student. When Hope's sister Alysha further disclosed details that suggested the children might not be properly cared for at home, I made the hotline call.

You asked for some background on these two students. Normally, I would prefer an in-person meeting, but since we are nearing the end of the school year, I couldn't find time on everyone's calendars. In lieu of that meeting, I reached out to the girls' teachers and received back the following reports, which I am attaching pursuant to your role as the children's Court Appointed Special Advocate.

I hope this information is helpful. We have worked with CASA in the past regarding several of our students, and I have valued the partnership. We have enjoyed having Hope and Alysha at Whittier Elementary and hope they can return next year.

Dr. Miguel Quintero
Principal
Whittier Elementary School
1012 Bales Ave.
Kansas City, MO 64127
Phone: (816) 555-3850

DATE: May 19, 2011

FROM: Mrs. Ellen Grayson
             1st Grade Teacher
             Whittier Elementary School

RE: Hope Washington

Hope is a shy, quiet girl who mostly keeps to herself in class. She has one "best friend," Cindy Hermosa, who she sits with during Circle Time and at lunch. She plays with the other girls during recess, but takes a back seat in most games – a follower, not a leader. Some days her older sister Alysha (3rd grade) walks her to class from the morning bus. I sometimes see them holding hands and getting on the bus together to go home after school.

Hope loves animals and is very attentive to the classroom pets – a hamster and a long-eared bunny. She likes to be the student chosen to feed them and fill their water bottles, and she has expressed concern more than once that she thought they were hungry.

I have become increasingly concerned that Hope is not getting proper care at home. She is sometimes listless in class and has fallen asleep twice during Morning Reading Time. She becomes anxious waiting for lunch time, and eats everything on her tray as soon as she sits down. Many of our children come from families with limited resources, but Hope's clothes have become increasingly dirty and wrinkled. Sometimes she wears the same outfit all week.

Hope's classroom behavior is age-appropriate and she is a good student who keeps up with her schoolwork. Last month when I complimented her on her math workbook, she said, "Tyrone helps me at night." I believe Tyrone is her older brother.

Hope is a very sweet girl. I hope things work out for her at home.

From the desk of Miss Carol Holman

Alysha is an excellent student. She is good at math, and she particularly excels in reading. She is already reading books at a 5th and 6th grade level and eagerly gobbles up the books that Mrs. Halifax, our school librarian, recommends. She is not a show-off, but she always raises her hand to answer questions in class, and she is very pleased when she is called upon. She also likes Specials, and is particularly happy during Art Period.

I was surprised at the home details that Alysha disclosed when we met with Mr. Quintero. She is a very serious, responsible child, and she always comes to school with her homework completed and well done. She shows a great deal of concern for her younger sister, Hope, who is in Mrs. Grayson's 1st Grade Class. She often goes to meet Hope by Mrs. Grayson's classroom after school to go to the bus together, and she seems to look out for her on the playground when our recess times coincide.

Please let me know if I can provide any additional information. Hope is an excellent student with a great deal of potential.

From: Jennifer Martina (jmartina@kcpublicschools.org)
Sent: Tuesday, May 24, 2011 3:19 PM
To: miriamkfine@gmail.com
Cc: Murray O'Neill (moneill@kcpublicschools.org)
Subject: RE: Tyrone Merritt - Confidential

Dear Ms. Fine,

Thank you for your inquiry regarding our student, Tyrone Merritt. We were very sorry to learn he and his sisters have been having trouble at home.

It is our policy to comply fully with all Family Court requests and to provide all relevant information to the Court Appointed Special Advocate and Guardian ad Litem for any students in enrolled in Central Middle School. However, we do not have a great deal of information to provide regarding Tyrone's academic performance. Year-end grades will be submitted in early June. His first semester grades were satisfactory. He was not failing any subjects, and he was excelling in Computer Lab, where he received an A- for the first half of the year.

I met Tyrone once at the required meeting with all incoming 7th grade students. My notes from that meeting indicate he was a polite, respectful young man. He did not suggest that there were any difficulties at home.

I made a note that he indicated he was interested in "building things" and planned to sign up for the after-school Engineering Club. I have not had the opportunity to follow up with Mr. Gayle, who is that club's faculty advisor, to learn if Tyrone followed through with that activity.

I am copying Mr. O'Neill, the 8th Grade counselor, on this email. He would be the appropriate person for further inquiries when the next school year begins in August.

Sincerely,

Jennifer Martina

Jennifer Martina
7th Grade Counselor
Central Middle School
"Home of The Warhawks"

3611 E. Linwood Blvd.
Kansas City, MO 64128
Phone: (816) 555-9375

The Mission of Central Middle School
is to pursue excellence in all areas by providing rigorous academics,
developing leaders, fostering creativity,
and empowering students with
the essential skills to navigate the 21st century.

 **Optima**™

Contact Log

Name	Fine, Miriam
Case Number	594
Activity Date	6/7/2011
Activity Type	Placement Visit
Subject	Child welfare
Location	Grandparents' Home
Contact Type	Face-to-face
Hours	1.00

Notes:

I went to visit mid-morning, since Mabel told me they were taking the kids to a church event in the afternoon. The house was a little more cluttered than last time -- you can tell the kids are out of school now and home much of the day. Shoes on the living room floor, toys in the front hallway. But it all seems like controlled chaos, relatively clean, and when I went in the kitchen to talk to Mabel, everything was straightened up and put away there. I saw no cause for concern.

I talked to Hope and Alysha individually outside sitting on the wicker chairs on the porch. Alysha was first, and I gave her the copy of Amelia Bedelia Means Business that I picked out from the collection at CASA. I told her it was a good book for smart girls her age, and if she liked it, there were more books about Amelia Bedelia I could bring or she could get at the library. She held the book tightly for the rest of my visit.

Alysha told me they saw their mother last weekend, when Ms. Harris took them to McDonald's. She told me she gave her mother a picture she drew in school, and that her mother promised they could all come home "really, really soon." She said that very fervently. I asked what she was going to do this summer, and she said there was another girl her age on the block and she hoped they could play together "until I go home to my real house with my mom."

Hope brought Mr. Snuggles out on the porch to talk with me. I read her Sandra Boynton's book But Not The Hippopatamus, and she actually laughed. That was so sweet - she's a lovely little girl when she isn't so sad. I told her she could keep the book, and we'd read it together again the next time I come visit. She leaned over and whispered in my ear: "I saw mommy."

I found Tyrone in his room again playing video games. I asked if he wanted to go outside to talk, and he shrugged, so we stayed there. I asked about the visit with their mom, and he just said, "It was good for Alysha and Hope. They miss her." When I asked if he missed her, too, he just looked away. I asked how it was living with his grandparents and he said "it's okay." He said there aren't any boys his age nearby but his grandfather said he would take him to his old street to play with his school friends soon.

I asked if he liked to read, and he shrugged. I left a copy of Percy Jackson's Lightning Thief on the bed. Maybe he'll pick it up. If not, I'll think of something else to engage him. He's the tough one to get close to.

I talked to Mabel on the way out. I asked if she needed anything, and she said the church was helping out with used summer clothes for the kids, so she was good for now. She said the visit with their mother was good for the children. She also confided she hopes her daughter can get her act together and get the kids back. I hope so, too.

Activity Status	Approved

From: Miriam Fine [mailto:miriamkfine@gmail.com]
Sent: Wednesday, June 8, 2011 8:17 AM
To: hgoldstein@laramyjones.com
Subject: Mom / Arielle / Frustrations / Books

You are good to check up on me, Haze. I'm doing ok, not great. Mom's not great at all. She's starting to forget things. Not just people and street names—that's been going on for decades. I mean whole new categories, like which fish she likes on the EBT menu, and—this really scared me!—what day she was going to get her hair done. I can't really talk to her about it; she just gets flustered and mean (my mom . . . mean . . . almost unbelievable), and then she reverts to charming and blows the whole thing off. ("Oh, honey, I just forgot to write it down when we changed that appointment. We were moving a bunch of things around, remember?")

I've made her an appointment with a geriatric specialist at Menorah Medical Center for next week. No way is she going to agree to this. I'm going to flat out have to trick her—tell her we're going shopping at Town Center, and then divert to Menorah instead. I feel like such a rat. But what choice do I have? Grrr . . . this is getting hard! And I have that awful, mean, guilty feeling that it's just beginning.

Thanks for the hilarious update on your real estate mogul client. What a hoot! It is very reassuring to know there are still people in the world who will throw their mistress(es) under the bus to save their bank account(s). Is he good looking? You probably can't say. If he weren't rich, would these women have ever slept with him in the first place? I bet he never gets laid again now—hah! Serves him right.

Did I tell you Arielle is coming home for the 4th of July weekend? Apparently things are quiet in the online world over the summer. I'll be very glad to see her—Larry, too. I know Chicago isn't that far away, but still . . . it's not the same as having her here. I know you know.

My CASA case is going okay—I'm (slowly) getting used to the idea that you can't just go get these kids whatever they need. It doesn't work like that. My job is to work through the system—or, I suppose, to prod the system to work through itself. That's not as easy as it sounds (does it sound easy?).

Right now my main focus is on getting to know them—and hoping they learn to trust me. I have to admit, if a bunch of strange grown-ups had taken me away from my mother, I don't think I'd trust anyone! But I think on some level they knew things weren't right at home—at least the older two did. You can see it in the way they tried to protect their little sister. So maybe they will grow to trust grown-ups trying to help. The little one just misses her mother.

I really think they need to see a therapist for some sort of evaluation, and we got the Commissioner to put that in the orders during that first PC hearing. But so far, it's just one roadblock after another. Finding a children's therapist with experience in trauma who takes Medicaid is hard. Finding one with an open appointment slot is harder. Finding one who can see all three . . . nigh impossible!

I'm not giving up, though—if annoying, persistent nagging can get these children the help they need, then I'm your gal.

You'll like this: I brought them books yesterday! We're not allowed to give the kids gifts—supposedly it confuses the relationship; we want them to think of us as their advocates, not their sugar daddies. But one of the staff at CASA has been collecting books for the volunteers to take when they go on visits. Since they aren't really from me, it's okay. (Do you think the kids actually know the difference?).

Anyway, I did my very best to pick out books I thought they would like, and—bingo!—I hit the nail on the head. I told mom, and she focused right in. Once a school librarian, always a school librarian. When she starts forgetting the names of books and authors, then I'll know we're in trouble.

I may be naïve, but I think if you bring a kid a book . . . (three points if you get the reference). I know it always worked for mom.

How are you—right now, today? Is Mr. Real Estate Mogul still keeping you up at night? (Hah—you wish!) Any chance you can lure Joshua or David (or both) home at the end of June? I know Arielle would love to see them! Me, too, of course.

Moms, our kids, other people's kids, money, sex . . .

Love you,

Miri

_____

Miriam Fine
(913) 555-8436

"If I can't dance, I don't want to be part of your revolution." -- Emma Goldman

June 9, 2011

<u>Family Support Team Meeting</u>

Case: Merritt-Washington
Facilitator: Camille Harris, Children's Division worker
Location: Library Conference Room, Jackson County CASA
In attendance:
      Tyrone Merritt – Juvenile
      Alysha Washington – Juvenile
      Hope Washington – Juvenile
      Joelle Merritt – Mother
      Martin Jaylon, Mother's Attorney
      Mabel Merritt – Maternal Grandmother
      Roger Merritt – Maternal Grandfather
      Camille Harris, CD Worker
      Duncan Walsh, CD Supervisor
      Miriam Fine, CASA Volunteer
      Anita Blackstone, CASA Case Supervisor (taking notes for the group)

This was the first FST Meeting for the Merritt-Washington case, so Camille Harris, CD worker, outlined the purpose, process, and guidelines for the group.

<u>Purpose</u>: CD is required by Missouri Statute and state policy to hold regular FST meetings. The purpose is to gather all parties to the case for a facilitated meeting to provide appropriate support for the children and the family. FST meetings also ensure all parties have the opportunity to communicate and share all relevant information between formal Court appearances. The goal is to ensure children are moved into safe, permanent homes as quickly as possible and all parties receive Court-ordered services on a timely basis.

<u>Process</u>: Meetings will occur at specified intervals: 30 days, 60 days, 90 days, and then every 3-4 months until the children are released from care. All parties to the case are invited and encouraged to attend. Mom and Dad(s) are encouraged to have counsel present. The placement provider is asked to bring the children if at all possible. Children will be excused from the room if sensitive matters come up for discussion. The placement provider is asked to bring an extra adult who can leave the room to monitor the children during these times.

Each person at the meeting will sign the attendance log and the confidentiality agreement. Everything said within the FST is confidential and will not be repeated to other parties not in attendance.

Each meeting will begin by going around the room and asking each person to talk about any relevant occurrences or activities since the previous meeting. Examples might include children's behavior and school performance; medical, dental or therapeutic appointments or findings; parent visits; parental access to Court-ordered services; issues involving the assigned placement and their family. Participants are encouraged to share good news and progress, in addition to identifying areas for improvement.

Following this roundtable, the facilitator will lead a general discussion about issues that need special attention. Participants are encouraged to focus on brain-storming solutions, not blaming others.

FST meetings usually last 1-2 hours.

Guidelines:

1. All parties will be respectful and appropriate at all times. Participants will listen when others speak without interrupting. Everyone will be given a chance to speak in turn.

2. Participants who raise their voices or yell will be asked to control their behavior and may be asked to leave the meeting until they can participate appropriately.

3. All statements made in the FST will be held confidential and will not be repeated to parties not in attendance.

4. Children will be asked to leave the room when the discussion is not appropriate for them.

5. The placement provider is responsible for bringing an extra adult to supervise the children when they are out of the room.

6. Placement providers are encouraged to bring books, toys, or video games to keep the children occupied during the meeting.

7. Drinks and food are not provided, but participants may bring their own. Placement providers are encouraged to bring drinks/snacks for the children appropriate for a 2-hour meeting.

8. No weapons of any kind will be permitted in the FST, including guns, knives, or other potentially threatening items.

Camille Harris passed around the attendance log / confidentiality agreement for everyone to sign.

She asked the children to begin, and said after their turns they would be excused for the remainder of the meeting. She said they should tell the group how they were doing and what they wanted to happen for their lives.

Tyrone Merritt – Reported finishing school with okay grades, happy for summer but misses his friends from the old neighborhood. Loves his grandparents, but wants to go back home. Spoke directly to his mother: "Please do everything they tell you to, so we can come home. The girls need you."

Alysha Washington – Reported finishing school with a strong grade card, already wishes she could be in the 4th grade. She has made a friend on her grandparents' street, and likes the room she shares with her sister. Said she wants to go home "as soon as possible."

Hope Washington – Sat on mother's lap during meeting. Said she liked her room with Alysha at her grandparents' house but wanted her mommy. Cried when asked to leave her mother's lap and exit the meeting room.

(Children left room with Roger Merritt, grandfather, to supervise – meeting continued.)

Joelle Merritt, mother – Had to be asked to speak louder so all could hear. Said she was still in pain from broken jaw, which wasn't healing well; doctors didn't understand she needed pain pills – that's why she was drinking. Still working at Taco Joe's, said they were promising more hours, so she would have more money soon to take care of her kids. Said she received no financial help from Jerome Washington (father of Alysha/Hope) since he went to jail and his parents, who used to help, have cut her and their granddaughters off since she testified against him. Spoke directly to Mabel and Roger Merritt, crying, and said: "Thank you for taking care of my kids." Said she missed her children and wanted them back.

Mabel Merritt, maternal grandmother – reported children were doing well in her home. Said they were well-behaved, did chores when asked, took care of their own rooms. Said money was tight, but they were managing. Reported children seemed sad, especially at night, and wanted to go home. Spoke directly to Joelle: "Honey, we really want you to get sober and get your kids back. Please get to your therapy appointment and get treatment help. Your kids need you."

Camille Harris, CD worker – Full home study completed on Mabel and Roger Merritt and placement approved. Children appear to be doing well in home. No appointments have been made yet for child psych evals. One supervised visit with mother at McDonald's on 6/4/11 went well, though children were very reluctant to leave at end of visit. Mother has declined CD efforts to schedule psych eval and drug screening/evaluation.

Duncan Walsh, CD Supervisor – nothing to add.

Miriam Fine, CASA Volunteer – Reported visiting children in grandparents' home and concurs this is a good placement. Expressed concern that children have not been scheduled for psych evals, as she feels they are traumatized from earlier domestic violence and neglect, and further traumatized by removal from their home. Stressed importance of keeping all three children in the same schools for next year, as they express strong affinity for their school environments and classmates.

Anita Blackstone – CASA Case Supervisor – nothing to add.

Discussion ensued about getting mom scheduled for psych eval and drug screening/evaluation. She was very resistant, said "don't push me, people are always pushing me." Her attorney reminded her that following Court orders and participating in services are the best ways to get her children back. She shrugged and became sullen and silent through remainder of meeting.

Group agreed on 7/15/11 for 60-Day FST prior to Adjudication Hearing. Anita will schedule with CASA to use the Library Conference Room again and will notify parties about time.

Meeting ended and Joelle went out to talk with children in hallway. When Mabel and Roger Merritt went to collect them to go home, it was difficult to pry them away from their mother, especially the younger girl.

AJB / uploaded to OPTIMA 6/9/11

Resource Home Study

DATE: June 2, 2011

PROSPECTIVE RESOURCE: Mabel and Roger Merritt
5980 Quincy St., Kansas City, MO 64128
Cell: (816) 555-3958

RELATION: Grandparents

HISTORY:

Mabel and Roger Merritt are the maternal grandparents for Tyrone Merritt, Alysha Washington, and Hope Washington. The children are very familiar with the prospective placement. Tyrone was raised in the home from birth to age 3, when his mother lived there. Mabel Merritt often provided child care during this time. All three children stayed overnight with Mabel and Roger Merritt on a semi-regular basis when their mother was fighting with Jerome Washington.

The case.net search revealed no criminal history for Roger Merritt.
The case.net search revealed no criminal history for Mabel Merritt.
There are no other adults in the home with a criminal history.

HOME:

The home is beige with white trim. The home is a two-story home, with two bedrooms on the ground floor and one bedroom (master) on the second floor. There are two bathrooms – one upstairs and one downstairs. The home has an electric furnace. There is no basement in the home. Mabel and Roger Merritt have lived in the home, which they own, for 37 years. They vouch that the home is in good condition. They have one adult child, the mother in this case, who moved out of the home in 2002.They have no other living children, and no other adults or children live in the home. Mabel Merritt states that there is enough room for Merritt-Washington children to live in the home. Alysha and Hope share a bedroom, and Tyrone has his own bedroom on the first floor. The children share a bathroom.

BACKGROUND INFORMATION:

Mabel Merritt was born August 28, 1949, in Biloxi, Mississippi. She is 5'8" and weighs 230 pounds. Her hair is black (graying) and she has dark brown eyes. Her ethnicity is African American. She married Roger Merritt on October 20, 1974, at the age of 25. Together they had one child, born April 14, 1980, who died in infancy of SIDS, and one adult child, Joelle Merritt, the mother in this case, born June 9, 1982, while the Merritts lived in this home.

Mabel's parents are deceased. She states that her father left the home by the time she was eight years of age. Mabel was the fifth of six children. She stated that she was very close to her mother and her siblings, and maintains contact with the four living siblings on a regular basis through phone calls and emails.

One memory that stands out in Mabel's childhood is Easter. She remembers being in the kitchen coloring Easter eggs with her mom and two sisters. She states Easter is still her favorite time of the year.

Roger Merritt was born February 19, 1945, in Bentonville, Arkansas. He is 5'11" and weighs 270 pounds. His hair is black (graying) and he has dark brown eyes. His ethnicity is African American. Roger's father is deceased. His mother has dementia and lives in a nursing home outside of Bentonville. He has two siblings who still live in Arkansas. He was raised in a stable, two-parent household.

EDUCATION:

Mabel graduated from Biloxi High School and Roger graduated from Bentonville High School. Roger also attended Northwest Arkansas Community College for three semesters.

EMPLOYMENT:

Mabel worked part-time at the local Walmart for many years. She is now a full-time homemaker. Roger works as a janitor for the Kansas City Public School District, where he has been employed for nine years. He worked at Westport High School until it closed in 2010 and now works at Northeast High School. He currently works from 7 a.m. until 4 p.m. five days a week.

HEALTH:

Mabel states that she is in good health and attends the doctor regularly or as needed. She takes Omeprazole for acid reflux. She takes no other medications. She has no mental health needs.

Roger states that he has Type 2 Diabetes, which is controlled with diet, exercise, and insulin shots, which he self-administers twice daily. He also takes Lisinopril and Metoprolol for high blood pressure and Lipitor for high cholesterol. He takes no other medications, except a low-dose aspirin (81 mg) daily. He has no mental health needs.

FINANCES:

Roger and Mabel report that they have yearly employment income of $28,620 and do not have any other sources of income. Their expenses are as follows:

Car insurance	$120/monthly
Water	$100/monthly
Electric	$150/monthly
Cell	$100/monthly
Food (with children in home)	$350/monthly
Clothing (does not include children)	$50/monthly
Car 1 – Loan paid off	-0-
Car 2 – Payment	$176/monthly
Gas (with children in home)	$220/monthly
Cable	$90/monthly
Health Insurance – Roger (Medicare)	$75/monthly
Health insurance – Mabel	$250/monthly
Medication	$120/monthly
Monthly Expenses	$1,801
Monthly Income (after 15% tax rate) + Social Security	$1,873

Both Roger and Mabel Merritt have valid Missouri driver's licenses. Neither has a revoked license. The Merritts own two vehicles.

MARRIAGE:

Roger and Mabel Merritt were married on October 20, 1974, in Kansas City, Missouri. They had two children within the marriage, one deceased and one living. They are still currently married. Neither Roger nor Mabel Merritt was previously married, and they had no children before this marriage.

DISCIPLINE:

Mabel stated that the children have needed very little discipline in the time she has known them. However, if needed she removes them from the situation. She states that if they didn't respond to that, then she uses time out and/or taking away privileges.

RELIGION:

The Merritts state that they are Baptist and regularly attend the Mt. Pleasant Baptist Church in Kansas City, Missouri. They intend to take the children to church and enroll them in Sunday School.

SPECIAL INTERESTS OR HOBBIES:

The Merritts state that they spend most of their free time at church activities. Roger likes to watch sports on TV, and Mabel likes to cook and knit when she has time.

DEALING WITH NATURAL PARENTS:

Mabel reports she will encourage visits with the natural mother as the court allows. She would be willing to supervise some visits. She does not anticipate any problems with the natural mother.

HOME STATUS PREPARATIONS FOR CHILDREN:

Mabel previously set up both bedrooms for the children's overnight visits. Since they have moved in, Roger has completed a new desk he was making for Tyrone as a gift/project. Mabel has also set up the first-floor bathroom for long-term use, purchasing additional towels and personal hygiene items for all three children. They are prepared for any medical or mental health needs. They stated they have talked to their pastor, who said the church would help and support the children being in the home with family.

Roger and Mabel are the grandparents of Tyrone, Alysha, and Hope. They have known them since they were born and would like to stay in their life and provide a safe home for as long as necessary.

Submitted By:

Camille Harris

Camille Harris   Date: June 1, 2011
Children's Service Worker III

Approved By:

Duncan Walsh

Duncan Walsh   Date: June 2, 2011
Children's Service Supervisor

From: Miriam Fine [mailto:miriamkfine@gmail.com]
Sent: Friday, June 10, 2011 9:15 AM
To: Camille.Harris@dss.mo.gov
Subject: *Confidential: Merritt—Washington—therapist

Hi, Camille. I was surprised to learn at yesterday's FST that there have still been no therapy appointments set up for the Merritt-Washington children. I wanted to check in to see what we can do to move that forward. When I visited them earlier this week at their grandparents' home, it seemed they remain very upset at the initial removal from their mother's home. That view was confirmed at yesterday's FST by the grandmother and my own observation of Tyrone's behavior at the CASA house.

As we discussed, the Commissioner ordered a therapy review for all three kids at the May 13th PC hearing. It's been four weeks. Is there anything I can do to assist?

Many thanks!

Miriam Fine
CASA Volunteer

Miriam Fine
(913) 555-8436
"If I can't dance, I don't want to be part of your revolution." -- Emma Goldman

From: Miriam Fine [mailto:miriamkfine@gmail.com]
Sent: Monday, June 20, 2011 2:37 AM
To: Camille.Harris@dss.mo.gov
Subject: *Confidential: Merritt—Washington—therapist—2nd request

Hi, Camille. I wanted to follow up to see how you were doing finding a therapist for the Merritt-Washington children.

Why is this taking so long?

Their grandmother called me over the weekend to tell me they are not doing well. She reports that Hope cries a lot, Alysha is having nightmares, and Tyrone won't come out of his room most days.

Can you let me know what we need to do to get these appointments set up? I know a first visit will hardly make a dent—but we need to get started!

I'm available to help in any way necessary.

Can you let me know the next steps right away?

Many thanks!

Miriam Fine
CASA Volunteer

_____

Miriam Fine
(913) 555-8436
"If I can't dance, I don't want to be part of your revolution." -- Emma Goldman

From: Miriam Fine [mailto:miriamkfine@gmail.com]
Sent: Sunday, June 26, 2011 8:14 AM
To: ablackstone@jacksoncountycasa-mo.org
Subject: *Confidential: Merritt—Washington—therapy appointments

Anita,

I'd like your advice. I'm very concerned that Camille Harris has not set up therapy appointments for an initial assessment for the Merritt-Washington children. It's now been six weeks since the PC hearing. That's forever in the life of a child!

I had really hoped we'd get this done before the July 15 Adjudication Hearing at Court.

I have emailed Camille twice (professional, I promise, but with an escalating sense of urgency), but she has not replied.

What can I do to make this happen?

These kids need to see a therapist!

Thanks!
Miri

Miriam Fine
(913) 555-8436

"If I can't dance, I don't want to be part of your revolution." -- Emma Goldman

From: Anita Blackstone [mailto:ablackstone@jacksoncountycasa-mo.org]
Sent: Monday, June 27, 2011 12:07 PM
To: miriamkfine@gmail.com
Cc: hmiller@jacksoncountycasa-mo.org
Subject: RE: *Confidential: Merritt—Washington—therapy appointments

Hi Miriam,

Thanks for letting me know about the lack of response from Children's Division. In Camille's defense, it can be really hard to find an available therapist—especially for three kids at once. I know this won't make you feel better, but a six-week wait is nothing. My hope would be to get this done before the three-month mark for these kids.

But Camille should respond to your emails—they don't sound excessive. Next time you might try copying me and Henrietta (hmiller@jacksoncountycasa-mo.org). Sometimes having the Guardian ad Litem on the email will get their attention.

Since we have the Adjudication Hearing coming up in two weeks, why don't we ask Henrietta to mention to the Commissioner that the children still haven't seen a therapist. It won't surprise him, but he can admonish CD to get that done—it might help move the timetable up just a bit.

I'm sorry I don't have a better suggestion. You'll get used to this—everything takes a long time. The services available for foster kids (and kids living with relatives) are in short supply. As is the money to pay for them. We do the best we can to prod CD to do the best they can.

Best,

Anita

Anita Blackstone
Case Supervisor
(816) 555-8236

SAVE THE DATE for Jackson County CASA's 7th Annual **Carnival for CASA** on Saturday, Sept 17, at Paradise Park in Lee's Summit. Email Carnival@jacksoncountycasa-mo.org to learn about Sponsorship opportunities and to purchase tickets for this family-friendly event.

From: Miriam Fine [mailto:miriamkfine@gmail.com]
Sent: Saturday, July 2, 2011 7:25 AM
To: ablackstone@jacksoncountycasa-mo.org
Cc: hmiller@jacksoncountycasa-mo.org
Subject: RE: RE: *Confidential: Merritt—Washington—therapy appointments

Anita,

The more I think about it, the angrier I get. What do you mean "a six-week wait is nothing"?!! A six-week wait is everything for a traumatized child.

One of the things Cherry stressed in our new volunteer training is how deeply the underlying abuse and neglect likely impact our CASA kids. We learned all about toxic stress and its short- and long-term effects on the developing brain and the child's health outcomes—even into adulthood.

What's the point of all that research and all that training and all these Court people and all these Children's Division workers and all these lawyers and all of us CASA volunteers if no one does anything for actual, real children? If we can't help them, then why did we take them away from their mother in the first place?

Sorry to vent . . . I know you're not the problem . . . but patiently waiting to get services for these kids is not okay. These kids need to see a therapist! Tell me what to do!

Miri

_____

Miriam Fine
(913) 555-8436

"If I can't dance, I don't want to be part of your revolution." -- Emma Goldman

From: Miriam Fine [mailto:miriamkfine@gmail.com]
Sent: Monday, July 4, 2011 9:53 PM
To: hgoldstein@laramyjones.com
Subject: I could be nicer

Yep, that's the theme of my weekend. I could be nicer.

First, I shot off an angry, disrespectful email on Saturday morning to my CASA Case Supervisor, essentially accusing the entire system of malfeasance when it comes to these kids.

Then I was—very—impatient and unkind at the pharmacy Sunday afternoon when I went to refill mom's meds. They couldn't find one of the scripts, the line was long and growing, the help was re-arranging products in the hair product aisle instead of coming to check-out customers, they wanted to confirm my phone number for notification texts, the system that captures my ExtraCare number was on extra slo mo, the credit card reader didn't like my magnetic strip, and—for reasons that completely escape me—they were spending time with each customer to personally push some buy-one-get-one special on private-label vitamins. And I lost it. I mean lost it. Classic short-tempered impatient bitch yelling at hapless retail clerk—and then storming out without the meds.

I was so pissed off when I got home that I snapped at Ariel—about nothing—and then I totally bit Larry's head off tonight when he suggested I might be over-reacting across the board. I hate it when that man is right.

So . . . let this be my mea culpa. I'm a bitch. I'm impatient. I want what I want—which includes having the world work efficiently and appropriately. And I want to be nicer. Now.

Miri

Miriam Fine
(913) 555-8436

"If I can't dance, I don't want to be part of your revolution." -- Emma Goldman

From: Hazel Goldstein [mailto:hgoldstein@laramyjones.com]
Sent: Monday, July 4, 2011 11:54 PM
To: miriamkfine@gmail.com
Subject: You are nice!

Hey, let yourself off the hook a little here. You hold it together more than most people I've ever met. You should see the attorneys here in the office—they scream all the time—and they're not even trying to care for aging parents.

I think you're mostly upset about your CASA kids. I know corporate America was slow and non-responsive, but it looks like a speed demon compared to the legal system. And God only knows about the state social service system—but let's reasonably assume it is ten times worse than that.

I know it's not my place to say, but try to put your upper-middle-class expectations of service delivery and response time on hold here and just move forward incrementally. Remember—when you first got these kids, they weren't eating regularly and they were going to school in dirty clothes. It's already better than that.

I think you are very nice.

Hazel

Hazel M. Goldstein
Laramy, Jones, & Haverford LLP
Direct Phone: (816) 555-3116 / Office Phone: (816) 555-3420 / Mobile Phone: (816) 555-3078
Fax: (816) 555-5298
Email: hgoldstein@laramyjones.com

From: Anita Blackstone [mailto:ablackstone@jacksoncountycasa-mo.org]
Sent: Tuesday, July 5, 2011 8:12 AM
To: miriamkfine@gmail.com
Cc: hmiller@jacksoncountycasa-mo.org
Subject: RE: RE: RE: *Confidential: Merritt—Washington—therapy appointments

Hi Miriam,

I'll call you later today. We're working on it over here.

I have a call into Camille and her CD supervisor, and Henrietta is preparing a motion in case we need it.

Just hold tight.

The kids are safe right now, and that's what matters most.

Anita

Anita Blackstone
Case Supervisor
(816) 555-8236

SAVE THE DATE for Jackson County CASA's 7th Annual **Carnival for CASA** on Saturday, Sept 17, at Paradise Park in Lee's Summit. Email Carnival@jacksoncountycasa-mo.org to learn about Sponsorship opportunities and to purchase tickets for this family-friendly event.

This e-mail is intended only for the addressee(s) named above. The Electronic Communications Privacy Act, 18 U.S.C. §§2510 et seq, protects this e-mail and any attachments. It is confidential and contains attorney-client privileged materials and/or attorney work product, all of which is protected from disclosure and legally privileged.

July 15, 2011

Family Support Team Meeting

Case:	Merritt-Washington
Facilitator:	Camille Harris, Children's Division worker
Location:	Library Conference Room, Jackson County CASA

In attendance:

    Tyrone Merritt – Juvenile
    Alysha Washington – Juvenile
    Hope Washington – Juvenile
    Joelle Merritt – Mother
    Martin Jaylon – Mother's Attorney
    Mabel Merritt – Maternal Grandmother
    Camille Harris – CD Worker
    Miriam Fine – CASA Volunteer
    Anita Blackstone – CASA Case Supervisor (taking notes for the group)

Camille Harris passed around the attendance log / confidentiality agreement for everyone to sign.

She reminded everyone that they would need to leave in 45 minutes to walk over to the Family Courthouse for the Adjudication Hearing, so asked all participants to be brief with their remarks.

Tyrone Merritt – Reported he feels safe at his grandparents' home and he likes his grandmother's cooking. He still misses his friends. He said he thought they would have moved back home by now.

Alysha Washington – Reported she is okay, but still "misses Mommy."

Hope Washington – Sat on her mother's lap again. She didn't choose to speak when it was her turn.

(NOTE: As Roger Merritt was unable to attend this FST, there was no one to supervise the children. They remained in the room for the entire meeting.)

Joelle Merritt, mother – Said she was looking forward to a planned visit with the children tomorrow at home. She said she had taken out some of their toys and games so they could all play together in the family room. When asked by Camille about last week's scheduled psych eval, she said she had to miss the appointment because she had to work.

Camille spoke sternly about that: "You need to get that done. We're paying for it, and the Court says you have to do it if you want your kids back. I'll set up another appointment, but don't miss it."

Mabel Merritt, maternal grandmother – Apologized that Roger was not able to come to the meeting. Said he has missed some work due to illness, and didn't feel he could be absent today. Reported children continued to do well in her home.

Camille Harris, CD worker – Children appear to be doing well in home. No appointments have been made yet for child psych evals. She has identified a therapist with open appointments in August, and is working to schedule. The next supervised visit with Joelle is scheduled tomorrow with a parent aide in the children's home of origin. Disappointed mother was a no-show for scheduled psych eval. No drug screening/evaluation has been set up yet.

Miriam Fine, CASA Volunteer – Next visit to see the children at grandparents' home is planned for 7/23/11. Stressed her concern that therapist appointments be made as soon as possible. Important to complete prior to school starting, when scheduling will become even more difficult.

Anita Blackstone, CASA Case Supervisor – nothing to add.

Group agreed on 8/16/11 for 90-Day FST. Anita will schedule with CASA to use the Library Conference Room again and will notify parties about time.

Meeting ended so participants could walk over to Court for Adjudication Hearing.

AJB / uploaded to OPTIMA 7/16/11

IN THE CIRCUIT COURT OF JACKSON COUNTY, MISSOURI
FAMILY COURT DIVISION

IN THE INTEREST OF:

TYRONE MERRITT

SEX: M   **BORN:** 19-FEB-1998

CASE NUMBER: 1416-JU0040987

LIFE NUMBER:
1416-JR57790

IN THE INTEREST OF:

ALYSHA WASHINGTON

SEX: F   **BORN**: 07-APRIL-2003

CASE NUMBER: 1416-JU0040988

LIFE NUMBER:
1416-JR57791

IN THE INTEREST OF:

HOPE WASHINGTON

SEX: F   **BORN**: 17-NOV-2004

CASE NUMBER: 1416-JU0040989

LIFE NUMBER:
1416-JR57792

ORDER UPON ADJUDICATION HEARING

Now on July 15, 2011 there being present:

CAMILLE HARRIS	-	Children's Division
JOELLE MERRITT	-	Mother
ABIGAIL NORRIS	-	Attorney for the Juvenile Officer
HENRIETTA MILLER	-	Guardian ad Litem (CASA)
MIRIAM FINE	-	CASA Volunteer
MARTIN JAYLON	-	Attorney for Mother
TYRONE MERRITT	-	Juvenile

The cause coming on for Adjudication Hearing on the allegations of the Petition filed on May 13, 2011:

Evidence adduced sustains the allegations.

Paternity has not been established on the alleged father of Tyrone Washington and his whereabouts are unknown. Therefore, counsel has not been appointed. Further, there is no allegation against him.

The father of Alysha Washington and Hope Washington has not requested appointed counsel, further, there is no allegation against him.

The next court hearing for the above action is scheduled for OCTOBER 26, 2011, at 09:00 AM in DIVISION 40 for Case Review.

Note Well: Each party is responsible for notifying their respective witnesses of the above date and time.

7-15-11	*Gerard E. Solomon*
DATE	JUDGE/COMMISSIONER, FAMILY COURT DIVISION

Copies to:

ABIGAIL NORRIS
Attorney for the Juvenile Officer

MARTIN JAYLON
Attorney for the Natural Mother

CAMILLE HARRIS
CHILDREN'S DIVISION

HENRIETTA MILLER
JACKSON COUNTY CASA

MARLIN THOMPSON
Putative Father – Tyrone Merritt

JEROME WASHINGTON
Natural Father – Alysha Washington, Hope Washington

JOELLE MERRITT
Natural Mother

From: Miriam Fine [mailto:miriamkfine@gmail.com]
Sent: Friday, July 15, 2011 9:42 PM
To: hgoldstein@laramyjones.com
Subject: Adduced

Hi, Hazel. Maybe I should have gone to law school instead of business school. Do you think I could have done it?

Today's Court hearing was bizarre. This was the "Adjudication Hearing," which happens 60 days after the "Protective Custody Hearing." Which happens within 72 hours of picking the kids up. (See—I was paying attention during all that volunteer training.)

My understanding is that this is the big one—where the AJO (Attorney for the Juvenile Officer) brings their case against the parent(s) to the Court. If the Commissioner agrees they have made their case, then the kids stay in custody and we proceed as outlined in the PC documents filed 60 days ago. If the Commissioner thinks the AJO has failed to make the case, then everyone says "oops—sorry!" and the kids are sent back home. Immediately. Like that day.

I gather that doesn't happen very often, which is a good thing, because imagine if we went through all of this—and took the kids away from their parents for two months—only to decide we were wrong. That would be a pretty big oops.

Our case was the easy kind. The mom "stipulated," which I gather means she decided not to fight the charges. But I still thought there would be some sort of evidence presented or discussion or something. We made the grandmother come down to the Court for the hearing, along with the three kids, mom, mom's attorney, the CD worker, the CD worker's boss, the CASA Case Supervisor, the CASA Staff Attorney (kids' Guardian ad Litem), and moi.

Plus, we used up the time of the AJO, the Commissioner, and the Court Reporter. And took up valuable real estate in that God-awful Court Waiting Room.

And do you know what we did with all those people? The Commissioner asked the AJO to read the charges. She said the mom stipulated. The Commissioner asked the CD worker if she had anything else to add. She said the Home Study on the grandparents was completed and approved. The Commissioner asked me and the CASA Staff Attorney if we had anything to add. I said I thought the children were doing well in their grandparents' home and it was a good place for them. I recommended they remain in that placement.

The Commissioner thanked everyone and said he would issue his ruling by the end of the day. Sure enough, around 5 p.m., CASA notified me we had the Court Order. This is what it said: Evidence adduced sustains the allegations.

Some other legal gobbledygook, but that was the only relevant sentence. Evidence adduced sustains the allegations. For that one sentence, we brought 11 people to the Family Court and made them fight for a parking spot, wait in that horrid waiting room, file into the courtroom, stand up when the Commissioner entered wearing his robes, and otherwise go through all the choreographed motions of this absurdist play.

There's so much I don't get about this system—it's like its own country, with its own language, history, geography, and indigenous peoples. And all the rest of us are just naïve tourists traveling through.

I had to look up adduce. Four years of college (majoring in English!) and a graduate degree from a darned good school, not to mention a full career in corporate marketing, and I had never heard it before. As far as I can tell it's just an intimidating way of saying "offered." (Per the Merriam-Webster website: adduce – transitive verb – to offer as example, reason, or proof in discussion or analysis.)

I keep thinking if these pronouncements make me feel stupid—and we will here stipulate that I didn't go to Harvard Law, but I'm still pretty educated and relatively literate, in my own bumbling way, and I do watch a lot of legal procedurals on TV (even more now that I'm retired)—then what must this look like to the children on my case? And their mom—who dropped out of high school at 16? And their grandparents, who are stand-up folks, but not highly educated?

We've built an entire "child welfare" system to take care of children and their families that is so arcane and incestuous that no one who gets swept up in it can possibly understand what the hell is going on. Is that justice?

I have an idea. Let's demand that all rules, regulations, Court orders, and official documents be written in plain English that anyone with a 4th grade education can understand. Then maybe this Harvard MBA would be able to understand them, too!

Enough. My CASA kids will stay with their grandparents where they are safe and cared for. Their mother will get counselling and drug treatment or she won't. And we'll see where it goes from here.

Shabbat shalom, dear Hazel—may peace be upon us all.

MKF

_____

Miriam Fine
(913) 555-8436

"If I can't dance, I don't want to be part of your revolution." -- Emma Goldman

From: Hazel Goldstein [mailto:hgoldstein@laramyjones.com]
Sent: Friday, July 15, 2011 11:52 PM
To: miriamkfine@gmail.com
Subject: Veritas

Yes, you could have gone to law school. You probably would have even made Law Review.

If it makes you feel any better, I don't understand Family Law either. I learned the basic principles in law school, but the actual practice is well beyond me. I think most people assume these cases play out like the stories you see on TV—wicked, evil parents torture their kids with belts and cigarette butts, are tried in criminal court, and go to jail. But those are just the very worst cases—the ones that make the news.

Here's what I remember learning in school: The vast majority of child abuse and neglect cases are tried in Family Court as this bizarre hybrid of property law and child welfare intervention. First and foremost, the child is property—belonging to the parents—and the state (in Missouri, that's the AJO) puts on a case to show why that property should be removed from its rightful owner. The parents have property rights—different from the rights of those accused of a crime, but rights nonetheless— and they have to be balanced against the state's claim that the parents are ruining their property.

The kids aren't the accusers here, and they aren't classic crime victims either (except in very few horrid cases noted above that actually go to criminal trial; you'll probably never see that; it's very rare). They aren't really even witnesses. They're property. Nobody ever calls them that. But it's how the law treats them.

At the same time, they are victims in the eyes of the (non-legal) child welfare system. So, really, we have lawyers trying to get judges to make decisions and issue orders that boss around the trained social workers. Think about that: people who went to law school—and never took a required course in child development or the sociology of poverty or youth counseling or the pathology of drug addiction or the symptoms and consequences of mental health issues—are the ones who get to decide what is best for these children.

I have never understood how that could make any sense at all. I'm a great lawyer—and I would probably make a great judge someday (God willing!). I would be a lousy children's social worker. But, in our American system, the legal folks (judges) trump the child welfare folks (social workers).

The whole thing is totally Through the Looking Glass bizarre. So, yes, you could have gone to law school. But I'm not sure it would help at all!

Hazel

Hazel M. Goldstein
Laramy, Jones, & Haverford LLP
Direct Phone: (816) 555-3116 / Office Phone: (816) 555-3420 / Mobile Phone: (816) 555-3078
Fax: (816) 555-5298
Email: hgoldstein@laramyjones.com

From: Hazel Goldstein [mailto:hgoldstein@laramyjones.com]
Sent: Saturday, July 16, 2011 9:03 AM
To: miriamkfine@gmail.com
Subject: Veritas—round two

You really got me thinking about this—I tossed and turned all night. I think it's the first time I've really focused on the bizarre Through the Looking Glass world of family law. White-collar crime looks so simple and clean (!) in contrast.

Did you know that in Missouri, cases in Family Court are decided based on "preponderance of the evidence," but all other legal matters are determined "beyond a reasonable doubt?" Try to explain that to a regular attorney like me! And hearsay is admissible as evidence in Family Court, but not anywhere else. Go figure.

What's really scary is that in Jackson County, the Family Court can order any attorney who is licensed to practice to represent a parent pro bono. That's how all those parents get free lawyers. So watch out for the mom's lawyer on your case. She might get one of the good ones—who do this a lot and know what they're doing. Or she could get a regular "put out my shingle" lawyer who knows a little criminal law, a little bankruptcy law, a little estate planning or real estate law, but never took a Family Court case in their life. And who certainly has no time to devote to a non-paying client who's probably a little difficult, to say the least.

That's also how kids get legal (Guardian ad Litem) representation if neither the Office of the Guardian ad Litem nor CASA can take them. I've heard that happens about 10% of the time. If any of the parents in the case have ever been in the system (which is pretty often, since child abuse and neglect are cyclical; about one-third of child victims will grow up to subject their own children to maltreatment), then they were most likely represented by either OGAL or CASA sometime in the past. It would be a legal conflict if the same institution that represented these individuals as children now represented the other side of the case (their own children) decades later.

So . . . if OGAL represented Dad back in the day, and CASA represented Mom back in the day, then neither can represent their kids now—and they get sent over to the private bar. Which means lawyers like me—who don't know a damned thing about family law—end up representing these kids.

That really makes you feel warm and fuzzy, doesn't it? Aren't you glad you asked?

Shabbat shalom to you, too . . . (really),

Hazel

Hazel M. Goldstein
Laramy, Jones, & Haverford LLP
Direct Phone: (816) 555-3116 / Office Phone: (816) 555-3420 / Mobile Phone: (816) 555-3078
Fax: (816) 555-5298
Email: hgoldstein@laramyjones.com

From: Miriam Fine [mailto:miriamkfine@gmail.com]
Sent: Wednesday, July 20, 2011 8:24 PM
To: hgoldstein@laramyjones.com
Subject: Life Number

Here's today's sad, sad fact:

I just got my hard copy of the Court paperwork from the kids' Adjudication Hearing earlier this month. Did you know that every child in the system has two numbers—a Case Number, which makes sense, and a "Life Number"—that's the number they keep forever, "just in case" they come back into the system after the current case is resolved?

Isn't that the saddest thing you've ever heard? These kids come back into care so often the system prepares for it up front. I am nauseous at the callous efficiency of whoever thought that up. I wish they could plan ahead in matters that might actually keep children and families together in the first place . . . augh . . . .!!

MKF

_____

Miriam Fine
(913) 555-8436

"If I can't dance, I don't want to be part of your revolution." -- Emma Goldman

Contact Log

Name	Fine, Miriam
Case Number	594
Activity Date	7/23/2011
Activity Type	Placement Visit
Subject	Child welfare
Location	Grandparents' Home
Contact Type	Face-to-face
Hours	1.00
Notes:	

Children were resting in their rooms when I arrived mid-afternoon. They had gone to a church lunch/picnic with both grandparents. I had a few minutes to speak with Mabel privately. She told me the children are doing pretty well. As planned, they were able to see their mother again last weekend with a parent aide at their home. Mabel said that mom constantly reassures the children they "will all be back together soon." She said it is hard when they come back to her house, but she still thinks it is good for the kids to get to see their mom.

I asked if she had any ideas about why Joelle wasn't getting help, and she said she thought she was too ashamed and still in denial. She said she doesn't believe Joelle when she says she is getting more hours at the restaurant. She thought she might be getting money from a new boyfriend. Otherwise, she couldn't figure out how she was paying the rent.

I asked if she had everything she needed for the children, and she said they were struggling, but getting by. She said she had forgotten how much children could eat -- especially teen-agers! I told her we had community partners who could help with Food Pantry referrals, but she brushed that idea away. "We can feed our own." She also mentioned that she was worried about Roger. His diabetes is getting harder to control and he has been complaining of numbness in his right foot. She said he is finding it harder to throw a football outside with Tyrone or walk with the girls to the park. She said he has been missing a lot of work.

I went outside on the porch with each of the girls again, which is becoming our custom. Hope was pretty groggy from her earlier nap and mostly leaned against me with Mr. Snuggles. She told me she had a hot dog at the picnic and "some really good cake." We read the Hippopatomus book again, and she seemed content, but she didn't laugh like before.

I gave Alysha another Amelia Bedelia book, which seemed to please her. We talked about asking her grandmother to take her to get her own library card so she could check out her own books over the summer. She said she was getting used to living with her grandparents and was relieved that she didn't have to worry about Hope all the time. Then she quickly added: "Of course, we all still want to go home to live with Mommy."

I had to go find Tyrone in his room again. He was deep into a video game, but politely put it down to talk to me. He still doesn't confide much, so I can't tell how he's doing. He said the girls are "much happier now," which I think might be a clue. He said Roger wasn't going outside with them after work anymore, but he had met two boys on the street to play hoops with. I asked if he liked summer better than the school year, and he shrugged. I asked if he needed anything, and he shrugged at that, too. It's hard for me to tell how much of his unwillingness to communicate stems from unhappiness or trauma and how much is normal teen-age behavior. He does seem clean, well-dressed, and healthy, and not in any kind of immediate emotional distress.

Activity Status   Approved

From: Miriam Fine [mailto:miriamkfine@gmail.com]
Sent: Sunday, July 24, 2011 10:30 PM
To: hgoldstein@laramyjones.com
Subject: What is wrong with this picture?

Dear Patient Hazel,

I'm so lucky to have you to rant and rave to. You are probably saving my marriage, not to mention the sanity of my CASA Case Supervisor. Thank you for always being that person. You can rave to me, too, you know. If you are ever appalled at the unjust way our society treats rich, white (white-collar) men.

Here's tonight's rant: I went to visit my CASA kids yesterday and got some time alone with their grandmother. She's a tough gal—caring, but down-to-earth. She is proud and self-sufficient. She won't beg, but she doesn't sugar-coat things either.

Bottom line: they are struggling financially. I get the feeling they were comfortably working class, raised their own kid as best they could, had a little set aside for retirement, but not enough, which is why the grandfather is still working well past retirement age. They were definitely not prepared to take on three more kids at this stage in their lives.

Are you ready to get pissed off? The state of Missouri pays a foster family $332 - $372/month per child, depending on their age. That's $4,454/year tops. And each child gets a clothing voucher for approx. $200 twice a year. That's right, $400/year to clothe a child (including shoes—don't these people know how much shoes cost??!)

Plus, children in foster care are automatically put on Medicaid, so their health care is covered. Considering the typical amount to raise a child in Missouri is $38,000/year (yes, I looked it up), that means the typical foster family is in the hole for something like $33,000/year per child.

Missouri ranks 48th in the United States for foster care reimbursement (I looked that up, too). Can you believe it? We're worse than Mississippi and West Virginia!

But, here's the real kicker: As awful and appalling as that is, the state provides absolutely no financial assistance to relatives who step up to care for children who have been removed from their homes! That's right—the state of Missouri pays foster families (complete strangers) to take care of kids, but they give nothing to relatives—people the kids already know and probably love. The children living with relatives are enrolled in Medicaid . . . that's it; nothing else.

So . . . some nice, good-hearted, but unfamiliar family would get $14,562 in cash assistance and clothing vouchers every year to care for my three CASA kids (which is not enough—see comments above), but their loving grandparents get bubkes. There is something really, really, really wrong with that.

Aren't you proud we live in the glorious United States of America . . . liberty and justice for all?

MKF

Miriam Fine
(913) 555-8436

"If I can't dance, I don't want to be part of your revolution." -- Emma Goldman

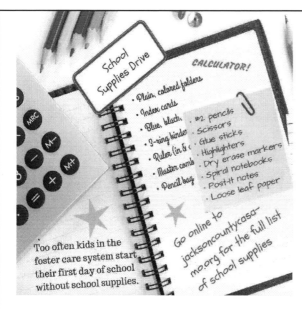

CASA School Supplies

Jackson County CASA
2544 Holmes - KC MO

Saturday, August 6
9 a.m. – 4 p.m.

Sunday August 7
11 a.m. – 4 p.m.

All CASA kids (Kindergarten – 12th grade) are invited to choose their own backpack and fill it with school supplies specifically for their grade and their school. On-site volunteers will have supply lists and be available to help the children. CASA Volunteers are welcome to attend.

If there are other biological or foster children living in the placement (bio parents, foster family, or relatives), they are also welcome to come get backpacks and school supplies. Children in residential placement will receive school supplies directly from their placement provider.

Email your CASA Case Supervisor to reserve a time for your CASA kids and any other kids in the home. Please provide: Child's First Name, Grade, School and Preferred Time(s).

This event is made possible by many generous companies, churches, synagogues, and individuals, as well as grant funding from The Edward G. and Kathryn E. Mader Foundation, the Grainger Foundation, and the Walmart State Giving Program.

From: Miriam Fine [mailto:miriamkfine@gmail.com]
Sent: Monday, August 1, 2011 11:38 AM
To: ablackstone@jacksoncountycasa-mo.org
Subject: *Confidential: Merritt—Washington—School Supplies

Anita,

Thank you so much for sending me the information about CASA's School Supply Drive. YES, please sign the Merritt-Washington children up to receive backpacks and school supplies. Would 1 p.m. on Sunday, August 7th work? That would let Mabel and Roger bring them over to CASA right after church. I'll come, too.

Here are the kids' grades and schools for the upcoming school year:

Hope Washington – 2nd grade – Whittier Elementary

Alysha Washington – 4th grade – Whittier Elementary

Tyrone Merritt – 8th grade – Central Middle School

I hope you hear back from all your CASA Volunteers about what a gift this is for our families. I know these kids' grandparents are doing their best, but they are working-class people who were headed towards retirement, and the added budget pressure of three kids has been really tough. I'm so glad to have something to offer them to help. Thanks for this!

Miri

_____
Miriam Fine
(913) 555-8436

"If I can't dance, I don't want to be part of your revolution." -- Emma Goldman

From: Miriam Fine [mailto:miriamkfine@gmail.com]
Sent: Friday, August 5, 2011 2:14 PM
To: ablackstone@jacksoncountycasa-mo.org
Subject: *Confidential: Merritt—Washington—School Supplies—Regrets

Anita,

I was planning to come to CASA on Sunday to help my kids pick out their school supplies when they come with their grandparents. I'm so sorry, but it looks like I'm not going to make it.

My mom—who has been struggling with a broad range of health issues and growing dementia related to aging—fell in her kitchen this morning and broke her hip. I am just back from the hospital, where she has been admitted, pending surgery on Monday morning. It looks like I will need to be at the hospital all weekend, and thus will miss the School Supply event at CASA.

Can you tell the staff and volunteers who are running the event? I'll call the grandma on my case; I know she'll get the kids there, and she is certainly capable of doing whatever is needed that day without me.

Let me know if you need anything else from me. I'm heading back to the hospital shortly, but I have my cell phone and my to-do list. And they have lots of coffee in the waiting room for sustenance.

Thanks for your understanding,

Miri

Miriam Fine
(913) 555-8436

"If I can't dance, I don't want to be part of your revolution." -- Emma Goldman

From: Miriam Fine [mailto:miriamkfine@gmail.com]
Sent: Monday, August 8, 2011 11:05 PM
To: hgoldstein@laramyjones.com
Subject: Why is it always a broken hip

We're finally home from the hospital. The nurse said mom is drugged out for the night—lots of supervision in the ICU—no need for us to stay. I hope that's right—you hear horror stories—but I'm exhausted and can't think of anything but my own bed. Not even a shower. Maybe tomorrow I'll want a shower.

Thank you for bringing dinner by—I know Menorah Hospital is way out of your way—and you're in the middle of that trial prep. But it meant the world to me to see a normal person from the normal world. All weekend in the hospital has totally weirded me out.

The doc came by after you left—he said so far, all signs point to a strong post-surgical recovery. They will even try to get her up tomorrow to stand on her new bionic hip. We'll see how that goes. She looks awful to me—gray and pallid and small. I guess we'll know she's better when she starts to pink up.

I'm mad and sad and worried and mad. Why does she have to go and get old on me? Why did she have to be so damned stubborn and try to reach that shelf when she could have yelled for Jonathan or called me or just let it go? It's her fault, it's not her fault, it's my fault, it's not my fault. I am pretty sure it is not your fault.

Thank you for coming. I love you. Good-night.

MKF

_____
Miriam Fine
(913) 555-8436

"If I can't dance, I don't want to be part of your revolution." -- Emma Goldman

From: Miriam Fine [mailto:miriamkfine@gmail.com]
Sent: Monday, August 15, 2011 11:26 AM
To: ablackstone@jacksoncountycasa-mo.org
Subject: *Confidential: Merritt—Washington—FST

Anita,

Thanks for checking up on me. My mom is doing better. She's out of intensive care, and the plan is to move her to rehab at the end of the week. I'm still spending a lot of time at the hospital, but I no longer have to be there every single minute.

Yes—I'll be at the FST for the Merritt-Washington kids tomorrow. I still haven't heard anything from Camille about setting the children up for that first therapist appointment. I want the opportunity to address that in person. As of today, these kids have been in custody for 96 days.

I'll see you tomorrow at CASA.

Miri

_____

Miriam Fine
(913) 555-8436

"If I can't dance, I don't want to be part of your revolution." -- Emma Goldman

August 16, 2011

Family Support Team Meeting

Case: Merritt-Washington
Facilitator: Camille Harris, Children's Division worker
Location: Library Conference Room, Jackson County CASA
In attendance:
    Joelle Merritt – Mother
    Martin Jaylon – Mother's Attorney
    Mabel Merritt – Maternal Grandmother
    Camille Harris – CD Worker
    Miriam Fine – CASA Volunteer
    Anita Blackstone – CASA Case Supervisor (taking notes for the group)

Camille Harris passed around the attendance log / confidentiality agreement for everyone to sign.

She asked Mabel Merritt where the children were today, and Mabel said they just started school on Monday, and she didn't want to take them out of class on their second day back. Camille noted that it is particularly important for adolescents to participate in FST meetings. She encouraged Mabel to remind the group to pick times for future meetings that would work for Tyrone to attend, and the girls when possible.

Mabel also said that Roger was unable to attend today's meeting, as he has not been feeling well.

Joelle Merritt, mother – Said she was sorry she had been "too busy with work" to see the children before they started school again. She had thought she would see them today and expressed annoyance that Mabel did not tell her the children would not be attending the FST. She was also angry that "the process is taking so long." She said she thought she would have her kids back by now.

Camille Harris asked Joelle if she was ready to reschedule a psych eval and set up a drug screening/evaluation appointment, and Joelle said yes, "when she could fit it in."

Camille Harris, CD worker – Reminded mother that regaining custody of her children would be accelerated if she participated in services. Asked mother's attorney to explain this to his client, as well. Reported that psych eval on children had been completed 8/10/11. Miriam Fine, CASA Volunteer, asked when she would get the report. Camille said it usually takes 2-3 weeks for the therapist to write up their notes and recommendations and send them to CD and other parties.

Mabel Merritt, maternal grandmother – Reported children were excited to start school and first day had gone well. Thanked CASA for the school supplies. Said kids had been excited to pick out their own backpacks, and she didn't know how she would have paid for everything the kids needed otherwise. "Children are so much more expensive than I remember."

Miriam Fine, CASA Volunteer – Visited children at their home on 7/23/11 – next visit scheduled for 8/29/11. Said she hoped the report from the therapist would come soon, as she was worried about Tyrone. While the girls appear to be adjusting reasonably well to life with their grandparents, Tyrone is becoming distant and uncommunicative. She is worried about him, and thinks therapy might be warranted. She said it is hard to tell how much of his behavioral changes are due to the uncertainty of his current situation and how much are "normal teen-age boy" moods, but she is concerned. Wants to hear the expert psych opinion.

The group agreed to meet in January for the next FST. Camille will work with Mabel Merritt to pick a time when the children will not be in school and will inform the others.

AJB / uploaded to OPTIMA 8-16-11

Alysha Washington

Mr. Jasper - Grade 4

August 19, 2011

My Summer Vacation

My summer vacation was not very nice. Right before we finished 3rd grade something really bad happened. The police and the social worker came to our house and took me and my brother and little sister away.

It was really scary and my little sister was crying. I was crying too. They took us to our Grandma and Grandpa and that made us feel better.

I live there now. I like my bedroom and the bunk bed I share with my sister. Our Grandma takes us to school which is easier than taking my sister on the bus. We have more food and Grandma helps with a lot of things. But I miss mommy a lot.

It was not a fun summer.

Recipient information

Name: Hope Washington
DOB: 11-17-04
Medicaid Number: 2897653

Name: Alysha Washington
DOB: 04-07-03
Medicaid Number: 2897652

Name: Tyrone Washington
DOB: 02-19-98
Medicaid Number: 2897651

Provider Information

Name: Kevin Osborne, Ph.D.
Medicaid Number: 3749022
Referral Date: 05-13-11
Appointment Date: 08-10-11
Report Date: 08-22-11

Diagnostic Assessment

Referral Source:

Hope Merritt, Alysha Merritt, and Tyrone Washington were referred by Children's Division based on an order from the Jackson County Family Court dated 5/13/11.

Client/Family/Referral Source statement of need and treatment expectations:

The Jackson County Family Court ordered this evaluation to determine the impact of long-term domestic violence and child neglect on the clients. The provider has also been asked to determine if ongoing mental health services or referral for psychotropic medications are recommended for any of the children.

All three children came to my office on 8/10/11 with their maternal grandmother, Mrs. Mabel Merritt. In a 90-minute session, I was able to speak individually with Mrs. Merritt, Hope, Alysha, and Tyrone. This report presents my findings from those interviews and my review of the documents provided by Children's Division relating to the open case in Family Court.

Legal Status:

All three children are in the care and custody of the Missouri Children's Division and have been placed in the home of their maternal grandparents, Roger and Mabel Merritt. Previously they were in the custody of their mother, Joelle Merritt. Hope and Alysha's father, Jerome Washington, is incarcerated. Tyrone's father is not confirmed and his whereabouts are unknown.

Family and Social Status (current & historical):

Joelle Merritt became pregnant at 16 and dropped out of high school to care for her newborn son, Tyrone. The father's paternity was never confirmed, and the boy that Joelle named on the birth certificate moved out of town the following year. Mrs. Merritt says there was no contact with that youth after Tyrone's birth.

Joelle lived with her parents for the next four years. They provided financial support for her and the baby, and Mabel Merritt provided day care for the child while Joelle worked at an area fast-food restaurant. Mrs. Merritt describes that time as stable and happy.

In 2001 Joelle began dating her shift boss, Jerome Washington, a man five years her senior. Mr. and Mrs. Merritt objected to the relationship and refused to babysit Tyrone while Joelle went out with her new boyfriend. There was escalating tension in the household, and Joelle, who was 20 at the time, eventually moved out of her parents' home to move in with Jerome, taking four-year-old Tyrone with her.

The relationship between Mr. and Mrs. Merritt and Joelle remained strained, though there was some contact in subsequent years, especially when Joelle needed someone to watch Tyrone. She asked for money on more than one occasion, but Mr. and Mrs. Merritt declined, believing that would only enable her relationship with Jerome Washington.

Joelle and Jerome had a child, Alysha, in 2003, but the relationship deteriorated after that. Jerome began to drink and lost his job at the fast food restaurant. He picked up day work, but the family struggled financially. Joelle became increasingly depressed and withdrawn, as Jerome became increasingly volatile. The police were called to the home on one occasion, and Mrs. Merritt says they believed there was additional unreported domestic violence. They later learned Jerome was on parole for a 1997 conviction of domestic assault against a previous girlfriend, who was pregnant at the time.

Sometimes Joelle would bring the children to stay with the Merritts for several nights at a time when she and Jerome were having a "big fight."

Joelle became pregnant again and gave birth to Hope on 11/17/04. The family now had an infant, a 19-month-old, and a 6-year-old living in a two-bedroom apartment with very little income. Joelle continued to work part-time at the taco restaurant, and Jerome did odd jobs, as well as part-time work at McDonald's.

The police were called to the home on 9/30/06 for a domestic disturbance, but Joelle refused to press charges. On 2/9/07 Jerome and Joelle fought in the parking lot of McDonald's, when Joelle confronted Jerome about spending his pay on liquor rather than supporting the family. Jerome assaulted Joelle, and the police were called. Joelle was taken to the Truman Medical Center ER where it was determined she had a broken jaw, along with other cuts and bruises.

Mrs. Merritt was not clear on what happened to Jerome after that, though CD records indicate he was convicted of assault and parole violation and is presently incarcerated in the Jackson County Detention Center. None of the children have been to see him since his arrest, and Mrs. Merritt did not believe that Joelle had visited either.

Mrs. Merritt believes that Joelle's substance abuse began with this domestic violence incident. She was given OxyContin at the hospital for pain from her injuries, and a local physician renewed the prescription twice. Mrs. Merritt said that Joelle was distraught when the doctor would not renew the OxyContin a third time and began to drink beer and cough syrup at home after work. Mrs. Merritt was not aware of any Diphenhydramine abuse, and said she was surprised that a bottle of Benadryl had been found near Joelle on the day the children were removed.

Mrs. Merritt told me that Joelle had gone to a local free health clinic seeking help for depression, but was told there was a four-week waiting list for an initial appointment. Mrs. Merritt does not believe that Joelle returned.

Since they were removed from the home three months ago, the children have had two supervised visits with their mother, once at McDonald's with the CD worker and once at Joelle's home with a parent aide. They have also seen her at the 30- and 60-Day FST meetings on this case.

Presenting problems and situation:

The three siblings, Hope (6), Alysha (8), and Tyrone (13), were removed from their home on May 11, 2011, following a report to the Child Abuse and Neglect Hotline made by the school principal at Whittier Elementary.

Hope's first-grade teacher, Mrs. Ellen Grayson, was concerned that Hope was coming to school in dirty/wrinkled clothes and that she was repeatedly falling asleep in class, especially in the morning. She was also concerned that Hope was not being fed adequately at home, noting that she exhibited a great deal of anxiety about when the school-provided free breakfast and lunch were going to be served each day. Hope is enrolled in the school's Harvester's BackSnack program, which provides food for children to eat over the weekend. One Friday when the class was on an afternoon field trip, Hope repeatedly asked Mrs. Grayson if they would be back to school in time to pick up their BackSnacks. Mrs. Grayson had difficulty reassuring Hope that there would be no problem with the pickup.

On 5/11/11, Mrs. Grayson took Hope aside in the school library and asked if everything was alright at home. Hope told her that her brother and sister take care of her because their mother is sick and always asleep. She said her mother doesn't fix dinner anymore, so Alysha and Tyrone have to find them food. Mrs. Grayson asked who washes her clothes, and she said that her sister washed both their clothes in the sink or the bathtub and put them out to dry on chairs in the kitchen.

Mrs. Grayson alerted the school principal, Mr. Quintero, to her concerns and together they spoke to Hope's sister, Alysha, in the third grade at the same school. Alysha was initially reticent, but eventually disclosed that their mother is frequently drunk when they return home from school, and she is often asleep in her room or on the family couch. Alysha said her mother sometimes brings food home from the fast-food restaurant where she works or the local store, but there is often no food for dinner.

She told the teacher and principal that the children "do okay" with the free breakfast and lunch they get at school, and she said when they get home on Fridays with their BackSnacks, they unpack them on the table and make a plan together for the weekend. She was very reluctant to "tell" on their mother, and expressed a great deal of concern that they would be taken away from their home and "sent to foster care."

Based on the information provided by both girls, Mr. Quintero made a hotline report. That afternoon, Children's Division and a KCPD officer went to the home and found the mother, Ms. Joelle Merritt, asleep on the couch. She was difficult to rouse, and there were signs of alcohol and drug abuse, including empty cough syrup bottles and empty beer bottles on the floor, and a partially empty bottle of Benadryl open on the coffee table. The home was filthy and disorganized, and there were cockroaches crawling among dirty dishes in the kitchen sink.

The three children were removed from the home and placed with their maternal grandparents, Roger and Mabel Merritt. All three children have been living there for the past three months. They were able to complete the school year at their respective schools (Whittier Elementary and Central Middle School), and all three children are enrolled to begin at the next grade level at these schools at the end of August.

Current Community Resources and Services:

Mr. and Mrs. Merritt are actively involved in the Mt. Pleasant Baptist Church, and all three children will begin Sunday School there in the fall. They have been attending events at the church this summer, including picnics and other social gatherings. The church appears to be an important source of support for the Merritts.

Assessment for Hope Merritt:

Current Symptoms/Behaviors:

Hope was removed from her home during the last two weeks of school, so there are no reports from her teacher or principal about her symptoms or behavior after she moved to her grandparents' home. Her grandmother, Mrs. Merritt, reports that she is well-behaved and offers no resistance to following instructions, such as getting ready for school or going to bed on time. Mrs. Merritt reports that she seems eager to please.

Mrs. Merritt also reports that Hope frequently asks about her mother and about when they can "go home." She cries at night and can only be consoled by her sister or brother. In general, Mrs. Merritt reports that Hope is very attached to both her older siblings and prefers to be in the same room with them at all times.

Hope presents as a well-adjusted 6-year-old, who is shy and speaks softly. When I first sat down with her at the play table, she was coloring, and she didn't look up until I addressed her. I asked if she would tell me about living with her grandparents, and she opened up quickly. Hope said she liked her room at the Merritt's house (she calls them Grandma and Grandpa), and she mentioned several times that she has the bottom bunk bed "with Alysha on the top." She made several comments that suggest she is very dependent on her older siblings. "Alysha and Tyrone get me breakfast." "Alysha and Tyrone help me with my homework." "Alysha reads books to me." She clearly considers them parental figures who take care of her basic needs.

When asked, Hope said she was not unhappy, but that she missed her mother. She asked twice if I knew when they would "go back home."

Hope displays no immediate physical signs of distress.

Psychiatric Treatment History (Include previous treatment by this provider):

Hope has had no previous mental health assessments, counseling, or treatment.

Substance Abuse Treatment History:

None reported. While there was alcohol, cough syrup, and OTC medications in the mother's home prior to the children's removal, there is no evidence that Hope was given any of these substances or took any on her own.

Recent (30 days) alcohol and drug use (history of use, duration, patterns & consequences):

There is no evidence of drug or alcohol use in the grandparents' home.

Current Medication Regimen:

Hope takes no medications.

Medication allergies/adverse reactions:

Hope reported that she is "allergic to bees." Mrs. Merritt said she had never heard Joelle mention this about any of the children, and she thinks Hope just means she is scared of bees. I did not see any indication of a prior allergic reaction to bees or other insects in Hope's file. This should be kept in mind in case an EpiPen or other medication is warranted in the future.

Otherwise, Hope has no known allergies or adverse reactions to psychotropic medications.

Vocational/Educational Status/Functioning:

Hope will enter the 2nd grade at Whittier Elementary School in two weeks. She does not have an IEP. Her grades from 1st grade are reported to be mostly "A"s and "B"s. She has had no detentions, suspensions, or significant behavior problems at school. She reported that she likes school and was particularly happy that they had a "soft bunny" in her previous classroom. She indicated that she will be glad to go back to school when summer is over so that she can play with her best friend again.

Personal and Social Resources and Strengths:

Hope has a limited perception of her current situation, but she understands that "the grown-ups" don't think it's a good idea to live with her mother right now. She does not seem to remember her father and did not ask about him. She likes living with her grandparents and feels safe there. Her primary supports remain her two older siblings, whom she is clearly very dependent upon.

The Merritts appear to be a stable placement for Hope. Their financial resources appear to be limited but sufficient to provide food, shelter, and clothing. There is evidence that the church will assist if needed.

Summary Recommendations:

Hope has not presented any clinical disorders or mental health diagnoses. She is sad and misses her mother, but the support of her siblings and grandparents has provided a buffer, and she is not deeply distressed. I do not recommend ongoing treatment or psychotropic medication.

Continued supervised visits with her mother would be in Hope's best interests. I do not recommend visits with her father at this time.

What Hope needs most is a stable placement in the same home as both her siblings, with minimal disruption to her school and home routine.

Assessment for Alysha Merritt:

Current Symptoms/Behaviors:

Alysha was removed from her home during the last two weeks of school, so there are no reports from her teacher or principal about her symptoms or behavior after she moved to her grandparents' home. Her grandmother, Mrs. Merritt, reports that she is very smart and sensitive, a quiet child who does well in school and likes to read.

Mrs. Merritt also reports that Alysha is hyper-vigilant concerning Hope and always makes sure that Hope is served first at the dinner table. She said that she often hears Hope crying at night, and when she enters the room she finds Alysha holding her sister on the bottom bunk and cuddling her back to sleep. Alysha also appears to be very close to Tyrone, deferring to him during dinner conversations or when talking in the car.

Alysha presents as a moderately-anxious 8-year-old who carries the weight of the world on her shoulders. She is very intelligent and eager to please. In many ways she "acts older than her age." She was reading a book in the waiting room while I talked with her sister and seemed reluctant to put it down when I asked her to join me in my office. When asked, Alysha said she liked the Merritts' house. She expressed guilt about being happy in her new situation and said she was sorry for "telling" on her mother. She asked if I knew when they would be allowed to return home. I asked if she thought that would be best, and she said "I think so. Tyrone and I can take care of Hope, and Mommy needs us, too."

She told me that Hope was very sad, and she often slept with her so she would feel safe.

Alysha displays no immediate physical signs of distress.

Psychiatric Treatment History (Include previous treatment by this provider):

Alysha has had no previous mental health assessments, counseling, or treatment.

Substance Abuse Treatment History:

None reported. While there was alcohol, cough syrup, and OTC medications in the mother's home prior to the children's removal, there is no evidence that Alysha was given any of these substances or took any on her own.

Recent (30 days) alcohol and drug use (history of use, duration, patterns & consequences):

There is no evidence of drug or alcohol use in the grandparents' home.

Current Medication Regimen:

Alysha wears glasses but takes no medications.

Medication allergies/adverse reactions:

Alysha has no known allergies or adverse reactions to psychotropic medications.

Vocational/Educational Status/Functioning:

Alysha will enter the 4th grade at Whittier Elementary School in two weeks. She does not have an IEP, though there was a note in her file that the school might consider testing her for the gifted program. Her grades from 2nd grade are excellent, primarily "A"s. She has had no detentions, suspensions, or significant behavior problems at school. She reported that she likes school, especially reading, history, and going to the library. She is very eager to begin the new school year.

Personal and Social Resources and Strengths:

Alysha is extremely bright, and her ability to understand and problem-solve around her family situation have been very helpful in keeping her anxiety under control. As she becomes increasingly comfortable at the Merritts' home and begins to trust that they will care for her and provide adult supervision and care for Hope, her hyper-vigilance should wane. Her guilt about her mother is likely to remain, but does not appear to be debilitating.

The Merritts appear to be a stable placement for Alysha. Their financial resources appear to be limited, but sufficient to provide food, shelter, and clothing. There is evidence that the church will assist if needed.

Summary Recommendations:

Alysha has not presented any clinical disorders or mental health diagnoses, other than moderate anxiety appropriate to her current situation. However, it is not in her best interests to continue to feel the primary parenting responsibility for her younger sister. The Merritts should be encouraged to fully take over as Hope's primary caregivers, so that Alysha can pursue more age-appropriate interests and activities.

I do not recommend ongoing treatment or psychotropic medication.

Continued supervised visits with her mother would be in Alysha's best interests. I do not recommend visits with her father at this time.

It is therapeutically important that Alysha remain in a stable placement in the same home as both her siblings, with minimal disruption to her school and home routine.

Assessment for Tyrone Washington:

Current Symptoms/Behaviors:

Tyrone was removed from his home during the last two weeks of school, so there are no reports from his teachers or principal about his symptoms or behavior after he moved to his grandparents' home. His grandmother, Mrs. Merritt, reports that he is a well-behaved young man, but has become increasingly withdrawn since he moved into their home three months ago. She reports that he prefers to be alone in his room, playing video games or listening to music, and is increasingly difficult to engage in family conversations or group activities at the church.

Mrs. Merritt also reports that Tyrone was upset following the most recent July visit with the children's mother. At that meeting Joelle told her children several times that they would be coming home to live with her soon, and Tyrone expressed anger at what he called "stupid lies." Of all the children, Mrs. Merritt feels that Tyrone best grasps the situation and understands that their mother would not be competent to care for them in her present state of depression and alcohol dependence.

Tyrone presents as a polite 13-year-old youth with a great deal of repressed sadness and anger. He did not make a lot of eye contact with me, but he spoke clearly and answered all of my questions. He told me that it had been very hard when they were living with his mother. He is old enough to remember the domestic violence in the home, and he said it was very scary when Jerome and Joelle fought. He said Jerome never hit him or either of the girls, but he was always afraid that might happen.

Tyrone said he was sorry Jerome was in jail, but he thought it was best for everyone – and he certainly felt they were all safer after the police arrested Jerome. He said it was very hard for him and Alysha to "take care of things" when their mother was too sad or too tired to manage (he did not mention the alcohol or medication abuse). He spoke of worrying about washing their clothes and finding food to eat. He clearly felt it was his responsibility to take care of Alysha and Hope and "keep the family together."

Tyrone has very mixed emotions about the current situation. He is angry at his mother for her inability to care for them, and he is very angry at the social worker and police who "took them away." But he is also very relieved to be living with the Merritts and hopes they can stay there.

Tyrone told me the girls often cry at night, but he feels safe now, and he thinks they are safe, too.

Tyrone said his asthma has gotten worse since moving in with the Merritts. He did not speculate on the cause.

Psychiatric Treatment History (Include previous treatment by this provider):

Tyrone has had no previous mental health assessments, counseling, or treatment.

Substance Abuse Treatment History:

None reported. While there was alcohol, cough syrup, and OTC medications in the mother's home prior to the children's removal, there is no evidence that Tyrone was given any of these substances or took any on his own. He reported he had tried beer at a friend's house but didn't like it.

Recent (30 days) alcohol and drug use (history of use, duration, patterns & consequences):

There is no evidence of drug or alcohol use in the grandparents' home.

Current Medication Regimen:

Tyrone has asthma and requires daily maintenance medication as well as an emergency inhaler for flare-ups.

Medication allergies/adverse reactions:

Tyrone has no known allergies or adverse reactions to psychotropic medications.

Vocational/Educational Status/Functioning:

Tyrone will enter the 8th grade at Central Middle School in two weeks. He does not have an IEP. His grades from 7th grade were satisfactory. He received all "B"s and "C"s, with one "A" in his computer elective. Tyrone has had no detentions, suspensions, or significant behavior problems at school. He reported that school is "okay – better than staying at home," and expressed neither anxiety nor anticipation about beginning the new school year.

Personal and Social Resources and Strengths:

Tyrone is a resilient young man who managed to keep his sisters and himself safe, fed, and clothed during many years of family turmoil and chaos. He is having some difficulty adjusting to his new home with the Merritts where he is no longer expected to function as the responsible adult in the home, but with each passing month, he is adapting to the more appropriate role of child in the household.

Stability and trust will be very important for Tyrone going forward, and he will respond best if there are no immediate disruptions to his home and school situation.

The Merritts appear to be a stable placement for Tyrone. Their financial resources appear to be limited but sufficient to provide food, shelter, and clothing. There is evidence that the church will assist if needed.

Summary Recommendations:

Tyrone has not presented any clinical disorders or mental health diagnoses, other than moderate anxiety and anger appropriate to his past and current situation. It is now in his best interests to relinquish parental responsibilities for his sisters to the Merritts and focus on his own development and education.

I do not recommend ongoing treatment or psychotropic medication, however, ongoing monitoring for anxiety and anger issues would be advisable.

Continued supervised visits with his mother would be in Tyrone's best interests, but they should be terminated if he begins to show increasing signs of anger or attempts to return to his previous caretaker role.

Stability and consistency are vital to Tyrone's well-being at this point, and disruptions to his home placement or school should be avoided at all costs.

Name/Title   Kevin Osborne, Ph.D.
Date   08/22/11

From: Miriam Fine [mailto:miriamkfine@gmail.com]
Sent: Monday, August 22, 2011 10:22 AM
To: hgoldstein@laramyjones.com
Subject: The Children and the Shrink

Dear Hazel,

Well I got what I asked for—sort of. After I asked and emailed and nagged and emailed some more, the CD worker finally got my CASA kids to a shrink. I don't know what I expected. I guess I just kept thinking of Carol—someone with experience and wisdom who would be with these kids while they go through this horrible process and protect them from being permanently and emotionally damaged.

I should have known it doesn't work like that for kids on Medicaid. The counsellor seems like a nice enough guy—he has a Ph.D. and a well-established practice. And his report was well written and thorough. But here's the upshot: He spent 90 minutes total with the grandmother and the three kids (about 20 minutes each), and basically wrote to the Court saying: "Their life has sucked. They're tough kids. If they can stay with their grandparents, I think they'll be okay in the end."

No ongoing therapy. No counselling for trauma. Nothing. We're sorry your mom got pregnant at 16 and had to drop out of high school, and we're sorry you watched your dad/step-dad beat your mom up, and we're sorry there were no free mental health services to help her, and we're sorry she got hooked on drugs and booze, and we're sorry you didn't have enough to eat and had to wash your own clothes in the bathroom sink, and we're sorry we had the cops come and drag you out of your house, but . . . we think you'll be okay in the end.

Honestly, Hazel—what is wrong with this world? I had a perfectly lovely, privileged, better-than-ordinary childhood with perfectly lovely, privileged, better-than-ordinary parents, and I still need to talk to a psychiatrist every other week just to keep from jumping out of my skin. How can we expect these kids to overcome this kind of trauma and become happy, successful adults without professional help?

My CASA Case Supervisor says kids are more resilient than we give them credit for, and so far she thinks the kids on my case are doing pretty well considering. Considering . . . that's the bar???

Do you get tired of hearing me blather? You can say so, you know . . . I won't stop. But you can say so.

Yours—always,

Miri

Miriam Fine
(913) 555-8436

"If I can't dance, I don't want to be part of your revolution." -- Emma Goldman

From: Miriam Fine [mailto:miriamkfine@gmail.com]
Sent: Monday, August 22, 2011 10:27 AM
To: hgoldstein@laramyjones.com
Subject: Mom

And I forgot to answer your question: yes, mom is doing better—thanks for asking. The rehab set-up at Village Shalom is pretty good. She knows people there. They know her. People she knows come by. That takes some of the entertainment burden off me.

Which is a good thing, because I'm running out of amusing things to say.

Jonathan comes every day and stays with her for hours, which is incredibly sweet. He can't be trusted to manage the medical/rehab stuff, but he's a doll and she loves him, and that's a blessing.

It's funny—when they first built Village Shalom ten years ago, mom was here every day—helping set up the library, organizing book discussion groups, going to committee meetings, visiting "older" friends. I know she always thought she was paying it forward—that someday, she would need their services, too. I just don't think she thought it would be this soon. But she's 85 (or she will be next week)—that isn't soon at all.

MKF

Miriam Fine
(913) 555-8436

"If I can't dance, I don't want to be part of your revolution." -- Emma Goldman

Welcome **miriam.fine**
Change Password   Log Off

Staff
Dashboard

Volunteers
Dashboard

Volunteers

Lookup
Tables

Cases

User
Administration

Reports

Contact Log

Name	Fine, Miriam
Case Number	594
Activity Date	8/29/2011
Activity Type	Placement Visit
Subject	Child welfare
Location	Grandparents' Home
Contact Type	Face-to-face
Hours	1.00

Notes:

The children have been back at school for two weeks, so I went to visit in the afternoon. The girls were sitting at the kitchen table eating a snack. They took turns joining me out on the porch like we've been doing.

Hope told me she "loves" the 2nd grade and "loves" her teacher, Miss Richardson. She said they have even more pets in this classroom -- an aquarium full of fish, a snake, and a hedgehog named Needles. She also said they will be going to the zoo later in the year. She showed me the new backpack she got at CASA -- decorated with bunny rabbits. This is the first time I've visited that she didn't talk about going home to her mother, and she didn't have Mr. Snuggles with her.

Alysha was also in a good mood. She said her new teacher, Mr. Jasper, put her in the highest reading group right away. He lent her a copy of Harry Potter and the Sorcerer's Stone, and she was very excited to be reading a hardcover book. I asked if she had everything she needed for school, and she replied that she did. She said that wasn't the case last year, and she seemed relieved that it was not going to be a problem this time. But then she quickly said, "I still think we should go home and live with Mommy. She misses us."

Alysha confided some of the girls in her class were starting Girl Scouts and she wanted to do that, too. She said she didn't want to ask her grandmother, because it would mean more driving and probably money for a uniform and some other stuff. I said I'd talk to Mabel and see what might be possible. No promises, though.

Tyrone went out to play with his friends down the street while I was talking to the girls. He walked past us on the porch, and I hollered: "You good?" and he yelled back "Yes, ma'am!" I thought it best to let him go. If I kept him back, I don't think he would have told me much more anyway.

The girls stayed outside to play, and I went in to talk to Mabel. She said it was a relief to have the kids back in school. It was hard to watch them all day by herself during the summer. I asked about Roger, and she said he wasn't feeling well, and had missed some more work at the school. I can tell she's worried.

She told me she had asked the CD worker again about financial assistance to help pay for gas to get the kids to/from school, and Camille told her CD didn't have any money to help. I told her I thought CASA might be able to assist and I would get back to her about that soon.

Otherwise, it was a very good visit. The kids are happy and stable right now.

Activity Status	Approved

From: Anita Blackstone [mailto:ablackstone@jacksoncountycasa-mo.org]
Sent: Tuesday, August 30, 2011 3:39 PM
To: miriamkfine@gmail.com
Cc: chaines@jacksoncountycasa-mo.org
Subject: RE: *Confidential: Merritt—Washington—gas card for grandmother

Hi Miriam. Thanks for your voice message this morning.

I saw Camille Harris in Court on another case and asked her if she had looked into CD funds to help pay for Mabel Merritt's expenses to transport the kids to school. She said she had asked her supervisor and been told no—that CD was completely out of money for transportation for the fiscal year. I believe her. We have two other cases where we have advocated for financial help for relatives and been turned down. I just don't think they have the money.

I am copying Cherry Haines on this email. She manages CASA's Emergency Assistance program. If you can send her an email explaining the need, she will see what she can do to help.

Thanks for your strong advocacy for these children.

Anita

Anita Blackstone
Case Supervisor
(816) 555-8236

SAVE THE DATE for Jackson County CASA's 7th Annual **Carnival for CASA** on Saturday, Sept 17, at Paradise Park in Lee's Summit. Email Carnival@jacksoncountycasa-mo.org to learn about Sponsorship opportunities and to purchase tickets for this family-friendly event.

From: Miriam Fine [mailto:miriamkfine@gmail.com]
Sent: Wednesday, August 31, 2011 9:03 AM
To: chaines@jacksoncountycasa-mo.org
Cc: ablackstone@jacksoncountycasa-mo.org
Subject: *Confidential: Merritt—Washington—Emergency Assistance Request

Cherry,

Anita Blackstone told me that I could ask you for assistance for the grandmother on my CASA case. There are three kids: Hope Washington (6), Alysha Washington (8), and Tyrone Merritt (13). They have been removed from their mother's home due to severe neglect and are placed with their maternal grandparents, Mabel and Roger Merritt.

We all agree it is in the children's best interests to remain in their schools of origin, especially since the case goal is reunification with mom. We do not think it makes sense to move the kids to new schools now and then just move them back if we are able to successfully reunify them. Hope and Alysha go to Whittier Elementary and Tyrone is an 8th grader at Central Middle School.

While the grandparents live relatively close to both schools, they are outside the boundaries for mandatory school bus service, so Mabel has been driving the children to/from school every day. She has said she is having trouble paying for this added expense. I did the math as follows:

6 miles from Merritt home to Central, then Whittier:
  x 2 for round-trip
  x 2 per day
  x 5 days per week
  x 4 weeks per month
  x 26 cents/mile
  = $125/month

Can CASA help this grandmother keep her kids in their original schools so we can minimize the disruption in their already difficult lives? I'd just pay for it myself, but I know you told us in training we can't do that.

Many thanks!

Miriam

Miriam Fine
(913) 555-8436

"If I can't dance, I don't want to be part of your revolution." -- Emma Goldman

From: Cherry Haines [mailto:chaines@jacksoncountycasa-mo.org]
Sent: Thursday, September 1, 2011 4:57 PM
To: miriamkfine@gmail.com
Cc: ablackstone@jacksoncountycasa-mo.org
Subject: RE: *Confidential: Merritt—Washington—Emergency Assistance Request

Dear Miriam,

I think we can help relieve some of the financial pressure on the grandparents of the Merritt-Washington children. We have a fund—given by private donors—that allows us to provide up to $300 in assistance for an individual family caring for children in care. The goal of this fund is to help keep children with relative placements rather than moving them into foster care and to help children under Court supervision lead "more normal" lives. I think this situation clearly meets both those goals.

I will approve three $100 QuikTrip Gas Cards for this family. I'll get the cards this weekend and you can pick the first one up next week. You can pick up the next two cards the first weeks of October and November.

After that, if the children remain in this placement, we can post on Facebook and see if individual or company donors offer to assist. We also have several community partners who can help this family with Food Pantry relief and other assistance. Let me know if you'd like referrals.

Let me know if you have any questions. Thank you for looking out for these children.

Cherry Haines
Director of Volunteer Programs
Jackson County CASA
www.jacksoncountycasa-mo.org
Direct: 816.555.8204

SAVE THE DATE for Jackson County CASA's 7th Annual **Carnival for CASA** on Saturday, Sept 17, at Paradise Park in Lee's Summit. Email Carnival@jacksoncountycasa-mo.org to learn about Sponsorship opportunities and to purchase tickets for this family-friendly event.

From: Miriam Fine [mailto:miriamkfine@gmail.com]
Sent: Tuesday, September 20, 2011 4:45 PM
To: hgoldstein@laramyjones.com
Subject: Flowers—thank you!

Oh, aren't you the very nicest? Thank you so much!

Mom loved the flowers—I think it made her homecoming official. Aren't they lovely?

It was hell on earth getting her discharged and transported back home. And that damned step up to her front door. Nothing, nothing, nothing is easy, is it? And we have insurance and money and friends who can help. I think working this CASA case has given me a new perspective— everything that is hard for us—imagine how much harder for them.

But mom's home now, dutiful Jonathan in loving attendance. I think they'll be okay the rest of the day without me.

I have come home for a glass of wine.

Which I deserve.

Thank you again.

_____
Miriam Fine
(913) 555-8436

"If I can't dance, I don't want to be part of your revolution." -- Emma Goldman

Contact Log

Name	Fine, Miriam
Case Number	594
Activity Date	9/24/2011
Activity Type	Placement Visit
Subject	Child welfare
Location	Whittier Elementary / Grandparents' Home
Contact Type	Face-to-face
Hours	2.25

Notes:

I met Mabel and the girls at Whittier Elementary this morning to cheer on Alysha in the school Spelling Bee. She placed third, and was only beaten out by two 6th graders. I introduced myself to her teacher, Mr. Jasper, who seemed very pleased with her performance and told me, "It's a pleasure to have Alysha in my classroom."

I was able to talk with Hope while we sat in the bleachers. She is starting to "act" like an ordinary 2nd grader -- not too clingy, a little fidgety, chatting about the school, Needles the Hedgehog, and her friend Sarah. She was very attentive during Alysha's spelling turns, and clapped very enthusiastically when her sister spelled a word correctly.

Mabel looks tired. I asked how things were going at home and she smiled, but didn't really answer. She told me that Roger had wanted to come watch Alysha today, but he wasn't leaving the house very much now. He missed work all last week because of numbness in his foot. She told me that she had talked to Alysha about the Girl Scouts and explained that they just couldn't swing that right now. They didn't have the money, and she couldn't manage the transportation with Roger's health concerns on her mind. I asked if she could maybe find another mother who would agree to drive Alysha if I could find the money (maybe CASA has a donor?). She basically said it was all too compllicated right now, and we should just let this go. "Alysha understands; she's a good girl."

Tyrone had stayed home, so I stopped by the house after the spelling bee. He was doing homework in his room, but he put down his book to chat with me. He said he likes 8th grade better than last year -- the computer class is more interesting. He said the Engineering Club had already met once for the new school year, and Mabel had let him stay late after school to attend. He said they had seen their mother a week ago, when Ms. Harris brought them "home." He wouldn't talk anymore about that. He mentioned that Roger wasn't feeling well, but he mostly wanted to talk about his computer class.

I had a chance to talk with Roger before Mabel and the girls arrived home. It is the first time we have spoken at length. He seems like a kind, mild-mannered man, who is obviously very sad about his daughter's alcohol problems and loves his grandchildren very much. He told me he is seeing the doctor early in the coming week to "get this foot fixed up so I can get back to work and play with my grandkids."

Activity Status   Approved

From: Miriam Fine [mailto:miriamkfine@gmail.com]
Sent: Tuesday, October 18, 2011 2:12 PM
To: hgoldstein@laramyjones.com
Subject: Books—always books!

Well, it's as if Mom has come back from the dead. Ever since we got her home, she's been gaining mobility and strength—and re-gaining personality! Her memory's still not great—it flickers out kind of randomly sometimes—but mostly she seems like herself again. I'm so relieved, and I can only imagine what it feels like to her.

In any event . . . Mom wants to do a project. And, being Mom, she wants to do a book project. It turns out that a (much) younger friend from her Jewish Book Fair days has actually written a book. Not Mom's favorite kind of book—meaning fiction—but a book nonetheless.

It's about KC Jewish business leaders-turned-philanthropists. It's actually pretty good—I just finished the advance copy Mom gave me—with some inspiring, true tales of early poverty turned to eventual fortune by hard work, guts, brains, and family support. I've lived in KC my entire life and never heard these stories.

Anyway—Mom wants to organize a book event for this friend, Marilyn Friedmann, at the Plaza Library, bring out a crowd, and get some recognition for the book. Just like she used to do for her beloved Jewish Book Fair. I asked if she wanted to host the event at the Jewish Community Center, but I think she's still a little hurt that they never kept the Book Fair going after she retired as its long-term volunteer manager (and funder, I have long suspected). What she said was: "Let's make this larger than just the Jewish community; let's go big."

I told her I'd email Crosby Kemper over at the public library to see if there's interest. Crosby went to Yale, which is almost like going to Harvard, which means I've met him at several All-Ivy events over the years. So I'm allowed.

I don't know if she's really up to this, Hazel, but she wants to do it, and I'm thinking if I do most of the heavy lifting, we can likely pull it off. How hard could it be?

I think Mom would like one final Big Book Event to her credit.

I'd be happy if I could give that to her.

Miri

Miriam Fine
(913) 555-8436

"If I can't dance, I don't want to be part of your revolution." -- Emma Goldman

Staff | Volunteers | Volunteers | Lookup | Cases | User | Reports
Dashboard | Dashboard | | Tables | | Administration

Contact Log

Name	Fine, Miriam
Case Number	594
Activity Date	10/25/2011
Activity Type	Placement Visit
Subject	Child welfare
Location	Grandparents' Home
Contact Type	Face-to-face
Hours	0.75

Notes:

I wanted to see the children before the 10/26/11 Case Review, so I visited after school today. It was too rainy to go out on the porch, so I asked Mabel if I could meet individually with each of the kids at the dining room table.

I told each child that there was a Court Hearing the next day to be sure they were doing okay and to see if it still made sense for them to visit with their mother in the hopes of moving back to live with her in the spring. I asked each child what they wanted to happen and what they wanted me to tell the Commissioner.

Hope said she liked living with her grandparents, but she missed her mommy and wanted to go home. She asked if they had to wait that long. She asked if they could all live together -- the three kids, her mom, and her grandparents. She thought if they did that maybe she could get a cat.

Alysha listened very quietly to what I had to say. She asked if I thought her mother was "getting better." I said I wasn't sure, and she nodded. She said I should tell the Commissioner that she thought she and Tyrone could take care of Hope and help their mother. "But I like living here," she said wistfully. "Even if Grandma can't take me to Girl Scouts, it's really good here."

Tyrone was the most talkative he has been with me. He was agitated and said he couldn't always be the one to take care of his younger sisters, that it was good with Mabel and Roger, and "couldn't we just leave it all alone." I told him that spring was a long time away, but he didn't seem mollified. Clearly, talk of reunification is upsetting to him.

Roger was upstairs in the grandparents' bedroom, but I was able to speak with Mabel in the kitchen while the children watched TV. She told me that Roger's foot problems had become severe -- a previously undiagnosed foot ulcer had become infected and he was going to have surgery in two weeks to amputate three of his toes on that foot. She said she hadn't told the children yet. She appears worried about taking care of the children and Roger, when he comes home from the hospital. She is also worried about money.

I asked if she felt she could still care for the children, and she said, "For now."

| Activity Status | Approved |

From: Miriam Fine [mailto:miriamkfine@gmail.com]
Sent: Tuesday, October 25, 2011 8:19 PM
To: hgoldstein@laramyjones.com
Subject: Lousy luck

Oh, Haze, this is just so sad. Just when my CASA kids were settling in with their grandparents—and leading something close to a "normal" life—their grandfather has gotten really sick and needs surgery. I can't go into details, but it totally sucks.

"Everything that is hard for us—imagine how much harder for them." Didn't I just say that? Well, crap!

Now their grandmother has to take care of the kids and her husband . . . I sure hope she can do it. This home is the only safe place these kids have ever known.

Your pissed-at-God-and-the-world friend,

Miri

_____

Miriam Fine
(913) 555-8436

"If I can't dance, I don't want to be part of your revolution." -- Emma Goldman

IN THE CIRCUIT COURT OF JACKSON COUNTY, MISSOURI
FAMILY COURT DIVISION

IN THE INTEREST OF:

TYRONE MERRITT

SEX: M BORN: 19-FEB-1998

CASE NUMBER: 1416-JU0040987

LIFE NUMBER:
1416-JR57790

IN THE INTEREST OF:

ALYSHA WASHINGTON

SEX: F BORN: 07-APRIL-2003

CASE NUMBER: 1416-JU0040988

LIFE NUMBER:
1416-JR57791

IN THE INTEREST OF:

HOPE WASHINGTON

SEX: F BORN: 17-NOV-2004

CASE NUMBER: 1416-JU0040989

LIFE NUMBER:
1416-JR57792

FINDINGS AND RECOMMENDATIONS

Now on October 26, 2011, there being present:

CAMILLE HARRIS	-	Children's Division
JOELLE MERRITT	-	Mother
ABIGAIL NORRIS	-	Attorney for the Juvenile Officer
HENRIETTA MILLER	-	Guardian ad Litem (CASA)
MIRIAM FINE	-	CASA Volunteer
MARTIN JAYLON	-	Attorney for Mother
TYRONE MERRITT	-	Juvenile

The cause comes on for Case Review pursuant to an order of JULY 15, 2011.

IT IS HEREBY ORDERED: that the juveniles continue to be committed to the custody of Children's Division for placement with the maternal grandparents or in another non-relative licensed placement, until further order of the Court.

IT IS FURTHER ORDERED:

1. Reasonable efforts were exercised by Children's Division including visits, therapy, parent aid and others, but the mother has not chosen to participate at the expected level. Specifically, she has not chosen to participate in the following voluntary services, which would be funded and provided by Children's Division:
   Psychological evaluation
   Substance abuse screening/evaluation
   Random drug testing

   The mother has participated in some supervised visits – approximately one/month – but has declined many opportunities to visit the children. Furthermore, she has sometimes appeared to be under the influence during visits.

   The mother has not addressed all the issues including sobriety and mental health concerns.

2. In all other respects the prior order remains in full force and effect.

The next court hearing for the above action is scheduled for JANUARY 18, 2012, at 03:00 PM in DIVISION 40 for Case Review.

Notice of Findings and Recommendation & Notice of Right to a Rehearing

The parties are notified that the forgoing Findings and Recommendations have been entered this date by a commissioner, and all papers relative to the care or proceeding, together with the Findings and Recommendation have been transferred to a Judge of the Court. The Findings and Recommendations shall become the Judgment of the Court upon adoption by order of the Judge. Unless waived by the parties in writing, at party in the case or proceeding heard by a commissioner, within fifteen days after the mailing of notice of the filing of the Judgment of the Court, may file a motion for rehearing by a Judge of the Court. If the motion for rehearing is not ruled on within forty-five days after the motion is filed, the motion is overruled for all purposes. Rule 130.13.

October 27, 2011	*Gerard E. Solomon*
Date	GERARD E. SOLOMON, Commissioner

Order and Judgment Adopting Commissioner's Findings and Recommendation

It is hereby ordered, adjudged and decreed the foregoing Findings and Recommendations entered by the commissioner are adopted and confirmed as a final Judgment of the Court.

October 27, 2011   *Suzanne M. Martell*
_____   _____
Date   Judge

NOTICE OF ENTRY OF JUDGMENT

You are hereby notified that on   OCT 28 2011,   the Family Court, Juvenile Division, of Jackson County, Missouri made and entered the above judgment in this case:

You are further notified that you may have a right of appeal from this judgment under Rule 120.01 and section 211.261, RSMo, which provides that:

1. An appeal shall be allowed to the juveniles from any final judgment made under the Juvenile Code and may be taken on the part of the juveniles by the custodian.

2. An appeal shall be allowed to custodian from any final judgment made under the Juvenile Code that adversely affects the custodian.

3. Notice of appeal shall be filed in accordance with Missouri law.

4. Neither the filing of a notice of appeal nor the filing of any motion subsequne to the judgment shall act to stay the execution of a judgment unless the court enters an order staying execution.

Corrine Adamson
_____
Deputy Court Administrator

Certificate of Service

This is to certify that a copy of the foregoing was hand delivered/faxed/emailed/mailed and/or sent through the eFiling system to the following on OCT 28 2011.

M R Jones
_____

Copies to:

ABIGAIL NORRIS
Attorney for the Juvenile Officer

MARTIN JAYLON
Attorney for the Natural Mother

CAMILLE HARRIS
CHILDREN'S DIVISION

HENRIETTA MILLER
JACKSON COUNTY CASA

MARLIN THOMPSON
Putative Father – Tyrone Merritt

JEROME WASHINGTON
Natural Father – Alysha Washington, Hope Washington

JOELLE MERRITT
Natural Mother

From: Crosby Kemper III [mailto:ckemper@kclibrary.org]
Sent: Friday, October 28, 2011 9:42 AM
To: Miriam Fine <miriamkfine@gmail.com>
Cc: Henry Fortunato <henryfortunato@kclibrary.org>
Subject: Marilyn Friedmann Book Event

Hi, Miriam.

Of course, I remember you. We had a great conversation at the Harvard Club "after party" the night Jill Lepore came to the Library to talk about her new book.

The Library would be delighted to have you and your mother organize a book event for Marilyn Fried-mann in the spring. How about the evening of Thursday, April 19, at the Plaza branch? We could do an author talk with Q&A and then a book signing. If you and your mom wanted to sponsor a reception beforehand, we have space for that, too. Whatever you think would be nice.

I'm copying Henry Fortunato, who can work with you on the publicity and reception details. In the meantime—can you send me a copy of the book to read? It sounds very interesting.

Thank you for thinking of the Library. I think this will be a terrific event.

All the best,

Crosby

Crosby Kemper III
Director, The Kansas City Public Library

Join us in Building a Community of Readers!

Staff Dashboard   **Volunteers Dashboard**   **Volunteers**   **Lookup Tables**   **Cases**   **User Administration**   **Reports**

Contact Log

Name	Fine, Miriam
Case Number	594
Activity Date	11/13/2011
Activity Type	Placement Visit
Subject	Child welfare
Location	Grandparents' Home
Contact Type	Face-to-face
Hours	0.75

Notes:

I stopped by the house mid-morning, as Mabel told me the family would not be attending church this Sunday since Roger just got home from the hospital. She opened the door looking haggard. She said it had been a rough few days following the surgery, but Roger was resting comfortably upstairs. She said the children seemed concerned, but were generally going about their usual routine. She did mention that Tyrone seemed "angry" at Roger for getting sick and becoming unavailable.

I talked to Tyrone first this time, since the girls were playing with a friend in the family room. He was in his room listening to music on his bed with his ear phones on. He sat up and engaged when I knocked on the door and asked if I could come in. I asked how school was going and he said "okay." I asked if they had seen their mom recently, and he said she had come to the hospital to see Roger after the surgery and they had talked some in the waiting room. He said "she was probably drunk," and I didn't ask more.

I asked if he was able to help his grandmother around the house while Roger was recuperating, and he said: "Yeah, sure. But who knows if the old guy is going to get better or not." This is the most anger I have seen Tyrone express. I told him most people recover well after having toes amputated, and he shoud give it a little time. He shrugged.

The girls' friend went home to her own house for lunch, and I took turns talking to the girls while they helped Mabel make sandwiches. Hope told me "Grandpa had his toes cut off so he'll feel better," and then she told me about the big fish tank in the hospital waiting room. She has a real eye for color and shape -- she described a lot of the fish in pretty clear detail. She didn't mention Joelle coming to the hospital, and I diidn't ask her.

Alysha wanted to talk about the book she was reading -- the second in the Harry Potter series. I asked her if she found the books scary and she looked at me like I was not very cool. "They are written for kids in 5th and 6th grade, but I'm good enough to read them." That wasn't my question, but I guess it was an answer anyway. I asked if she had talked to her mom at the hospital, and she said yes. "I think it made her sad that Grandpa needed surgery. She looked worried about him." She also told me Hope and Tyrone were worried about their grandfather. I asked if she was worried, and she said: "Grandma says he'll be okay, and I believe her." I think she does; she did not seem upset or worried. Mabel called her to bring lunch up to Roger, and she moved quickly to help.

I did not stay long, as Mabel had lunch ready, and it seemed the family had enough going on without an added guest.

Activity Status   Approved

From: Miriam Fine [mailto:miriamkfine@gmail.com]
Sent: Tuesday, November 15, 2011 8:00 AM
To: ablackstone@jacksoncountycasa-mo.org
Subject: *Confidential: Merritt—Washington—Christmas gifts

Anita,

Thank you so much for letting me know about CASA'S Holiday Project. That will be a God-send for the Merritt-Washington kids! For their grandmother, too. She mentioned the other day that she was worried about Thanksgiving and Christmas for the children. She tries to put on a good face, but I think money is really tight since Roger went on disability.

His foot surgery was last week, and I'm sure there are out-of-pocket expenses related to that, as well. I know he has Medicare, but even that doesn't cover everything. And they certainly never expected to be raising three kids at this stage in their lives!

So I will let Mabel know that I will bring Christmas gifts for the children when I visit in December. She can decide if she wants to put them under the tree "from Santa Claus" or handle it a different way. It is lovely to learn that companies and individuals from all over the city help "adopt" CASA kids for Christmas. It warms my Jewish heart.

I've filled out the form for all three kids attached. Can you give it to Cherry or whichever CASA Christmas Elf organizes this project? If anyone donates food, I know that would be a big help, too. I don't think there's much for a special Christmas meal at the Merritt home this year.

Thanks, Anita!

Yours in the Holiday Spirit,

Miri

Miriam Fine
(913) 555-8436

"If I can't dance, I don't want to be part of your revolution." -- Emma Goldman

Holiday Wish List

CASA Case Volunteer: Miriam Fine
CASA Case Supervisor: Anita Blackstone
CASA Staff Attorney: Henrietta Miller
Date Submitted: 11/15/11

1. Hope, female, age 6 (will be 7 by Christmas) – 2nd grade
   a. Shoe size: children's size 12
   b. Clothing size: size 6X/7 (small/medium)
   c. Clothing notes: receives pass-down clothes/coat from sister, but needs new underwear and socks (likes Dora the Explorer and The Little Mermaid) – also warm shoes for winter
   d. Favorite color: aqua
   e. Toy wish list:
      i. Stuffed animal – likes animals, especially cats and rabbits
      ii. Soft snuggly blanket – plush or flannel
      iii. My Little Pony playset
      iv. Baby Doll – African American

2. Alysha, female, age 8 – 4th grade
   a. Shoe size: youth junior size 4
   b. Clothing size: size 8 (medium)
   c. Clothing notes: needs warm winter coat and boots for school. Also sweaters or warm shirts. Needs new underwear and socks.
   d. Favorite color: purple/pink
   e. Toy wish list:
      i. Books – reads above grade level – books for 5th or 6th grade girl – very sensitive – no dark themes
      ii. Craft kit
      iii. Art supplies – crayons, colored pencils, markers
      iv. Barbie doll & accessories/clothes – African-American

3. Tyrone, male, age 13 – 8th grade
   a. Shoe size: men's size 10
   b. Clothing size: large / size 16
   c. Clothing notes: needs tennis shoes for school – suggest gift card to Payless or Kohl's or Walmart. Hoodie to wear to school.
   d. Favorite color: dark blue
   e. Toy wish list:
      i. GameStop gift card
      ii. Axe deodorant / body spray / other hygiene products
      iii. LEGO set
      iv. Wallet

From: Miriam Fine [mailto:miriamkfine@gmail.com]
Sent: Thursday, December 1, 2011 8:19 PM
To: hgoldstein@laramyjones.com
Subject: plus ça change

Hi – any chance you guys are free for dinner Saturday night? Maybe something easy and early—that new place on the Plaza that just opened in the space where the other new place just closed? Larry said some of the lawyers at the firm had lunch there the other day and really liked it.

I've been nuts over here. My CASA case, of course, which isn't requiring a lot of actual work at the moment, but always has me mildly worried and on edge. It feels like the other shoe is always about to drop. It must feel like that for the kids, too. What a way to spend your childhood.

Did you know there's even a term for what this constant uncertainty does to children? It's called "toxic stress," and it basically describes the short-term and long-term effects on kids' brains of ongoing anxiety about threats to their safety and well-being. They think this stuff can actually change brain chemistry and re-wire neural pathways, so these kids could have challenges to overcome for the rest of their lives.

They say the faster we can get these kids into a safe, permanent home, the less damage they will suffer. And yet . . . the whole system moves so damned slow. We know we need quick resolution to prevent permanent brain damage. But the system is constructed out of obstacles. What sense does that make?

Enough! On to more pleasant projects. Mom and I are actually making a lot of progress on our book event. She sure knows how to work with authors! It's wonderful to watch her negotiate and coach: No, you shouldn't talk for the full hour; yes, save time for Q&A; no, don't read out loud for more than a paragraph. Etc. This is Mom's wheelhouse, and she's in heaven.

Here's what's a little harder: the publicity. Mom thinks we should print fliers and make phone calls. She's not wrong—those are good ideas. Old ideas, but good. But she has no patience with my insistence on using technology, too. So, against her objections, I set up an event Facebook page and crafted an email to send out to everyone we know. Well, everyone I know, since I don't think Mom could possibly manage a group email to her friends. I'm not even sure she knows their email addresses.

Oh, well, it doesn't matter. Together we have the skills to pull this off. And it's a real pleasure to talk to her about something fun and concrete and happy, instead of just illness and injury and recovery. Mom is at her best when she feels competent. Aren't we all?

Miri

Miriam Fine
(913) 555-8436

"If I can't dance, I don't want to be part of your revolution." -- Emma Goldman

Staff
Dashboard

Volunteers
Dashboard

Volunteers

Lookup
Tables

Cases

User
Administration

Reports

Contact Log

Name	Fine, Miriam
Case Number	594
Activity Date	12/19/2011
Activity Type	Placement Visit
Subject	Child welfare
Location	Grandparents' Home
Contact Type	Face-to-face
Hours	0.75

Notes:

The children are home from school for winter break, so Mabel said I should visit in the morning. I told her I was bringing the Christmas gifts from CASA, and she said she had told the kids I would be bringing them, so I didn't have to sneak in. She said Hope thinks I'm delivering "presents from Santa Claus," but the other kids know they are from friends at CASA.

The family that "adopted" the kids for the holiday toy project was very generous, so I had several boxes of wrapped gifts and a box of food, too. The kids helped me bring them in from the car. Tyrone was pretty quiet, but he carried the heavy box of food into the kitchen when I asked him to help, before disappearing into his room. Hope and Alysha got busy arranging the presents in attractive piles in one corner of the living room (I didn't see a tree), while Mabel and I talked in the kitchen.

She looks very, very tired. She told me Roger's foot wound had become re-infected, and he was back in the hospital. She didn't know when he would be released; she hoped before Christmas. She was very grateful for the gifts for the kids, said she didn't have the time or the money to shop for Christmas, and she didn't think Joelle would be buying them anything. She said that Camille had promised to take the children to see Joelle before Christmas, but it hadn't been arranged yet. She said her phone conversations with Joelle caused her to have a lot of concerns that she was still drinking. She did not elaborate.

I asked how the kids were handling Roger's medical situation, and she said she thought the girls were fine. They were both happy in school and had made friends in the neighborhood. She said Tyrone was getting moodier and harder to handle, and that he no longer helped around the house as easily or politely as before, and sometimes talked back to her. Last week when she asked him to take out the trash, he growled "You're not my mother, and you can't make me!" She said he yells at the girls if they knock on his door or come into his room, and spends most of his time playing video games or listening to music on his bed.

I left Hope guessing what was in the big gift box with her name on it, and talked with Alysha in their bedroom. She told me it was scary when Roger had to go back to the hospital. Apparently, he developed a very high fever while Mabel was out getting groceries, and started thrashing and ranting. I didn't get the full story, but it sounds like Tyrone called 911, and the ambulance arrived just as Mabel was returning home. I think she took it from there, but Alysha seemed pretty shook up about the incident. She told me her grandmother was sad and tired, and Tyrone was yelling all the time. She said she just wanted it to be Christmas and for everyone to be happy, and she hoped she got some new books as presents.

Hope was hard to disengage from her examination of the gift boxes and bags, but she came to talk to me for a few minutes. She told me she had given Mr. Snuggles to Mabel to bring to her grandfather to help him feel better. She said she was really looking forward to Christmas, and she hoped "getting presents would make Tyrone happy."

Tyrone wouldn't talk when I first knocked on his bedroom door. I did get him to tell me that he had called 911 when Roger's fever got bad, and I complimented him on his quick thinking. "Yeah," he grunted. "A lot of good that'll do." But he was generally polite with me (he always is), and thanked me again for the presents before he went under with his headphones again.

Activity Status	Approved

From: Miriam Fine [mailto:miriamkfine@gmail.com]
Sent: Tuesday, December 20, 2011 9:13 AM
To: ablackstone@jacksoncountycasa-mo.org
Cc: hmiller@jacksoncountycasa-mo.org; Camille.Harris@dss.mo.gov
Subject: *Confidential: Merritt—Washington—concerns about grandparent placement

I wanted to apprise the team of concerns that have emerged from my recent visit to see the Merritt-Washington children in their grandparents' home.

As you all know, Roger Merritt had surgery in early November to partially amputate several toes due to complications from his chronic diabetes. He was recovering at home when his wound became infected, and was taken by ambulance back to Research Medical Center on 12/14/17. He remains in the hospital with an unknown discharge date, likely in 7-10 days.

I am concerned about Mabel Merritt's ability to continue to provide appropriate care for the children in addition to caring for her husband when he comes home from the hospital. I am concerned about the family's financial situation now that is it is clear that Roger Merritt, the sole breadwinner in the household, will be unable to work for several months. He receives long-term disability, but this is only 60% of his previous salary, and the family was struggling on 100%. They have limited savings.

I am also becoming increasingly concerned about Tyrone's attitude and behaviors. He was always the most traumatized of the children, as he was old enough to witness the early DV and also took on the primary parenting role to protect his younger sisters. He was doing well in the Merritt home, but the threat of "losing" another father figure has rattled his trust and feelings of stability. He is acting out, and Mabel is having trouble managing his behaviors along with all the other issues in the household. I do not know if she can handle this level of stress for much longer.

As we approach our 1/18/12 Case Review over at Court, I would like the team to begin thinking about where we will place the children (or just Tyrone?) if Mabel becomes unable to care for them. Can we discuss at the FST following our January Court hearing?

Sincerely,

Miriam

Miriam Fine
(913) 555-8436

"If I can't dance, I don't want to be part of your revolution." -- Emma Goldman

From: Anita Blackstone [mailto:ablackstone@jacksoncountycasa-mo.org]
Sent: Thursday, December 22, 2011 5:10 PM
To: miriamkfine@gmail.com
Cc: hmiller@jacksoncountycasa-mo.org; Camille.Harris@dss.mo.gov
Subject: RE: *Confidential: Merritt—Washington—concerns about grandparent placement

Miri,

Thank you for your email alerting the team to your concerns about the grandparent placement for the Merritt-Washington children. I have booked the CASA Library for 4:30 p.m. on January 18 so that we can all discuss following the Case Review at 3 p.m. at Court.

Camille—since we will be discussing potentially sensitive matters at this FST, can you bring a parent aide to supervise the children during the parts of the meeting where they need to be excused?

Since the holidays are nearly upon us, I assume we won't be doing much to identify alternative placement options this week or next. Let's plan to bring our best ideas to the 1/18/12 meeting and brainstorm at that time. I think it will be helpful to include the grandmother in the discussions.

Miri—it would be very helpful if you could visit the home again prior to that meeting and bring us a current view of Mabel's ability to manage the children. We can hope that the situation has improved by then, and they can remain in this placement, where they have clearly done well. It will be difficult to find another placement to take all three children, and it would be a shame to separate them if we can avoid it.

Thank you to all for your efforts on behalf of these children.

Anita

Anita Blackstone
Case Supervisor
(816) 555-8236

From: Hazel Goldstein [mailto:hgoldstein@laramyjones.com]
Sent: Tuesday, December 27, 2011 11:09 PM
To: miriamkfine@gmail.com
Subject: God bless us, every one!

Ah, Miriam. You made my day. Thanks so much for telling me about the call from your CASA kids' grandmother. You know, with both boys gone and just John and me in our empty nest, it's easy to forget what it feels like to watch kids open presents on Christmas. Of course, it wasn't Christmas at our house, but you know what I mean. We still had presents.

It broke my heart when you told me your teen-age boy put deodorant on his wish list. At that age, Joshua and David were asking for their own cell phones and skate boards and all kinds of tech toys that only John could figure out how to buy! Also CDs put out by very obscure—and probably inappropriate—bands.

Of course, that was also the year of the grand Twin Bar Mitzvot so they got more loot than any 13-year-olds deserve. Not to mention the cash. And you're working with a 13-year-old who puts basic hygiene items on his Christmas Wish List. Jesus! Or something.

I hope our kids appreciate how lucky they are. I hope we appreciate how lucky we are.

I never thought about African-American girls wanting dolls that look like them. Of course—that makes perfect sense. Then why don't I see more black dolls in the stores? (I suppose you'll remind me that I live in Mission Hills, where the homeowners' covenants still prohibit "Negroes and Jews" from owning a home. But I do shop at the Costco in mid-town—truly I do.)

Next year, I'm calling CASA and signing up for my own set of kids to shop for. I think we all need to remember what it was like to buy a kid just the right present—even if it's deodorant. Especially if it's deodorant.

I love you. I'm glad you and Larry are coming over tomorrow night to celebrate the last night of Hanukkah. I want to try the new dripless beeswax candles I bought online, and Joe's going to make his world-famous latkes. Not those sorry baked sweet potato ones he tried last year, but the real thing—dripping in oil—I promise. What's the point of being married to a doctor if you can't enjoy clogging up your arteries now and then?

Here's to the Maccabees! And to your CASA kids! And to our moms—dead and alive.

Hazel

Hazel M. Goldstein
Laramy, Jones, & Haverford LLP
Direct Phone: (816) 555-3116 / Office Phone: (816) 555-3420 / Mobile Phone: (816) 555-3078
Fax: (816) 555-5298
Email: hgoldstein@laramyjones.com

Central Middle School

3611 Linwood Blvd., Kansas City, MO 64128

January 5, 2012

TO: Mrs. Mabel Merritt

FROM: Mr. Murray O'Neill
         8th Grade Counselor - Central Middle School

RE: Tyrone Merritt – attendance issue

Dear Mrs. Merritt,

Per Kansas City School District policy, I am providing this written documentation as a follow-up to our phone conversation on January 5, 2012. As we discussed on the phone, Tyrone Merritt was absent from his 4th, 5th, and 6th period classes on Tuesday, January 4, 2012, with no approved excuse.

As you know, Central Middle School takes school attendance very seriously. We believe that attending class:

- Helps avoid delays in learning caused by needing to make up work
- Provides skill development and practice time
- Improves students' chances of achievement
- Helps students learn the value of discipline, dedication, and perseverance

Our policy for first offenses is to ask parents/caregivers to address this issue with their student and to stress the importance of school attendance. If the student repeats the transgression, the counsellor and principal will ask both the student and the parent/caregiver to meet to discuss the appropriate punishment and to further stress that school attendance is critical for academic success.

In addition to the educational risks of skipping class, students who are found outside school premises may face additional punishments:

> Students under the age of 16 who are found outside of school during regular class hours will be penalized according to city truancy ordinances.
> - The first offense will result in a warning to parents, guardians, or anyone having control or custody of the offending youth.
> - Two or more offenses could result in a fine of up to $500 or recommending the youth enter a pretrial diversion program for truant offenders.

We trust that you will speak with your student to ensure this situation does not arise again. Please don't hesitate to call me at (816) 555-2100 if I can assist in any way.

The Mission of Central Middle School is to pursue excellence in all areas by providing rigorous academics, developing leaders, fostering creativity, and empowering students with the essential skills to navigate the 21st century.

Central Middle School

3611 Linwood Blvd., Kansas City, MO 64128

January 10, 2012

TO: Mrs. Mabel Merritt

FROM: Mr. Murray O'Neill
             8th Grade Counselor - Central Middle School

RE: Tyrone Merritt – attendance issue – 2nd warning

Dear Mrs. Merritt,

Per Kansas City School District policy, I am providing this written documentation as a follow-up to our phone conversation on January 10, 2012.

As we discussed on the phone, Tyrone Merritt was absent from his 3rd, 4th, 5th, and 6th period classes on Monday, January 9, 2012, with no approved excuse.

This is this student's second attendance transgression in six days. In light of this serious second offense, we ask that you and Tyrone come to a meeting with myself and the school principal, Ms. Joyce Brown, on Thursday, January 12, 2012, at 3 p.m., immediately following the end of the school day. I understand from our phone conversation that Mr. Roger Merritt, the boy's grandfather, with whom he also lives, is recovering from surgery and will be unable to attend.

Recurring unexcused absences are a very serious offense, and we hope to speak with you and Tyrone about ways to assure this does not happen again. Please don't hesitate to call me at (816) 555-2100 if you would like to speak prior to our meeting on Thursday.

The Mission of Central Middle School is to pursue excellence in all areas by providing rigorous academics, developing leaders, fostering creativity, and empowering students with the essential skills to navigate the 21st century.

Staff   Volunteers   Volunteers   Lookup   Cases   User   Reports
Dashboard   Dashboard   Tables   Administration

Contact Log

Name	Fine, Miriam
Case Number	594
Activity Date	1/12/2012
Activity Type	Placement Visit
Subject	Child welfare
Location	Grandparents' Home
Contact Type	Face-to-face
Hours	1.50

Notes:

I arrived at the Merritt home at 7 p.m., just as the family was clearing the table from dinner. Alysha went upstairs to bring down the dinner tray from Roger, who remains bedridden following his release from the hospital earlier this month. Mabel immediately sent all three children to their rooms to do homework and asked to speak with me in the family room.

Mabel told me that Tyrone had skipped school twice in the last two weeks -- the first time in the afternoon, and the second time for most of the day. She had taken him to meet with the school counselor and the principal as a precondition of avoiding suspension, but she said he was sullen during the meeting and uncommunicative. I asked her what she thought was going on, and she said she didn't know, that she didn't have any experience with teen-age boys, but she thought it was related to his grandfather's illness and what he perceived as the "threat" of the children returning home to their mother even though she was still drunk all the time. She also mentioned Tyrone had been hanging around with a "bad crowd" after school, and it was getting harder for her for to control him. She said he was even mean to the girls mosts of the time now.

Mabel told me that the parent aide had come on Saturday to take the childlren to see Joelle for the afternoon. She said Tyrone was resistant, but finally went because Hope started crying. Mabel is not sure if these visits are good for the children.

She said that Hope reported, "Mommy fell asleep on the couch so we had to leave."

Tyrone growled, "Drunk bitch," and went immediately to his room and put on his headphones. Mabel asked if we should talk to the Court about limiting or stopping the children's visits with their mom, as she believes they are disruptive and her daughter is not taking any action to get sober.

I talked briefly to Alysha and Hope, taking each one to the now-cleared dining room table to speak individually. Alysha told me that she really likes her teacher and school is going very well. She has been asked to become a "library assistant" one day a week, and she is very pleased about this. I asked her about their visit with mom, and she became very quiet. She whispered, "it's not getting better," but she wouldn't say more. I gave her a book I got from CASA (Meet Kit from the American Girl series) and told her if she liked it there were a lot more books about Kit and other girls in the American past. Alysha held the book tightly as we said good-night.

Hope is just fine. I didn't ask about their visit with mom, but she volunteered that "Tyrone got really mad at Mommy." I asked if she was mad at her mother, too, and she said, "no, Mommy said we'd be coming home soon." I asked if she was still happy here with her grandparents, and she said yes. She told me there was a new girl in her class at school, and she thought they would be friends because she had a pet dog at home. I gave her a new book about rabbits and bunnies, and she scurried off to ask Alysha to read it to her.

Tyrone opened the door to his room when I knocked, but he was very sullen. I asked if he wanted to tell me what was going on with school, and he said "I'm sure she told you all about it." I said I'd like to hear his version of the story, and he said that school was stupid and he'd rather be with his friends. He said "no one cares if I graduate anyway." I told him I thought his grandparents cared, and I knew I certainly cared. I told him I had brought a form he could use to tell the Commissioner how he felt and what he wanted. I said if he filled it out before I left today, I would give it to the Commissioner before our hearing next week. He said he thought the Commissioner should know that his mother was still a drunk and he would fill out the form. I asked if there was anything else he wanted to say, and he just shrugged. I gave him one of the LEGO sets CASA gets from The Giving Brick and he said thank you - that was the best I got out of him during this visit. He brought me the form before I left, but he didn't say anything about it - just put it on the table and said, "here it is."

Activity Status	Approved

CHILD'S REPORT ON PLACEMENT

Court Date: _____1/12/12_____

Child's Name: _____Tyrone Merritt_____

Current Placement:___Grandparents – Roger and Mabel Merritt_____

This form gives you, the child involved in this case, an opportunity to express your feelings and any facts concerning your present placement. This form may be used by the Guardian ad litem, and the Judge or Commissioner as allowed by law. It is possible that all the information will be made available to all the parties, including the placement provider. Please be fair, open and honest.

1. Are you generally satisfied with your current placement?

_____X_____ yes   _____ no

Please explain:

My grandparents are nice and I
like living with my sisters. I do not
want to live with my mother again.
She is a drunk. My grandfather
is very sick.

2. Does the placement provider help with your goal, whether it is reunification with a parent, independent living, relative placement or other plan?

_____X_____ yes   _____ no

Please explain:

I think so. We all want to
stay here together.

3. Please describe how you get along with the other children, if any, in your placement.

I love my sisters.
Sometimes they bug me.

4. Please name the school you are going to and explain what you like about it or don't like about it.

Central Middle School
I like my friends. We all think our classes are mostly boring and stupid.

5. Please talk about how you are disciplined when you do something you are not supposed to, or violate rules of the home.

My grandmother is very sad when I am mean or skip school. She grounds me. My grandfather is too sick to care.

6. If you have visits with brothers or sisters, please explain how that is going and how it could be better.

7. Do you have any health concerns that you feel like are not being taken care of? If so, explain:

I get asthma attacks. I have my inhaler now.

8. Please explain how visits, if any, are going with your parent(s), and what could be done to make them better.

Mom is drunk when we see her. I don't want to go any more.

9. Do you get a chance to participate in things you want to, like sports, music, dance, and other activities? Please explain:

Sometimes I go to Robot Club at school. I hang with my friends unless grandma is mad at me.

10. How do you get along with your social worker, and do you feel that they understand your needs and situation? Please explain:

Ms. Harris is nice, but she makes us visit mom.
Ms. Fine is my friend and CASA and listens to me.

11. Do you know of any relatives or other adults you might be able to live with? If yes, please list their name(s) and how you know them.

No. My father split.

12. Do you know of any help that you need that you are not getting right now? If yes, please explain.

I need my grandma to get off my back.

13. If you are in counseling, do you think it is helping? Please explain.

Only one time.
I don't know.

14. Would you like for your court hearing to be scheduled so that you don't have to miss school to attend?

_____X_____ yes   _____ no

15. Do you have a photo you would like for the judge or commissioner to have? If so, be sure to bring it to court.

11. Please explain anything about your situation that you think is important and that has not been asked.

Our mother is still a
mess. She cannot take
care of us. Let us stay
here. Please.

From: Anita Blackstone [mailto:ablackstone@jacksoncountycasa-mo.org]
Sent: Monday, January 16, 2012 9:26 AM
To: miriamkfine@gmail.com
Cc: hmiller@jacksoncountycasa-mo.org; Camille.Harris@dss.mo.gov
Subject: RE: *Confidential: Merritt—Washington—concerns about parent visits

Miri,

Thank you for your email conveying the grandmother's concerns about parent visits for the Merritt-Washington children and for sending over the Child Placement Report from Tyrone.

Camille Harris confirms that the mother has not been participating in Court-ordered services and never re-scheduled her psych eval. She has also declined to accept a referral to a substance abuse treatment facility and has refused to provide Court-recommended urine tests through MedLabs.

Nonetheless, as you know, reunification remains the goal for the first 12 months of almost all child abuse and neglect cases in Missouri. In order to provide the greatest possible opportunity for successful reunification, parental visits are important (and are the parent's legal right). In fact, CD has tried to provide more supervised visits with Joelle and the kids, though mom is often hard to reach and/or cancels at the last minute.

Even if the Merritt-Washington children do not reunify with their mother, these visits may prove significant later during the mediation process to seek a permanent home for the children. If we decide to pursue Termination of Parental Rights (TPR) to release the children for adoption after the 12-month mark, the mother's lawyer would have grounds to contest if we had interfered with parental visits during this initial one-year timeframe.

We can talk more about this on Wednesday when we meet with the full team after the Case Review at Court. However, it is generally true that unless a parent exhibits violent or threatening behavior during a visit, CD will continue the visits and the Court will support that decision.

Don't let this dissuade you from making the most persuasive case you can for the children's best interests as you see them. That's your job. I just want you to know the legal context that influences how CD and the Court approach this situation.

Anita

Anita Blackstone
Case Supervisor
(816) 555-8236

IN THE CIRCUIT COURT OF JACKSON COUNTY, MISSOURI
FAMILY COURT DIVISION

IN THE INTEREST OF:	**CASE NUMBER:** 1416-JU0040987
TYRONE MERRITT	
	LIFE NUMBER:
SEX: M BORN: 19-FEB-1998	1416-JR57790

IN THE INTEREST OF:	**CASE NUMBER:** 1416-JU0040988
ALYSHA WASHINGTON	
	LIFE NUMBER:
SEX: F BORN: 07-APRIL-2003	1416-JR57791

IN THE INTEREST OF:	**CASE NUMBER:** 1416-JU0040989
HOPE WASHINGTON	
	LIFE NUMBER:
SEX: F BORN: 17-NOV-2004	1416-JR57792

FINDINGS AND RECOMMENDATIONS

Now on January 18, 2012, there being present:

CAMILLE HARRIS	-	Children's Division
JOELLE MERRITT	-	Mother
ABIGAIL NORRIS	-	Attorney for the Juvenile Officer
HENRIETTA MILLER	-	Guardian ad Litem (CASA)
MIRIAM FINE	-	CASA Volunteer
MARTIN JAYLON	-	Attorney for Mother
TYRONE MERRITT	-	Juvenile
ALYSHA WASHINGTON	-	Juvenile
HOPE WASHINGTON	-	Juvenile

The cause comes on for Cases Review pursuant to an order of OCTOBER 26, 2011.

IT IS HEREBY ORDERED: that the juveniles continue to be committed to the custody of Children's Division for placement with the maternal grandparents' or in another non-relative licensed placement, until further order of the Court.

IT IS FURTHER ORDERED:

1. Reasonable efforts were exercised by Children's Division including visits, therapy, parent aid and others, but the mother continues not to participate at the expected level. Specifically, she has not chosen to participate in the following voluntary services, which would be funded and provided by Children's Division:
    Psychological evaluation
    Substance abuse screening/evaluation
    Random drug testing

    The mother has participated in some supervised visits – approximately one/month – but continues to decline offered opportunities to visit the children and to cancel some scheduled visits. Furthermore, she has sometimes appeared to be under the influence during visits.

    The mother has not addressed all the issues including sobriety and mental health concerns.

2. In all other respects the prior order remains in full force and effect.

The next court hearing for the above action is scheduled for MAY15, 2012, at 10:00 AM in DIVISION 40 for Permanency Hearing.

Notice of Findings and Recommendation & Notice of Right to a Rehearing

The parties are notified that the forgoing Findings and Recommendations have been entered this date by a commissioner, and all papers relative to the care or proceeding, together with the Findings and Recommendation have been transferred to a Judge of the Court. The Findings and Recommendations shall become the Judgment of the Court upon adoption by order of the Judge. Unless waived by the parties in writing, at party in the case or proceeding heard by a commissioner, within fifteen days after the mailing of notice of the filing of the Judgment of the Court, may file a motion for rehearing by a Judge of the Court. If the motion for rehearing is not ruled on within forty-five days after the motion is filed, the motion is overruled for all purposes. Rule 130.13.

January 19, 2012
_____
Date

Gerard E. Solomon
_____
GERARD E. SOLOMON, Commissioner

Order and Judgment Adopting Commissioner's Findings and Recommendation

It is hereby ordered, adjudged and decreed the foregoing Findings and Recommendations entered by the commissioner are adopted and confirmed as a final Judgment of the Court.

January 19, 2012   *Suzanne M. Martell*

Date   Judge

NOTICE OF ENTRY OF JUDGMENT

You are hereby notified that on   JAN 20 2012,   the Family Court, Juvenile Division, of Jackson County, Missouri made and entered the above judgment in this case:

You are further notified that you may have a right of appeal from this judgment under Rule 120.01 and section 211.261, RSMo, which provides that:

1. An appeal shall be allowed to the juveniles from any final judgment made under the Juvenile Code and may be taken on the part of the juveniles by the custodian.

2. An appeal shall be allowed to custodian from any final judgment made under the Juvenile Code that adversely affects the custodian.

3. Notice of appeal shall be filed in accordance with Missouri law.

4. Neither the filing of a notice of appeal nor the filing of any motion subsequent to the judgment shall act to stay the execution of a judgment unless the court enters an order staying execution.

Corrine Adamson

Deputy Court Administrator

Certificate of Service

This is to certify that a copy of the foregoing was hand delivered/faxed/emailed/mailed and/or sent through the eFiling system to the following on JAN 20 2012,

M R Jones

Copies to:

ABIGAIL NORRIS
Attorney for the Juvenile Officer

MARTIN JAYLON
Attorney for the Natural Mother

CAMILLE HARRIS
CHILDREN'S DIVISION

HENRIETTA MILLER
JACKSON COUNTY CASA

MARLIN THOMPSON
Putative Father

JEROME WASHINGTON
Natural Father – Alysha Washington, Hope Washington

JOELLE MERRITT
Natural Mother

January 18, 2012

Family Support Team Meeting

Case: Merritt-Washington
Facilitator: Camille Harris, Children's Division worker
Location: Library Conference Room, Jackson County CASA
In attendance:
        Tyrone Merritt – Juvenile
        Alysha Washington – Juvenile
        Hope Washington – Juvenile
        Joelle Merritt – Mother
        Martin Jaylon – Mother's Attorney
        Mabel Merritt – Maternal Grandmother
        Camille Harris – CD Worker
        JoAnne Whittaker – parent aid
        Miriam Fine – CASA Volunteer
        Anita Blackstone – CASA Case Supervisor (taking notes for the group)

Camille Harris passed around the attendance log / confidentiality agreement for everyone to sign.

She asked the children to begin, and said after their turns they would be excused for the remainder of the meeting.

Tyrone Merritt – Defiant and angry during meeting, said he didn't know why he still had to see his mother when she was always drunk. He said the Court hearings were stupid because "nothing changes anyway, no matter what I want." He also said school was stupid, but he was going because he had to.

Alysha Washington – Reported school was going well, but wouldn't say more. Seemed upset at Tyrone's outbursts.

Hope Washington – Sat next to her mother, but wouldn't sit on her lap this time. She squirmed away when Joelle reached down to pick her up. She said she had a new friend at school who had a dog, and she liked her teacher. She said she wished that "Tyrone wouldn't yell all the time like Daddy." This seemed to surprise both Joelle and Mabel.

(Children left room with parent aid to supervise – meeting continued.)

Mabel Merritt, maternal grandmother – Reported she had taken Tyrone to meet with school counsellor and principal after truancy incidents. She said he was going to school at the present time, she thought to avoid suspension, but admitted she was having trouble controlling his behavior. She said she thought it would be better when Roger's health improved and he could help with Tyrone, but right now she was having trouble taking care of Roger and managing the children on her own, especially with Tyrone acting out.

Camille asked Mabel if she wanted CD to start looking for another placement for the children, and Mabel said absolutely not. She said, "You mean put them in foster care with strangers?" Camille asked if there were any other relatives who might be appropriate, but Mabel said Joelle was their only living child and the children's great-aunts and uncles lived out of state. She said the children's paternal grandparents had been out of the picture since Joelle testified against Jerome Washington at the domestic assault trial.

Camille asked what other resources might help the situation, and Mabel said she would reach out to her pastor to see if some of the church members could help with meals and driving the kids while Roger was still laid up. Everyone agreed that sounded like a good idea. Camille encouraged Mabel to reach out to the team at any time if she needed more help or felt she could not safely care for the children.

Mabel said, "I won't ever let these kids go to foster care – I'll make it work."

Joelle Merritt, mother – Seemed very upset by the proceedings and began to cry. Told the group she promised to get sober and take care of her children. "My kids don't belong in foster care."

Camille Harris, CD worker – Reminded Joelle that the first step to reunification was for her to access the services the Court had ordered. She told Joelle she would call her tomorrow to schedule a psych eval and drug screening, and Joelle nodded in assent.

Miriam Fine, CASA Volunteer – Reported the girls continue to thrive in their grandparents' home. Continuing in this stable placement and their school situations remained her top priority for their well-being. She didn't know what to do about Tyrone, asked if CD would consider another visit to the therapist since the situation appeared to be getting worse.

Camille said she didn't think that was warranted yet, but it should remain a future option.

Anita Blackstone, CASA Case Supervisor – nothing to add.

Group agreed on 3/15/12 for next FST. Anita will schedule with CASA to use the Library Conference Room and will notify parties about time.

Mabel exited the room and took the children away before Joelle could say good-bye to them.

AJB / uploaded to OPTIMA 1-18-12

Optima™

Welcome **miriam.fine**
Change Password   Log Off

**Staff
Dashboard**

**Volunteers
Dashboard**

Volunteers

**Lookup
Tables**

Cases

**User
Administration**

Reports

Contact Log

Name	Fine, Miriam
Case Number	594
Activity Date	1/24/2012
Activity Type	School Visit
Subject	School Attendance / Performance
Location	Central Middle School
Contact Type	Face-to-face
Hours	1.50

Notes:

I joined Camille Harris at a meeting with Mabel Merritt and the principal and 8th grade counsellor at Central Middle School to discuss Tyrone's continuing truancy. He skips class several times a week -- sometimes just one period -- other times a full or half day.

We explained Tyrone's traumatic history of domestic violence and neglect and difficult home situation. While sympathetic, both Mr. O'Neill and Ms. Brown indicated these are not excuses for poor behavior or failure to attend school. Ms. Brown stated several times that in her experience "giving students in difficult situations slack" only leads to further problems. She feels that students who have been raised in chaos need structure, discipline, and firm rules.

The school has agreed to keep Tyrone enrolled through the next month. However, if Mabel is unable to persuade (force?) him to attend class on a regular basis, then he will be suspended for 3 weeks. The school does not plan to call the police or take action to place Tyrone in juvenile detention.

I walked Mabel out to her car, and she was distraught. I do not believe she knows how to convince Tyrone to go to school, nor does she know where he spends the time when he is not in class.

Activity Status	Approved

From: Miriam Fine [mailto:miriamkfine@gmail.com]
Sent: Wednesday, February 8, 2012 11:42 PM
To: chaines@jacksoncountycasa-mo.org
Cc: ablackstone@jacksoncountycasa-mo.org
Subject: RE: *Confidential: Merritt—Washington—Emergency Assistance Request

Cherry,

I'm writing to ask for more help for Mabel Merritt, the grandmother who is driving her three grandkids to their original schools so their education won't be disrupted. You previously provided three $100 Gas Gift Cards that got the family through September, October, and November.

You mentioned at that time we could possibly reach out to the CASA donor network via social media for more help if needed.

I'd like to do that if you're still willing. The family is really struggling. The grandfather, who was the sole breadwinner, had major surgery in November and has not been able to return to work. The older sibling, a teen-age boy, has begun skipping school, and I would like to help this grandmother as much as possible so she doesn't give up and ask us to put the kids in foster care, which would definitely not be in their best interests.

I'm available to pick up Gas Gift Cards from the CASA house or directly from donors and get them to the family.

Also—you mentioned in your previous email that you could provide referrals to other social service agencies to help with food assistance. I will pass along any information you can provide. I am hopeful that if we all pull together we can keep these kids in this family placement and avoid the disruption of a new home setting and new schools.

Many thanks!
Miriam

Miriam Fine
(913) 555-8436

"If I can't dance, I don't want to be part of your revolution." -- Emma Goldman

Posts

Jackson County MO CASA

February 9 at 10:44 a.m.

We have three CASA kids who need your help. They are living with their grandparents who have been working hard to be sure they can remain in their original schools, so that their education won't be disrupted. This takes a lot of driving, and that means a lot of added expense for an older couple. If you can help provide a Gas Card so these loving grandparents can continue to provide for these three kids, it would be a great gift. To help, email Cherry Haines at <u>volunteer@jacksoncountycasa-mo.org</u>.

From: Cherry Haines [mailto:chaines@jacksoncountycasa-mo.org]
Sent: Monday, February 13, 2012 2:49 PM
To: miriamkfine@gmail.com
Cc: ablackstone@jacksoncountycasa-mo.org
Subject: *Confidential: Merritt—Washington—Gas Card Donations / JFS Referral

Dear Miriam,

Our CASA supporters are so generous! We had a very good response from our Facebook post asking for Gas Cards to help the grandmother continue to get the Merritt-Washington kids to school. We have received several cards for $25 and $50, and two local businesses took up employee collections and brought in about $250 in cash. I will purchase Gas Cards with that money, so you can have those, too.

Our policy at CASA is to provide assistance on an "as needed" basis. We have had unfortunate experiences in the past with families selling gift/gas cards on the open market and then using the cash for drugs. Also, since CASA children can be moved from their placement with little notice, we want to be sure the family has the children in their home when they use the assistance we provide.

In keeping with this policy, I will keep the Gas Cards here at CASA, and you can pick them up before your monthly visits. If I'm not in the office when you come, both Angela and Marcus know where we keep the key to my cabinet.

I spoke with our contact at Jewish Family Services (JFS) and they would be happy to fast-track Mabel Merritt for an assessment to receive monthly Food Pantry assistance. In our experience, families that take advantage of that opportunity to "shop" for free food each month experience considerable budget relief. Also, the JFS staff can help her sign up for food stamps through SNAP (Supplemental Nutrition Assistance Program). You should have Mabel call Lorraine at (816) 555-6702 and say she was referred by CASA. Lorraine knows to expect her call.

I know you said the grandmother was very independent and didn't believe in taking "welfare," but now that her husband is disabled, perhaps she will be willing to access this assistance for the benefit of the children. You might tell her that the staff at JFS is very knowledgeable and very respectful, and I think she will find there is no loss of dignity in the process. You might also tell her it would cost the state a lot more to put the kids in foster care (which is no one's preference), so accessing SNAP benefits might actually be saving the government money. See if that persuades her.

Let me know if you have any questions. I know these situations are very difficult. Thank you for looking out for these children.

Cherry Haines
Director of Volunteer Programs
Jackson County CASA
www.jacksoncountycasa-mo.org
Direct: 816.555.8204

Staff   Volunteers   Volunteers   Lookup   Cases   User   Reports
Dashboard   Dashboard   Tables   Administration

Contact Log

Name	Fine, Miriam
Case Number	594
Activity Date	2/20/2012
Activity Type	Placement Visit
Subject	Child welfare
Location	Grandparents' Home
Contact Type	Face-to-face
Hours	1.00
Notes:	

The children had a three-day weekend for President's Day, so I was able to visit mid-morning. Joelle had visited the day before, the first time she had come over to the Merritt's house since the children moved there. Mabel said Joelle spent most of the vist watching TV with Roger, who is now able to come downstairs and sit in his easy chair in the living room. She did play Go Fish! and Crazy 8's with the girls at the dining room table, and she let Hope show her their bedroom.

She tried to talk to Tyrone, but he left the house and did not come back until she was gone.

Mabel told me that she did not agree with CD's policy to continue these parent visits. I explained to her again about the "12 month" rule, but she remains convinced these visits are not good for the children, and she sees no sign that that they are motivating Joelle to get sober. She said Joelle was not drunk during the visit, but when she called her on the phone later that night, she was slurring her words and speaking incoherently.

I gave Mabel three Gas Cards totaling $100 for the coming month and she said thank you repeatedly. Every small bit of encouragement seems to help in her difficult situation. I also gave her Lorraine's number at Jewish Family Services and told her that CASA highly recommends their services. I explained that Lorraine could help figure out if the family was eligible for food stamps while Roger was unable to work, and -- either way -- she could shop in the JFS Food Pantry one week every month to get free, nutritious food to feed the kids.

She seemed particularly interested when I told her they also had toilet paper and shampoo and other basic items. I think those are the "extras" she finds very hard to pay for with three additional people in the household.

I only had a few minutes alone with each of the girls, but they seem to be doing just fine. They were happy to have a day off from school (Hope told me they were allowed to sleep late and help make pancakes for breakfast), though they both told me they didn't mind going back to class tomorrow.

Tyrone told me that he has been going to class because "my grandmother is going to kick my ass out if I don't." I told him it is a teenager's job to go to school, and I was glad he was taking his responsibility seriously and also minding his grandmother. He grumbled under his breath, but he didn't talk back to me. I think it's possible that the threat of suspension scared him into compliance. He showed me the "robot" he made from the LEGO kit I brought last time. Building things remains his one consistent interest.

Activity Status   Approved

From: Miriam Fine [mailto:miriamkfine@gmail.com]
Sent: Wednesday, February 22, 2012 7:59 PM
To: hgoldstein@laramyjones.com
Subject: 10 Things You Can't Buy with Food Stamps

So today I'm over at the condo visiting Mom, talking about the book event (57 days to go!) and Marilyn Friedmann's thesis about why Jews choose to give charity beyond our own faith community.

I'm telling Mom how proud I am that our Jewish Family Services has this state-of-the-art Food Pantry, where even non-Jews—like my CASA family—can get help. I say something like, "I just read in the Jewish Post that even people that get food stamps can access our Food Pantry to help them get through the month. The article said the Missouri SNAP food stamp program provides $128.54 per person per month. That's $4.28 a day. I spent more than that on the latte I picked up on my way over here."

And she says: "I don't like food stamps because poor people might use them to buy cigarettes, and I feel like my tax dollars are enabling their bad behavior."

I could have fallen through the floor. My kind, generous, philanthropic, always-voted-Democrat mother thinks that poor people use food stamps to buy cigarettes! I was so taken aback that I immediately hopped onto her computer and googled food stamps, so she could see it in writing.

Households may not use SNAP (Supplemental Nutrition Assistance Program) benefits to purchase:

- Beer, wine, liquor
- Cigarettes or tobacco products
- Pet foods
- Soaps, including dishwasher detergent or washing machine soap
- Paper products, including toilet paper or paper towels
- Feminine hygiene products, including pads or tampons
- Diapers
- Shampoo, deodorant, toothpaste, dental floss, mouth wash, or hand lotion
- Vitamins and medicines
- Prepared, hot foods

To mom's credit, she was immediately contrite. I think it really got to her that a poor woman couldn't use public benefits to buy diapers or toilet paper. It is pretty appalling when you think about it: We'll feed you, but God forbid you want to put a clean diaper on your baby or wipe your kids' butts. Or your own.

You know, I'm learning a lot from my CASA work. What it looks like to be poor, but doing your best in a situation you never thought you'd be in. I truly believe if every well-off, well-meaning, entitled person (insert my mom's name here; hell, insert my name here) got to meet one poor person in their home, on their turf, and learned their name and their story, we would have a lot more charity and a lot better public services than we do today.

End of sermon. Tomorrow I'm going to donate toilet paper to the JFS Food Pantry.

Miri

_____

Miriam Fine
(913) 555-8436

"If I can't dance, I don't want to be part of your revolution." -- Emma Goldman

March 15, 2012

Family Support Team Meeting

Case:	Merritt-Washington
Facilitator:	Camille Harris, Children's Division worker
Location:	Children's Division offices – 615 E. 13th St., KC MO
	Upstairs Conference Room

In attendance:

      Tyrone Merritt – Juvenile
      Alysha Washington – Juvenile
      Hope Washington – Juvenile
      Joelle Merritt – Mother
      Martin Jaylon – Mother's Attorney
      Mabel Merritt – Maternal Grandmother
      Camille Harris – CD Worker
      Duncan Walsh – CD Supervisor
      Miriam Fine – CASA Volunteer
      Anita Blackstone – CASA Case Supervisor (taking notes for the group)

Camille Harris passed around the attendance log / confidentiality agreement for everyone to sign.

She asked the children to begin and said after their turns they would be excused for the remainder of the meeting. She told them they could sit in chairs in the hallway until the adults were done.

Tyrone Merritt – Very angry about the threat of school suspension and told the group, "Everyone cuts classes – I don't see why this is such a big deal." He said he thought coming to all these meetings was stupid, and "nothing ever gets better anyway." Joelle (mother) tried to talk to him, but he cut her off and refused to engage.

Alysha Washington – Reported she is doing very well in school. Said she is getting used to living with her grandparents and is glad her grandfather is feeling better now.

Hope Washington – Seemed intimidated by the new setting. Sat with grandmother and wouldn't talk.

(Children left room to sit in hallway – meeting continued.)

Mabel Merritt, maternal grandmother – Reported that Roger's health continues to improve, which is a help with the children. She hopes he can go back to work soon, which will help with the bills. Said both Hope and Alysha continue to do well. She said they are enjoying Sunday School and continue to do well in their elementary school classes. "They are such good girls, especially when you consider what they've gone through." Reported Alysha needed new glasses, since she broke her current frames while playing at school. Asked CD for help navigating the process to get new glasses under Medicaid. Reported Tyrone continues to be sullen and difficult to manage. "He is going to school, but he puts up a fight. It is really hard on all of us." She said it gets worse after visits with his mother. She said she thinks Joelle is continuing to drink and doesn't understand why she doesn't get help so she can get her kids back.

Camille Harris, CD worker – Told group that the Permanency Hearing was set for May 15 at which time CD would likely recommend goal change to adoption since "we have seen no effort by Joelle to access services." She encouraged Joelle to talk to her attorney to be sure she understood the consequences of not participating in the reunification process.

Joelle Merritt, mother – Accused the group of ganging up on her. "You don't know what it's like. It's impossible to work and do everything you want me to. You all just want to take my kids away."

Miriam Fine, CASA Volunteer – Reported the girls continue to do well in their grandparents' home and continuing this placement is in their best interests. Expressed ongoing concern about Tyrone's escalating behaviors. Said she was having trouble getting through to him now, but agreed he should stay with Roger and Mabel as long as they can manage, especially since keeping the siblings together remains a top priority. Said she agreed the goal should be changed to adoption if there was no significant progress in the next two months; she would make that recommendation in her report to the court.

Anita Blackstone, CASA Case Supervisor – nothing to add.

Group agreed to set next meeting time pending results of the Permanency Hearing.

Children were sitting in hallway when group adjourned, and Mabel took them home.

AJB / uploaded to OPTIMA 3-15-12

From: Miriam Fine [mailto:miriamkfine@gmail.com]
Sent: Friday, March 16, 2012 10:44 AM
To: ablackstone@jacksoncountycasa-mo.org
Cc: hmiller@jacksoncountycasa-mo.org
Subject: *Confidential: Merritt—Washington—do we have to meet at CD again?

Hi, Anita,

I wanted to follow up after yesterday's FST at the CD offices downtown.

Not to be too crass, but . . . why is the Children's Divisions such an incredibly ugly place?? I was expecting something like Children's Mercy Hospital—where the walls are pastel and the decorations are kid-friendly and the furniture (at least some of it) is soft and comfy and kid-sized. Not some concrete bunker with nothing on the walls except posters with rules and regulations and meeting rooms with old metal tables and folding chairs. And no windows. Why is the government so thoroughly opposed to meeting rooms with windows?

I was horrified we were bringing the children to a building like this. There's nothing at all to suggest it is a place meant to help them. I have two questions to follow, but first: I'd like to ask that we never, ever meet at CD for an FST again. I know the CASA conference rooms were booked yesterday, but going forward, if CASA is unavailable, I am advocating to reschedule the meeting. It is NOT in these children's best interests to be re-traumatized by walking through scary hallways and sitting in dismal rooms on hard grown-up chairs twice their size while their futures are decided.

My two questions:

1. Is it okay that we made the kids sit out in the hall unattended while we talked in a room with a closed door? What if Hope had to go to the bathroom? What if Tyrone decided to bolt? What if a violent dad on another case came down the hallway? The place is probably safe, but we had to go through a metal detector to get in the building, so someone is obviously worried about security. I know when we meet at CASA, we require an adult be present to supervise the children. Why doesn't this rule apply when we're at CD?

2. How can I expedite getting Alysha new glasses? Mabel has put tape around the bridge of her old ones to hold them together, but they aren't very stable, and I don't want the other kids to make fun of her. Let me know how to make that happen as quickly as possible.

Thanks always!

Miriam

_____
Miriam Fine
(913) 555-8436

"If I can't dance, I don't want to be part of your revolution." -- Emma Goldman

From: Camille.Harris@dss.mo.gov
Sent: Monday, March 27, 2012 4:45 PM
To: ablackstone@jacksoncountycasa-mo.org; hmiller@jacksoncountycasa-mo.org;
cc: miriamkfine@gmail.com
Subject: *Confidential: Merritt—Washington—Tyrone moved to Gillis

I am writing to inform the CASA team that Tyrone Merritt was moved to the Gillis School this morning after a violent outburst last night at his grandparents' home.

Earlier that day I took the children to McDonald's to visit with their mother. She was obviously intoxicated, and Tyrone was upset throughout the visit.

I returned the children to their grandparents' home around 3:30 p.m. Mabel Merritt called my cell phone at 9 p.m. to tell me that Tyrone had left the house after dinner (around 6:30 p.m.) and had not returned. She was going out to look for him. Mabel called again at 10:30 p.m. to say that she had found Tyrone at a friend's house where they had been drinking beer and smoking marijuana. She made him get in the car and drove him home, where he began yelling, waking up both the girls. The argument got heated, and Tyrone shoved Mabel; she hit the doorframe and bruised her arm. She eventually got him to go to bed, where he passed out.

Mabel said she could no longer keep Tyrone in her home. She was afraid for her safety and for the girls. Fortunately, Gillis had an open bed in their teen program, and I drove Tyrone there this morning.

I have notified the principal at Central Middle School that Tyrone has been moved to Gills.
If you would like to make arrangements to visit, you can call the Residential Placement Director at (816) 555-5617.

The mission of the Children's Division is to partner with families, communities and government to protect children from abuse and neglect and to assure safety, permanency and well being for Missouri's children.

Staff
Dashboard

Volunteers
Dashboard

Volunteers

Lookup
Tables

Cases

User
Administration

Reports

Contact Log

Name	Fine, Miriam
Case Number	594
Activity Date	3/29/2012
Activity Type	Placement Visit
Subject	Child welfare
Location	Gillis School
Contact Type	Face-to-face
Hours	0.75
Notes:	

I contacted the Residential Placement Director at Gillis to visit Tyrone, and they recommended letting him settle in for a few days. We met today in one of the conference rooms they use for therapy, family visits, and visits with the child's Guardian ad Litem. I was relieved that it is comfortable (easy chairs, coffe table, lamp lighting, and decent-sized windows) and not as institutional as I feared.

Tyrone looks awful -- not at all like the worried, but holding-it-together young man I met at CASA nearly a year ago. He has grown a lot, of course, and has the beginnings of facial hair now, but what is most changed are his eyes and his demeanor. He is now hyper-vigilant, with a lot of controlled (and uncontrolled) anger. I would be scared of him if I didn't know him so well.

I asked if I could sit and talk for a while, and he nodded. I asked if he wanted to tell me what happened, and he shrugged. I asked if there was anything he needed, and he did respond to that. He told me the CD worker had still not brought his asthma inhaler or his LEGO set -- and he needed them both. I told him I would bring them over the weekend if she didn't bring them before then. I think he trusts me to keep my word to him.

He asked if I knew what would happen to him. I told him I didn't know for sure, but I had talked with the Residential Placement Director, and it looked like he would stay at Gillis for 60 days to help him get his behaviors under control.

I told him he would have tutors there, and if he completed his schoolwork satisfactorilly, he could likely enroll in Central High in the fall with his classmates.

He asked if he could see his sisters, and I said I would ask Ms. Harris about arranging for a sibling visit. When he realized that might take some time, I think it really got to him. Up until then, I'm not sure he understood how significantly his circumstances had changed.

I promised I would follow up about the asthma inhaler and the LEGO set and would come back soon. He looked so defeated when I left, I felt very sorry for him.

Activity Status   Approved

Staff
Dashboard

Volunteers
Dashboard

Volunteers

Lookup
Tables

Cases

User
Administration

Reports

Contact Log

Name	Fine, Miriam
Case Number	594
Activity Date	3/29/2012
Activity Type	Placement Visit
Subject	Child welfare
Location	Grandparents' Home
Contact Type	Face-to-face
Hours	0.75

Notes:

I was able to visit the Merritt's home this afternoon to look in on the girls after school. I did not speak with them individually but talked to them at the dining room table while they were eating a snack Mabel had prepared.

I told them I had visited Tyrone in the new school where he was going to live for a few months and reassured them that he was okay. I told them I had walked around the school, and I thought it was very nice -- with brick buildings and a lot of grass and trees. Alysha asked if it looked like Hogwarts, and I told her it was nice, but it was not a castle. I think she was disappointed. She also told me about breaking her glasses on the playground. She feels guilty about the added worry for her grandmother, but she told me she "really needs new glasses so I can see."

Both girls asked when they could see Tyrone, and I told them I thought it would be a few weeks. Hope went and got Mr. Snuffles from her room when I said that, and brought him back to her chair at the table. This is the first time in several months that she has held him while we talked.

Alysha asked if it was their mother's fault that Tyrone got sent away, and I said that Tyrone just needed to live in a place that could help him be less angry. She nodded but didn't say anything more.

The girls went to their rooms to start their homework, and I talked with Mabel and Roger, who had come downstairs. Roger is not doing very well. He told me the doctors think he might need surgery on his other foot. Both grandparents are very concerned about Tyrone. They are clearly relieved that he has been placed somewhere with more supervision and therapeutic options, but they feel badly they couldn't take care of him. They are particularly worried about the girls and how this disruption will impact them.

We discussed the fact that the case is coming up on the 12-month mark. They agree with my current view that CASA should recommend Joelle's rights be terminated. They say they would like to adopt the children when the time comes. I just hope Roger's health does not get worse.

Activity Status   Approved

From: Camille.Harris@dss.mo.gov
Sent: Friday, March 30, 2012 10:14 AM
To: ablackstone@jacksoncountycasa-mo.org; hmiller@jacksoncountycasa-mo.org;
cc: miriamkfine@gmail.com
Subject: *Confidential: Merritt—Washington—Tyrone at Gillis

I am writing to confirm that I was able to pick up Tyrone Merritt's asthma inhaler from his grandmother's house and deliver it to Gillis this morning. Thank you to Miriam for alerting me about that. The staff there will be sure it is available as needed for any asthma flare-ups.

Regarding Miriam's question about sibling visits between Tyrone and his sisters, I do not know when we will be able to make that happen. The girls have school during the day, but I will talk to Mabel Merritt about possibly taking them to visit on the weekend if Gillis will allow. We'll see if we can't make that happen within the next few weeks.

> *The mission of the Children's Division is to partner with families, communities and government to protect children from abuse and neglect and to assure safety, permanency and well being for Missouri's children.*

From: Miriam Fine [mailto:miriamkfine@gmail.com]
Sent: Saturday, March 31, 2012 11:12 PM
To: hgoldstein@laramyjones.com
Subject: Kidnapping

Well, this has been my best and worst week as a CASA Volunteer. Here's the worst: CD picked up the teen-age boy on my case and swept him away to a residential placement. I'm not saying they were wrong. He has become increasingly hard to handle and became physically disruptive earlier in the week—nearly hurting his grandmother and scaring everyone in the house. There's no doubt he needs more structure and therapeutic help than she can provide right now.

But the way they do this! They just show up and grab the kid and whatever clothes and personal items someone thinks to pack in the chaos, and they're off with the kid and a suitcase (if he's lucky) and a bunch of trash bags filled with stuff. It's barbaric. The grandmother told me he didn't even get to say good-bye to his sisters.

Can you imagine? For years, this boy and his 8-year-old sister were each other's only support system, working together to take care of their baby sister and keep themselves alive. And now he's been moved with no notice, and he didn't get to say good-bye to his sisters, the most important people in his life (and vice versa). Tell me how that will reduce his trauma and help him find safety, peace, and the trust to build functional relationships and develop good behaviors?!

I went to visit him in the residential placement yesterday. It's an okay place—the physical campus is nice, and the staff seems experienced with kids his age. They have a lot of foster kids there, so they won't be surprised by anything my teen does.

But, oh, Hazel—the changes in this child! It's been less than a year since I first met him, but he has gone from a kind, clever young man, able to get food for his siblings and get himself to school every day, to a sullen, angry teen. I'm sure some of this is just adolescence, but it's easy to see that state intervention didn't make his life any better.

His grandparents are really good people, but the initial disruption was devastating, and the ongoing visits with their mother (required by law and CD policy) upset him on a monthly basis. I can't help but wonder: Why doesn't society reallocate the money we spend on CD and the Court system (all that payroll!) to mental health services and drug treatment for the parents before they get into so much trouble? Really—wouldn't that make more sense? I bet if some clever Harvard MBA ran the ROI, it would be obvious.

So, here's where I got to make a difference. It turns out that in the rush to pick up my kid and get him to his new placement, the CD worker forgot to grab his asthma inhaler. He doesn't need it all the time, but stress tends to trigger his asthma attacks—and being grabbed and hustled off to a residential placement certainly qualifies as stress. I guess no one else cared or asked, but thank God he told me when I went to see him. I called the CD worker on my cell phone as I was leaving the school, and she got on it right away. I think it scared her to realize this kid (in their care and custody!) might have an asthma attack and not have his emergency meds—because she screwed up.

She also forgot his LEGO set—one of his few important possessions—and even when I called, she didn't pick that up to deliver it with the inhaler. But I can get it tomorrow and use it as an excuse to visit again.

I'm also pissed that the CD worker thinks it may take "several weeks" to set up sibling visits between this teen and his sisters. I'm sure she's over-worked (I read the other day that the turnover at CD is horrible, and everyone is carrying caseloads way over the legal maximum), but keeping these kids apart traumatizes both my teen and the younger girls—who were just starting to get better.

I swear, Hazel—the more I learn about this system, the angrier I get. When you read in the paper about child abuse, you think the parents are the villains. But, really . . . it's all of us.

Enough, enough, enough. I got a kid his asthma medicine this week. I'll have to be content with that. Breathe . . . breathe . . . breathe . . .

MKF

_____
Miriam Fine
(913) 555-8436

"If I can't dance, I don't want to be part of your revolution." -- Emma Goldman

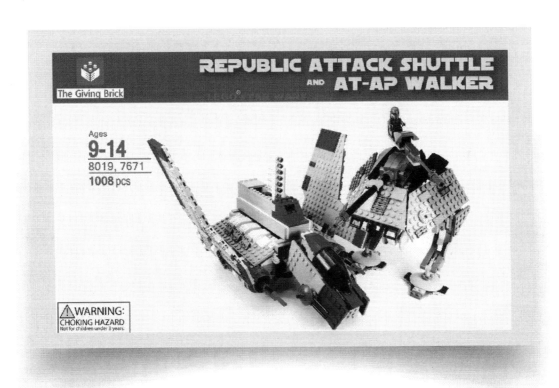

REPUBLIC ATTACK SHUTTLE AND AT-AP WALKER

The Giving Brick

Ages
9-14
8019, 7671
1008 pcs

WARNING:
CHOKING HAZARD
Not for children under 3 years.

Contact Log

Name	Fine, Miriam
Case Number	594
Activity Date	4/1/2012
Activity Type	Placement Visit
Subject	Child welfare
Location	Gillis School
Contact Type	Face-to-face
Hours	0.75

Notes:

I called ahead and the Residential Placement Director at Gillis made arrangements for me to meet Tyrone in the same conference room as before. He did not look any better. I asked how he was settling in and he shrugged. He said his roommate was older (15) and had been there about 4 months so he was "showing me the ropes."

He told me the CD worker had brought his asthma inhaler, and I told him I knew. I gave him his LEGO set, and he seemed visibly pleased. It is strange how that is the thing this kid cares the most about. I hope it also mattered that I kept my promise to him. I very much want him to believe that there are some adults who can be counted on to keep their word.

I told him I had seen Alysha and Hope and gave him a picture that Hope had drawn for him. He got a little shaky at that. He asked when he could see them, and I told him the CD worker was trying to get that arranged.

He seemed pretty interested in taking his LEGO kit back to his room, so I signed off. I told him I'd be back in a few weeks, but he could ask the Residential Director to contact me any time it was important. That I was his advocate, and he had a legal right to see me if he wanted to. I hope that made him feel better. Poor kid.

Activity Status   Approved

From: Miriam Fine [mailto:miriamkfine@gmail.com]
Sent: Saturday, April 7, 2012 7:59 PM
To: hgoldstein@laramyjones.com
Subject: 12 days and counting

We're almost there. I have to admit, planning this book thing with mom has been a lot more fun than I expected. She's annoying for sure (isn't that a mother's primary job? Even when her children are mothers themselves?), but she's also really smart and really good at this. I had forgotten. It's been a real treat to see her work her magic on everyone involved—the mildly self-important author, the slightly officious library marketing manager, the moderately difficult caterer, and—she would say—the ridiculously promotion-obsessed daughter.

But in the end, it's really coming together. Mom's talent for taking everyone seriously and making even the gal who runs the reception desk at the library feel important is a pleasure to watch. It's authentic, which is why it works. I could learn from that.

We have over 200 people who have RSVP'd, and the library tells me they usually get 25% who just show up, so we'll fill the hall, maybe even go a little into the overflow space. I've managed to get a little coverage in The Star and some other print and online calendars, and the Jewish Post has promised a story after the event. And—don't tell Mom—the Facebook event page is doing really well, with lots of likes and general engagement.

You've been a big help, too. Thanks for spreading the word in your legal circles and with your book club. I recognized a lot of the names on the RSVP list from your contacts. It would be great if you can come early and help me manage greeting people at the reception—thanks for offering!

And we just got terrific news—both Arielle and Isaac are going to come in for the event. That makes me really happy—it is a lovely way to honor their grandma. And they'll stay the weekend, which is even better.

You know, I became a CASA Volunteer to distract me from Mom. And now I've helped plan an entire book event with Mom to distract me from CASA.

I'm sure there's a lesson in there somewhere . . .

Miri

Miriam Fine
(913) 555-8436

"If I can't dance, I don't want to be part of your revolution." -- Emma Goldman

Dr. Ben Arielto   (816) 555-2905

NAME: Tyrone X. Merritt
ADDRESS: The Gillis School, 8150 Wornall Rd., KC MO 64114
DATE: 4/10/12

ABILIFY for 60 days -
        2 mg Day 1 and 2
        5 mg Day 3 and 4
        10 mg Day 5 – continue at this level

2 refills

SIGNED: *Dr. B Arielto* _____ M.D.

From: Miriam Fine [mailto:miriamkfine@gmail.com]
Sent: Thursday, April 12, 2012 9:15 AM
To: hgoldstein@laramyjones.com
Subject: Drugs!

They warned us about this in Training—and now it's happened to my kid. The contract psychiatrist for the residential facility who's supposed to provide counseling and support for my CASA teen has put him on psychotropic meds—after a 15-minute visit and no effort at talk therapy—or anything!

The drug is Abilify. I looked it up (emphasis mine):

> Abilify is FDA approved to treat schizophrenia, bipolar disorder in some adolescent and teens, as well as irritability associated with autism spectrum disorder. But the drug is prescribed off-label in children as a mood stabilizer and to treat ADHD symptoms.

So this poor teen, who has been traumatized since the age of four by domestic violence and impacted by his mother's mental illness, alcoholism, and—mostly—poverty, and who probably needs way more therapy than any of us, is . . . put on drugs. Drugs that are intended for very serious disorders (which he does not have) and drugs which have been shown to produce suicidal tendencies in children!!!

I had heard that children in foster care and residential placements were much more likely to be put on psychotropic meds. Read this from a policy brief put out in October by the American Bar Association Center on Children and the Law (author: JoAnne Solchany, PhD, ARNP):

> Multiple studies and reports have found that children in foster care are vulnerable to inappropriate or excessive medication use. The issues vary but the underlying concern that children in care are more vulnerable to improper psychotropic medication use remains the same.

I asked my Case Supervisor what we could do, and she said our best bet is to get him stable and get him out of residential. Then his grandmother can advocate directly for a more appropriate therapeutic approach. I swear to God, Hazel, this whole "care and custody" thing stinks. There's plenty of custody. But where's the care?

I'm beginning to wonder if there is also overuse of psychotropic meds by CASA Volunteers—or at least overuse of red wine. I'll let you know . . .

MKF

Miriam Fine
(913) 555-8436

"If I can't dance, I don't want to be part of your revolution." -- Emma Goldman

Giving Back:
How Jewish Business Leaders
Shaped Kansas City's Philanthropic Landscape
Past and Present

by Marilyn Friedmann

The Kansas City Public Library
Plaza Branch
Thursday, April 19, 2012

Reception (hosted by Esther Fine and Miriam Fine)	6 p.m.
Author Talk and Q&A	7 p.m.
Book Signing	8 p.m.

Marilyn Friedmann, local historian and author, will highlight four Kansas City Jewish families who used their business success to help fund social justice priorities in the general community:

The Oppenstein Brothers Foundation was established in 1941, after the death of Louis Oppenstein, a millionaire who made his fortune in the retail jewelry business. At the age of fourteen, Oppenstein left school when his father died to support his mother and six siblings. With his brothers as partners, he purchased the Herman Streicher Watch and Jewelry Company at 1017 Main Street. The Oppenstein Brothers jewelry business became quite successful, and Louis began investing in downtown real estate. Today, the Oppenstein Brothers Foundation, managed by Commerce Bank, funds many religious, charitable, scientific, and educational activities in Kansas City.

The H&R Block Foundation was established in 1974 to improve the quality of life of Kansas Citians through thoughtful, innovative, and responsible philanthropy. According to Henry Bloch, Chairman of the Foundation, who co-founded the H&R Block tax preparation company with his brother in 1955: *"Kansas City saw my company through the lean years, and I'm grateful for the opportunity to give back."* The Foundation has provided millions of dollars to nonprofit organizations in the areas of Arts and Culture; Neighborhood Revitalization; Education; and Health and Human Services.

The Sosland Foundation was created by descendants of Russian Jewish immigrants who came to America and settled in Kansas City in the late 19th century. In the early years, family members suffered from extreme poverty, eventually starting a business that was to become Sosland Publishing Co. The business thrived, giving the family the opportunity to pursue their charitable responsibilities both as a moral and religious obligation. The children, grandchildren, and great-grandchildren of Sosland Foundation founders now carry on this philanthropic tradition.

The Gould Charitable Foundation was created in 1988 as a memorial to the late Robert (Bob) Gould by his family. A leader in the mutual fund industry, Gould moved from Boston to Kansas City to work for DST, where he served as President from 1984 until his death. The Foundation focuses on projects that reflect Gould's values and interests and the family's own evolving concerns in both Kansas City and Boston. Priority areas include Elder Services, Environmental Stewardship, Health Care, Preservation of Personal Rights, Training for the Disadvantaged, Welfare and Education of Children, and Women's Issues.

The Kansas City
Jewish Post

Thursday, 26 April 2012

Local author highlights Jewish leaders giving back to the community

More than 250 audience members gathered on Thursday night, April 19, at the Plaza Branch of the Kansas City Public Library to hear local author and historian Marilynn Friedmann talk about how Jewish business leaders have impacted community philanthropy in Kansas City.

While Friedmann's book touches on many successful Jewish business men and women who went on to become significant philanthropists, her talk last week spent particular time focusing on the history of four families who chose to expand their giving beyond the Jewish community to the broader Kansas City community as a whole.

The history of four family foundations provided the basis for Friedmann's book talk and the ensuing Q&A session: The Oppenstein Brothers Foundation, the H&R Block Foundation, the Sosland Foundation, and the Gould Charitable Foundation.

Friedmann, who holds an M.A. in History from Brandeis University and a B.S. in Journalism from the University of Missouri in Columbia, teaches history at Avila College and helps prepare students for Bar and Bat Mitzvah at Congregation Shir Shalom. She co-founded the Jewish Book Fair at the Jewish Community Center with Esther Fine in 1994 and was very active in its growth for many years.

"I have always been fascinated by the way Jews, in particular, believe that financial success carries an obligation to give back," Friedmann said. "This book was an opportunity to explore how very important business leaders in our Kansas City history chose to use their wealth to make the community better for all of us."

Esther Fine and her daughter Miriam Fine, also members of Congregation Shir Shalom, organized the library event and hosted a pre-talk reception for the community to personally meet Friedmann and discuss her book.

"I think it's important to showcase local authors whenever we can," Esther Fine said. "It's always a thrill to see how much talent we have right here in Kansas City."

From: Miriam Fine [mailto:miriamkfine@gmail.com]
Sent: Friday, April 27, 2012 11:35 PM
To: hgoldstein@laramyjones.com
Subject: Drugs—why is it always drugs?

Hey, thanks for taking my panicked call this afternoon. I've calmed down. Mom has been admitted at Menorah, so someone much smarter than me is now managing this. When I left after dinner, she was on an IV drip for the dehydration and seemed oriented again. At least she knew who she was, and who I was, and where she was ("the damned hospital again").

You were right to tell me to look in the medicine cabinet. Yep—mom has a nearly empty bottle of Bactrim in there, dated 10 days ago. She couldn't—or wouldn't—tell me why, but Jonathan thinks she went to one of those Minute Clinics complaining about a urinary tract infection, and they probably gave her the prescription. Given the timing, I'm betting she just didn't want to be sick for our book event. It meant so much to her to be there and be at her very best. Just like old times.

But . . . a week on that antibiotic, and here comes the diarrhea. It's predictable.

They're running tests now, but of course it's the C. Diff. That son-of-a-bitch just waits for an opportunity and gallops on in. I wish we could get mom to acknowledge how careful she needs to be with meds. It's getting harder and harder to reason with her all the time. And Jonathan's no match for her when she gets like this. Not his job, anyway. It's mine. Sigh.

So—mom's safe—if you can call a hospital safe when you're at risk for C. Diff—and I'm home. Safe. Everyone's safe. You did your job today, dear friend. Thanks.

And—no small footnote—we made it through the book event. And mom was at her very best. Just like old times. So I did my job too. She loved the article in the Post. They even quoted her. Yay.

Miriam Fine
(913) 555-8436

"If I can't dance, I don't want to be part of your revolution." -- Emma Goldman

Contact Log

Name	Fine, Miriam
Case Number	594
Activity Date	5/1/2012
Activity Type	Placement Visit
Subject	Child welfare
Location	Grandparents' Home
Contact Type	Face-to-face
Hours	0.75

Notes:

I stopped by to visit the girls at the Merritts late afternoon. The house was very calm -- things put away -- Mabel cooking dinner in the kitchen -- the girls working on schoolwork at the dining room table. I helped cut up salad ingredients so I could talk to Mabel for a bit. She seems much steadier. She said that things had settled down quite a bit since Tyrone left, that the girls missed him, but everyone seemed relieved without all the drama. She said she had taken the girls to Gillis twice to see Tyrone, and she thought it was helpful for them to see where he was, especially since the campus is so pretty. She said she thought he was doing better, he seemed genuinely glad to see her and was not exhibiting so much obvious anger. I asked about Roger, and she said he is still facing medical issues, but is at least back at work half time! I'm sure that is a big relief -- both emotionally and financially.

Mabel said she took the girls to meet Joelle at the park a couple of weeks ago on a Saturday mid-morning. She said it was one of their best visits yet. She doesn't think Joelle has stopped drinking, but she wasn't drunk that day, and the girls enjoyed being outside and playing with her. We talked briefly about the upcoming Permanency Hearing at court in two weeks. She had a lot of questions, and I told her I'd get clarification from my Case Supervisor and we could speak that morning before we went into the courtroom. She also mentioned that she had not heard back from Camille Harris about getting new glasses for Alysha.

The weather was warm, so Alysha and I went outside to our usual place on the porch. She told me about visiting with both her mother and Tyrone. She was matter-of-fact about both, and seemed calm and happy about the visits.

She reported that things continued to go well at school. She thinks her final report card will reflect all A's. I told her that was a real achievement, and something to be very proud about. I told her there is an upcoming Court hearing in two weeks when the Commissioner will decide where she and her siblings should live permanently. I asked her what she wanted me to tell him, and she said, "We all miss Mommy, but it's really good here. I want to stay." I told her I agreed with her assessment and would pass her view along with my recommendation for that outcome.

Hope was in a good mood, too. She chatted about her class, her friend, the visit to the park, and her visit to "the pretty school" to see Tyrone. I told her I would be going to court in a couple of weeks and asking the Commissioner if she and Alysha could stay with her grandparents for good. I asked if she would like that, too. She said "Yes -- but Tyrone has to be with us, too."

This was the most positive visit I have had with Mabel and the girls to date. Everyone agrees they would like to move forward to make this situation permanent, and with Roger getting back to work I think it will be much easier all around.

Activity Status   Approved

 **Optima™**

Staff   Volunteers   Volunteers   Lookup   Cases   User   Reports
Dashboard   Dashboard   Tables   Administration

Contact Log

Name	Fine, Miriam
Case Number	594
Activity Date	5/3/2012
Activity Type	Placement Visit
Subject	Child welfare
Location	Gillis School
Contact Type	Face-to-face
Hours	0.75

Notes:

I met Tyrone in the front office and we took a walk around the Gillis grounds. He is very subdued -- I think a side-effect of the meds -- but much calmer and less agitated. He told me he likes his Gillis tutor and feels like he is keeping up with his studies. He said he really wants to start high school in the fall, so he is working for that.

We talked about the visits from Mabel and his sisters. He said he really misses them and feels badly that his behavior meant he had to "abandon them." I told him it was most important that he focus on getting control of his emotions and actions, and he would have a lifetime ahead to be close to his siblings. I reminded him that Mabel and Roger were the kind of adults who could properly care for his sisters.

He did not ask about his mother, and I did not bring her up.

I told him about the Permanency Hearing in two weeks and explained that his is when the Commissioner will decide their long-term goal for a safe, permanent home. I told him that at 14 he was old enough to have a say in that decision. He said he had thought a lot about it. He didn't think he could ever go home to live with his mother again. He was just too angry at her for failing to take care of them and for not getting sober when she was given the chance.

He said he liked living with Mabel and Roger, and would like to "go home there" to live with his grandparents and sisters as soon as he could leave Gillis. I asked if he would like the Merritts to adopt him, and he seemed surprised. He said he might be a little old for that, but he would like to live with them anyway.

I said good-bye, and told him I would let him know what the Commissioner decided. For now, he should focus on getting better and doing his schoolwork. It was a good visit.

Activity Status   Approved

From: Anita Blackstone [mailto:ablackstone@jacksoncountycasa-mo.org]
Sent: Wednesday, May 16, 2012 2:23 PM
To: miriamkfine@gmail.com
Cc: hmiller@jacksoncountycasa-mo.org; Camille.Harris@dss.mo.gov
Subject: RE: *Confidential: Merritt—Washington—Permanency Hearing

Miri,

I'm responding to your email seeking clarification about tomorrow's hearing, so you can better explain them to Roger and Mabel Merritt before we go to court.

You are correct that the primary purpose of the Permanency Hearing, held 12 months into the case, is for the court to determine the ultimate goal for the children. This is required by law so that children do not languish for years in the system with no plan for a safe, permanent home.

In the case of the Merritt-Washington children, we had all hoped that the mother would seek counseling and drug treatment services, so we would be on a path to send the children home by now. As you have noted many times, this is one of those cases that looked like it would work out well, once mom got the help she needed. However, that has not happened, for a variety of reasons that you probably understand better than anyone. One thing I have learned over the years is that poverty, mental illness, and substance abuse are a toxic triangle, sometimes not easily untangled, even with the best of intentions. And late intervention can be as ineffective as no intervention at all.

That being said, these kids are amazingly lucky to have such great grandparents, who are willing to take them. At tomorrow's hearing, the AJO will recommend that the goal be changed from reunification to adoption. The supporting evidence will come from Children's Division testimony, among others, as well as the reports you have been submitting via OPTIMA for the past year, many of which have been submitted to the court via the children's social file. The Merritts will likely be called to the stand to testify about their ability and willingness to continue to care for the children. Someone from Gillis may be called to testify, as well.

As the children's Guardian ad Litem, CASA Staff Attorney Henrietta Miller will concur with this recommendation. We don't expect mom's attorney to object—they have no grounds.

Just to be clear, this is only the beginning of the process, not the end. The court will schedule a Permanency Review in 6-12 months. If mom has still not made any progress with services and if nothing else has happened to change the situation, then the court will move to set a date for the TPR (Termination of Parental Rights) hearing. This may or may not be held in conjunction with the adoption. It mostly depends if Joelle consents or if we have to go to trial. We'll need Jerome Washington's consent on Alysha and Hope, as well.

You'll notice tomorrow that we are just asking for a goal change to adoption—the decision to select Roger and Mabel as the adoptive parents will take place as part of the CD adoption staffing process. I don't foresee any issues with their selection—grandparents are a strong choice, and I don't see anyone else coming forward to seek custody—but that part isn't what the court is deciding tomorrow. You might want to be sure they understand that.

Tomorrow is a very big step in this case. Now that the mandatory 12-month period of required reunification efforts are over, things will start to move a little more quickly for these kids. At least we can hope so.

Thanks again for all you do—see you tomorrow at court!

Anita

Anita Blackstone
Case Supervisor
(816) 555-8236

IN THE CIRCUIT COURT OF JACKSON COUNTY, MISSOURI
FAMILY COURT DIVISION

IN THE INTEREST OF:	CASE NUMBER: 1416-JU0040987
TYRONE MERRITT	
	LIFE NUMBER:
SEX: M BORN: 19-FEB-1998	1416-JR57790

IN THE INTEREST OF:	CASE NUMBER: 1416-JU0040988
ALYSHA WASHINGTON	
	LIFE NUMBER:
SEX: F BORN: 07-APRIL-2003	1416-JR57791

IN THE INTEREST OF:	CASE NUMBER: 1416-JU0040989
HOPE WASHINGTON	
	LIFE NUMBER:
SEX: F BORN: 17-NOV-2004	1416-JR57792

FINDINGS AND RECOMMENDATIONS

Now on May 15, 2012 there being present:

CAMILLE HARRIS	-	Children's Division
JOELLE MERRITT	-	Mother
ABIGAIL NORRIS	-	Attorney for the Juvenile Officer
HENRIETTA MILLER	-	Guardian ad Litem (CASA)
MIRIAM FINE	-	CASA Volunteer
MARTIN JAYLON	-	Attorney for Mother
TYRONE MERRITT	-	Juvenile

The cause comes on for Permanency Hearing.

IT IS HEREBY ORDERED: that the juveniles Alysha Washington and Hope Washington are committed to the custody of Children's Division for placement with Mabel and Roger Merritt, until further order of the Court.

The juvenile Tyrone Merritt is committed to the custody of Children's Division for placement at the Gillis School as long as therapeutically recommended. When released he will be placed with Mabel and Roger Merritt or other licensed placement approved by Children's Division, until further order of the Court.

The mother, Joelle Merritt, may have supervised visitation that may be supervised by the Children's Division or custodians, in their discretion.

The efforts of the Children's Division to achieve reunification were reasonable, including offered counseling, psychological evaluation, and drug testing. The efforts were unsuccessful in part due to the mother's refusal/inability to participate in the offered services, and her apparent continuing substance abuse. The mother shall continue to be offered services.

The Court orders that the permanency plan in this case is adoption. This permanency plan is the most appropriate permanency plan and is in the best interests of the children. The court reaches this determination based on all of the reports and information received. The Children's Division is ordered to complete an adoption staffing in this case within 30 days.

At the hearings on October 26, 2011, and January 18, 2012, the Court received documentary evidence, including the social file of the juvenile containing reports and recommendations from the Children's Division since the inception of the case, the Guardian ad Litem's reports and recommendations, the CASA Volunteer's reports and recommendations, the psychological evaluations of the children, and the relative kinship home study of Mabel and Roger Merritt, dated June 2011.

The Court heard the testimony of Camille Harris, Children's Division worker from the inception of this case to the present, and reviewed her affidavit. The court found the testimony of Ms. Harris provided a reasonable foundation for the recommendation of that agency for placement of the children. The Court recognizes, as noted by the worker, that this recommendation is based on section 210.565 RSMo, which provides a preference for placement with relatives, if at all possible:

> Relative care is the least restrictive family-like setting for children requiring out-of-home placement. Relative care reinforces the social status that comes from belonging to a family of one's own and the sense of identity and self-esteem that is inherent in knowing one's family history and culture. Regardless of which of the five permanency options: Reunification, Adoption, Guardianship, Placement with Fit and Willing Relative, or Another Planned Permanent Living Arrangement (APPLA), is being considered for a foster youth, relative care is the placement of preference and should, if at all possible, be pursued prior to making any other type of out-of-home placement, unless a court determines that placing a foster youth with a relative is not in the best interest of that foster youth. (Child Welfare Manual; Section 4: Out of Home Care; Chapter 12: Relative or Kinship Care; effective date September 7, 2010).

The court also heard the testimony of Mr. and Mrs. Merritt, the maternal grandparents of the children. The children have been placed with the Merritts since they were picked up on May 11, 2011. The evidence showed that Alysha and Hope Washington have thrived in their placement with the Merritts. The testimony and evidence clearly showed that they are a wonderful placement for the children.

The testimony and evidence also showed that the Merritts were a good placement for Tyrone Washington until the last several months, when his behavior became disruptive, beginning on or about January 4, 2012.

The court heard the testimony of Leroy Jenkins, Residential Placement Director at the Gillis School, where the juvenile has been placed since March 27, 2012. The testimony and evidence presented by Mr. Jenkins showed that Tyrone is getting needed therapeutic treatment at Gillis and his behaviors are improving. The staff hopes to recommend release on or about June 30, 2012. At that time the recommendation is for the juvenile to return to the Merritts' home, as the placement was previously working. All parties in this case recommend keeping the siblings together if at all possible.

The court notes that it is always unfortunate when reunification plans are not successful. However, it is in the best interests of these children to move forward with a plan for permanency in a reasonable time frame. Since the mother has been unwilling/unable to participate in services to allow her to regain custody of her children, the goal is changed to adoption.

The next court hearing for the above action is scheduled for OCTOBER 23, 2012, at 02:00 PM in DIVISION 40 for Case Review prior to Permanency Review.

Notice of Findings and Recommendation & Notice of Right to a Rehearing

The parties are notified that the forgoing Findings and Recommendations have been entered this date by a commissioner, and all papers relative to the care or proceeding, together with the Findings and Recommendation have been transferred to a Judge of the Court. The Findings and Recommendations shall become the Judgment of the Court upon adoption by order of the Judge. Unless waived by the parties in writing, at party in the case or proceeding heard by a commissioner, within fifteen days after the mailing of notice of the filing of the Judgment of the Court, may file a motion for rehearing by a Judge of the Court. If the motion for rehearing is not ruled on within forty-five days after the motion is filed, the motion is overruled for all purposes. Rule 130.13.

May 17, 2012	*Gerard E. Solomon*
Date	GERARD E. SOLOMON, Commissioner

Order and Judgment Adopting Commissioner's Findings and Recommendation

It is hereby ordered, adjudged and decreed the foregoing Findings and Recommendations entered by the commissioner are adopted and confirmed as a final Judgment of the Court.

May 17, 2012	*Suzanne M. Martell*
Date	Judge

NOTICE OF ENTRY OF JUDGMENT

You are hereby notified that on   MAY 18 2012,   the Family Court, Juvenile Division, of Jackson County, Missouri made and entered the above judgment in this case:

You are further notified that you may have a right of appeal from this judgment under Rule 120.01 and section 211.261, RSMo, which provides that:

1. An appeal shall be allowed to the juvenile from any final judgment made under the Juvenile Code and may be taken on the part of the juvenile by the custodian.

2. An appeal shall be allowed to custodian from any final judgment made under the Juvenile Code that adversely affects the custodian.

3. Notice of appeal shall be filed in accordance with Missouri law.

4. Neither the filing of a notice of appeal nor the filing of any motion subsequent to the judgment shall act to stay the execution of a judgment unless the court enters an order staying execution.

Corrine Adamson
Deputy Court Administrator

Certificate of Service

This is to certify that a copy of the foregoing was hand delivered/faxed/emailed/mailed and/or sent through the eFiling system to the following on MAY 18 2012,

M R Jones

Copies to:

ABIGAIL NORRIS
Attorney for the Juvenile Officer

MARTIN JAYLON
Attorney for the Natural Mother

CAMILLE HARRIS
CHILDREN'S DIVISION

HENRIETTA MILLER
JACKSON COUNTY CASA

MARLIN THOMPSON
Putative Father
Address Unknown

JEROME WASHINGTON
Natural Father – Alysha Washington, Hope Washington

JOELLE MERRITT
Natural Mother

Care & Custody
Part Two

"Grandma said we've had a goal change. What does that mean? Is it like half-time when we play soccer?"

"I think so – maybe. Ms. Fine said it means the grown-ups have changed their minds about letting us go home to live with Mommy. We get to stay here now. I think."

"What about Tyrone? He's not here."

"Ms. Fine said he can come home to live with us really soon. She said he's not as mad anymore."

"What about Mommy? Is she mad?"

"I don't know, Hope. I don't have all the answers."

"I like it here with Grandma and Grandpa. Do we get to stay for good? Is this the last time the goal changes?"

"I don't know. Maybe if the grown-ups don't change their minds again. Let's try to go to sleep, okay? We'll pretend everything's okay."

Dear Ms. Fine,

   You said we could tell you if we needed anything. I need new glasses. I am really sorry I broke my old pair on the playground. Grandma keeps taping them but they are falling apart.

   Can you help me get new glasses so I can see the board at school?

Thank you.
Alysha

From: Miriam Fine [mailto:miriamkfine@gmail.com]
Sent: Wednesday, May 16, 2012 10:14 AM
To: Camille.Harris@dss.mo.gov
Cc: ablackstone@jacksoncountycasa-mo.org; hmiller@jacksoncountycasa-mo.org;
Subject: *Confidential: Merritt—Washington—Alysha's glasses

Dear Camille,

I'm writing to enlist your help to expedite the process to get new glasses for Alysha Washington.

As you'll recall, the grandmother, Mabel Merritt, first called this to our attention at the 10-month FST held at Children's Division two months ago on March 15. Alysha had broken her glasses on the school playground, and Mabel was asking for help to request a new pair through Medicaid or with a CD voucher.

While we were waiting for the Permanency Hearing yesterday, I asked Mabel if she had ordered the new glasses yet. She told me that she hasn't heard back from you. She has had to "re-tape" Alysha's glasses frames three times, and she is afraid they are now so unstable it is affecting Alysha's vision. She also told me Alysha is embarrassed about the way her broken glasses look and has started avoiding play dates with other children. Last weekend she refused to go to a classmate's birthday party.

I know the Permanency Hearing was a big project and an important milestone in this case. And I am also well aware of the time and energy everyone is putting in to helping Tyrone get stabilized at Gillis. However, while all these very important issues are being addressed, this simple, but significant, need remains unmet for this 9-year-old girl.

Please let me know what I can do to move this forward.

Miriam

Miriam Fine
(913) 555-8436

"If I can't dance, I don't want to be part of your revolution." -- Emma Goldman

From: Duncan.Walsh@dss.mo.gov
Sent: Thursday, May 17, 2012 9:13 AM
To: ablackstone@jacksoncountycasa-mo.org; hmiller@jacksoncountycasa-mo.org;
cc: miriamkfine@gmail.com
Subject: *Confidential: Merritt—Washington—Change in CD Worker

I am writing to inform the CASA team that Camille Harris is leaving Children's Division to take a position as a social worker with Cornerstones of Care. Her last day with CD will be May 25.

We have assigned a new worker, Marlie Verlet, to the Merritt-Washington case. Marlie graduated in December from the University of Missouri with a degree in social work and started at CD about a month ago. She is still in training for the next few months. During that time, I will be handling the Merritt-Washington case. We will introduce Marlie to the team when she begins working cases, probably at our scheduled FST in July. In the meantime, please direct all case-related correspondence and concerns to my attention.

Please let me know if you have any questions.

Duncan Walsh
Supervisor – Children's Division
Missouri Department of Social Services
(816) 555-9805

The mission of the Children's Division is to partner with families, communities and government to protect children from abuse and neglect and to assure safety, permanency and well being for Missouri's children.

From: Anita Blackstone [mailto:ablackstone@jacksoncountycasa-mo.org]
Sent: Friday, May 18, 2012 3:10 PM
To: miriamkfine@gmail.com
Cc: hmiller@jacksoncountycasa-mo.org
Subject: RE: *Confidential: Merritt—Washington—Change in CD Worker

Miri,

Thanks for your phone call concerning Camille Harris's departure from CD. I'm really sad about this, too. Camille was a very good worker. She stayed on top of her cases and did her best to get necessary resources for her families and kids. I know you were sometimes frustrated with the pace of things, but, trust me, your children/family got services much more quickly than most—in part thanks to Camille. I think she truly believed in her work and really cared about the kids.

I think we're just going to have to wait to meet the new worker. You're not off base to be concerned that she is brand new to CD—in my experience, most workers spend their first several months on the job just figuring out the policies and procedures of that internal bureaucracy. They rarely even know the names of the kids on their cases. But I think Duncan Walsh will keep us on a steady path for now, and we will just have to keep an eye on things as we transition to the new worker.

Honestly, we were lucky to have Camille on the case for this long. Most CD workers barely make it nine months in their positions. The good ones get promoted or take better jobs elsewhere (like Camille just did) or quit and get out of this work entirely. And the bad ones get shuffled around or fired. I know it is hard to start over with a new worker—and introduce a new "caring" adult into the kids' lives. But it is really the normal course of things in the child welfare world.

On your specific concern about Alysha's glasses: I will call Duncan today to let him know that Camille said she was working on that and to ask him to please get Mabel Merritt information ASAP. I appreciate your concern that Alysha should not have to continue to manage with broken glasses just because CD is experiencing staff turnover.

Thanks for your vigilance to be sure nothing else important slips through the cracks.

Anita

Anita Blackstone
Case Supervisor
(816) 555-8236

From: Miriam Fine [mailto:miriamkfine@gmail.com]
Sent: Sunday, May 20, 2012 10:34 AM
To: hgoldstein@laramyjones.com
Subject: plus ça change

Hello, ever constant Hazel. What a pleasure to join you at the Women's Bar Association Luncheon on Friday—thank you so much for inviting me to sit at your table. What smart, funny, engaged women you work with; I was delighted to be among them.

The speaker was very powerful—it was interesting to think about that expanded definition of human trafficking—and horrifying to realize women and teens are still being enslaved in our own country today. Thanks for opening my eyes to that issue.

Today we will turn our attention to turnover. Not the flakey pastry kind. The flakey staff kind.

Mom has been doing so much better with the home health aide coming in every day. She likes her and seems willing to take orders from her—much better than she does with me. But, just two weeks in, the gal up and quits. I don't think it's anything mom did—she apparently quit the agency, got a better job in Topeka. So . . . we start over again. Which is not that easy to do with mom. Sigh . . .

And then I heard last week that the CD worker on my CASA case has quit. Everything I read in the media suggests this is part of a much bigger problem at CD. Here, I quote: ". . . news reports from the western part of the state point to a child protection system in Jackson County that is struggling under high caseloads, rampant employee turnover, and poor training of rookie caseworkers." I read somewhere else that turnover in CD statewide is approaching 50 percent.

A number half that size would have gotten immediate attention from the very highest levels at H&R Block. The company was always fixated on how managing turnover kept costs down, led to higher customer satisfaction, and improved the quality of service delivery. And that was for tax preparation!

With CD we're talking about kids' lives. Kids who have already undergone way too much trauma and disruption—who have no reason at all to trust adults—and who need stability and consistency more than anything in the world. So we introduce them to their CD case worker, tell them this is the person responsible for their safety and happiness, and then turn around and say, "Sorry, that person quit. Here's a new person. Trust them instead." Like that is going to work!

I'm pissed off and worried for mom and pissed off and worried for my CASA kids.

But I love you.

Miri

Miriam Fine
(913) 555-8436

"If I can't dance, I don't want to be part of your revolution." -- Emma Goldman

From: Duncan.Walsh@dss.mo.gov
Sent: Tuesday, May 22, 2012 9:13 AM
To: ablackstone@jacksoncountycasa-mo.org; hmiller@jacksoncountycasa-mo.org; miriamk
fine@gmail.com
cc: martin.jaylon@hollandgrain.com
Subject: *Confidential: Merritt—Washington—Mom accesses services

I am writing to inform the CASA team that Joelle Merritt requested a rescheduled psychological evaluation and complied with the appointment we set up with a therapist on 5/21/17. I will forward the written report from that provider as soon as we receive it here.

Joelle also presented today at MedLabs, our contract provider for drug and alcohol screening, and left a sample.

Based on my recent conversations with Joelle Merritt, it appears the goal change on this case has motivated her to participate in services. She hopes to make sufficient progress to move towards reunification before the AJO files to terminate her parental rights.

Duncan Walsh
Supervisor – Children's Division
Missouri Department of Social Services
(816) 555-9805

The mission of the Children's Division is to partner with families, communities and government to protect children from abuse and neglect and to assure safety, permanency and well being for Missouri's children.

From: Anita Blackstone [mailto:ablackstone@jacksoncountycasa-mo.org]
Sent: Wednesday, May 23, 2012 9:25 AM
To: miriamkfine@gmail.com
Cc: hmiller@jacksoncountycasa-mo.org
Subject: RE: *Confidential: Merritt—Washington—Mom seeks services

Miri,

I'm sorry I missed your call this morning. I'm heading over to Court for an adoption, but wanted to respond to your voice mail as quickly as I could.

First—don't panic. Just because Joelle has gone to a psych eval and dropped for a drug test doesn't mean anything about the case is changing right away. There are a lot of steps between here and sending the kids back home.

We'll have to see if Joelle is serious about seeking help for her mental health and addiction issues. I've seen a lot of parents freak out after the goal is changed to adoption. Some are truly motivated to take the necessary steps to get their kids back. But a lot of others fail to stick with the program, and the TPR/adoption process moves forward with little delay. I'd say at this point we have no idea if Joelle will be one of the moms who gets it together or not.

Either way our job is to protect the best interests of the kids. And that almost always means reunification—even if it comes late in the case. I know you have become close to the grandmother and developed a view that the children would be better off living with her and their grandfather. But if Joelle can get clean and sober and address her mental health issues, the kids are most likely better off returning home.

For the time being, let's work on being sure the kids will be okay either way. Supporting a healthy relationship between Joelle and the grandparents can help ensure they will have all three adults in their lives—one way or the other.

Call back if you need to talk this through some more. Most cases have twists and turns before the kids reach permanency. This is pretty much par for the course.

Anita

Anita Blackstone
Case Supervisor
(816) 555-8236

Staff   Volunteers   Volunteers   Lookup   Cases   User   Reports
Dashboard   Dashboard   Tables   Administration

Contact Log

Name	Fine, Miriam
Case Number	594
Activity Date	6/4/2012
Activity Type	Placement Visit
Subject	Child welfare
Location	Playground
Contact Type	Face-to-face
Hours	1.00
Notes:	

Mabel told me she was taking the girls to the neighborhood playground, so I met them there mid-morning. Roger was there, too, mostly sitting down, but clearly doing much better.

While the girls were playing on the equipment, I talked with Mabel about recent changes on the case. She expressed distress that Duncan Walsh had called to inform her of Camille Harris's departure from CD; he explained he would be visiting the children monthly until Camille's replacement was fully trained.

Mabel said she felt like Camille understood the issues in the case, and the kids liked her and were used to her. She wasn't sure how they would respond to a new worker, especially Tyrone. I told her I was going to see Tyrone later in the afternon at Gillis, and we would just have to see about the new CD worker. I promised to do my best to be sure the case stayed on track and that nothing fell through the cracks during the CD staff transitions.

On that point, Mabel said Duncan Walsh told her he had gotten a voucher to pay for new glasses for Alysha and would bring it later in the week when he came on his home visit. She sounded very relieved about that. "Though I have no idea why these things take so long!"

We also discussed the news that Joelle was showing more interest in participating in services since she realized she might lose custody of her children for good.

Mabel seems skeptical ("I've seen this rodeo before"), but she is genuinely hopeful that her daughter can get help and get well. We agreed that we wouldn't talk to the children about this just yet. If Joelle makes consistent progress over time, then we will talk about how to address it together.

Mabel said she had brought the girls to see Tyrone again after school let out in May. She said it breaks her heart to see them cling to each other when it's time to leave. She said she knows it will be hard, but she'd like to try to have Tyrone back in the home again when he completes his stay at Gillis.

I talked with Alysha while Hope played on the monkey bars. She was very pleased to tell me that she did, in fact, finish the school year with a perfect report card. She said the family had all gone to the library last week, and she had a stack of books to start off the summer, so she was happy. She also told me that her grandmother thought she would have new glasses soon, and thanked me for my help with that. Mabel is definitely teaching them excellent manners.

Hope was all energy and giggles today. She clearly likes being outside, and chases down every butterfly or squirrel that crosses her path. We didn't talk much, because she didn't want to sit still, but I pushed her on the swings, and she seems to be doing quite well.

Activity Status   Approved

Welcome **miriam.fine**

Change Password   Log Off

Staff   **Volunteers**   **Volunteers**   **Lookup**   **Cases**   **User**   **Reports**
Dashboard   **Dashboard**   **Tables**   **Administration**

Contact Log

Name	Fine, Miriam
Case Number	594
Activity Date	6/4/2012
Activity Type	Placement Visit
Subject	Child welfare
Location	Gillis
Contact Type	Face-to-face
Hours	0.75

Notes:

I met Tyrone in the main Gillis lobby and we walked around the campus while we talked. He is clearly more comfortable moving around than just sitting in a conference room.

He remains subdued, but it is hard to tell if that is from the meds or his placement situation. Either way, he is much calmer and seems to have his anger under control. I told him about the Permanency Hearing, and he said Mabel had already told him about the goal change to adoption. He seemed relieved. He said he could no longer picture going home to live with his mother.

He asked if I thought he would be able to leave Gillis and go back home to live with his grandparents and sisters, and I said I hoped so -- that was the treatment goal.

He told me he had completed his school work with the tutor and really hoped he could go to high school in the fall. I asked about his life at Gillis, and he said he had two friends. He had really liked his roommate, but he got into trouble and was sent to a locked facility, so Tyrone didn't see him anymore. He has a new roommate that he doesn't know very well yet. "You don't want to get to know people here too well," he said. "They leave all the time."

I told Tyrone there was another FST scheduled in about 6 weeks, but I would come see him again before then. I asked if he needed anything, and he just shrugged.

Activity Status   Approved

Recipient information	Provider Information
Name: Joelle Merritt	Name: Marilyn Crossfield, Ph.D.
DOB: 6-09-82	Medicaid Number: 3757972
Medicaid Number: none	Referral Date: 05-13-11
	Appointment Date: 05-21-12
	Report Date: 06-14-12

Diagnostic Assessment

Referral Source:

Joelle Merritt was referred by Children's Division based on a voluntary order from the Jackson County Family Court dated 5/13/11. This appointment is a reschedule of a previously cancelled appointment in 2011.

Client/Family/Referral Source statement of need and treatment expectations:

The Jackson County Family Court ordered this voluntary evaluation to determine the mental health status of the client. The provider has also been asked to determine if ongoing mental health services, referral for psychotropic medications, or addiction evaluation/treatment are recommended.

The client's three children (Tyrone Merritt, Alysha Washington, and Hope Washington) were removed from her home on 5/11/11 and remain in the care and custody of Children's Division. The provider has been asked to evaluate whether the client's mental health status would allow her to provide safe and appropriate care for the children if they are returned to her home.

Ms. Joelle Merritt came to my office on 5/21/12. In a 60-minute session, I was able to speak with her about her history, current situation, and view of her parenting responsibilities for her three children. This report presents my findings from that interview and my review of the documents provided by Children's Division relating to the open cases in Family Court.

Legal Status:

Ms. Merritt is not incarcerated, is not on parole, and has no outstanding charges or warrants against her. She has never been arrested for, or convicted of, a crime. Her three children are in the care and custody of the Missouri Children's Division due to findings of neglect. Alysha and Hope Washington are currently placed in the home of their maternal grandparents, Roger and Mabel Merritt. Tyrone Merritt is currently placed at the Gillis School due to behavioral issues while living with the Merritts.

Ms. Merritt is allowed two supervised visits/month with the children. She has participated in approximately half of the visits offered, claiming work or other scheduling conflicts prevented her from participating in the rest.

Ms. Merritt was also ordered by the Court to participate in voluntary drug screening/evaluation, which she has not done.

Hope and Alysha's father, Jerome Washington, is incarcerated. Tyrone's father is not confirmed, and his whereabouts are unknown.

Family and Social Status (current & historical):

Joelle Merritt reports that she was a happy and active teen, with many friends from both her church and the school volleyball team. She was doing well in her high school classes and hoped to attend Penn Valley Community College and then matriculate to get a four-year degree. She wanted to be a nurse.

At the end of her sophomore year in high school Joelle became pregnant. Her boyfriend at the time, Marlin Thompson, wanted her to have an abortion. However, Joelle felt that would be going against her church, and her parents, Roger and Mabel Merritt, encouraged her to keep the baby. When Joelle agreed to carry the pregnancy to term, the boyfriend broke up with her and refused to have anything further to do with Joelle or the baby. His family moved away that summer, and Joelle has not heard from him since. When the baby, named Tyrone, was born in February, Joelle put Marlin Thompson's name on the birth certificate as the child's father.

It is clear that Joelle still thinks of her high school boyfriend as her "one true love," and was deeply hurt by his betrayal and abandonment. Despite the intervening years, she talks about the day he will return to marry her and be a father to her children.

Joelle continued in school for several months after Tyrone was born. However, it became too difficult to care for the baby and complete her school work, and she dropped out. Money was tight with the added expense of a baby, and Mabel Merritt agreed to provide child care for Tyrone while Joelle went to work to contribute financially to the household. Joelle got a minimum wage job at Taco Joe's and worked as many hours as she could get to help the family.

Joelle describes these years as a happy time. She did not like working in the fast food restaurant, and she was sad about giving up her college dreams. She also missed Marlin Thompson, almost to the point of obsession. But she felt safe and secure living with her parents, and enjoyed watching Tyrone grow up to be a healthy and very happy toddler.

Around the time Tyrone was three, Joelle's boss at Taco Joe's, Jerome Washington, asked her out. He was an older man, five years her senior, and good-looking, and she was flattered by the attention. She said after Marlin left she thought no man would ever want her again. Joelle began to see Jerome regularly after work, which angered her parents. They did not trust him and thought he was too old for Joelle. Moreover, they were concerned that her new infatuation left little time to spend with her son, whose care fell more and more on Mabel Merritt.

Joelle and her parents fought continually during this time, and the once-pleasant home began to feel overly restrictive to the 20-year-old. Within a few months, Joelle moved out of her parents' home, taking Tyrone with her to live in Jerome's two-bedroom apartment.

Joelle reported being happy in the early months living with Jerome. The neighbor next door, a young mother herself, cared for Tyrone while Joelle worked, and she reduced her hours somewhat, relying on Jerome's higher wages to pay most of the bills and buy things for Tyrone. She noted that Jerome liked playing with the little boy after work, and bought him "fun trucks and action figures" to play with together. Joelle reported that she brought Tyrone over to stay with her parents a few times, but they kept pressuring her to leave Jerome and come back home, so she stopped visiting.

In the summer of 2002 Joelle became pregnant. She reported that Jerome was pleased and treated her very well throughout the pregnancy. On April 7, 2003, Joelle gave birth to their daughter, Alysha. Things were good for the small family for a while, but Jerome grew jealous of the time Joelle spent with the new baby. He was also angry that she cut back further on her hours at work and expressed resentment at having to "buy everything for you and those damned brats."

Joelle said that Jerome started staying out late after work "drinking with his buddies," and often came home drunk and mean. He began going into work late or hungover, and eventually lost his management job at Taco Joe's. He blamed Joelle for his dismissal and became increasingly abusive, yelling whenever one of the children got in his way or Joelle did something he didn't like.

Jerome took on day work to pay the rent and also worked part time at the local McDonald's. Money was tight, but he didn't want Joelle to take on more hours "with those assholes at Taco Joe's." Joelle reached out to her parents for money to buy diapers and formula for the baby, but they said they would only help if she left Jerome and came back home with the children.

During this time Joelle reports becoming increasingly sad and tired, finding it very difficult to get out of bed in the morning and to care for the children's needs. She said she began to believe that Jerome was right, it was her fault he drank and lost his job. She felt that no one loved her – not Marlin, not Jerome, and not her parents. Only the children were a comfort, and there wasn't enough money to take care of them. She said her neighbor helped sometimes, but often she had to skimp on diaper changes and water down Alysha's formula to make it last longer.

Joelle reports that Jerome now came home drunk most nights and yelled whenever he was in the apartment, often threatening to hit her or one of the children. She said she took Tyrone and Alysha to stay with her parents when Jerome was especially upset, and they agreed to take them in, because they were worried about their safety. They continued to plead with Joelle to leave Jerome, but she didn't see how she could manage that and felt that it would be wrong to "take his baby away from him."

Joelle said she called the police once during the winter when Jerome had choked her and she worried he would do something more violent. However, by the time the police arrived, he had apologized, and she believed he was truly sorry, so she sent them away without filing a report.

After that incident with the police, Joelle said Jerome tried harder to make things work at home. He stopped haranguing her about working at Taco Joe's and even stayed home with the children so she could pick up more hours. Joelle became hopeful again that things would work out and said she even started to talk to Jerome about possibly getting married.

In March Joelle discovered she was pregnant again, and she said Jerome treated her pretty well and was nice to Tyrone and Alysha. But when the new baby was born right before Thanksgiving in 2004, Jerome was disappointed that it was another girl and seemed to lose interest again.

When describing the next part of her story, Joelle began to cry. She said the two-bedroom apartment was very cramped with an infant, a 19-month-old, and a 6-year-old. It was hard to find someone to take care of three children, so Joelle worked very few hours at Taco Joe's. She felt stuck inside with the children, while Jerome spent all of his time either working or out drinking with friends. When he came home, he was usually drunk or angry or both.

She said she thought having his children would make him love her, but it wasn't working out that way. Joelle describes the next several years as a blur. She isn't quite sure how they managed to pay the rent or buy food, and she remembered several times when they had to ask neighbors for help. Once she went to Catholic Charities when the electricity was cut off, and they worked with the utility company to get it turned back on. Her parents still took the children "when things were bad with Jerome," but they continued to refuse financial help unless Joelle left him and moved back home.

At one point when the baby was almost two-years-old, Joelle told Jerome she had enough of his abuse and she was moving out. He screamed at her and began throwing things – on the floor and at Joelle. The neighbors must have heard the fight, because they called 911, and the police arrived. As before, Joelle told the officers it was "just a misunderstanding," and they left.

After that, Joelle describes a constant cycle of accusations, fights, violence, and apologies. She doesn't remember much about the children during this time – only that when it got really bad, she would take them over to her parents for a few nights.

In February 2007 things were at their lowest point. The utility company was threatening to turn off the heat again, there was little food in the apartment, and Jerome had not come home for several days. Joelle took the children to her parents' house and then drove to the McDonald's where Jerome worked. She confronted him in the parking lot, accusing him of drinking away his paycheck when they needed the money to pay the bills. Jerome lost his temper and attacked Joelle, breaking her jaw in the ensuing brawl.

A bystander called the police, who called an ambulance. Jerome was arrested, and Joelle was taken to the ER at Truman Medical Center.

Joelle said "that did it" with Jerome, and, with the support of a local domestic violence shelter, she got the nerve to testify against him in court. He had a prior assault conviction against a former girlfriend, which she said she hadn't known about, and the combination of her testimony and his parole violation got him six years.

Joelle said she hadn't seen him since the trial and had no interest in visiting him in jail. She said she certainly didn't think the children should be around him, because he was "a bad influence." She said Jerome's parents, who had previously seen the children occasionally and provided some financial support when the rent was late, were very angry about her testimony and cut off all contact and help. She felt that was wrong, "as they are their grandkids."

Joelle described her broken jaw in very dramatic terms and said the pain was excruciating. They gave her OxyContin at the hospital, which she said made it bearable, and she was able to renew that prescription twice, which got her through the month after the incident.

Joelle went back to work during that time, leaving Alysha and Hope with a neighbor while Tyrone was in school. Her parents helped her more now that Jerome was out of the picture, and she cobbled together a living for herself and the kids. When her medication renewals ran out, she said "the pain was terrible, and no one would help me." She admits she turned to liquor to "take the edge off" so she could sleep at night. She insisted she did not take illegal drugs, though she admitted to using Benadryl as an additional sleep aid "on the really bad nights."

Joelle vehemently denies having a substance abuse problem and believes the Children's Division butted in unnecessarily. She said she didn't have a lot of money, but she loved her kids, and "they were doing okay." She desperately wants them back.

Presenting problems and situation:

Joelle's three children, Hope (7), Alysha (9), and Tyrone (14), were removed from her home on May 11, 2011, by Children's Division, based on a hotline report by the school principal at Whittier Elementary. The hotline report alleged that the children were neglected, with insufficient adult supervision, and lacking basic necessities such as food and clean clothing.

When Children's Division and the KCPD arrived at the home, Joelle was difficult to arouse from her deep sleep on the couch, and there were indications of alcohol and OTC drug use around the room. The apartment was in disarray, and there were basic hygiene concerns.

The three children were removed from the home and immediately placed with Joelle's parents, Roger and Mabel Merritt. The children initially thrived in their new home, and Alysha and Hope continue to do well there. Tyrone began exhibiting behavioral problems in January 2012, including school truancy, and he was moved to the Gillis School in March after an incident involving physical aggression against his grandmother.

During the 13 months that the children have been out of her home, Joelle has not accessed Court-ordered services for psychological evaluation or drug/alcohol screening and treatment. She has participated in 8 supervised visits with the children, although the Court orders allow more than twice that number. She has also seen the children at FST meetings facilitated by Children's Division and some Court hearings on the case.

Based on Joelle's failure to participate fully in the Court plan for reunification with her children, the Court changed the case goal to TPR/Adoption on May 15, 2012.

Joelle said this was a "wake up call," which is why she came to see me. She said she also plans to go to the drug screening center to drop next week. She said she will do anything she has to in order to get her children back.

Current Community Resources and Services:

Joelle is very isolated, with few friends and no formal support structure. She has some support from her parents, Roger and Mabel Merritt, though they are increasingly focused on gaining full custody of the children to raise on their own. It does not appear they will cut Joelle off, however, they are now prioritizing the grandchildren over their daughter.

There is a neighbor in the apartment building who provides some child care and other assistance on an occasional basis. Joelle does not have good access to social service agencies, although she has gone to Catholic Charities for utility help.

Current Symptoms/Behaviors:

Joelle says she is "very sad" about her abandonment by both Marlin and Jerome, and she misses her children very much. Like many victims of domestic violence, she does not blame Jerome for the assault that put him in jail or the prior abuse; she blames herself. She presents with very low self-esteem and depression, likely starting when she had her first child at 16 and dropped out of high school, later compounded by domestic abuse over a number of years.

Joelle refuses to admit she has a substance abuse problem, but she does say she continues to use liquor to deal with residual jaw pain from her injury and Benadryl for ongoing sleep issues. She has not accepted that her actions caused the children to be removed from her home, and still believes she is prepared to care for them.

She continues to work at Taco Joe's; however, she said she sometimes "needs sleep" and has to miss her shift. She does not correlate these instances with alcohol or OTC drug abuse.

Psychiatric Treatment History (Include previous treatment by this provider):

Joelle has had no previous mental health assessments, counseling, or treatment.

Substance Abuse Treatment History:

Joelle has received no assessment or treatment for her use of alcohol or other drugs.

Recent (30 days) alcohol and drug use (history of use, duration, patterns & consequences):

Joelle admits to drinking beer and wine almost every day for many years, but she does not believe her use of alcohol is a problem. She states that her "occasional" use of Benadryl as a sleep aid causes no problems.

Current Medication Regimen:

Joelle takes no prescription medications.

Medication allergies/ adverse reactions:

No known allergies or adverse reactions to medications.

Vocational/Educational Status/Functioning:

Joelle left high school during her junior year to care for her baby. She did not return to formal schooling and has not completed her GED. She presents as intelligent and literate, but not well educated. She has held the same job at Taco Joe's for more than a decade and expresses little ambition to seek more lucrative employment or return to school.

Personal and Social Resources and Strengths:

Joelle is an intelligent and resourceful woman, who has become defeated by circumstances, domestic abuse, and substance addiction. Despite many setbacks and great adversity, she managed to care for her children for many years and maintains an optimistic resilience even after they have been removed from her home.

Summary Recommendations:

Joelle needs intense inpatient services to treat her depression and low self-esteem, as well as her alcoholism and possible drug addiction. I recommend admission to ReCovery's residential program for 60-90 days, so that she can receive treatment for her co-occurrence of mental health and substance use disorders.

Name/Title   Marilyn Crossfield, Ph.D.   Date   06/14/12

MedLabs
3274 Broadway
Kansas City, MO 64111

Sample Provided by: Joelle Merritt / DOB 06/09/82

Date of Sample: May 31, 2012

Test Results Reported: June 5, 2012

Referred by: Children's Division – Jackson County

Responsible Payor: Children's Division – Jackson County

Results Sent to: Children's Division – Jackson County

Test Ordered

10 Panel + Alcohol Urine Drug Test

AMP-Amphetamines (MAMP-Methamphetamine, MDMA-Ecstasy), COC-Cocaine, OPI-Opiates (including heroin, codeine and morphine), PCP-Phencyclidine, THC-Marijuana, BZO-Benzodiazepines, BAR-Barbiturates, MTD-Methadone, PPX-Propoxyphene, Meth – Methaqualone, ETH – Alcohol.

Results

Positive for ETH – Alcohol – within last 80 hours
Negative for all other substances

MedLabs is affiliated with the Drug and Alcohol Testing Industry Association (DATIA) and the Substance Abuse Program Administrators Association (SAPAA). We have been in the drug and alcohol testing business for 20 years. Our procedures include a comprehensive program that provides the highest quality services, focusing on accuracy, integrity, and professionalism.

Our mission is to provide affordable lab screening to help reduce drug and alcohol abuse, while empowering individuals and companies to manage their health and wellness.

June 20, 2012

To: Duncan Walsh – Children's Division
        Abigail Norris – Attorney for the Juvenile Office
        Henrietta Miller – Guardian ad Litem
        Miriam Fine – CASA

From: Martin Jaylon, attorney for Joelle Merritt

Re: Joelle Merritt – Admission to ReCovery

This letter will inform the parties in the Family Court cases of Tyrone Merritt, Alysha Washington, and Hope Washington that the children's mother, Joelle Merritt, entered ReCovery today for a 30-day stay for evaluation and treatment for possible mental health and substance use disorders.

It is Ms. Merritt's intention to complete this course of treatment and all recommended follow-up steps so that she can once again safely parent her children. We anticipate asking the Court to reunify this family as soon as possible.

We will inform Children's Division when ReCovery staff thinks it is therapeutically appropriate to re-initiate visits with the children.

Please let me know if you have any questions on this or any other matter relating to this case.

Martin Jaylon

Martin Jaylon
Partner
Holland, Grain, & Shaw LLC

From: Miriam Fine [mailto:miriamkfine@gmail.com]
Sent: Friday, June 22, 2012 8:43 AM
To: hgoldstein@laramyjones.com
Subject: Back and forth

OMG, Hazel—I don't know what to think! Without going into too much detail, here's the gist: the mom on my CASA case has decided to get clean.

I guess it finally dawned on her that she really was going to lose her kids. It's fairly astounding that it took her this long to grasp that basic fact. Though, I have to admit, the system's focus on "reunification" for the first 12 months could easily confuse someone without a lot of sophistication. When everyone on the case is talking about reunification as the goal, maybe the mother just doesn't get that it might not happen.

This mom has clearly always loved her kids—I never doubted that for a minute. She was just too impaired to do anything about it. I guess the prospect of permanently losing her children created that "hitting bottom wake-up call" they say can jolt an addict into seeking treatment.

So . . . she's been jolted. I just learned she's admitted herself into an inpatient treatment facility for co-occurrence of mental illness and alcoholism.

Who knows how this will play out? The research says that approximately 90% of alcoholics will experience at least one relapse in the four years following treatment. That means there's only a 10% chance my CASA mom will stay clean while her kids are living with her.

And what happens to the kids when she relapses? Maybe by then she'll have married a good, stable man who can take care of them. Maybe she'll be a "functional alcoholic"—drinking, but still able to meet her kids' basic needs. Maybe they'll muddle through like they did before she was caught the first time. Maybe they'll end up back in the system. But I don't think the Court is asking this question. If she can get clean, even for 30 or 60 days, I think they'll try to send my kids back home.

That is good news, of course. Or it should be good news. It was always what we hoped would happen— mom would get help / kids would go home. But all I can think is that just when these kids have found some consistency and stability in their lives, we are threatening to turn it all upside down again.

I know all the evidence points to reunification at all costs, save the actual safety of the children. And you really do want to root for this mom—she's been through hell and back. And now she's trying to get clean. Which is hard work under the best of circumstances; and her circumstances are not the best.

But surely there should be some consideration of the trauma on the children, the toxic stress, caused by this back-and-forth jockeying. "Your mom is bad, we're taking you away. Your mom might get better, let's wait and see. Your mom didn't get better, we're filing to free you for adoption. Your mom just decided to try harder, you might go home." Auuuggghhh.............!!

I'm officially naming this the Yo-Yo Syndrome. And I declare it unkind and unwise, and likely a violation under the Geneva Convention.

I assume your firm feels differently when you represent parents pro bono, and I'm sure there are very good reasons to give parents back their children. But my heart aches for these kids, who were so close to permanency. Once again, they will have to wait and see if the adults in their lives can get it right.

Miri

_____
Miriam Fine
(913) 555-8436

"If I can't dance, I don't want to be part of your revolution." -- Emma Goldman

From: Duncan.Walsh@dss.mo.gov
Sent: Friday, June 29, 2012 11:25 AM
To: ablackstone@jacksoncountycasa-mo.org; hmiller@jacksoncountycasa-mo.org;
cc: miriamkfine@gmail.com
Subject: *Confidential: Merritt—Washington—Tyrone released from Gillis

I am writing to inform the CASA team that Tyrone Merritt was released from Gillis this morning and returned to the home of his grandparents Roger and Mabel Merritt. It is the opinion of the Gillis team that Tyrone is now stable enough to move to this less restrictive setting.

The Gillis psychiatrist recommends that Tyrone continue on his medication regimen, and the prescription is authorized for refills through the next 14 weeks.

Our next FST on this case is in two weeks, on July 16. We will use this opportunity to learn more about how Tyrone's re-entry into the Merritt household is progressing and how it is affecting the other two children.

Duncan Walsh
Supervisor – Children's Division
Missouri Department of Social Services
(816) 555-9805

The mission of the Children's Division is to partner with families, communities and government to protect children from abuse and neglect and to assure safety, permanency and well being for Missouri's children.

Contact Log

Name	Fine, Miriam
Case Number	594
Activity Date	7/3/2012
Activity Type	Placement Visit
Subject	Child welfare
Location	Grandparents' Home
Contact Type	Face-to-face
Hours	1.00
Notes:	

This was an excellent visit. The family is very happy to be "reunited" -- Tyrone is happy to be "back home," the girls are happy to have Tyrone back, and Roger and Mabel are very optimistic about their ability to make it all work for everyone. The shadow of a potential disruption if Joelle asks to get the children back is very subterranean right now. Mabel has not discussed this possibility with the children, and they are operating under the assumption that this current intact family of five will be their long-term reality. All three children are happy and safe for the first time since this case began.

I spoke with Tyrone who told me he has "turned over a new leaf." He told me he met a lot of boys at Gillis who had no functional or available family at all, and he came to realize how lucky he was to have grandparents who wanted to care for him and his sisters. He said he very much wanted this to work out, and he was determined not to blow it.

We talked about the upcoming start of high school, and Tyrone is very eager for that. I would say Tyrone is in a very good place right now, and we need to do everything we can to maintain stability and consistency for him to continue to heal and thrive.

Alysha told me she is very happy to have Tyrone back home now that he is "not so mad all the time." She is up to Book Four in the Harry Potter series and happy to have lots of time to read this summer.

Her best news: She finally, finally, finally has new glasses! As promised, Duncan Walsh delivered a voucher to Mabel, who took Alysha the same day to order new glasses. They aren't fancy or high-end designer frames, but they are perfectly attractive and serviceable. Alysha said she could read much better now and was quite pleased.

Hope told me she was "just happy that it's summer." She is an outdoors child, happiest playing with her friends in the front yard or her sister at the park or playground. She said it was "fun" to have Tyrone home and asked me if he could stay. I told her I hoped so.

None of the children asked about their mother, and I did not bring her up.

Activity Status   Approved

July 15, 2012

Family Support Team Meeting

Case: Merritt-Washington
Facilitator: Duncan Walsh, Children's Division Supervisor
Location: Library Conference Room, Jackson County CASA
In attendance:
      Tyrone Merritt – Juvenile
      Alysha Washington – Juvenile
      Hope Washington – Juvenile
      Joelle Merritt – Mother
      Martin Jaylon – Mother's Attorney
      Mabel Merritt – Maternal Grandmother
      Roger Merritt – Maternal Grandfather
      Marlie Verlet – CD Worker
      Miriam Fine – CASA Volunteer
      Anita Blackstone – CASA Case Supervisor (taking notes for the group)

Duncan Walsh passed around the attendance log / confidentiality agreement for everyone to sign.

He introduced Marlie Verlet to the team and explained she was taking over for Camille Harris. After today's meeting, Marlie will be the CD worker and primary contact for this family.

Duncan asked the children to begin, and said after their turns they would be excused for the remainder of the meeting. Mabel said that Roger would step out with the children.

Tyrone Merritt – Reported that he has been back home with his grandparents and sisters for two weeks and is much happier there. Said Gillis was "okay" but some of the boys were weird or scary and he missed his regular friends from school. He said he liked Dr. Arielto, the psychiatrist at Gillis, and asked if he could keep seeing him. Duncan Walsh explained that leaving Gillis probably meant Tyrone wouldn't be seeing Dr. Arielto anymore. Tyrone seemed distressed by that information.

Miriam Fine, CASA Volunteer, asked if Duncan could explain that more fully, since it would probably be best for Tyrone to continue in a therapeutic relationship with a provider he trusted. Duncan said Dr. Arielto had his own private practice and came to see youth at Gillis based on a contract with the facility. Since his private practice schedule was likely full, there was no mechanism for asking him to take on Tyrone as a Medicaid patient through CD.

Miriam asked how CD planned to find a therapist for Tyrone for ongoing treatment, and Duncan said Marlie would look for a psychiatrist to monitor his meds.

Alysha Washington – Reported that she was having a good summer and was very happy to have her brother back home. She said her new glasses were great.

Hope Washington – Said she was glad Tyrone was home and glad it was summer.

(Children left room with Roget Merritt to supervise – meeting continued)

Joelle Merritt, mother – Reported she had completed 25 days at ReCovery and felt the program was extremely beneficial. She expected to be released in 5 days, moving to outpatient treatment and regular AA meetings. She said she had learned a lot about how to manage her depression and avoid violent personal relationships and felt she could maintain sobriety with strong support and constant vigilance. She asked the group to explain how she could regain custody of her children.

Mabel Merritt, maternal grandmother – Visibly conflicted by Joelle's comments. She told her daughter she was very happy to see her looking so well and to hear she was clean and sober. She said she would support her in every possible way to stay clean. But she was not sure the children should go home to live with her. She said they are finally stable and happy, doing well in school and behaving well at home, and she worried about the impact of another disruption on their lives. She asked Joelle to consider leaving them with her and Roger, at which point Joelle became visibly angry and an argument ensued.

Duncan Walsh, CD Supervisor – Stepped in to reduce the escalating verbal conflict. Said there was a process which he would describe, so everyone knew where they stood. He said CD would likely approve renewed supervised visits between Joelle and the children after she was released from ReCovery. If those went well – and if Joelle continued to drop clean – then they would move to unsupervised visits and eventually overnight stays. Duncan said that CD would not consider asking the court to send the children home for at least 6 months. Even then, the children would remain under the care and custody of CD for another 6 months, providing for state oversight and CASA visits until the case was released.

Duncan asked both Joelle and Mabel if they could work on providing productive supervised visits for the children without fighting between themselves, and they both agreed they would work to do that.

Miriam Fine, CASA Volunteer – Noted that this seemed like a very critical time for the family, with Tyrone just released from Gillis and Joelle anticipating release from ReCovery. She said the children had been very happy to have their futures "settled" when the court changed the goal to adoption, and she thought too much change too quickly could really upset their equilibrium, especially Tyrone. She wanted to be sure that the focus remained on the children and any emerging needs in this period of uncertainty. She said moving them to permanency as soon as possible needed to remain top of mind for all the adults concerned.

Anita Blackstone, CASA Case Supervisor – nothing to add.

Group agreed on 10/15/12 for next FST. Anita will schedule with CASA to use the Library Conference Room and will notify parties about time.

AJB / uploaded to OPTIMA 7-16-12

ReCovery

8720 Blue Ridge Blvd, Kansas City, MO 64138

July 20, 2012

To the Jackson County Family Court,

This letter will confirm that Ms. Joelle Merritt was a resident patient at ReCovery from 6/20/12 to 7/20/12. During this time, she received treatment for depression, alcoholism, and substance abuse.

Ms. Merritt successfully completed her program and has been clean and sober for 30 days.

Ms. Merritt is being released to leave our inpatient setting and move to bi-weekly therapy and substance monitoring at our out-patient clinic. We also highly recommend that she attend daily meetings of Alcoholics Anonymous.

If approved by the Family Court, we believe that visits with her children will be therapeutically beneficial to Ms. Merritt, and she will not be a threat to their safety.

Dr. M. L. Thompson

M. L. Thompson, Ph.D.
Director of Clinical Services - ReCovery

ReCovery provides substance abuse and mental health services to individuals and families in the Kansas City area to help them enjoy happier, healthier, and more productive lives.

Contact Log

Name	Fine, Miriam
Case Number	594
Activity Date	8/3/2012
Activity Type	Placement Visit
Subject	Child welfare
Location	Grandparents' Home
Contact Type	Face-to-face
Hours	1.25

Notes:

I was scheduled to visit the children on Wednesday, but Mabel called to tell me she was taking them to see Joelle and asked if I could reschedule for today (Friday). The family was planning on attending a church picnic in the afternoon, so I came over mid-morning.

Mabel and I were able to speak first, and I asked about the supervised visit with Joelle two days earlier. She said it went better than she expected, and that Joelle was sober and much clearer than she had been in a long time. She said there was some awkwardness -- it was hard for the group to figure out exactly what to do at first. But Joelle had brought in the fixings for pizza, and she was able to engage the kids in cooking in the kitchen. Even Tyrone put out paper plates and drinks on the table and stayed relatively connected to the conversation. Mabel said it made her feel hopeful.

I reminded her about the upcoming CASA School Supply Drive, and she said she had that on the calendar. She was especially glad, since Tyrone needed a calculator and padlock for his locker at the high school, and she knew they would be expensive.

Tyrone was in his room playing video games. He is still a bit subdued, but seems to be completely settled back to living in the Merritt's home. He talked about reconnecting with his friends and starting high school, and he sounded excited. I asked what it was like to visit his mom after such a long break. He shrugged, but then said, "She's not so bad when she's not drinking."

Alysha was playing outside, but came in to talk with me. She is very eager for school to start and told me they were going to CASA to pick out backpacks "and all the supplies I need for 5th grade." She volunteered that they had been to see their mother on Wednesday. I asked how that went, and she said "it was really pretty good. I was nervous at first, but she just seemed like mommy." She asked if they were still going to live with their grandparents, and I said that was the plan for the time being. She didn't ask more.

Hope wanted to play "tea party" with her stuffed animals, so we talked while we had tea. She remains a very sunny child, and does not express a lot of worries or concerns. She told me about "making pizza with mommy and Alysha," and didn't express any surprise that it had been so long since they had seen Joelle.

I told Mabel I'd swing by again after school started to see how everyone was doing. Right now the family seems well adjusted, without any major disruptions caused by visiting with Joelle.

Activity Status   Approved

MedLabs
3274 Broadway
Kansas City, MO 64111

Sample Provided by: Joelle Merritt / DOB 06/09/82

Date of Sample: August 2, 2012

Test Results Reported: August 7, 2012

Referred by: Children's Division – Jackson County

Responsible Payor: Children's Division – Jackson County

Results Sent to: Children's Division – Jackson County

Test Ordered

10 Panel + Alcohol Urine Drug Test

AMP-Amphetamines (MAMP-Methamphetamine, MDMA-Ecstasy), COC-Cocaine, OPI-Opiates (including heroin, codeine and morphine), PCP-Phencyclidine, THC-Marijuana, BZO-Benzodiazepines, BAR-Barbiturates, MTD-Methadone, PPX-Propoxyphene, Meth – Methaqualone, ETH – Alcohol.

Results

Negative for ETH – Alcohol – within last 80 hours
Negative for all other substances

MedLabs is affiliated with the Drug and Alcohol Testing Industry Association (DATIA) and the Substance Abuse Program Administrators Association (SAPAA). We have been in the drug and alcohol testing business for 20 years. Our procedures include a comprehensive program that provides the highest quality services, focusing on accuracy, integrity, and professionalism.

Our mission is to provide affordable lab screening to help reduce drug and alcohol abuse, while empowering individuals and companies to manage their health and wellness.

Staff   Volunteers   Volunteers   Lookup   Cases   User   Reports
Dashboard   Dashboard   Tables   Administration

Contact Log

Name	Fine, Miriam
Case Number	594
Activity Date	9/3/2012
Activity Type	Placement Visit
Subject	Child welfare
Location	Grandparents' Home
Contact Type	Face-to-face
Hours	1.00
Notes:	

Everyone was home for Labor Day and Mabel invited me over for lunch for my monthly visit. The family ate together at the dining room table, and it was lively and playful. There was a lot of good-natured kidding about Mabel's annual insistence on watermelon salad for Labor Day, which no one seems to appreciate except Mabel.

She sent the kids outside so we could talk while cleaning up the kitchen. Roger joined us, which was unusual. He told me he was back at work full time, feeling much better, hoped to keep his diabetes at bay by more diligent medication and diet complicance. He said Mabel had taken the kids to see Joelle twice since we met last. While he is supportive of Joelle's efforts to get clean, he said he seriously doubts her ability to care for the children over the long run. "It's harder than it looks during an afternoon visit."

Mabel seconded that sentiment. They are both clearly worried that Joelle might be able to convince the Court she can look after the kids, but her history suggests that will be very hard to sustain. They are also pretty frustrated that the Court changed the goal to adoption, but now reunification is back on the table. I suggested we give it some time, since we've just started supervised visits again, and there are still a lot of steps before Joelle could request regaining custody. We agreed to keep an eye on the kids and see how things go.

Mabel asked if I could help with Tyrone's medication. She said the renewal prescription that came home with him from Gillis expires in 4 weeks and CD still hadn't gotten him an appointment with a new doctor to renew the meds. She is concerned that there won't be time to get a new prescription before he runs out of pills. She's been online and seen the warnings about "cold turkey" withdrawal from this drug. I said I would talk to Marlie to see where CD is in the process of finding a psychiatrist for Tyrone.

I took time on the porch to speak to each of the children privately. Alysha reported she "loves" 5th grade, "loves" her teacher, "loves" her classroom, and "loves" her friends. She is clearly happiest when school is in session, and she can excel in her own world. I asked about visiting her mom, and she was thoughtful with her response. "It's much better, and she really wants us back. It's just that ... well, we're happy here. It's hard to think about moving again." She also mentioned that Mabel had indicated she would try to manage Girl Scouts this year. I can tell Alysha is very hopeful about that. She just wants to do what the other girls in her class are doing.

Hope told me that 3rd grade was going to be a lot of fun. She has Miss Carol Holman, who is the same teacher Alysha had for 3rd grade (the year the children were brought into care). Hope is very excited about having "Alysha's teacher," and tells me she is doing well in both reading and math.

Tyrone seems to be doing quite well, though it's hard to tell what is fact and what is posturing with a 14-year-old boy. He seems so much bigger and older than when he was picked up a year-and-a-half ago. He did not mention the visits with Joelle, and I decided not to ask. We talked about his new school instead, and he told me high school was "interesting," and he felt like his tutoring at Gillis had kept him even on his studies. I asked if there was a Robotics or Engingeering Club at Central Academy. He said he thought they had both, but he hadn't checked them out yet. He did tell me, with some pride, that Central was they oldest high school in Kansas City and both Walt Disney and Casey Stengel had gone there. Also a rapper named Kutt Calhoun, who I had never heard of, but seemed to make a big impression on on Tyrone. He told me Calhoun just released an album called Red-Headed Stepchild. Go figure. But it's good to see Tyrone engaged in his environment again.

Activity Status   Approved

From: Miriam Fine [mailto:miriamkfine@gmail.com]
Sent: Tuesday, September 4, 2012 8:43 AM
To: Marlie.Verlet@dss.mo.gov
Cc: Cc: Duncan.Walsh@dss.mo.gov; ablackstone@jacksoncountycasa-mo.org;
    hmiller@jacksoncountycasa-mo.org;
Subject: *Confidential: Merritt—Washington—Medication for Tyrone

Hi, Marlie. I'm writing to check in to see how you're doing with getting a psychiatrist appointment for Tyrone Merritt. You'll recall that Duncan Walsh told the group at our July 15 FST meeting that you would be setting that up now that Tyrone has been discharged from Gillis.

I visited the children yesterday; their grandmother said she has not yet heard from you about this appointment. She reminded me that Tyrone's prescription for Abilify will run out on October 9, and she is very concerned about the risks of cold-turkey withdrawal for a teen on such a powerful psychotropic medication. We have 5 weeks to get Tyrone into an appointment to be sure his medication regimen is appropriately monitored. What can I do to assist?

Many thanks!

Miriam Fine
CASA Volunteer

_____

Miriam Fine
(913) 555-8436

"If I can't dance, I don't want to be part of your revolution." -- Emma Goldman

From: Miriam Fine [mailto:miriamkfine@gmail.com]
Sent: Tuesday, September 11, 2012 7:12 AM
To: Marlie.Verlet@dss.mo.gov
Cc: Duncan.Walsh@dss.mo.gov; ablackstone@jacksoncountycasa-mo.org;
      hmiller@jacksoncountycasa-mo.org;
Subject: *Confidential: Merritt—Washington—Medication for Tyrone—URGENT

Dear Marlie,

I have had no response from my email to you on September 4 about a psychiatric appointment for Tyrone Merritt to renew his Abilify prescription and/or prescribe a regimen to taper off the medication. Mabel Merritt, the youth's grandmother and current placement, informs me that she has not heard from you either. **This matter is now extremely urgent.**

I am attaching information that explains the severity of the risks facing Tyrone Merritt, who is only 14 years old, and whose brain is still developing, if he is forced by CD incompetence to go through cold-turkey withdrawal from this powerful psychotropic medication. I have highlighted the most relevant sections.

You have had more than enough time to work on this issue, as shown in the following timeline:

1. Tyrone was released from Gillis on June 29 (74 days ago).
2. At the July 15 FST, Duncan Walsh told the group in your presence that you would work this issue (58 days ago).
3. Mabel Merritt has asked you repeatedly over the past 2 months to help on this problem.
4. I wrote to you on September 4 to ask about the status of Tyrone's medical/therapeutic services (7 days ago).

I am not sure what your priorities are at CD or what obstacles you face, but I do know this young man deserves better attention and help from the state agency that removed him from his mother in the first place. I am beseeching you to please focus on the "care" in "care and custody" and move immediately to find a psychiatrist for Tyrone Merritt before his psychotropic medication prescription runs out on October 9 (in 28 days).

Sincerely,

Miriam Fine
CASA Volunteer

Miriam Fine
(913) 555-8436
"If I can't dance, I don't want to be part of your revolution." -- Emma Goldman

Abilify – Withdrawal
Abilify (Aripiprazole) is a second-generation antipsychotic prescription medication, used to treat certain mental/mood disorders in adults and adolescents, including depression, schizophrenia, bipolar disorder, Tourette's disorder, and irritability associated with autistic disorder.

Abilify is a partial dopamine agonist, delivered in tablets, orally disintegrating tablets, oral solution, or injection for intramuscular use. Serious side effects can be associated with withdrawal from the medication, which should always be done under medical supervision. Consult with your doctor/psychiatrist about the proper withdrawal plan and what drug to use for replacement.

Factors That Can Influence Withdrawal
The factors that can influence withdrawal from Abilify include length of time on the medication, dosage, individual factors, and tapering. Tapering is highly recommended when withdrawing from Abilify, as it gives the body time to adjust to the new chemical balance in the brain. Quitting "cold turkey" is never recommended.

Abilify Withdrawal Symptoms
There are numerous symptoms associated with withdrawal from Abilify. They will vary based on the factors noted above. Many are short term and will pass with time. Some may have more serious long-term consequences.

> **Depression** -- Patients taking Abilify for symptoms of depression may find these symptoms recur after the drug is withdrawn. Sometimes the symptoms are more extreme than they were prior to taking the medication. Adolescents may be at increased risk for suicidal thinking and behaviors.

> **Concentration Problems and Dizziness** -- Withdrawal from Abilify reduces dopamine levels in the brain, which can reduce both concentration and cognitive functioning.

> **Headaches and Insomnia** -- Some patients experience headaches while withdrawing from Abilify. These may be mild or severe, and may mirror the symptoms of migraine headaches. Some patients report lack of sleep while withdrawing from Abilify, caused by night-time feels of restlessness and anxiety.

> **Dizziness and Diarrhea** -- Withdrawal from Abilify can cause feelings nausea and dizziness. This is most severe in patients who withdraw cold turkey. Some patients report several days of diarrhea while withdrawing from Abilify.

> **Other Withdrawal Symptoms** -- Many other withdrawal symptoms have been reported. It is very important for patients to remain in close contact with their physician/psychiatrist while implementing a withdrawal plan from Abilify so that all symptoms can be monitored and managed.

How Long Do Abilify Withdrawal Symptoms Last?
Abilify can remain in the system for up to 34 days, which will moderate withdrawal symptoms. When the drug is no longer in the system, withdrawal symptoms typically get worse in appearance and duration and can last for several weeks to several months. Staying in touch with the prescribing doctor/psychiatrist will allow proper observation and treatment of all withdrawal side effects.

Content sponsored, but not endorsed, by: *General America Pharmaceutical, Inc.*

From: Anita Blackstone [mailto:ablackstone@jacksoncountycasa-mo.org]
Sent: Wednesday, September 12, 2012 10:36 AM
To: miriamkfine@gmail.com
Cc: hmiller@jacksoncountycasa-mo.org;
Subject: RE: *Confidential: Merritt—Washington—Medication for Tyrone—URGENT

Miri,

Slow down and take a deep breath. I know you're working hard to be sure that Tyrone gets in to see the psychiatrist before his meds run out. We are all grateful for your passionate advocacy.

But pissing off CD won't help. They can pick and choose which kids to focus on at any given time—their caseloads are sufficiently overwhelming that they can always justify "missing" something on a particular kid. Let's do our best to be sure they don't get so annoyed with us that Tyrone becomes one of those kids.

I think Marlie is just too new to know what to do. She's probably swamped and anxious and scared that if she asks for help, she'll look incompetent. I've seen it before.

Let's try this: Why don't we have Henrietta write an email to Duncan to see if we can't get some movement on this issue? Sometimes a nudge from the Guardian ad Litem can move mountains. We have a Case Review scheduled in five weeks on this case, and I'm betting that Duncan won't want us to file a prior motion with the Court informing the Commissioner of this lapse on their part.

Shall we try that?

Anita

Anita Blackstone
Case Supervisor
(816) 555-8236

From: Miriam Fine [mailto:miriamkfine@gmail.com]
Sent: Wednesday, September 12, 2012 11:19 AM
To: hgoldstein@laramyjones.com
Subject: Spanking—and not the good kind

Well, it was bound to happen. I got an email this morning from my CASA Case Supervisor essentially telling me to back off.

It reminded me of that time the synagogue Religious School Director told me to stop hounding Isaac's 5th grade Sunday School teacher to put deeper religious content in the classroom curriculum—actually, I believe I said "any religious content—and arts and crafts don't count." Remember the hub-bub . . .? I think that one went all the way to the synagogue board.

It's pretty interesting the things I thought mattered before I met these CASA kids. Talk about perspective.

Anyway . . . I've been on a mission since July to get CD to set up a psychiatric appointment for my CASA teen so he won't run out of psychotropic meds and get thrown into cold-turkey withdrawal.

The staff change on the case predictably slowed everything down (and nothing was ever that fast to begin with!). I was nice for a really long time, I promise. Insistent, but nice. But I finally lost my cool yesterday and wrote an email essentially accusing the new worker of blatant disregard for the well-being of this child. I was a bitch.

I know this stuff happens all the time—the residential facilities put these kids on powerful drugs to control their behaviors (I'm pretty sure the operative word here is "control"); then the kids get released to foster parents or family members or bio mom with a few days or weeks of medication and maybe one refill if they're lucky; then the meds run out before CD finds a psychiatrist to see the kids and renew the script.

And—boom!—these kids, who have already suffered trauma from the original abuse, trauma from being removed from their homes, and trauma from being put in residential, are thrown into cold-turkey withdrawal from very powerful drugs that were probably not appropriate for adolescent brains in the first place!

Is it any wonder so many kids in the system end up acting out and getting in trouble?

Anyway . . . I guess I let my frustration show, because my Case Supervisor asked me to chill. She's going to have our GAL approach CD with a more "legalistic" request. Which is probably a good thing, because I was only getting started on yelling at that worker. Which was likely not going to make anything better.

You don't think I'm an irredeemable bitch, do you?

Mom used to always tell me I let my passion get ahead of my common sense. "Keep the end goal in mind," she's been saying since I was a kid. I'm trying . . .

In the meantime, I actually just left a voice message for Carol to see if she'll write an Abilify prescription for me off-label. I can fill it and get the meds to the grandmother—just to tide the kid over until CD does their job. I'm pretty sure this falls in the category of both illegal and unethical. Not to mention well outside the boundaries for a CASA Volunteer. But it's ridiculous that everyone knows what the kid needs, and the Gillis shrink has already put him on the meds, and we all know the serious consequences of sudden withdrawal, and it's just bureaucratic inertia that is keeping him from getting the goddamn pills!

I'll be very curious to see what Carol says. Could the solution be this simple? Hah—fat chance! Would you visit me in jail?

Miri

_____

Miriam Fine
(913) 555-8436

"If I can't dance, I don't want to be part of your revolution." -- Emma Goldman

From: Miriam Fine [mailto:miriamkfine@gmail.com]
Sent: Wednesday, September 12, 2012 2:20 PM
To: hgoldstein@laramyjones.com
Subject: Saved by the shrink

Well, that didn't take long.

Carol called me back within the hour. And basically said no, no, and hell, no.

She was very sympathetic. Said it was a crying shame that the system couldn't get the mental health treatments and meds right for these kids. But reminded me—which I knew, of course—that she could lose her license for prescribing medication for me that she knew I planned to give to someone else. And I could certainly get in trouble for giving prescription medication to a minor who is not in my care. And, though she didn't know the exact rules, she guessed the CASA people would fire me pronto if they ever even learned I had asked.

So . . . professional as always . . . she pulled me back from the abyss, reminding me that my job is to do what I can do. And not to jeopardize that good work by breaking the rules—or the law.

She asked if I wanted to move my next appointment up a week earlier.

I said yes.

Miri

Miriam Fine
(913) 555-8436

"If I can't dance, I don't want to be part of your revolution." -- Emma Goldman

From: Henrietta Miller [mailto:hmiller@jacksoncountycasa-mo.org]
Sent: Thursday, September 13, 2012 4:55 PM
To: Duncan.Walsh@dss.mo.gov
Cc: ablackstone@jacksoncountycasa-mo.gov; miriamkfine@gmail.com
Subject: RE: *Confidential: Merritt—Washington—Medication for Tyrone—URGENT

Dear Duncan,

I am writing to follow up on the matter of arranging for medical/psychiatric services for Tyrone Merritt (Case Number 1416-JU0040987).

Tyrone was released from the Gillis School on June 29, 2012, and returned to his grandparents' home, under the care and custody of Children's Division. While at Gillis, the facility's contract psychiatrist, Dr. Ben Arielto, prescribed Abilify to help with Tyrone's clinical disorders and behavior issues. That prescription was for 180 days of medication, ending on October 9, 2012.

You made assurances at our July 15, 2012, FST Meeting that CD would be arranging for a follow-up appointment with an off-site psychiatrist so that Tyrone would receive uninterrupted mental health services and monitoring. We also noted at the time that Tyrone would need an ongoing medication treatment/withdrawal plan, since his Abilify prescription would be expiring.

It has now been 76 days since Tyrone was discharged from Gillis, and no appointment has been made for him to see a psychiatrist. Furthermore, repeated requests from our CASA Volunteer Miriam Fine to the CD Worker Marlie Verlet for information on this issue have gone unanswered. I believe you were copied on those emails of September 4, 2012, and September 11, 2012, but I can forward them again if necessary.

To recap, Tyrone Merritt's prescription for the powerful psychotropic medication Abilify will expire in 26 days, and we have become extremely concerned about his psychological and physical well-being after that point. It is imperative that Tyrone sees a psychiatrist before that 26-day window closes, so that he can be assessed for either medication continuation or planned, medically-supervised withdrawal.

I would prefer to handle this matter directly with CD, based on our longstanding and productive relationship. However, we feel this matter has now become urgent, and this youth's health and safety are at risk. If I do not hear from you within three business days that an appointment has been arranged for Tyrone Merritt to see a psychiatrist prior to October 9, 2012, then I will be forced to file a motion asking the Family Court to intervene on the child's behalf.

Henrietta

Henrietta Miller
CASA Staff Attorney / Guardian ad Litem
(816) 555-8209
Fax: (816) 555-5252

MedLabs
3274 Broadway
Kansas City, MO 64111

Sample Provided by:	Joelle Merritt / DOB 06/09/82
Date of Sample:	September 11, 2012
Test Results Reported:	September 14, 2012
Referred by:	Children's Division – Jackson County
Responsible Payor:	Children's Division – Jackson County
Results Sent to:	Children's Division – Jackson County

Test Ordered

10 Panel + Alcohol Urine Drug Test

AMP-Amphetamines (MAMP-Methamphetamine, MDMA-Ecstasy), COC-Cocaine, OPI-Opiates (including heroin, codeine and morphine), PCP-Phencyclidine, THC-Marijuana, BZO-Benzodiazepines, BAR-Barbiturates, MTD-Methadone, PPX-Propoxyphene, Meth – Methaqualone, ETH – Alcohol.

Results

Negative for ETH – Alcohol – within last 80 hours
Negative for all other substances

MedLabs is affiliated with the Drug and Alcohol Testing Industry Association (DATIA) and the Substance Abuse Program Administrators Association (SAPAA). We have been in the drug and alcohol testing business for 20 years. Our procedures include a comprehensive program that provides the highest quality services, focusing on accuracy, integrity, and professionalism.

Our mission is to provide affordable lab screening to help reduce drug and alcohol abuse, while empowering individuals and companies to manage their health and wellness.

Contact Log

Name	Fine, Miriam
Case Number	594
Activity Date	10/3/2012
Activity Type	Placement Visit
Subject	Child welfare
Location	Grandparents' Home
Contact Type	Face-to-face
Hours	1.25

Notes:

I had planned to visit the children after school, but Mabel asked me to come early so we could speak privately. Roger was at work, but she told me they had conferred and were in agreement about their request to slow down on the supervised visits with Joelle. Mabel said Joelle was doing well and seemed to be staying on her sobriety program, however the increased pace of visits is difficult for Mabel to manage. She said it isn't easy for an "older couple" to raise three children under the best of circumstances, and their efforts to both care for the children and manage the now twice-weekly visits with their mother were exhausting.

She also said the kids were becoming resistant to the visits. Not because they didn't want to see Joelle, but because they had their own lives to lead -- school, schoolwork, hobbies, friends. Alysha just started Girl Scouts, and Mabel said she is very excited about that. Mabel is trying really hard to get her to those meetings and events. She said fitting in visits with Joelle just made the kids feel imposed upon and was a continual reminder that other children lived with their parents, while they did not.

I told her there wasn't a lot I could do -- now that she is accessing services in line with Court orders, Joelle has a legal right to see more of her kids. I did suggest to Mabel that she tell the CD worker that she was no longer able to supervise the visits. Then Marlie would have to provide a Parent Aide or supervise the vistis herself.

Mabel snorted and basically said, "Marlie doesn't know her nose from her elbow" (her comment wasn't that nice). I told her it wasn't her job to provide services that CD required but couldn't manage to arrange. If she didn't think she had the capacity to organize and implement supervised visits, she could leave it on CD's doorstep and see what happens.

I also reminded her of a previous conversation with our CASA Case Supervisor and Staff Attorney. If Joelle isn't given sufficient access to the children, after those visits are ordered by the Court, then her attorney will have grounds to fight at any future TPR trial. If Mabel's long-term view is that Joelle's parental rights will probably be terminated so the children can be adopted, then it makes sense to faciliate as many visits as possible now.

Mabel also told me that Duncan Walsh had contacted her with the name of a psychiatrist who would be taking Tyrone's case. Mabel had called his office immediately, and was told they had a three-week waiting list. She has made an appointment for Tyrone on Oct. 25. This is 16 days after Tyrone runs out of meds. Mabel is very upset about this. Frankly, I am, too.

The children were tired when they arrived home from school. I asked if anyone needed to talk with me about anything, but all three said they had homework and looked like they wanted their snacks. This is the first visit where I have not spoken with each child individually. However, I observed that they appeared healthy and safe.

Activity Status   Approved

October 15, 2012

Family Support Team Meeting

Case: Merritt-Washington
Facilitator: Marlie Verlet, Children's Division supervisor
Location: Library Conference Room, Jackson County CASA
In attendance:
      Tyrone Merritt – Juvenile
      Alysha Washington – Juvenile
      Hope Washington – Juvenile
      Joelle Merritt – Mother
      Martin Jaylon – Mother's Attorney
      Mabel Merritt – Maternal Grandmother
      Marlie Verlet – CD Worker
      Miriam Fine – CASA Volunteer
      Anita Blackstone – CASA Case Supervisor (taking notes for the group)

Marlie Verlet passed around the attendance log / confidentiality agreement for everyone to sign.

Marlie suggested the group begin with the children.

Tyrone Merritt – Reported enjoying first year in high school. Feels he is doing well in math and keeping up in history, English, and his other classes. He has joined the Robotics Club and likes the other kids who are doing that. There is a "late bus" that gets him pretty close to home, and he can walk the rest of the way, so Mabel doesn't have to make an extra trip to get him. Said he likes visiting his mom, but sometimes he "has things to do," and it isn't convenient.

Alysha Washington – Very happy in 5th grade and reports her early assignments all received A's. Said she liked visiting her mom "since she got well," but seemed to be choosing her words carefully. She did not make eye contact with either Joelle or Mabel Merritt while speaking.

Hope Washington – Sat next to Joelle during the meeting, and wanted her to admire a picture she was drawing while the others talked. Reported she likes 3rd grade a lot and is doing well. She is very happy to have "Alysha's teacher." She asked Marlie Verlet if "we are going home to Mommy now." Marlie answered "it's too soon to talk about that."

(Children left room. Since they are comfortable at the CASA house and getting older, no supervision needed. Anita Blackstone confirmed it would be okay with the CASA staff if the children remained in the hall attending to their schoolwork. They could knock on the conference room door if they needed anything.)

Joelle Merritt, mother – Said she is following her recovery program and keeping all therapist appointments, as well as attending AA meetings twice weekly. She continues to work at Taco Joe's and has been promoted to a supervisory position, which pays slightly more. Said she has been clean and sober since leaving ReCovery and enjoying visits with the children. She said she hoped the Court would soon allow her unsupervised and overnight visits with her kids. "I've licked this thing, and I want them back home."

Mabel Merritt, maternal grandmother – Said Roger was at work today and couldn't get the time off.

Reported she was very glad that the visits with Joelle were going well, but the added stress of providing transport and supervision for these visits was too much. She said she had asked Marlie several times to provide a Parent Aide to take the kids, but hadn't heard back. Marlie responded that CD is out of budget for Parent Aides through the end of the quarter. Mabel became angry and said: "Well, the Court has ordered you to get these kids to the visits, not me. I'm done."

Martin Jaylon, mom's attorney, suggested that perhaps Joelle could drive over to the Merritts house to visit the kids after work, perhaps while Mabel is in the home doing housework or preparing dinner. That compromise seemed to calm the group, and Mabel said, "You could even stay for dinner sometimes."

Mabel reported that the new psychiatrist for Tyrone did not have any openings until October 25. She said he took his last pill on October 9 and was beginning to complain about headaches and difficulty concentrating. She said she was worried about his schoolwork if this continues. She accused CD of "dragging their feet" in getting Tyrone the needed appointment, but Duncan Walsh said he thought it would all work out in the next ten days or so.

Marlie Verlet, CD worker – Reminded the group that the next Case Review is scheduled for next week and the Commissioner would like to see all three children present. She asked Mabel if she would be able to take them out of school, and Mabel said yes.

Reported that CD would be recommending moving to unsupervised visits, followed by overnight visits with a goal of reunification if Joelle continued to follow Court orders for psychiatric treatment, substance abuse treatment, and regular drug/alcohol testing.

Provided copies of Section 4, Chapter 10 (Permanency Through Reunification) of the Child Welfare Manual for the State of Missouri Department of Social Services, which notes that:

> Whenever possible, the goal of out-of-home care will be a timely family reunification.

> Family reunification may be recommended as soon as the family has met the treatment goals and the Family Support Team/PPRT determines that:

> - The family can meet the minimal physical and emotional needs of the child with supportive services if needed; and

> - Needed supportive services are available and the family will utilize such services.

Miriam Fine, CASA Volunteer – Said she would concur with CD's recommendation for increased visits with Joelle, but wanted to be sure everyone was taking the children's needs into account in scheduling these visits. "They need to proceed with as little disruption to their lives as possible. They deserve to live like regular kids." She also expressed very strong reservations about the "rush to reunification" and urged everyone to take their time with such an important change in the children's lives. Said this might well be the right permanency plan for the children, but Joelle has not been out of ReCovery very long and time is needed to be sure she has the long-term ability to safely care for three children in her home.

Miriam also said she wanted the record to show that she was appalled that it took so long to schedule a psychiatrist for Tyrone. "This kid has enough problems without suffering drug withdrawal because the adults couldn't get it together."

Anita Blackstone, CASA Case Supervisor – nothing to add.

Group agreed on 2/15/13 for next FST. Anita will schedule with CASA to use the Library Conference Room and will notify parties about time.

AJB / uploaded to OPTIMA 10-15-12

MedLabs
3274 Broadway
Kansas City, MO 64111

Sample Provided by:	Joelle Merritt / DOB 06/09/82
Date of Sample:	October 11, 2012
Test Results Reported:	October 17, 2012
Referred by:	Children's Division – Jackson County
Responsible Payor:	Children's Division – Jackson County
Results Sent to:	Children's Division – Jackson County

Test Ordered

10 Panel + Alcohol Urine Drug Test

AMP-Amphetamines (MAMP-Methamphetamine, MDMA-Ecstasy), COC-Cocaine, OPI-Opiates (including heroin, codeine and morphine), PCP-Phencyclidine, THC-Marijuana, BZO-Benzodiazepines, BAR-Barbiturates, MTD-Methadone, PPX-Propoxyphene, Meth – Methaqualone, ETH – Alcohol.

Results

Negative for ETH – Alcohol – within last 80 hours
Negative for all other substances

MedLabs is affiliated with the Drug and Alcohol Testing Industry Association (DATIA) and the Substance Abuse Program Administrators Association (SAPAA). We have been in the drug and alcohol testing business for 20 years. Our procedures include a comprehensive program that provides the highest quality services, focusing on accuracy, integrity, and professionalism.

Our mission is to provide affordable lab screening to help reduce drug and alcohol abuse, while empowering individuals and companies to manage their health and wellness.

CHILD'S REPORT ON PLACEMENT

Court Date: _____ 10/23/12 _____

Child's Name: _____ Hope Merritt _____

Current Placement: __ Grandparents – Roger and Mabel Merritt _____

This form gives you, the child involved in this case, an opportunity to express your feelings and any facts concerning your present placement. This form may be used by the Guardian ad litem, and the Judge or Commissioner as allowed by law. It is possible that all the information will be made available to all the parties, including the placement provider. Please be fair, open and honest.

1. Are you generally satisfied with your current placement?

_____X_____ yes _____ no

Please explain:
I like living with Grandma and Grandpa and Alysha and Tyrone.

2. Does the placement provider help with your goal, whether it is reunification with a parent, independent living, relative placement or other plan?

_____X_____ yes _____ no

Please explain:
Grandma helps with everything.

3. Please describe how you get along with the other children, if any, in your placement.

I like my sister and brother.

4. Please name the school you are going to and explain what you like about it or don't like about it.

Whittier Elementary I like my teacher a lot. She was Alysha's teacher before.

5. Please talk about how you are disciplined when you do something you are not supposed to, or violate rules of the home.

We get Time Out.

6. If you have visits with brothers or sisters, please explain how that is going and how it could be better.

Tyrone is home with us now. I like that.

7. Do you have any health concerns that you feel like are not being taken care of? If so, explain:

8. Please explain how visits, if any, are going with your parent(s), and what could be done to make them better.

I like to see Mommy.
It makes Grandma tired.

9. Do you get a chance to participate in things you want to, like sports, music, dance, and other activities? Please explain:

I like to play with Alysha. I want a cat but Grandma says no.

10. How do you get along with your social worker, and do you feel that they understand your needs and situation? Please explain:

Ms. Camille Harris went away.
Ms. Verlet is new.
Ms. Fine takes care of us.

11. Do you know of any relatives or other adults you might be able to live with? If yes, please list their name(s) and how you know them.

We lived with Mommy before.

12. Do you know of any help that you need that you are not getting right now? If yes, please explain.

I am happy.

13. If you are in counseling, do you think it is helping? Please explain.

_____
_____
_____
_____
_____

14. Would you like for your court hearing to be scheduled so that you don't have to miss school to attend?

___X___ yes   _____ no

15. Do you have a photo you would like for the judge or commissioner to have? If so, be sure to bring it to court.

11. Please explain anything about your situation that you think is important and that has not been asked.

I want to stay with Alysha and Tyrone.

CHILD'S REPORT ON PLACEMENT

Court Date:_____10/23/12_____

Child's Name:_____Alysha Merritt_____

Current Placement:__Grandparents – Roger and Mabel Merritt_____

This form gives you, the child involved in this case, an opportunity to express your feelings and any facts concerning your present placement. This form may be used by the Guardian ad litem, and the Judge or Commissioner as allowed by law. It is possible that all the information will be made available to all the parties, including the placement provider. Please be fair, open and honest.

1. Are you generally satisfied with your current placement?

_____✓_____ yes   _____ no

Please explain:
_____It is very nice living with_____
_____my grandparents_____
_____
_____
_____

2. Does the placement provider help with your goal, whether it is reunification with a parent, independent living, relative placement or other plan?

_____ yes   _____ no

Please explain:
_____I don't know how to answer_____
_____this. We would like to stay_____
_____together here. I think our_____
_____grandparents want that, too._____
_____But our Mom wants us back._____

3. Please describe how you get along with the other children, if any, in your placement.

All three of us get along extremely well together.

4. Please name the school you are going to and explain what you like about it or don't like about it.

Whittier Elementary School I love my class and my teachers and my friends.

5. Please talk about how you are disciplined when you do something you are not supposed to, or violate rules of the home.

We would get time out but very rarely. We are pretty good kids.

6. If you have visits with brothers or sisters, please explain how that is going and how it could be better.

It was sad when Tyrone went to the Bill's School, but he's back home now.

7. Do you have any health concerns that you feel like are not being taken care of? If so, explain:

I like my new glasses, I can see the board really clearly now.

8. Please explain how visits, if any, are going with your parent(s), and what could be done to make them better.

I like to see Mom, and she is much better now. Sometimes I have homework and it's hard to get everything done.

9. Do you get a chance to participate in things you want to, like sports, music, dance, and other activities? Please explain:

I go to the Library and also get lots of books at school. I really love Girl Scouts!!

10. How do you get along with your social worker, and do you feel that they understand your needs and situation? Please explain:

I do not think our new CD social worker knows us very well. We miss Mrs. Harris who helped us a lot.

11. Do you know of any relatives or other adults you might be able to live with? If yes, please list their name(s) and how you know them.

Our other grandparents don't see us anymore. Our father is in jail.

12. Do you know of any help that you need that you are not getting right now? If yes, please explain.

13. If you are in counseling, do you think it is helping? Please explain.

_____
_____
_____
_____
_____

14. Would you like for your court hearing to be scheduled so that you don't have to miss school to attend?

_____✓_____ yes   _____ no

15. Do you have a photo you would like for the judge or commissioner to have? If so, be sure to bring it to court.

11. Please explain anything about your situation that you think is important and that has not been asked.

We love Mommy, but moving is hard and we are settled with Grandma and Grandpa. Could we stay here and still see Mommy sometimes?

CHILD'S REPORT ON PLACEMENT

Court Date: _____10/23/12_____

Child's Name:_____Tyrone Washington_____

Current Placement:__Grandparents – Roger and Mabel Merritt_____

This form gives you, the child involved in this case, an opportunity to express your feelings and any facts concerning your present placement. This form may be used by the Guardian ad litem, and the Judge or Commissioner as allowed by law. It is possible that all the information will be made available to all the parties, including the placement provider. Please be fair, open and honest.

1. Are you generally satisfied with your current placement?

_____✗_____ yes   _____ no

Please explain:

I have been happy with my
grandparents since getting released
from Gillis.

2. Does the placement provider help with your goal, whether it is reunification with a parent, independent living, relative placement or other plan?

_???_____ yes   _____ no

Please explain:

I would like to stay with my
grandparents but they make
us visit our mother. I would
like to have a say.

3. Please describe how you get along with the other children, if any, in your placement.

I love my sisters very much.

4. Please name the school you are going to and explain what you like about it or don't like about it.

Central Academy
I am doing well in school this year. I like math more than English.

5. Please talk about how you are disciplined when you do something you are not supposed to, or violate rules of the home.

I would get grounded or sent back to Gillis if I am very bad.

6. If you have visits with brothers or sisters, please explain how that is going and how it could be better.

It is important for us all to stay together.

7. Do you have any health concerns that you feel like are not being taken care of? If so, explain:

Ms. Fine makes sure I have my inhaler.
I ran out of pills and get headaches.

8. Please explain how visits, if any, are going with your parent(s), and what could be done to make them better.

It is hard to find time to visit Mom. I would rather be with my friends.

9. Do you get a chance to participate in things you want to, like sports, music, dance, and other activities? Please explain:

I do Robotics unless we have to visit Mom after school

10. How do you get along with your social worker, and do you feel that they understand your needs and situation? Please explain:

There have been changes. I think Ms. Harris quit. I rely on Ms. Fine.

11. Do you know of any relatives or other adults you might be able to live with? If yes, please list their name(s) and how you know them.

_No._

12. Do you know of any help that you need that you are not getting right now? If yes, please explain.

I need to have my pills renewed. I'm scared about that

13. If you are in counseling, do you think it is helping? Please explain.

_Because Ms. Harris quit I
don't get to see a
councillor._

14. Would you like for your court hearing to be scheduled so that you don't have to miss school to attend?

    X   yes !!!!   no

15. Do you have a photo you would like for the judge or commissioner to have? If so, be sure to bring it to court.

11. Please explain anything about your situation that you think is important and that has not been asked.

_I am worried my pills ran
out and I feel wierd.
I want to stay with Grandma
and Grandpa and not go
back to Gillis._

IN THE CIRCUIT COURT OF JACKSON COUNTY, MISSOURI
FAMILY COURT DIVISION

IN THE INTEREST OF:	**CASE NUMBER:** 1416-JU0040987
TYRONE MERRITT	
	LIFE NUMBER:
SEX: M BORN: 19-FEB-1998	1416-JR57790

IN THE INTEREST OF:	**CASE NUMBER:** 1416-JU0040988
ALYSHA WASHINGTON	
	LIFE NUMBER:
SEX: F BORN: 07-APRIL-2003	1416-JR57791

IN THE INTEREST OF:	**CASE NUMBER:** 1416-JU0040989
HOPE WASHINGTON	
	LIFE NUMBER:
SEX: F BORN: 17-NOV-2004	1416-JR57792

FINDINGS AND RECOMMENDATIONS

Now on October 23, 2012 there being present:

MARLIE VERLET	-	Children's Division
DUNCAN WALSH	-	Children's Division
JOELLE MERRITT	-	Mother
ABIGAIL NORRIS	-	Attorney for the Juvenile Officer
HENRIETTA MILLER	-	Guardian ad Litem (CASA)
MIRIAM FINE	-	CASA Volunteer
MARTIN JAYLON	-	Attorney for Mother
TYRONE MERRITT	-	Juvenile
ALYSHA WASHINGTON	-	Juvenile
HOPE WASHINGTON	-	Juvenile

The cause comes on for Case Review pursuant to an order of MAY 15, 2012.

IT IS HEREBY ORDERED: that the juveniles Tyrone Merritt, Alysha Washington, and Hope Washington are committed to the custody of Children's Division for placement with Mabel and Roger Merritt, until further order of the Court.

The Court has reviewed all documentary evidence presented, including the social file of the juvenile containing reports and recommendations from the Children's Division since the inception of the case, the Guardian ad Litem's reports and recommendations, the CASA Volunteer's reports and recommendations, Placement Reports filled out by the juveniles, and all records pertaining to the mother's treatment at ReCovery and subsequent drug/alcohol testing results.

Based on the mother's compliance with all Court orders and 90-day record of negative UAs, the Court hereby changes the permanency plan from adoption to reunification. The mother, Joelle Merritt, may have increased supervised visitation up to three times weekly, moving to unsupervised visitation and overnight visits at the discretion of the Children's Division.

The Court takes notice of the concerns of the Guardian ad Litem and the CASA Volunteer regarding this goal change, as well as the wishes expressed by the juveniles in their Placement Reports. Nonetheless, Missouri State guidelines strongly prefer reunification if the children's safety is not compromised, both to protect the biological parents' legal rights and in accordance with longstanding research on the best interests of children.

The court reaches this determination based on all of the reports and information received. The Children's Division is ordered to move towards reunification within the next 90 days.

The next court hearing for the above action is scheduled for JANUARY 15, 2013 at 02:00 PM in DIVISION 40 for Case Review prior to Permanency Review.

Notice of Findings and Recommendation & Notice of Right to a Rehearing

The parties are notified that the forgoing Findings and Recommendations have been entered this date by a commissioner, and all papers relative to the care or proceeding, together with the Findings and Recommendation have been transferred to a Judge of the Court. The Findings and Recommendations shall become the Judgment of the Court upon adoption by order of the Judge. Unless waived by the parties in writing, at party in the case or proceeding heard by a commissioner, within fifteen days after the mailing of notice of the filing of the Judgment of the Court, may file a motion for rehearing by a Judge of the Court. If the motion for rehearing is not ruled on within forty-five days after the motion is filed, the motion is overruled for all purposes. Rule 130.13

October 25, 2012

Gerard E. Solomon
_____

Date   GERARD E. SOLOMON, Commissione

Order and Judgment Adopting Commissioner's Findings and Recommendation

It is hereby ordered, adjudged and decreed the foregoing Findings and Recommendations entered by the commissioner are adopted and confirmed as a final Judgment of the Court.

October 25, 2012   *Suzanne M. Martell*
_____   _____
Date   Judge

NOTICE OF ENTRY OF JUDGMENT

You are hereby notified that on   OCT 26 2012,   the Family Court, Juvenile Division, of Jackson County, Missouri made and entered the above judgment in this case:

You are further notified that you may have a right of appeal from this judgment under Rule 120.01 and section 211.261, RSMo, which provides that:

1. An appeal shall be allowed to the juvenile from any final judgment made under the Juvenile Code and may be taken on the part of the juvenile by the custodian.

2. An appeal shall be allowed to custodian from any final judgment made under the Juvenile Code that adversely affects the custodian.

3. Notice of appeal shall be filed in accordance with Missouri law.

4. Neither the filing of a notice of appeal nor the filing of any motion subsequne to the judgment shall act to stay the execution of a judgment unless the court enters an order staying execution.

Corrine Adamson
_____
Deputy Court Administrator

Certificate of Service

This is to certify that a copy of the foregoing was hand delivered/faxed/emailed/mailed and/or sent through the eFiling system to the following on OCT 26 2012,

M R Jones
_____

Copies to:

ABIGAIL NORRIS
Attorney for the Juvenile Officer

MARTIN JAYLON
Attorney for the Natural Mother

MARLIE VERLET
CHILDREN'S DIVISION

HENRIETTA MILLER
JACKSON COUNTY CASA

MARLIN THOMPSON
Putative Father

JEROME WASHINGTON
Natural Father – Alysha Washington, Hope Washington

JOELLE MERRITT
Natural Mother

Contact Log

Name	Fine, Miriam
Case Number	594
Activity Date	11/3/2012
Activity Type	Placement Visit
Subject	Child welfare
Location	Grandparents' Home
Contact Type	Face-to-face
Hours	1.25

Notes:

Things were pretty chaotic at the Merritts' home this Saturday morning. Last night was the first time Joelle picked the kids up for an unsupervised visit. She took them to Minsky's for pizza after work (Mabel said she gave her money), and apparently it took everyone a while to settle down when they returned around 8 p.m. I asked Mabel what she thought about the evening, and she admitted to being very conflicted. She said it was great to see the kids and their mom together and heading out the door, but she worried the entire time they were gone. She also said it was one thing to have a "pizza night out" paid for by Grandma, and another for Joelle to manage the children on her own full time.

Mabel reported that she took Tyrone out of school on Oct 25 to see the new psychiatrist. She said he was very concerned that Tyrone's Abilify prescription had expired and explained to them both that this was a very helpful drug, but also very powerful, and had to be managed very carefully. He started a new prescription at the previous dosage and said they would discuss a taper plan to get Tyrone off the meds at their next appointment in 90 days. Mabel noted that it was possible the children would be back living with Joelle by then -- she wondered if her daughter would be able to manage getting Tyrone to his appointment.

I worked with Mabel to fill out the Holiday Wish List to turn in to CASA. She said she was very grateful to have gifts for the children again this year.

I spoke with each of the children individually and focused on asking about the unsupervised time with Joelle. Tyrone said it was "pretty weird" to be out with his mom like that. He said he never remembered going to a restaurant with her before, so the whole thing seemed pretty contrived. He also thought he would rather be out with his friends on a Friday night than hanging out with his mother and sisters. But he acknowledged the evening went well, Joelle seemed better, and it was actually fun to have a family night out. He said he just "wanted it all settled once and for all, so we know where we belong."

Alysha also said the evening went well, but she was anxious about the uncertainty in their lives. "Other kids know where they are going to live," she said. She again noted her concern about getting to stay in Girl Scouts ("I'm working on my Junior First Aid badge") and about not changing schools or teachers. I reassured her that Joelle lived in her school district and nothing would change there. "What if Mom decides to move or gets kicked out of the apartment?" she asked. I didn't have an answer for that.

Hope is happy-go-lucky as always. She told me about going out "with my whole family" and said it was "a lot of fun." She didn't express any concerns, and I didn't press her.

I told the kids I would see them before Christmas.

Activity Status   Approved

Holiday Wish List

CASA Case Volunteer: Miriam Fine
CASA Case Supervisor: Anita Blackstone
CASA Staff Attorney: Henrietta Miller
Date Submitted: 11/15/12

1. Hope, female, age 7 (will be 8 by Christmas) – 3rd grade
   a. Shoe size: children's size 13
   b. Clothing size: size 8 (medium)
   c. Clothing notes: receives hand-me-downs from her sister (coat/pants/shirts), but would love something new and pretty all her own. Needs underwear and socks (likes Dora the Explorer or anything with animals on it). Desperately needs warms shoes/boots for winter in correct size.
   d. Favorite color: aqua
   e. Toy wish list:
      i. Barbie doll – African American – and clothes/accessories
      ii. Age-appropriate craft sets
      iii. Princess costume / dresses / accessories
      iv. Bike

2. Alysha, female, age 9 – 5th grade
   a. Shoe size: youth junior size 5
   b. Clothing size: size 10/12 (large)
   c. Clothing notes: immediate need for boots and warm coat for winter. Also needs new underwear and socks. **Would love Girl Scout socks and/or Girl Scout hoodie.
   d. Favorite color: purple/pink
   e. Toy wish list:
      i. Books – reads at 6th/7th grade level – she would like the Golden Compass books and a green Girl Scout journal (with logo)
      ii. New LEGO Friends set for girls
      iii. Shampoo (for African-American hair) / soap / hairbrush
      iv. Bike

3. Tyrone, male, age 14 – high school freshman (9th grade)
   a. Shoe size: men's size 12
   b. Clothing size: x-large / size 18-20
   c. Clothing notes: needs tennis shoes in larger size for school – gift card to Payless would be best. Needs warm coat for winter.
   d. Favorite color: dark blue
   e. Toy wish list:
      i. Axe deodorant / body spray / other hygiene products
      ii. LEGO set – likes large, complicated sets
      iii. Basketball
      iv. Duffel bag for gym clothes for school

MedLabs
3274 Broadway
Kansas City, MO 64111

Sample Provided by: Joelle Merritt / DOB 06/09/82

Date of Sample: November 12, 2012

Test Results Reported: November 15, 2012

Referred by: Children's Division – Jackson County

Responsible Payor: Children's Division – Jackson County

Results Sent to: Children's Division – Jackson County

Test Ordered

10 Panel + Alcohol Urine Drug Test

AMP-Amphetamines (MAMP-Methamphetamine, MDMA-Ecstasy), COC-Cocaine, OPI-Opiates (including heroin, codeine and morphine), PCP-Phencyclidine, THC-Marijuana, BZO-Benzodiazepines, BAR-Barbiturates, MTD-Methadone, PPX-Propoxyphene, Meth – Methaqualone, ETH – Alcohol.

Results

Negative for ETH – Alcohol – within last 80 hours
Negative for all other substances

MedLabs is affiliated with the Drug and Alcohol Testing Industry Association (DATIA) and the Substance Abuse Program Administrators Association (SAPAA). We have been in the drug and alcohol testing business for 20 years. Our procedures include a comprehensive program that provides the highest quality services, focusing on accuracy, integrity, and professionalism.

Our mission is to provide affordable lab screening to help reduce drug and alcohol abuse, while empowering individuals and companies to manage their health and wellness.

MedLabs
3274 Broadway
Kansas City, MO 64111

Sample Provided by:	Joelle Merritt / DOB 06/09/82
Date of Sample:	December 17, 2012
Test Results Reported:	December 20, 2012
Referred by:	Children's Division – Jackson County
Responsible Payor:	Children's Division – Jackson County
Results Sent to:	Children's Division – Jackson County

Test Ordered

10 Panel + Alcohol Urine Drug Test

AMP-Amphetamines (MAMP-Methamphetamine, MDMA-Ecstasy), COC-Cocaine, OPI-Opiates (including heroin, codeine and morphine), PCP-Phencyclidine, THC-Marijuana, BZO-Benzodiazepines, BAR-Barbiturates, MTD-Methadone, PPX-Propoxyphene, Meth – Methaqualone, ETH – Alcohol.

Results

Negative for ETH – Alcohol – within last 80 hours
Negative for all other substances

MedLabs is affiliated with the Drug and Alcohol Testing Industry Association (DATIA) and the Substance Abuse Program Administrators Association (SAPAA). We have been in the drug and alcohol testing business for 20 years. Our procedures include a comprehensive program that provides the highest quality services, focusing on accuracy, integrity, and professionalism.

Our mission is to provide affordable lab screening to help reduce drug and alcohol abuse, while empowering individuals and companies to manage their health and wellness.

**Staff
Dashboard**

**Volunteers
Dashboard**

Volunteers

**Lookup
Tables**

Cases

**User
Administration**

Reports

Contact Log

Name	Fine, Miriam
Case Number	594
Activity Date	12/22/2012
Activity Type	Placement Visit
Subject	Child welfare
Location	Grandparents' Home
Contact Type	Face-to-face
Hours	1.25

Notes:

I stopped by the Merritts' home mid-mornign to deliver the CASA Christmas presents for the kids. There was a tree this year, so the wrapped presents went there. I didn't see much point in trying to hide the bikes for the girls -- the house is pretty tight with five people, so I guess those just became early gifts. I went ahead and gave Tyrone the box with his basketball, so he wouldn't be left out.

The weather was mild, so Roger took the girls outside to try out their bikes -- I don't think they ever had bikes before! I talked to Mabel while Tyrone called up a friend to shoot hoops.

Mabel said the children had been staying overnight at Joelle's on Friday nights, and they had stayed two nights over the long Thanksgiving weekend. She said it seemed okay to her -- the more the kids were there, the more "normal" it seemed. She said she was very grateful they lived so near each other -- she wondered aloud what it must be like for families with a greater distance to travel. Mabel said she cooked Thanksgiving dinner with the girls, and Joelle came over to eat with the family. Mabel said it was their first holiday together in a very long time.

I asked how she felt about the growing possibility of reunificaiton for the kids. She said she could tell how hard Joelle was trying, she just didn't think she was strong enough for the daily trials of raising three kids on her own.

I also asked about Tyrone's behaviors, and she said he had mellowed out again once he was back on his meds. I asked how long the psychiatrist thought that should continue, and said she wasn't sure, but he seemed to be recommending a taper regimen begin after his next appointment in mid-January.

I went outside to watch the girls ride their bikes. They don't have it down yet, but Roger was helping them very patiently. I waved and asked if anyone wanted to talk, but they didn't want to leave their bikes, and I didn't want to interrupt. They seemed so happy. I told Mabel I'd call Tyrone to check in after Christmas -- he was off with his friends, and I didn't want to embarrass him by chasing him down.

Activity Status   Approved

Staff   Volunteers   Volunteers   Lookup   Cases   User   Reports
Dashboard   Dashboard   Tables   Administration

CONTACT LOG DETAILS

Back

Contact Log

Name	Fine, Miriam
Case Number	594
Activity Date	12/28/2012
Activity Type	Placement Visit
Subject	Child welfare
Location	Grandparents' Home
Contact Type	Phone Call
Hours	0.25

Notes:

I called Tyrone to check in, but he was out with friends. He called me back later in the day, which is a first. I'm glad he has my cell number and is willing to call. I told him he could always use that number if he needed something or was in trouble in any way. As we move toward reunification, I really want the kids to have a lifeline if they need it.

Tyrone's pretty awkward on the phone, but he told me he liked his Christmas gifts and thanked me for bringing them. He said it was great to be on vacation, and he was sorry they had to go back to school so soon. I asked about the times they were spending with his mom, and he said he thought it might work out, he wasn't sure, he hoped so. He said he was mostly glad his sisters seemed happy, and he was really glad he wasn't going to have to change schools no matter what. He seems well settled in at Central Academy, with friends and classes he likes.

He wished me a Happy New Year when we signed off, which was very sweet.

Activity Status   Approved

From: Marlie.Verlet@dss.mo.gov
Sent: Tuesday, January 11, 2013 9:52 AM
To: Anorris@courts.mo.gov
Cc: ablackstone@jacksoncountycasa-mo.org; hmiller@jacksoncountycasa-mo.org; Duncan.
Walsh@dss.mo.gov; miriamkfine@gmail.com; martin.jaylon@hollandgrain.com
Subject: *Confidential: Merritt—Washington—Recommendation for Reunification

Children's Division wishes to notify the Attorney for the Juvenile Office and the Family Court that we are recommending Tyrone Washington, Alysha Merritt, and Hope Merritt be reunified with their mother, Joelle Merritt, as soon as possible.

The Family Support Team (FST) has been serving as the Permanency Planning Review Team (PPRT) for these children while they have been in out-of-home care with their grandparents since their initial removal on May 15, 2011.

The CASA Volunteer and the children's Guardian ad Litem do not agree that the children should be moved at this time, however their recommendation is based on minimizing disruption to the children's lives, rather than specific safety concerns.

Lacking safety concerns, and based on the mother's compliance with all treatment goals as well as our determination that she can meet the minimal physical and emotional needs of the children with supportive services, Children's Division is therefore putting forward this recommendation of reunification to be considered at the Case Review Hearing for these children on January 15, 2013.

The mission of the Children's Division is to partner with families, communities and government to protect children from abuse and neglect and to assure safety, permanency and well being for Missouri's children.

IN THE CIRCUIT COURT OF JACKSON COUNTY, MISSOURI
FAMILY COURT DIVISION

IN THE INTEREST OF:	CASE NUMBER: 1416-JU0040987
TYRONE MERRITT	
	LIFE NUMBER:
SEX: M BORN: 19-FEB-1998	1416-JR57790

IN THE INTEREST OF:	CASE NUMBER: 1416-JU0040988
ALYSHA WASHINGTON	
	LIFE NUMBER:
SEX: F BORN: 07-APRIL-2003	1416-JR57791

IN THE INTEREST OF:	CASE NUMBER: 1416-JU0040989
HOPE WASHINGTON	
	LIFE NUMBER:
SEX: F BORN: 17-NOV-2004	1416-JR57792

FINDINGS AND RECOMMENDATIONS

Now on January 15, 2013 there being present:

MARLIE VERLET	-	Children's Division
DUNCAN WALSH	-	Children's Division
JOELLE MERRITT	-	Mother
ABIGAIL NORRIS	-	Attorney for the Juvenile Officer
HENRIETTA MILLER	-	Guardian ad Litem (CASA)
MIRIAM FINE	-	CASA Volunteer
MARTIN JAYLON	-	Attorney for Mother
TYRONE MERRITT	-	Juvenile
ALYSHA WASHINGTON	-	Juvenile
HOPE WASHINGTON	-	Juvenile

The cause comes on for Permanency Hearing.

IT IS HEREBY ORDERED: that the juveniles Tyrone Merritt, Alysha Washington, and Hope Washington are committed to the physical custody of their parent Joelle Merritt with legal custody remaining with Children's Division until further Court review to be held in not less than 6 months.

The Court has reviewed all documentary evidence presented, including the social file of the juveniles containing reports and recommendations from the Children's Division since the inception of the case, the Guardian ad Litem's reports and recommendations, the CASA Volunteer's reports and recommendations, Placement Reports filled out by the juveniles, and all records pertaining to the mother's treatment at ReCovery and subsequent drug/alcohol testing results.

Based on the mother's compliance with all Court orders and her record of negative UAs over the past six months, the Court hereby grants reunification for this family.

The Court once again takes notice of the concerns of the Guardian ad Litem and the CASA Volunteer for this placement change. However, the Court believes all treatment goals for this case and the minimum standards for the children's safety have been met.

The court reaches this determination based on all of the reports and information received. The Children's Division is ordered to place the children with their parent within 7 days.

The next court hearing for the above action is scheduled for JULY 10, 2013 at 01:00 PM in DIVISION 40 for Case Review and possible Case Release.

Notice of Findings and Recommendation & Notice of Right to a Rehearing

The parties are notified that the forgoing Findings and Recommendations have been entered this date by a commissioner, and all papers relative to the care or proceeding, together with the Findings and Recommendation have been transferred to a Judge of the Court. The Findings and Recommendations shall become the Judgment of the Court upon adoption by order of the Judge. Unless waived by the parties in writing, at party in the case or proceeding heard by a commissioner, within fifteen days after the mailing of notice of the filing of the Judgment of the Court, may file a motion for rehearing by a Judge of the Court. If the motion for rehearing is not ruled on within forty-five days after the motion is filed, the motion is overruled for all purposes. Rule 130.13

January 17, 2013

Gerard E. Solomon

Date

GERARD E. SOLOMON, Commissioner

Order and Judgment Adopting Commissioner's Findings and Recommendation

It is hereby ordered, adjudged and decreed the foregoing Findings and Recommendations entered by the commissioner are adopted and confirmed as a final Judgment of the Court.

January 17, 2013   _Suzanne M. Martell_
_____   _____
Date   Judge

NOTICE OF ENTRY OF JUDGMENT

You are hereby notified that on   JAN 18 2013, the Family Court, Juvenile Division, of Jackson County, Missouri made and entered the above judgment in this case:

You are further notified that you may have a right of appeal from this judgment under Rule 120.01 and section 211.261, RSMo, which provides that:

1. An appeal shall be allowed to the juvenile from any final judgment made under the Juvenile Code and may be taken on the part of the juvenile by the custodian.

2. An appeal shall be allowed to custodian from any final judgment made under the Juvenile Code that adversely affects the custodian.

3. Notice of appeal shall be filed in accordance with Missouri law.

4. Neither the filing of a notice of appeal nor the filing of any motion subsequne to the judgment shall act to stay the execution of a judgment unless the court enters an order staying execution.

Corrine Adamson
_____
Deputy Court Administrator

Certificate of Service

This is to certify that a copy of the foregoing was hand delivered/faxed/emailed/mailed and/or sent through the eFiling system to the following on JAN 18 2013,

M R Jones
_____

Copies to:

ABIGAIL NORRIS
Attorney for the Juvenile Officer

MARTIN JAYLON
Attorney for the Natural Mother

MARLIE VERLET
CHILDREN'S DIVISION

HENRIETTA MILLER
JACKSON COUNTY CASA

MARLIN THOMPSON
Putative Father

JEROME WASHINGTON
Natural Father – Alysha Washington, Hope Washington

JOELLE MERRITT
Natural Mother

From: Miriam Fine [mailto:miriamkfine@gmail.com]
Sent: Tuesday, January 15, 2013 11:02 APM
To: hgoldstein@laramyjones.com
Subject: Property law prevails

Remember when you told me that Family Law is a bizarre hybrid of property law and child welfare intervention? Well, property law trumped today.

Even though my CASA kids are happily settled with their grandparents . . . and even though this mom did absolutely nothing to get her act together for a full 12 months after they were taken out of her home . . . and even though she only spent 30 days in in-patient mental health and substance abuse treatment (the original psych eval recommended 60-90) . . . and even though she's only been clean and sober for six months . . . the Commissioner has ordered my kids to move back in with their mom within 7 days.

Over my recommendation. Over the recommendation of the Guardian ad Litem. Over the stated (in writing) preference of the kids.

How can this possibly be justice, Hazel? How can this possibly be in the best interests of the children? Everything else in this damned system works like molasses. With this, they have to rush . . . ?

As mom would say: Nu, would it have hurt to wait, Big Macher? You have to be in such a hurry?

Despondently yours,

Miri

_____

Miriam Fine
(913) 555-8436

"If I can't dance, I don't want to be part of your revolution." -- Emma Goldman

Staff
Dashboard

Volunteers
Dashboard

Volunteers

Lookup
Tables

Cases

User
Administration

Reports

Contact Log

Name	Fine, Miriam
Case Number	594
Activity Date	2/3/2013
Activity Type	Placement Visit
Subject	Child welfare
Location	Mother's apartment
Contact Type	Face-to-face
Hours	1.00

Notes:

The children have settled back into Joelle's apartment and all seems relatively calm. Alysha and Hope showed me their room, which is small, but adequate. Tyrone used to sleep there, as well, in a sleeping bag, but he is now sleeping on the living room couch.

I asked him how that was working out, and he said it isn't very comfortable, but he's doing okay. He said he misses having his own room like he did at his grandparents' house. I asked him if there was anything else he wanted me to know, and he said he's "out of pills again."

I asked Joelle, and she said she had gotten confused with all the commotion around the move and had missed taking Tyrone out of school for his psychiatrist appointment. She said she hadn't known what to do about that, and I told her I would let the CD worker know so they could reschedule the appointment. I told her it was very important that she keep all the medical and therapeutic appointments the children needed, and she could ask CD for help if she got confused again.

I spoke briefly with each of the girls. Hope seems just fine. Alysha told me it is good to be back home, but her mom has not been able to get her to Girl Scouts, due to her work schedule and everything going on with settling back in. She was stoic about it, but her underlying sadness is very clear. She waited a long time for that opportunity, and I hope there is a way Joelle can continue to let her participate with her friends and classmates. They otherwise seem safe and well cared for.

Activity Status   Approved

From: Marlie.Verlet@dss.mo.gov
Sent: Tuesday, February 5, 2013 4:39 PM
To: miriamkfine@gmail.com
Cc: ablackstone@jacksoncountycasa-mo.org; hmiller@jacksoncountycasa-mo.org; Duncan.
Walsh@dss.mo.gov
Subject: *Confidential: Merritt—Washington—Tyrone's Appt/Meds

Miriam,

Thank you for notifying us that Joelle Merritt missed taking Tyrone to his psychiatrist appointment last week to get his meds renewed. CD had not been informed by either Ms. Merritt or the physician about the missed appointment.

I will begin the process of rescheduling that visit for Tyrone. It might take a few weeks, but we will move as quickly as we possibly can.

The mission of the Children's Division is to partner with families, communities and government to protect children from abuse and neglect and to assure safety, permanency and well being for Missouri's children.

February 15, 2013

Family Support Team Meeting

Case:	Merritt-Washington
Facilitator:	Marlie Verlet, Children's Division worker
Location:	Library Conference Room, Jackson County CASA

In attendance:

Tyrone Merritt – Juvenile
Joelle Merritt – Mother
Martin Jaylon, Mother's Attorney
Mabel Merritt – Maternal Grandmother
Marlie Verlet – CD Worker
Duncan Walsh – CD Supervisor
Miriam Fine – CASA Volunteer
Anita Blackstone – CASA Case Supervisor (taking notes for the group)
Henrietta Miller – Guardian ad Litem (CASA)

Marlie Verlet passed around the attendance log / confidentiality agreement for everyone to sign.

Joelle said that the girls had a school-wide assembly today, so she only brought Tyrone. Marlie asked if he would like to stay for the entire meeting, and he said yes. The Guardian ad Litem agreed, based on his age, and asked if he would like to begin.

Tyrone Merritt – Reported getting adjusted to living back home with mom. Said he misses having his own room and bed at Grandma's, but he's "doing okay with it." Reported he is out of his pills and that worries him, because the last time he ran out he got really sick.

Henrietta Miller, CASA Staff Attorney, Guardian ad Litem – Asked the adults to explain the issue with Tyrone's medication so she could better understand the situation.

Joelle Merritt, mother – Said it had been very hectic when the children returned home. She didn't have a lot of notice and it had been hard to get everything ready in time. She forgot about Tyrone's appointment, which was just four days after the kids moved back in. She said she had called Marlie to ask for help rescheduling the appointment but that hadn't happened yet.

Marlie Verlet, CD worker – Said she had left three messages on the psychiatrist's answering machine, but had not heard back. Said this was a top priority, and she was working it.

Miriam Fine, CASA Volunteer – Expressed anger and frustration that this was taking so long. Reminded the group that taking care of the children's medical and safety needs was a requirement of the reunification plan.

Duncan Walsh, CD Supervisor – "We're working on it. There's no need to be aggressive here. Let's move on to other matters."

Joelle Merritt, mother – Said she was very busy taking care of the children, adding hours at work, and getting to her own therapy appointments and AA meetings. She said Mabel came over often to help, and Roger came over on the weekends. She "was managing."

Mabel Merritt, maternal grandmother – Said she was trying to get over to Joelle's as much as she could to help with the kids. Noted it was easier for her to take care of them in her own home, but she was trying to help make this work for the children and for her own daughter. Alysha told her that Joelle couldn't get her to Girl Scouts because of work, and she had missed a meeting and an important event, so Mabel was going to try to do the driving for this. She said Girl Scouts had been very important to Alysha, and she didn't want to see her have to drop out.

Marlie Verlet, CD worker – Repeated that she was working to reschedule the psychiatrist appointment for Tyrone. Noted there are no immediate needs for the girls, who seem to be doing well.

Miriam Fine, CASA Volunteer – Said she hoped the group would get their act together and figure out the appointment issue. Asked if anything could be done to get Tyrone a proper bed to sleep on, but there was no response.

Anita Blackstone, CASA Case Supervisor – nothing to add.

Group agreed on 6/18/13 for next FST. Anita will schedule with CASA to use the Library Conference Room and will notify parties about time.

AJB / uploaded to OPTIMA 2-16-13

 **Optima**™

Welcome **miriam.fine**

Change Password   Log Off

Staff   Volunteers   Volunteers   Lookup   Cases   User   Reports
Dashboard   Dashboard   Tables   Administration

Contact Log

Name	Fine, Miriam
Case Number	594
Activity Date	3/3/2013
Activity Type	Placement Visit
Subject	Child welfare
Location	Mother's apartment
Contact Type	Face-to-face
Hours	1.00

Notes:

I am very concerned about Joelle's ability to provide appropriate care and supervision for the children. I suspect she may be drinking again. There was a beer can in the trash in the kitchen, and Hope told me "Tyrone and Alysha help me with my homework when Mommy doesn't come home."

Joelle told me she is working a lot of hours at Taco Joe's, but she was very defensive.

She told me there is an appointment for Tyrone set up later in the month, but she didn't have the exact date. She said he is "getting hard to manage," and I observed that he appears very anxious and twitchy. I asked how he was doing, and he said he wasn't sleeping much and school was "getting hard and stupid again."

Overall, I am very concerned about the children's safety in this placement.

Activity Status   Approved

POLICE REPORT

Case No:	730862-198	Date:	3/15/13
Reporting Officer:	Helena Juarez	Prepared By:	same
Incident/Issue:	Single-vehicle car accident/driver intoxicated		

Description of Accident/Issue:

Police were called by bystanders at 9:37 p.m. after vehicle ran through red light at 31st and Main and hit streetlight. Driver, dazed but uninjured, was the sole occupant of car. It was determined that driver was under the influence. There was considerable damage to the car and city property (street light), but no pedestrians or bystanders were injured, and no other cars were involved.

Actions Taken:

Witnesses called 911 at 9:37 p.m. to report a vehicle had run a red light at 31st and Main, barely missing several cars in cross traffic, then crashing into a street light on the north side of 31st Street. Officer Helena Juarez and Officer James Fortino were dispatched and arrived on the scene at 9:42 p.m. Driver was outside car sitting on the curb. She was disoriented but did not appear to be injured. Officer Juarez asked for her Driver's License. She said her purse was in the car, and gave her name as Joelle Merritt. This was confirmed by her Driver's License, which was later recovered from the purse in the front seat of the car.

Ms. Merritt appeared intoxicated, slurring her words and appearing disoriented. Officer Juarez asked if she had been drinking. Ms. Merritt nodded and began to sob. Officer Juarez asked her to perform a Portable Breath Test, which registered a BAC over .16.

Officer Fortino observed two beer cans on the floor of the front passenger side of the car, though he was unable to tell if they were full or empty. The brand was not immediately apparent.

Ms. Merritt was arrested on site. She was read her Miranda rights and taken by Officers Juarez and Fortino in their squad car to the KCPD station for booking.

From: Merlie.Verlet@dss.mo.gov
Sent: Friday, March 15, 2013 6:07 PM
To: ablackstone@jacksoncountycasa-mo.org; hmiller@jacksoncountycasa-mo.org;
cc: miriamkfine@gmail.com; Duncan.Walsh@dss.mo.gov
Subject: *Confidential: Merritt—Washington—Children removed from home

I am writing to inform the CASA team that I picked up all three children at their mother's home this afternoon after school. Their mother, Joelle Merritt, went out the night before and did not return home. The children did not inform anyone at their respective schools, but mid-morning we received a call that Joelle was in the KCPD Holding Facility at the Jackson County Detention Center on a DUI charge.

We were able to reach Mabel and Roger Merritt, the children's grandparents and their previous placement by cell phone, but they are currently in Bentonville, dealing with a family crisis related to Roger's mother, who lives in a nursing home there. They will be back in Kansas City next Wednesday, March 20, and can take the children back into their home at that time.

In the meantime, Alysha and Hope Washington were taken to the Salvation Army Children's Shelter at 3637 Broadway. The shelter is very full right now, and has no beds for a teen boy, so Tyrone went to a temporary foster placement with Rachel and Marcus Treeman at 10973 E. 28th St. in Independence.

While very upset, all three of the children appear to be in good physical condition, with no obvious injuries or medical issues.

I will collect the children again on March 20 and take them to the Merritts' home in Kansas City.

The mission of the Children's Division is to partner with families, communities and government to protect children from abuse and neglect and to assure safety, permanency and well being for Missouri's children.

Contact Log

Name	Fine, Miriam
Case Number	594
Activity Date	3/17/2013
Activity Type	Placement Visit
Subject	Child welfare
Location	Salvation Army Children's Center
Contact Type	Face-to-face
Hours	0.75

Notes:

I went to the Salvation Army Children's Center this afternoon to see Alysha and Hope. They are sharing a room there, and staff assured me their basic needs are being met. Children's Division brought a change of clothes for each of the girls, but not sleepwear, toothbrush, etc. Staff said that is common, and they keep a clothes closet and hygiene supplies for kids who might need them.

It was crowded at the Center with all of the children out of school, but I was allowed to speak to the girls in "their" room. They were inseparable today, with Hope refusing to leave Alysha's side. We talked about what had happened. Alysha said it wasn't the first time Joelle had gone out at night, but she always came back home, and "I didn't ever want to tell on her again."

She told me there was a bus that took all the Shelter kids to their various schools, so she and Hope would be able to go to school on Monday. She said she had some homework that was due, but it was back at Joelle's. I told her to explain privately to her teacher what had happened. I think she really doesn't want to do that, but she likes this teacher, so I think she can advocate for herself on this one. She asked if I had seen Tyrone yet, and I told her I was going out to his temporary foster home later today.

She asked if it was true they would all be going home to their grandparents' house later in the week, and I reassured her that I had spoken to her grandmother and it was all arranged.

She asked about their mother, and I said they were keeping her safe in the city jail right now, but I didn't know about later. She had been working hard to hold it together while we talked, but she started crying then. That set Hope to crying, too, so we all just sat on one of the twin beds for a while.

They calmed down after 20 minutes or so, and I left. They are physically safe but I am worried they are very sad and scared. It is also very important that all three children be reunited as soon as possible.

Activity Status   Approved

Contact Log

Name	Fine, Miriam
Case Number	594
Activity Date	3/17/2013
Activity Type	Placement Visit
Subject	Child welfare
Location	Foster Home
Contact Type	Face-to-face
Hours	0.75

Notes:

I talked to Tyrone on the living room couch. He is miserable, even worse than when he was at Gillis. He told me the children had agreed not to "report" Joelle when she didn't come home, so it was a shock to find CD waiting for them when they got home from school on Friday. I asked how long she had been drinking again, and he shrugged. "We were taking care of ourselves okay," he said.

I told him I had just come from visiting Alysha and Hope at the Children's Shelter. He was very anxious about them, and seemed to calm somewhat when I said they were okay and would be able to go to school tomorrow. He said the foster mom, Rachel, had already explained to him that they wouldn't be able to drive him to Central Acadamy on Monday, because Marcus had to go to work and she had to take care of the younger foster kids. Since he would only be living there a few days, she told him he could just stay home and study by himself. Since he doesn't have his books or class materials here, that didn't make any sense, but I just asked how he felt about that, and he shrugged again: "Nothing matters now, does it? It's all falling apart."

I told him to hang in there -- by the end of the week he would be back with his sisters at Mabel and Roger's and back with his classes and friends at his high school. He seemed unconvinced. "They just keep moving us around -- who knows what they'll try next. I'm stuck here with a bunch of babies, mom's in jail, and I can't sleep or think or anything."

I am very concerned that Tyrone is expressing new feelings of despair. I am also very concerned that these placement changes have completely disrupted efforts to get his medication regimen stabilized. He is clearly showing symptoms of withdrawal again. We must move him back with Mabel and Roger as quickly as possible and get him to a psychiatrist to review/renew his medication plan without delay.

| Activity Status | Approved |

From: Merlie.Verlet@dss.mo.gov
Sent: Monday, March 18, 2013 5:18 PM
To: ablackstone@jacksoncountycasa-mo.org; hmiller@jacksoncountycasa-mo.org;
cc: miriamkfine@gmail.com; Duncan.Walsh@dss.mo.gov
Subject: *Confidential: Merritt—Washington—Tyrone on run

I am writing to inform the CASA team that Tyrone Merritt has gone on run.

Rachel Treeman, temporary foster placement, called to report that she went to the grocery store mid-morning with the two younger foster children. When she returned, Tyrone was gone. He left no note. When he had not returned by the time the other children arrived home on the school bus, she called CD.

I have spoken with Mabel and Roger Merritt, the principal at Central Academy, and the staff at the Salvation Army Children's Shelter. No one has heard from Tyrone.

We have informed the Attorney for the Juvenile Office and the Family Court. We have also asked KCPD to put out a capias, and hopefully he will be picked up soon.

If Tyrone contacts CASA, we would appreciate knowing his whereabouts.

The mission of the Children's Division is to partner with families, communities and government to protect children from abuse and neglect and to assure safety, permanency and well being for Missouri's children.

From: Anita Blackstone [mailto:ablackstone@jacksoncountycasa-mo.org]
Sent: Monday, March 18, 2013 8:10 PM
To: miriamkfine@gmail.com
Cc: hmiller@jacksoncountycasa-mo.org
Subject: RE: *Confidential: Merritt—Washington—Tyrone on run

Miri,

Thanks for returning my phone call about Tyrone. I'm sorry I missed you.

Yes, you're right, this is not good. Tyrone might be staying with a friend, but the fact that he hasn't contacted anyone, even Mabel or Roger, is not a good sign. I know you said he was upset when you visited him yesterday, but I didn't get the sense he would do anything this drastic. He knew the foster placement was only temporary and he would be going home to his grandparents in a couple of days. I am—mostly—surprised that he would run out on his sisters during this difficult time. He must be more upset that we realized.

I particularly appreciate your concern that Tyrone is now probably suffering significant withdrawal symptoms from the Abilify. There's nothing to be done about that until we find him and bring him in.

Most kids who go on the run end up "couch surfing" with friends. Some get into trouble—hanging out with a bad crowd, running drugs, joining a gang. The really sad cases end up being trafficked, even the boys.

Let's hope that Tyrone lands somewhere with a competent adult who chooses to call CASA or CD before they call the police. The Commissioner does not like to put kids in detention just for running. If we can find Tyrone and get him situated again—either with the Treemans or with his grandparents—I think we can get this back under control very quickly.

Sometimes kids on the run make their first outreach to their CASA Volunteer. Let me know if Tyrone calls, and we'll see what we can do to bring him in safely.

Anita

Anita Blackstone
Case Supervisor
(816) 555-8236

Welcome **miriam.fine**

Change Password   Log Off

Staff Dashboard   **Volunteers Dashboard**   **Volunteers**   **Lookup Tables**   **Cases**   **User Administration**   **Reports**

Contact Log

Name	Fine, Miriam
Case Number	594
Activity Date	3/23/2013
Activity Type	Placement Visit
Subject	Child welfare
Location	Grandparents' Home
Contact Type	Face-to-face
Hours	0.75

Notes:

Visited girls back at their grandparents' this afternoon. Mabel had taken them back to Joelle's apartment in the morning, and the landlord had let them in so they could collect their clothes, school materials, and other items. They were unpacking and settling back into their bedroom when I arrived.

Mabel told me it was all pretty bad. She and Roger had been in Arkansas because his mother had a heart attack. She was just going into surgery, when CD called to tell them Joelle had been arrested. Mabel said they came back as quickly as they could; she clearly felt terrible that the girls spent time in a shelter, and she is racked by guilt over Tyrone. I asked if she had any idea where he might have gone, but she said she didn't know a lot about his friends or who might have taken him in.

She told me that Joelle was going to be released on probation later in the week and would be going back to live in her apartment. She said it was going to be a while before she felt like she could see Joelle -- or let the girls see her again.

The girls both seem tired and dazed and very upset that Tyrone has run away. Alysha told me it is very hard to concentrate on her schoolwork with so much going on in their family -- getting picked up again by CD, five nights in the shelter, now moving back in with her grandparents.

"I don't think it will ever feel normal," she told me. "I just want Tyrone to come back so we can be a family again." I asked if she had everything she needed, and she said Mabel helped her pack up everything when they went to the apartment that morning. "I didn't have that much, you know."

Hope asked me repeatedly about Tyrone. She said she knew he wouldn't abandon her "like Mommy." She sticks pretty close to Alysha most of the time. I asked her about school, but she wouldn't engage.

Roger asked me if I knew what would happen next with Joelle. I told him I hadn't heard, but I'd ask. He's pretty mad at the recent turn of events: "That judge should have known she wasn't ready to take care of three kids. Alcoholics don't just get better like that. Now she's worse off, and the girls are worse off, and no one even knows where Tyrone is."

Activity Status   Approved

From: Miriam Fine [mailto:miriamkfine@gmail.com]
Sent: Sunday, March 24, 2013 11:03 PM
To: ablackstone@jacksoncountycasa-mo.org
Subject: *Confidential: Merritt—Washington—Tyrone has made contact

Anita,

I tried to call your cell, but it went straight to voice mail. I hope you get this email first thing in the morning and call me back asap.

Tyrone called about an hour ago. He said he's "with a friend" and has food and somewhere to sleep. I told him I was really worried about him, and asked if we could meet somewhere. I said I wouldn't call the cops or turn him in—I just wanted to know he was okay. I said his grandparents and sisters were pretty worried, too.

He apologized for upsetting everyone—said he just couldn't stand the idea of being a foster child and would rather be on his own since nothing else worked out. He said he'd call me again and maybe we could meet. "Please tell Alysha and Hope that I'm just fine. I'm old enough to make it on my own."

Anita—tell me what to do. I'm really scared for him.

Miriam Fine
(913) 555-8436

"If I can't dance, I don't want to be part of your revolution." -- Emma Goldman

Staff
Dashboard

Volunteers
Dashboard

Volunteers

Lookup
Tables

Cases

User
Administration

Reports

Contact Log

Name	Fine, Miriam
Case Number	594
Activity Date	4/15/2013
Activity Type	Placement Visit
Subject	Child welfare
Location	Whittier Elementary
Contact Type	Face-to-face
Hours	1.00

Notes:

I went with Mabel to see the girls in the school Spring Assembly. They both had speaking parts and did a fine job. I was able to congratulate them both afterwards and give them flowers -- they seemed very surprised and pleased by that. Alysha said "we've never had flowers before!"

Mabel told me that things are settling down again. Both girls are doing well in their classes and she hears good reports from their teachers. Alysha is back in her beloved Girl Scouts. She said neither one asks about Joelle anymore.

She knew that Joelle was home on probation from her DUI sentence. I asked if she thought we should ask the Court to resume supervised visits, and she said she wasn't ready for that quite yet. "I'd just like to move forward with the adoption plans. These kids need some long-term stability. Frankly, Roger and I do, too." I told her we'd take it up again at the next FST, but that I would be happy to advocate for proceeding towards TPR/Adoption as soon as possible.

She asked if I had heard from Tyrone since that first call. I said no, and promised to call her immediately if I did. She's very worried about him and still feels guilty they were in Arkansas when the kids were picked up from Joelle's. "Any other time, and we'd have been here."

Activity Status   Approved

From: Miriam Fine [mailto:miriamkfine@gmail.com]
Sent: Wednesday, April 17, 2013 12:13 AM
To: ablackstone@jacksoncountycasa-mo.org
Subject: *Confidential: Merritt—Washington—Tyrone has made contact (2)

Anita,

Tyrone called again tonight. There was a lot of background noise, and he said he was "hanging out with friends"—maybe outside, I couldn't tell for sure?

He said "there are a lot more kids out here like me than you realize," but when I asked him to tell me more, he pretty much clammed up. I asked if anyone was hurting him or making him do things he didn't want to do, and he scoffed: "I'm smarter than that, Ms. Fine. I know the score on the streets."

I asked if he'd be willing to meet me for a cup of coffee or a meal, and he said "not yet—maybe soon." I think he mostly called to ask about his sisters. I told him they were doing well at their grandmother's house, and I knew everyone would want to see him.

He put me off, but I hope I'm making a little progress. I told him I really appreciate the calls, and hope he'll stay in touch.

What else we can do?

Miriam Fine
(913) 555-8436

"If I can't dance, I don't want to be part of your revolution." -- Emma Goldman

**Staff   Volunteers   Volunteers   Lookup   Cases   User   Reports
Dashboard   Dashboard   Tables   Administration**

Contact Log

Name	Fine, Miriam
Case Number	594
Activity Date	5/10/2013
Activity Type	Placement Visit
Subject	Child welfare
Location	Grandparents' Home
Contact Type	Face-to-face
Hours	1.00
Notes:	

I joined the family for dinner. Other than Tyrone's absence ("the big elephant in the room") it now seems like a perfectly normal family with two children at the dinner table. I have hope that we are coming close to a happy, permanent solution for the two girls, at least.

Alysha told me Mabel has signed her up for a summer camp for gifted kids run by the school district. She is very excited about that. Hope wanted to talk about last week's school trip to the zoo. She told me she had decided to be a veterinarian when she grows up -- "maybe for really big animals like tigers and elephants."

Mabel said she had hoped we'd hear from Tyrone again and maybe he would consider "turning himself in." We agreed we would just have to cross our fingers and wait.

"And pray," Mabel said.

Activity Status   Approved

Miriam,
We were so sorry to hear about
the loss of your mother.

Sending warm thoughts,
The Staff of Jackson County CASA

From: Miriam Fine [mailto:miriamkfine@gmail.com]
Sent: Monday, May 20, 2013 10:13 AM
To: hgoldstein@laramyjones.com
Subject: Thanks for all your help

Ah, Hazel, thank you for all your help this weekend. I don't think I'd have made it through without you.

I thought the service was really lovely yesterday; didn't you? Naomi gave a beautiful eulogy—she always does. You could tell she really knew Mom—that she wasn't just repeating stories other people had told her. She's a good rabbi; we're lucky to have her. And so many of mom's friends came—she would have liked that.

I am beyond wiped out. Those crazy three days and nights in the hospital when we didn't have a clue if she was getting better or dying. And then the horrible moment when I had to tell the nursing staff we were ready to turn off the vent. I know she wasn't there anymore—but it was still hard. The most grownup thing I've ever done. Mom always said she gave me medical power of attorney because I'm not sentimental; I'd do what had to be done. So I did.

I'm really glad Arielle and Isaac got here in time to say good-bye. I don't know if Mom could hear, but I think it was important for them. It will make this next hard part easier. And she would have wanted that for her beloved grandchildren.

I thought people would never leave after shiva tonight—maybe the food was too good. I'm going to put out less tomorrow night and hope they go home early. I've got to pace myself if I'm going to do two more nights of this. How do Orthodox Jews manage a full week of shiva? I can't imagine.

I found the package you left on the counter with the notecards. Thank you—they're perfect. I've already got a million thank-you notes to write—so many lovely donations in mom's memory. I always loved the notecards you used when your mom died. Thanks for making some for me. And thanks for making the poppies orange. Mom would have loved that.

You know what I keep thinking about, over and over? That book event last year at the library. Mom was so delighted and so gracious and so proud. So herself. I think it's the last time I saw her truly happy. I'll always be grateful I agreed to do that with her. That night is my last cherished memory.

Mostly, I feel astoundingly disoriented. Like I'm in a Murakami novel. You turn the corner and there's a black cat. And your mother's dead.

I know you know. Thanks for being my guide in this world we did not want to inhabit.

Miri

Miriam Fine
(913) 555-8436

"If I can't dance, I don't want to be part of your revolution." -- Emma Goldman

IN THE CIRCUIT COURT OF JACKSON COUNTY, MISSOURI,
JUVENILE DIVISION

IN THE INTEREST OF:

Tyrone X. Merritt	1416-JU0040987	1416-JR57790
NAME	**PETITION NUMBER**	**LIFE NUMBER**

Alysha M. Washington	1416-JU0040988	1416-JR57791
NAME	**PETITION NUMBER**	**LIFE NUMBER**

Hope S. Washington	1416-JU0040988	1416-JR57792
NAME	**PETITION NUMBER**	**LIFE NUMBER**

ENTRY OF APPEARANCE

Comes now _____Jeremy Verona_____ and hereby enters

his/her appearance in the above-captioned cause on behalf of _____Jerome Washington_____

Name	Jeremy Verona
Address	1604 18th Street, KC MO 64108
Telephone Number	(816) 555-6703
Bar Number	498204
FAX Number	(816) 555-6704

From: Anita Blackstone [mailto:ablackstone@jacksoncountycasa-mo.org]
Sent: Monday, May 27, 2013 11:03 AM
To: miriamkfine@gmail.com
Cc: hmiller@jacksoncountycasa-mo.org
Subject: RE: *Confidential: Merritt—Washington—Jerome Washington

Hi, Miri. How are you doing?

Everyone here sends their very best wishes. I know we received several donations in your mom's memory—what a lovely tribute to her early work with CASA and your ongoing commitment to the organization. Henrietta said she really enjoyed meeting your mom at the book event on the Plaza last month. I'm so glad you'll have that wonderful event to remember.

I didn't want to intrude during this difficult time for your family, but I thought you should know about an unexpected development in your case. We have been notified that a local attorney has filed notice that he will be representing Jerome Washington in this matter. Apparently, Jerome has now been released from the Jackson County Detention Center, and my guess is that he intends to ask to see his daughters.

I know you'll ask, so I'll just go ahead and answer your main question: yes, parents who have been released from jail, even those who were convicted of violent crimes, have the legal right to ask to see their children. The Court often grants such requests.

I just wanted you to be prepared, since I'm sure there is more to come. We can decide what steps we want to take—and what we want to ask the Court—when we know a little bit more about why Jerome has retained counsel.

I hope you are able to find comfort right now in the love and care of family and friends. Please count the CASA team among those who care deeply for you.

Anita

Anita Blackstone
Case Supervisor
(816) 555-8236

From: Miriam Fine [mailto:miriamkfine@gmail.com]
Sent: Saturday, June 1, 2013 10:19 PM
To: hgoldstein@laramyjones.com
Subject: Falling apart

Hazel,

It's all falling apart. Or I'm falling apart. Or both. I know Carol would tell me it's only been a few weeks since Mom died—to give it all time, to give myself time. But here's the thing—time marches on, whether you're ready for it or not.

My CASA Supervisor wrote earlier in the week that the asshole father on my case (that's a technical term) is out of jail and has hired an attorney. He probably wants to see his daughters. I could go on and on about the idiocy of a system that would let a man who beats the crap out of his wife have access to small children. But I'll save that for another day. I intend to do everything in my power to keep that creep away from these girls—and I'm holding out hope the system will do the right thing. So we'll save that rant for another day—and hopefully one that will never come.

But tonight I need to confess. I need you to swear (really, pinky swear) that you will never, ever, ever tell a living soul what I'm about to say. You've kept big secrets for me before; this one is bigger.

I was at the midtown Costco today picking up soda and toilet paper, and I ran into my CASA teen! I couldn't believe it. I turned into the aisle, headed towards those little stations where the nice ladies in hairnets put out food samples. You know, the ones that don't have any calories in them, because they're free. And there he was, picking up those little samples just as quickly as the ladies set them out and gobbling them down. He saw me right away, froze, but didn't walk away.

How in the world did he get in the door without showing a Costco card? Hard to say . . . and I wasn't about to ask. If there are urban survival tricks, apparently he's had time to learn them.

My heart was really pounding, but I kept my cool. I walked up slowly, like you do when you don't want to spook a stray puppy. It was an effort not to put my hand out. I said I was really glad to see him— asked if we could go over to the snack area—the real part, not the free part—and maybe get a bite to eat and a cold drink. He must have been really hungry, because he said yes. I just left my cart right there in the aisle; it didn't seem to matter anymore.

I bought one of those big pepperoni pizzas and a couple of extra-large sodas, and we sat on those horrid red-and-white painted steel picnic tables. Boy, can that kid eat. I don't think he's had a decent meal in a long time—he's lost weight, and his clothes, just jeans and a tee-shirt, are really loose. I tried to think of stories to tell him about his younger sisters—he liked hearing about their recent School Assembly. And I told him my mother had died. I think that's the first time it ever occurred to him that I was a person with a life independent of my connection to him. "I'm really sorry to hear that, Ms. Fine. I know how awful it is to live without your mom." Oh, man, how's that coming from a kid?

I had to really resist peppering him with questions about where he was living and what he was doing. I didn't want him to shut down. He talked about a few friends—someone named Mark and someone named Jenny. I couldn't tell if they were on the streets, too, but I think so.

Finally, with the last piece of pizza going down fast—God help me, it just seemed like the only decent thing to do—I blurted out: "Do you want to come home with me for a few days?"

He didn't bolt, so I kept going: "You could sleep in one of our spare bedrooms and get a hot shower and have real food. I won't tell anyone but my husband. It would be our secret. You can't stay forever, but it would give you a chance to figure things out."

And so . . . he did. I don't know why. But he did. He got in my car—which he's never done before—and directed me to a kind of encampment under a freeway bridge by downtown, where he retrieved a duffel bag. Then we drove home. Conversation was pretty awkward—I put on the radio, and he was happy to find a music station he liked. I pulled into the garage and showed him Isaac's old room, which is now well set up as a guest room, with its own bathroom, matching towels, and hotel-sized toiletries. All the amenities I thought mattered so much. I doubt a kid who's been living on the streets cares if the towels match.

And that's where he is now. Sound asleep in Isaac's bedroom. I have just broken two of the biggest CASA rules in the book. Never put a kid in your car, and never, ever, ever, ever take a kid home with you. If my CASA Supervisor ever finds out, she will fire me on the spot. Which means I will never get to see the two girls again, let alone my teen.

But what was I supposed to do? A dirty, hungry kid—and I have a spare bedroom, and a good shower with hot water (and matching towels), and a full refrigerator.

Larry was surprisingly good about it. He's been pretty worried about me since Mom died. So he wasn't going to put up a fuss. He's actually sleeping on the couch in the living room tonight, so he'll hear if my kid gets up and needs something (or, I suppose, tries to steal something). And, hopefully, by morning, I'll figure out what to do next.

I couldn't help it, Hazel. Truly, I couldn't.

I think you would have done the same.

Miri

Miriam Fine
(913) 555-8436

"If I can't dance, I don't want to be part of your revolution." -- Emma Goldman

From: Miriam Fine [mailto:miriamkfine@gmail.com]
Sent: Monday, June 3, 2013 10:19 PM
To: hgoldstein@laramyjones.com
Subject: He's gone

Thanks for your reassuring words, Haze. It made me feel better for you to say that I wasn't totally nuts—that any decent person would have brought the kid home, too. I know that's not really true. Honestly, I don't think I would have done it if I weren't so unhinged from Mom's death. I'm normally much more rule-abiding than this. But I did it. And I don't regret it.

And, anyway, it's over now.

He hung around the house all day Sunday watching TV and sleeping and pretty much cleaning out the refrigerator. I told him anything in the kitchen was fair game, and he took me at my word. Larry found some old jeans and a tee-shirt from Isaac's basement stash, so he could wash and dry his clothes. That, along with the shower, helped some with the smell.

Another full night's sleep, with Larry still on the couch, and then he got up this morning, ate breakfast, and asked me for a ride back to his camp under the bridge. I suggested a million alternatives—calling his grandmother, looking for a bed at reStart, talking to the minister at his grandparents' church—but he's smart enough to know any of those options mean coming back into protective custody. Which he is clearly not ready to do. He's got some new bravado around being independent and self-sufficient—which I guess is well-deserved, since he has now managed to keep himself alive for months on the run.

So . . . I found another duffel bag to stuff with more of Isaac's old clothes and some granola bars. I put in some deodorant, because I remembered he once asked for that for Christmas. And I drove him back to the bridge.

In the car, I told him the time at our house had to remain our secret. That I wouldn't be putting the info in my CASA reports or telling the CASA staff or anyone at CD or the Court that I'd seen him. That I was worried I wouldn't be allowed to help his sisters anymore if anyone found out I had broken the rules by bringing him home. He got that right away. I know he wouldn't do anything to jeopardize his sisters' chances to get the help they need. I hope it's not wishful thinking, but I believe he'll keep our secret.

And I reminded him he can call me—anytime. He thanked me—he's always been good at that—and then he grabbed both duffel bags and hopped out.

I have never been sadder than watching that kid walk away from my car.

Not even at Mom's funeral.

Miri

Miriam Fine
(913) 555-8436

"If I can't dance, I don't want to be part of your revolution." -- Emma Goldman

June 18, 2013

Family Support Team Meeting

Case: Merritt-Washington
Facilitator: Marlie Verlet, Children's Division worker
Location: Library Conference Room, Jackson County CASA
In attendance:

    Alysha Washington – Juvenile
    Hope Washington – Juvenile
    Joelle Merritt – Mother
    Martin Jaylon – Mother's Attorney
    Jerome Washington – Father
    Jeremy Verona – Father's Attorney
    Mabel Merritt – Maternal Grandmother
    Roger Merritt – Maternal Grandfather
    Marlie Verlet – CD Worker
    Duncan Walsh – CD Supervisor
    Miraim Fine – CASA Volunteer
    Anita Blackstone – CASA Case Supervisor (taking notes for group)

Marlie Verlet passed around the attendance log / confidentiality agreement for everyone to sign. She noted that Tyrone Merritt is still on run and has made only occasional contact (two phone calls) with the CASA Volunteer. No one else has heard from him or seen him since he left his temporary foster placement on March 18, three months ago.

Joelle Merritt now out on probation from the DUI conviction, asked if anything more could be done to locate Tyrone. Marlie said that CD had asked the Court to issue a capias, so he will be brought in if he is stopped for some other reason, such as a traffic or vagrancy violation. However, the police do not conduct pro-active searches for youth who have run away.

Marlie noted that Jerome Washington was with the group for the first time, along with his attorney. She asked everyone to please go around the room and introduce themselves before they start the meeting.

Marlie asked the children to speak first, before being excused with Roger, who agreed to supervise.

Alysha Washington – spoke directly to Joelle and said she did not want to leave her grandparents' house again and she hoped Joelle wouldn't make them. Said she was doing well in school and very happy to be back with her Girl Scout troop and wanted to keep it that way. Said she was working on her Scribe and Drawing badges and it was important to finish them. She would not make eye contact with Jerome or speak to him, and said she didn't like sitting near him. Marlie asked him to move to the opposite side of the table for today, which he did. Alysha visibly relaxed.

Hope Washington – refused to sit by Joelle and stayed very close to Alysha. She wouldn't speak and began to cry as they left the room with Roger.

Marlie asked the group to please try to proceed in a calm and organized manner.

Joelle told the group she is back at her AA meetings and believes she will soon be able to see the children again. Mabel said she wasn't sure that was such a good idea. The group agreed to put this discussion on hold for a few months and revisit as Joelle continued to make progress on her sobriety.

Jerome Washington told the group he had served his time and was out of jail now, on probation. He said he was staying at a friend's apartment and was now working at a different McDonald's. He said he worked on his anger management issues while incarcerated and felt he was ready to reinitiate a relationship with his children.

Joelle objected very loudly, but her lawyer quieted her.

"I have a right to see my kids," Jerome said. "Lots of the guys in lockup talk about their kids—how it ain't right for the moms to have them whenever they want and we don't even get to see them. I wanna see my kids. I won't hurt them or nothing. I just want to see them. I got that right."

Marlie said that CD would consider recommending an initial supervised visit at the Case Review with the Court later in the month. If that went well, more visits would be considered.

Mabel became visibly upset and said she would never allow "that man in my home or near these children." Marlie reminded her that Jerome had legal rights, and it would be up to the Court to decide, but visits could be held outside of her home and she need not be present.

Miriam Fine, CASA Volunteer – Said she would speak with the children and make her recommendation on visits with Jerome directly to the Court. Reminded the group that the children's best interests needed to be paramount.

Mabel Merritt, maternal grandmother – Reported the girls were doing very well now that they were back at home. She hoped everyone would work to keep their situation as stable as possible.

Anita Blackstone, CASA Case Supervisor—nothing to add.

Group agreed on 10/18/13 for next FST. Anita will schedule with CASA to use the Library Conference Room and will notify parties about time.

AJB / uploaded to OPTIMA 6-18-13

Welcome **miriam.fine**

Change Password   Log Off

Staff | **Volunteers** | **Volunteers** | **Lookup** | **Cases** | **User** | **Reports**
Dashboard | **Dashboard** | | **Tables** | | **Administration** |

Contact Log

Name	Fine, Miriam
Case Number	594
Activity Date	6/20/2013
Activity Type	Placement Visit
Subject	Child welfare
Location	Grandparents' Home
Contact Type	Face-to-face
Hours	1.00

Notes:

I visited the children in the afternoon. Alysha had just gotten home from the gifted camp she is enrolled in for the summer. She was excited to tell me about the science experiments they have been working on and the speakers who have come each week to tell them about different careers. She was particularly taken with the librarian who came from the KC Public Library and told them about all the different kinds of jobs in that field. If we can just keep Alysha around books, she will be happy.

She told me it was scary to see Jerome at the FST and didn't want to see him again. I told her we could fill out another Child Placement Report so she could tell the Commissioner, but I couldn't promise how it would work out. She asked if I would help her fill it out the Placement Report on the computer. "Maybe they'll pay more attention that way -- no one cared about what I said before."

I reminded her that Jerome might have changed, and it might be good to see him. She seemed very skeptical. She asked if I could please be sure she and Hope didn't have to be alone with him, and I told her I thought we could manage that, even if we couldn't prevent visits altogether.

I asked if she wanted to see her mom, and she said, "Maybe -- but not right now. Seeing them both in that room together was really hard. I just want to go on with my life here with Grandma and Grandpa. I'm tired of being scared and so much uncertainty -- for me and for Hope."

She asked if I had heard from Tyrone again, but wasn't surprised that I had not. I think she is resigned that he's really run away.

Hope had swim lessons at the Y earlier in the day and proudly told me she was learning the backstroke. I asked her about Jerome and Joelle, and she pretty much repeated what Alysha had said. She's scared of Jerome and heistant about Joelle. "But I'll do whatever Alysha does," she said. "Can't we just stay here and make a happy family with Grandma and Grandpa? And Tyrone, if he'll come back to us. I don't think he'll come back if we have to see Daddy. They fought too much, and Tyrone's even bigger now."

I spent some time with Mabel while she was starting to get dinner ready. She is very worried and angry. "After all this time and and all they've been through, those people still want these kids to have to see that man? How could that be a good thing?" I told her I agreed, and would do my best to recommend no visits with Jerome, but the Court would have to protect his legal rights too. She sniffed at that: "Man beats his girlfriend, drinks the rent money, goes to jail and doesn't take care of his kids ... what right does he have to legal rights?"

We agreed to just wait and see how it all played out. In the meantime, she asked me again if there was anything more we could do to find Tyrone and bring him home. Sadly, I am out of ideas.

Activity Status   Approved

CHILD'S REPORT ON PLACEMENT

Court Date: _____ 7/1/13 _____

Child's Name: _Alysha Merritt (assistance from CASA Miriam Fine)_____

Current Placement: __Grandparents – Roger and Mabel Merritt_____

This form gives you, the child involved in this case, an opportunity to express your feelings and any facts concerning your present placement. This form may be used by the Guardian ad litem, and the Judge or Commissioner as allowed by law. It is possible that all the information will be made available to all the parties, including the placement provider. Please be fair, open and honest.

1. Are you generally satisfied with your current placement?

_____X !!!!!_____ yes   _____ no

Please explain:

I am very happy living with my grandparents, Roger and Mabel Merritt. We were happy here before, but were reunified with our mother. That didn't work out. She started drinking again, and my brother and I had to take care of our little sister like before. It is a relief to be living with our grandparents again, where our needs are cared for. I miss my brother Tyrone a lot. He ran away after our mother got into trouble with the police. I hope we find him soon.

Most important: I DO NOT WANT TO SEE MY FATHER, JEROME WASHINGTON. He is a bad, mean man, who hit my mother and yelled at us all the time. Please, please, please don't make me see him or let him anywhere near Hope. We are scared of him.

2. Does the placement provider help with your goal, whether it is reunification with a parent, independent living, relative placement or other plan?

____X_____ yes   _____ no

Please explain:

I am not sure what our goal is anymore, but I know Grandma and Grandpa would like us to live here, and that's what we want, too. They are afraid of Jerome Washington, too, and have said he can't come in their house.

3. Please describe how you get along with the other children, if any, in your placement.

I love my sister and really miss Tyrone. I wish he would come home.

4. Please name the school you are going to and explain what you like about it or don't like about it.

It is summer vacation now, but I will be in the 6th grade at Whittier Elementary next year. I like school a lot. It is the best thing in my life.

5. Please talk about how you are disciplined when you do something you are not supposed to, or violate rules of the home.

I try very hard to be good and not break any rules.

6. If you have visits with brothers or sisters, please explain how that is going and how it could be better.

_____
_____
_____
_____
_____
_____

7. Do you have any health concerns that you feel like are not being taken care of? If so, explain:

Things are fine since I got a new pair of glasses. I am being very careful not to break this pair.

8. Please explain how visits, if any, are going with your parent(s), and what could be done to make them better.

I don't think Mommy wants to see us yet. I hope we can see her again soon, maybe if she stops drinking again. I DO NOT WANT TO SEE MY FATHER, JEROME WASHINGTON. That is why I am writing this Form, to tell you that. He is bad and scary and violent and mean. Do not make us do that. Please.

9. Do you get a chance to participate in things you want to, like sports, music, dance, and other activities? Please explain:

I like my summer camp for gifted children a lot.

10. How do you get along with your social worker, and do you feel that they understand your needs and situation? Please explain:

There have been changes. Ms. Verlet was not our worker when things started. Does she understand why Jerome Washington is a bad man? Our CASA, Ms. Fine, understands and is trying to help. She is helping me write out this report on the computer.

11. Do you know of any relatives or other adults you might be able to live with? If yes, please list their name(s) and how you know them.

_____
_____
_____
_____
_____

12. Do you know of any help that you need that you are not getting right now? If yes, please explain.

We need protection from our father. I am worried we will not get that.

13. If you are in counseling, do you think it is helping? Please explain.

_____
_____
_____
_____
_____

14. Would you like for your court hearing to be scheduled so that you don't have to miss school to attend?

_____X_____ yes   _____ no

15. Do you have a photo you would like for the judge or commissioner to have? If so, be sure to bring it to court.

11. Please explain anything about your situation that you think is important and that has not been asked.

Keep our father away from us.

IN THE CIRCUIT COURT OF JACKSON COUNTY, MISSOURI
FAMILY COURT DIVISION

IN THE INTEREST OF:	CASE NUMBER: 1416-JU0040987
TYRONE MERRITT	LIFE NUMBER:
SEX: M BORN: 19-FEB-1998	1416-JR57790

IN THE INTEREST OF:	CASE NUMBER: 1416-JU0040988
ALYSHA WASHINGTON	LIFE NUMBER:
SEX: F BORN: 07-APRIL-2003	1416-JR57791

IN THE INTEREST OF:	CASE NUMBER: 1416-JU0040989
HOPE WASHINGTON	LIFE NUMBER:
SEX: F BORN: 17-NOV-2004	1416-JR57792

FINDINGS AND RECOMMENDATIONS

Now on July 1, 2013 there being present:

MARLIE VERLET	-	Children's Division
MARLIE VERLET	-	Children's Division
JOELLE MERRITT	-	Mother
ABIGAIL NORRIS	-	Attorney for the Juvenile Officer
HENRIETTA MILLER	-	Guardian ad Litem (CASA)
MIRIAM FINE	-	CASA Volunteer
MARTIN JAYLON	-	Attorney for Mother
ALYSHA WASHINGTON	-	Juvenile
HOPE WASHINGTON	-	Juvenile
JEROME WASHINGTON	-	Father
JEREMY VERONA	-	Attorney for Father

The cause comes on for Cases Review pursuant to an order of JANUARY 15, 2013.

IT IS HEREBY ORDERED: that the juveniles are not safe in the physical custody of their mother, Joelle Merritt, so are hereby recommitted to the custody of Children's Division for placement with the maternal grandparents' or in another non-relative licensed placement, until further order of the Court. The Court notes that the capias for Tyrone Merritt, currently on the run, remains in place.

IT IS FURTHER ORDERED: that based on successful completion of his sentence at the Jackson County Detention Center and participation in anger management programs while incarcerated, Jerome Washington will be granted supervised visitation with Alysha and Hope Washington, at the discretion of Children's Division.

The Court notes that the Guardian ad Litem and CASA Volunteer have submitted recommendations asking that such visits be denied in the best interests of the children; however, we find no legal grounds based on the evidence presented.

The next court hearing for the above action is scheduled for OCTOBER 1, 2013, at 2:00 PM in DIVISION 40 for Permanency Hearing.

Notice of Findings and Recommendation & Notice of Right to a Rehearing

The parties are notified that the forgoing Findings and Recommendations have been entered this date by a commissioner, and all papers relative to the care or proceeding, together with the Findings and Recommendation have been transferred to a Judge of the Court. The Findings and Recommendations shall become the Judgment of the Court upon adoption by order of the Judge. Unless waived by the parties in writing, at party in the case or proceeding heard by a commissioner, within fifteen days after the mailing of notice of the filing of the Judgment of the Court, may file a motion for rehearing by a Judge of the Court. If the motion for rehearing is not ruled on within forty-five days after the motion is filed, the motion is overruled for all purposes. Rule 130.13

July 3, 2013
_____
Date

Gerard E. Solomon
_____
GERARD E. SOLOMON, Commissioner

Order and Judgment Adopting Commissioner's Findings and Recommendation

It is hereby ordered, adjudged and decreed the foregoing Findings and Recommendations entered by the commissioner are adopted and confirmed as a final Judgment of the Court.

July 3, 2013   *Suzanne M. Martell*
_____   _____
Date   Judge

NOTICE OF ENTRY OF JUDGMENT

You are hereby notified that on   JUL 3, 2013,   the Family Court, Juvenile Division, of Jackson County, Missouri made and entered the above judgment in this case:

You are further notified that you may have a right of appeal from this judgment under Rule 120.01 and section 211.261, RSMo, which provides that:

1. An appeal shall be allowed to the juveniles from any final judgment made under the Juvenile Code and may be taken on the part of the juveniles by the custodian.

2. An appeal shall be allowed to custodian from any final judgment made under the Juvenile Code that adversely affects the custodian.

3. Notice of appeal shall be filed in accordance with Missouri law.

4. Neither the filing of a notice of appeal nor the filing of any motion subsequent to the judgment shall act to stay the execution of a judgment unless the court enters an order staying execution.

Corrine Adamson
_____
Deputy Court Administrator

Certificate of Service

This is to certify that a copy of the foregoing was hand delivered/faxed/emailed/mailed and/or sent through the eFiling system to the following on JULY 5 2013.

M R Jones
_____

Copies to:

ABIGAIL NORRIS
Attorney for the Juvenile Officer

MARTIN JAYLON
Attorney for the Natural Mother

JEREMY VERONA
Attorney for the Natural Father

MARLIE VERLET
CHILDREN'S DIVISION

HENRIETTA MILLER
JACKSON COUNTY CASA

MARLIN THOMPSON
Putative Father

JEROME WASHINGTON
Natural Father – Alysha Washington, Hope Washington

JOELLE MERRITT
Natural Mother

From: Miriam Fine [mailto:miriamkfine@gmail.com]
Sent: Tuesday, July 2, 2013 4:27 PM
To: hgoldstein@laramyjones.com
Subject: Emerging

Hi, Hazel. Thanks for checking on me. I think I'm doing a little better. Sloshim is over, and the sages must not have been idiots, because 30 days does seem like some kind of meaningful marker. I still feel like there's this big hole in the world—and I might fall through it if I get too close to the edge—but mostly things are starting to rearrange themselves into something that looks like normal.

I've written most of the required thank-you notes on your beautiful stationery—so many generous donations! There was one to buy a tree in Israel. That totally cracked me up. Here's the TY note I did not write:

> *Dear Sophie,*
>   *Thank you so much for the lovely donation in mom's memory to buy a tree in Israel. As you know, mom was pretty indifferent about trees and barely ever talked about Israel. She thought the American Jewish obsession with a homeland in the Middle East was very strange. In fact, I think she mostly sympathized with the displaced and oppressed Palestinians.*
>   *But since none of her social justice causes right here in Kansas City caught your eye, I'm glad you felt moved to honor her in this way. Mom always said you were a bit of an odd duck.*
>   *Fondly,*
>   *Miriam*

Hah—that would get the Jewish tongues wagging! I'm afraid grief is not making me a nicer person.

I'm also currently inclined to throw some sort of incendiary device in the direction of the Jackson County Family Court. Do you know what those jerks have done? They are granting visitation to the dad on my case, even though he spent six years in prison for violent assault and his mere presence in the room totally terrifies my kids. The older one even had me help her write a report to the Court asking them to keep him away from her.

But do they listen to these kids? No. They just "follow the law." Which in this case means forcing these girls to "visit" with the man who broke their mother's jaw. Oh, yeah, and did I mention he was on probation at the time from another domestic assault? So this two-time loser has more legal rights than these child victims. I swear, Hazel . . . none of this is any good. Not any good at all.

I think about my CASA teen all the time—I wonder what he's doing now.

Miri

Miriam Fine
(913) 555-8436

"If I can't dance, I don't want to be part of your revolution." -- Emma Goldman

POLICE REPORT

Case No:	730629-506	Date:	7/2/13
Reporting Officer:	Tom Willens	Prepared By:	same
Incident/Issue:	Juvenile Shoplifting		

Description of Accident/Issue:

Manager of CVS on Independence Avenue called police after catching young man attempting to leave the store without paying for merchandise stuffed in his pockets – aspirin, band aids, cookies, and potato chips.

Actions Taken:

Store manager Jason Karr called 911 at 10:17 a.m. to report stopping a youth leaving the CVS without paying for merchandise. When Officer Tom Willens arrived at the store at 10:32 a.m. the youth was being held in the manager's office at the back of the store.

He identified himself as Tyrone Merritt and confessed to attempting to steal the items in question. He said he was hungry and needed the first aid supplies for blisters. When questioned, the youth said he had no permanent address, but stayed with friends or slept in the park. He said his mother was in jail, and he had been living with his grandparents until he was sent to foster care.

Officer Willens called into the station and was notified there was a capias out on Mr. Merritt. He arrested the youth, read him his Miranda rights, and took him to the KCPD station for booking. En route he drove through McDonald's to get food for Mr. Merritt.

Youth is presently in Juvenile Detention awaiting Family Court hearing.

Staff   Volunteers   Volunteers   Lookup   Cases   User   Reports
Dashboard   Dashboard   Tables   Administration

Contact Log

Name	Fine, Miriam
Case Number	594
Activity Date	7/5/2013
Activity Type	Placement Visit
Subject	Child welfare
Location	Juvenile Detention
Contact Type	Face-to-face
Hours	0.50

Notes:

I met Tyrone in the common area, which seems to be where most meetings take place in detention. I haven't seen him since March in his temporary foster placement, and he has lost a lot of weight in the four months he's been on run. He sat pretty passively in one of those plastic chairs while we talked, more defeated than angry or nervous. I think he was relieved to see me -- maybe even relieved that he got caught and finally had a bed and regular meals for a while.

He asked right away about Alysha and Hope -- wanted to hear "all the news" about them. I told him they were back with Mabel and Roger and that Joelle was home on probation, but not yet ready to have visits. "She just couldn't do it, could she?" he said. "She loves us, but she can't take care of us. I guess now we know that for good."

I told him that Jerome had been released from jail and was asking to see Alysha and Hope for supervised visits. He got very angry at that -- the only time he was aggressive during my visit. "No! That can't be right. He'll just scare them and maybe even hurt them! You have to stop that!" I told him we were all doing our best to protect his sisters, and he'd just have to trust the adults. He snorted at that. I guess I can't blame him.

I asked what he could tell me about his time away. He was pretty vague. Mentioned a friend named Mark from school whose cousin let him crash on the sofa. And a girl named Jenny.

Also a group of kids he met (from where?) who sometimes squat in an abandoned house in Independence. He said he didn't know the address, but I think he was just protecting them. He said they got food from soup kitchens and panhandling and dumpster diving. And, under his breath, shoplifting. I think there's an encampment under a downtown freeway bridge where a lot of them hang out, too -- not as sure about those details.

I told him I was really glad he had called me while he was on his own, and I hoped he'd always do that, no matter where he was or what was going on. I reminded him we could trust each other.

We talked about his upcoming hearing - I explained he would get a Court-appointed lawyer for the criminal charges, separate from Henrietta as his Guardian ad Litem. The AJO had already told me she was going to ask for probation and release back to Gillis. I asked Tyrone if he wanted me to recommend he be placed back with Mabel and Roger instead. "Not if Jerome is coming 'round!" he said. "I might have to really fight him this time."

I told him Mabel and Roger would come to his hearing, and he could talk to them then about visiting him if he wanted. He asked if they were mad at him, and I said, "more worried than mad. I think you can make it right with them."

Activity Status   Approved

Staff   Volunteers   Volunteers   Lookup   Cases   User   Reports
Dashboard   Dashboard   Tables   Administration

Contact Log

Name	Fine, Miriam
Case Number	594
Activity Date	7/10/2013
Activity Type	Placement Visit
Subject	Child welfare
Location	Juvenile Detention
Contact Type	Face-to-face
Hours	0.50

Notes:

Oddly, Tyrone looks much better after a week in detention. I have been told the food is quite good here, and he is clearly putting on weight with regular meals. I asked how he was doing, and he said he was bored, but happy to be safe and have a bed to sleep on. He also said it was good to be able to watch TV again.

He told me that Mabel had visited on Monday and she wasn't mad ("at least not anymore"), just worried about him. She had provided updates about his sisters, which seemed to mean a lot to him.

We talked about his hearing coming up on Friday on the shoplifting charge. He said he had met his "new lawyer" and thought she was very young, but would be fine. He was in agreement with the plan to return to Gillis if he could get "released from jail."

I asked if he needed anything else, and he just sighed. I think his basic needs for health and safety are being met. I told him I'd be at the hearing on Friday and would see him then. If all worked out and he went to GIllis, I would visit soon. "And maybe bring some more of those LEGO sets?" he asked hopefully. There is still a child hidden inside this now-tough, now juvenile delinquent, teen.

Activity Status   Approved

From: Anita Blackstone [mailto:ablackstone@jacksoncountycasa-mo.org]
Sent: Monday, July 15, 2013 4:33 PM
To: miriamkfine@gmail.com
Cc: hmiller@jacksoncountycasa-mo.org
Subject: RE: *Confidential: Merritt—Washington—Tyrone back to Gillis

Miri,

Once again, thank you so much for coming to Tyrone's juvenile hearing on Friday. We know from experience how important it is for these youth to have the consistent presence of their CASA Volunteer as they go through these difficult situations.

We got word from the Court today that the Judge agreed with the AJO's recommendation, and Tyrone will be put on probation and released to Gillis. Marlie Verlet will be moving him tomorrow morning.

I noted from your OPTIMA report that Tyrone has asked to see the Gillis psychiatrist. I'm sure that will be an early agenda item on their treatment plan. Hopefully, now that he is back in a therapeutic residential facility, we can get him the consistent treatment and medication he needs to stabilize his behaviors again.

Since this will be a longer-term residential placement, Tyrone will begin classes at the Gillis School in August. Hopefully, a tutor can work with him this summer to help him make up the coursework he missed while he was on run. If not, he will have to repeat freshman year.

I'm sure you can visit Tyrone as soon as it can be arranged. As before, just contact Gillis to make arrangements.

Oh, and on your other question—I checked with Cherry, and she still has some great LEGO sets for older youth in inventory. Why don't you reach out to her directly to pick something up at the CASA office on your way out to Gillis to visit?

Anita

Anita Blackstone
Case Supervisor
(816) 555-8236

Dr. Ben Arielto   (816) 555-2905

NAME: Tyrone X. Merritt
ADDRESS: The Gillis School, 8150 Wornall Rd., KC MO 64114
DATE: 7/17/13

ABILIFY for 60 days -
     2 mg Day 1 and 2
     5 mg Day 3 and 4
     10 mg Day 5 – continue at this level

2 refills

        SIGNED: *Dr. B Arielto* _____M.D.

Contact Log

Name	Fine, Miriam
Case Number	594
Activity Date	7/18/2013
Activity Type	Placement Visit
Subject	Child welfare
Location	Grandparents' Home
Contact Type	Face-to-face
Hours	1.00

Notes:

Things were in a bit of an upheaval when I visited the girls at their grandparents' this afternoon. For the first time in two years, Alysha shut herself in their bedroom and refused to talk to me. Hope was outside with a girlfriend, but wouldn't stop to come greet me.

Mabel told me they had their first supervised visit with Jerome over the weekend and both had been acting out since then. I asked for more details, and she said she had taken them to McDonald's to meet Jerome after his work shift. He had bought Happy Meals for the girls and coffee for her, and sat down to talk. She said the girls were both very scared -- wouldn't talk to Jerome despite his cajoling. Alysha finally muttered: "You hurt Mommy and then we all had to go away. Now Tyrone is in trouble, too. Why should I talk to you?"

Mabel said Jerome looked so stricken she almost felt sorry for him. Then he got angry and stomped off, and she took the girls home. She told me again that she thought seeing him was very bad for the girls. I told her I would tell Henrietta and the Court again that my recommendation was to delay these visits and encouraged her to tell all the details to Marlie, too. I think if CD feels the visits are unsafe for the girls they will change their recommendation.

I asked about Joelle, and she said she talks on the phone with her and sometimes the girls talk, too. She thinks it will take more time before anyone is ready to resume those visits. She doesn't think the girls are scared of Joelle -- they just don't trust her anymore. "Can you blame them?" she asked.

We talked about Tyrone, and she said she was going to see him at Gillis. She wanted to go alone first, before she asked about bringing the girls. She said they talk about him sometimes, but less all the time. That makes her sad. "All those kids had was each other -- now they don't even have that." I reminded her that they had her and Roger, and she thanked me for that encouragement. "Not many people appreciate what we're doing," she said. "Except for the folks at the church. They are really good to all of us."

I tried to talk to Alysha again before I left, but she wouldn't open the door. I told her I'd be back again soon. I don't want her to think her anger will keep me away. Hope waved when I left -- a slightly better sign.

Activity Status   Approved

Man stabbed inside local bar, suspect arrested

KANSAS CITY, MO - A fight broke out early Thursday inside a midtown bar, leaving one man seriously hurt, according to Kansas City Police.

The incident occurred about 2:30 a.m. after a dispute involving a game of pool at One More Shot at 2503 Prospect Avenue.

A woman called police and said her boyfriend had been stabbed by another patron after he was accused of cheating during a pool game. She said the argument escalated into a fist fight. The alleged attacker then drew a switch blade and began slashing the victim.

Police arrived and found two men restraining the alleged attacker. They spoke with another bar patron and the bartender, who said they witnessed the stabbing.

One man, Tom Mahoney, 32, was taken by ambulance to Truman Medical Center with stab wounds to his neck and arm. Hospital officials said the cuts were life-threatening.

Jerome Washington, 35, was arrested on site and later booked on suspicion of parole violation and assault with a deadly weapon. He was out on parole for two previous domestic violence incidents, including an attack on his girlfriend in a local McDonald's parking lot.

Welcome **miriam.fine**

Change Password   Log Off

Staff   Volunteers   Volunteers   Lookup   Cases   User   Reports
Dashboard   Dashboard   Tables   Administration

Contact Log

Name	Fine, Miriam
Case Number	594
Activity Date	8/10/2013
Activity Type	Placement Visit
Subject	Child welfare
Location	Gillis School
Contact Type	Face-to-face
Hours	0.75

Notes:

I visited Tyrone at Gillis this afternoon. He continues to put on weight and look better since his time on the street. He told me he had seen the Gillis psychiatrist again and was back on his meds. I can tell he is relieved -- he seems to want some external watch/control to help him keep it together.

I don't have the medical background to know if the problem is underlying mental illness or the abrupt cut-off of the Abilify when he left Gilllis a year ago or the subsequent trauma of the failed reunification with his mother and his time on the run, but Tyrone clearly needs ongoing monitoring and treatment now. I'm just relieved he is complying with his medication regimen without complaint.

We talked about the Gillis plan for the tutor to start working with him next week, when the new school year begins. I cautioned Tyrone not to be frustrated if he had forgotten some things -- I reminded him that he is smart and good at school and should be able to regain the lost ground if he works at it.

We spent most of the visit starting on the new LEGO set that I brought over from CASA. I'm not very good at LEGOs, which amuses Tyrone to no end. I think he likes to be the expert at something, and he seems to enjoy showing me up.

Mabel had brought the girls to visit, and he wanted to tell me about that. He seemed very relieved that Jerome was back in custody. "He is a bad, bad man -- and he's very bad for the girls. I worry that he'll hurt them, and Grandma and Grandpa are too old to stop him." He did not ask about Joelle.

Overall, I think Tyrone is in a safe, appropriate place -- where he can concentrate on regaining his own mental health and balance, without worrying about the safety of Alysha, Hope, or Joelle. What he needs most right now is consistency and the reassurance that the adults will manage things. That is very hard for him to grasp or believe, but I hope over time he will come to trust that he is still too young to care for himself -- and he shouldn't be expected to care for others.

Activity Status   Approved

From: Merlie.Verlet@dss.mo.gov
Sent: Thursday, August 15, 2013 8:04 AM
To: Anorris@courts.mo.gov
Cc: ablackstone@jacksoncountycasa-mo.org; hmiller@jacksoncountycasa-mo.org;   miriamk
        fine@gmail.com; Duncan.Walsh@dss.mo.gov;   martin.jaylon@hollandgrain.
    com; JeremyVerona@aol.com
Subject: *Confidential: Merritt—Washington—Jerome Washington pleads guilty

I am writing to inform the Family Court that Children's Division has been notified by the Jackson County Prosecutor that Jerome Washington has agreed to plead guilty to Assault in the Second Degree.

The Prosecutor has confirmed this is a Class C felony, punishable by up to seven years in prison, a fine of up to $5,000, or both (Mo. Ann. Stat. § § 565.060, 558.011, 560.011). Mr. Washington is presently incarcerated in the Jackson County Detention Center pending sentencing. CD is recommending no further contact between the juveniles Alysha Washington and Hope Washington and their father, Mr. Washington.

Mr. Washington's attorney has indicated that he is willing to consider signing away parental rights to release the girls for adoption. I will keep you informed as we learn more about this possible offer.

The mission of the Children's Division is to partner with families, communities and government to protect children from abuse and neglect and to assure safety, permanency and well being for Missouri's children.

Welcome **miriam.fine**

Change Password   Log Off

Staff Dashboard   Volunteers Dashboard   Volunteers   Lookup Tables   Cases   User Administration   Reports

Contact Log

Name	Fine, Miriam
Case Number	594
Activity Date	8/16/2013
Activity Type	Placement Visit
Subject	Child welfare
Location	Grandparents' Home
Contact Type	Face-to-face
Hours	1.00

Notes:

The girls are eager for school to start next week. They both showed me their new CASA back packs and their school supplies. Alysha is very proud that she now owns a calculator.

Alone, I explained to each of the girls that Jerome was going back to jail. They both expressed great relief. Alysha asked if they could finally stay with their grandparents for good. I told her I thought it might be possible. They are both desperate for resolution, certainty, and permanence.

Mabel seemed very relieved that Jerome was again out of the picture. She said her conversations with Joelle on the phone had been going well -- she thinks it might be time for her to start seeing the girls again. She talked about visiting Tyrone at Gillis: "That boy's in the best place he can be right now."

Activity Status   Approved

MISSOURI DEPARTMENT OF SOCIAL SERVICES
CHILDREN'S DIVISION
GENERAL CONSENT TO TERMINATION OF PARENTAL RIGHTS AND ADOPTION
(FOR USE IN CASES FILED PURSUANT TO SECTIONS 211.444 AND 453.030, RSMO)

IN THE ___40 TH___ DIVISION
OF THE CIRCUIT COURT OF THE CITY/COUNTY OF ___JACKSON___
STATE OF MISSOURI

In re the Matter of ___ALYSHA WASHINGTON___) 1416-JU0040988
___HOPE WASHINGTON___) Case No ___1416-JU0040989___
("CHILD")

GENERAL CONSENT TO TERMINATION OF PARENTAL RIGHTS AND ADOPTION

My name is ___JEROME MARCUS WASHINGTON___
(FULL LEGAL NAME)

I reside at ___19034 MAPLE AVE. KC MO 64128___
(NOW DETENTION CENTER) (ADDRESS)

I am a (☒ male ☐ female) person and my date of birth is ___10/24/87___. I acknowledge the following statements
are completed by me and each statement is true, complete, and correct to the best of my knowledge: 4/7/2003

1. ☒ The Child, ___ALYSHA / HOPE WASHINGTON___ was born on ___11/17/2004___
(FULL LEGAL NAME)

in ___KANSAS CITY JACKSON COUNTY MISSOURI___
(CITY/COUNTY/STATE)

2. My relationship to the Child is:

   ☒ (A) I am the (☐ mother ☒ father) of the Child. I OR

   ☐ (B) I have been named as a possible birth father for the Child. I deny I am the birth father of the Child; however, in order to
   facilitate the location of a stable and secure home for the Child, I am willing to execute this Consent and do so with the full
   understanding that its terms will apply to me if it turns out I am in fact the birth father of the Child. **I understand if I deny
   paternity, but consent to adoption, I waive any future interest in the child.**

3. ☒ Because I believe it is in the best interest of the Child and his or her future welfare, I **voluntarily and of my own free will forever
   consent to the termination of parental rights and obligations and consent to the lawful adoption of the child.**

**I UNDERSTAND AND INTEND THAT THIS CONSENT TO TERMINATION OF MY PARENTAL RIGHTS AND CONSENT TO ADOP-
TION IS FINAL AND IRREVOCABLE ONCE IT IS EXECUTED BY ME UNLESS, PRIOR TO A FINAL DECREE OF ADOPTION, I
ALLEGE AND PROVE BY CLEAR AND CONVINCING EVIDENCE THIS CONSENT WAS NOT FREELY AND VOLUNTARILY GIVEN.**

4. ☒ I understand as the parent of the Child, I may have the primary right to custody of the Child if I so choose, even if I am a minor,
   and by signing this Consent I am giving up any such right along with all my other parental rights and obligations.

5. I have completed ___12___ years of education.

6. ☒ I read and understand the English language; or

   ☐ I understand English and this Consent form was read to me by:

   _____   _____ ; or
   (FULL LEGAL NAME)   (TITLE)

   ☐ this Consent form was read to me in my native language of _____
   by _____
   (NAME OF INTERPRETER)

1

7. Check and complete all that apply:

☐ At the time of the Child's birth, I was married to _____.
   (FULL LEGAL NAME)

☐ I was married to _____ within the last 300 days prior to the child's birth.
   (FULL LEGAL NAME)

☒ I am not married.

☐ My marriage to _____ was legally dissolved on _____.
   (FULL LEGAL NAME)   (DATE)

8. Indian Child Welfare Act:

☒ As far as I know, neither I, nor any member of my family, including the Child, is a member of or eligible for membership in a federally recognized American Indian Tribe or Alaskan Native Village.

OR

☐ Either I, or a member of my family, including the Child, is a member of or eligible for membership in a federally recognized American Indian Tribe or Alaskan Native Village.

9. I understand I have the right to be represented by my own attorney. I understand the court may appoint an attorney to represent me if I request counsel, and if hiring my own attorney would cause a financial hardship. I also understand I may review this document and seek the advice of an attorney before signing this Consent.

☒ I have talked to and am represented by _JEREMY   VERONA_____ regarding this Consent.
                                         (NAME OF ATTORNEY)

OR

☐ I HEREBY WAIVE MY RIGHT TO AN ATTORNEY.

10. ☐ The Child is currently under the jurisdiction of the juvenile court/family court in _JACKSON_____ County,
    _MISSOURI_____, in case number _1416-JU0040988 /89_
    (STATE)

11. By completing and signing this Consent, I certify to the Court that I am of sound mind and:

☒ i. Hereby submit to the jurisdiction of the Court of the State of Missouri.

☒ ii. Understand this Consent will be filed with the juvenile court/family court in _JACKSON_____ County, Missouri and any other court in which proceedings concerning the Child may be pending.

☒ iii. Have had enough time to carefully consider whether or not consent to termination of parental rights and adoption is in my own best interest and the best interest of the Child.

☒ iv. Have given careful thought to my decision to proceed with this Consent.

☒ v. Am not under the influence of any drug, medication, or other substance which might affect my reasoning or judgment.

☒ vi. Have signed this Consent to termination of parental rights and adoption of my own free will and without any duress or undue influence from anyone.

☒ vii. Have not been given any money or gifts, and no one has promised to provide me any money or gifts in exchange for my consent other than payment of expenses allowed by law.

12. I choose to:

☒ waive service of summons and a copy of any petition seeking the termination of my parental rights and/or adoption of the child that may be filed in any court of competent jurisdiction. I hereby waive my right to appear in any such proceedings and consent to a hearing thereof, at any time, without further notice to me;

OR

☐ reserve the right to receive service of summons and a copy of any petition seeking the termination of my parental rights and/or adoption of the child as may hereafter be filed in any court of competent jurisdiction.

13. ☒ I understand the importance of identifying all possible fathers of the child and may provide the names of all such persons:

_____I AM   THEIR   FATHER._____

2

14. ☐ I am the birth mother, and I have not misrepresented to any man who could be the father of this child that:

_____ i. I was not pregnant;

_____ ii. the pregnancy was terminated;

_____ iii. the child has died; or

_____ iv. the child is not his.

I CERTIFY BY MY SIGNATURE BELOW THAT I HAVE READ, CONSIDERED, AND UNDERSTAND ALL THE ABOVE STATEMENTS.

I, _____ JEROME   MARCUS   WASHINGTON , hereby acknowledge that the statements provided above.
(FULL LEGAL NAME)

are true, complete and correct.

SIGNATURE OF PARENT	DATE	TIME
J Washington	8/30/13	1:50 pm
SIGNATURE OF PARENT'S ATTORNEY OR INTERMEDIARY	DATE	TIME
J Verom	8/30/13	2:00 P.M.
SIGNATURE OF PARENT'S GUARDIAN AD LITEM (IF REQUIRED BY § 453.030.9 RSMO OR OTHER APPLICABLE LAW)	DATE	TIME

ACKNOWLEDGMENT OR WITNESSES TO PARENT'S CONSENT
THIS CONSENT MUST BE:
A) EXECUTED IN FRONT OF A JUDGE, OR B) ACKNOWLEDGED BEFORE A NOTARY PUBLIC OR TWO ADULT WITNESSES

JUDGE

On this _____ day of _____, in the year _____, before me personally
                              (MONTH)

appeared _____ known to me to be the person who executed this
                    (FULL LEGAL NAME OF PARENT)

Consent to Termination of Parental Rights and Adoption and acknowledged to me that she/he executed the same for the purposes herein stated, and I have advised the consenting parent of the consequences of the consent.

_____
                                                                Judge

NOTARY

STATE OF MISSOURI   )

)

COUNTY OF _____)

On this _____ day of _____, in the year _____, before me personally
                              (MONTH)

appeared _____ known to me to be the person who executed this
                    (FULL LEGAL NAME OF PARENT)

Consent to Termination of Parental Rights and Adoption and acknowledged to me that she/he executed the same for the purposes herein stated.

_____
                                                         Notary Public

My Commission Expires: _____

3

WITNESSES

THE UNDERSIGNED WITNESSES CERTIFY BY THEIR SIGNATURES THAT _Jerome Marcus Washington_

(FULL LEGAL NAME OF PARENT)

SIGNED THE CONSENT AND THE CONSENT WAS KNOWINGLY AND FREELY GIVEN. WE FURTHER CERTIFY WE ARE NOT THE PROSPECTIVE ADOPTIVE PARENTS OF THE ABOVE NAMED CHILD.

PRINTED NAME AND DATE OF BIRTH OF WITNESS ONE	DATE	TIME
John Watkins	8/30/13	2:10 pm
SIGNATURE OF WITNESS ONE	FULL ADDRESS OF WITNESS ONE	
John Watkins	8409 Fifth St. KC MO 64108	
PRINTED NAME AND DATE OF BIRTH OF WITNESS TWO	DATE	TIME
Colleen R. Harris	8/30/13	2:15 pm
SIGNATURE OF WITNESS TWO	FULL ADDRESS OF WITNESS TWO	
Colleen Harris	125 Angel Drive Lee's Summit MO 64014	

4

From: Miriam Fine [mailto:miriamkfine@gmail.com]
Sent: Wednesday, September 4, 2013 9:55 PM
To: hgoldstein@laramyjones.com
Subject: Happy ending . . . ? Part One

Ah, Hazel, it's been such a day. I'm happy, sad, happy, sad. You know. Both, neither, nothing, everything.

We had our long-awaited Mediation with the mom on my CASA case this morning. We've been meeting as a team for over two years now—but this was different. Everyone in the room knew where it was going. And everyone was equal parts relieved, anxious, sad, guilty, happy. So hard.

Dad signed away his parental rights last week. He never wanted these kids anyway. He was just being macho and asserting "his rights." And the grandparents have been fighting for years to adopt these kids. So, really, there was nothing else standing in the way of a safe, permanent home for these kids except today's proceedings.

First, my kudos to your profession. The lawyer assigned to the mediation was top notch. Sandra Gallois – have you met her? Trim, put together red-head, about our age, maybe a bit younger. One of those professional gals who exudes calm confidence and a sense of fair play. *I don't have a dog in this fight— just here to help*—you know the type.

I liked her immediately, and I think everyone else did too. She was pretty straightforward from the start: "Our goal today is to find an agreement that works for everyone in this room. This is not about winning and losing. It's about a group of adults doing their very best to agree to a situation that will be best for the children they all care very much about." She had us all nodding, and then we were off.

I didn't realize mediation looks more like therapy than a legal proceeding. Everyone taking their turn, the mediator working to be sure everyone else hears and affirms them—not their *position*, but their *feelings*. There were a lot of feelings in the room today.

In the end it was astoundingly sweet. I think this mom has known for a while now that she can't take care of her kids—she's just too broken herself. If she hadn't had her first kids at 16 . . . if she hadn't dropped out of high school . . . if she hadn't left home . . . if she hadn't partnered up with an abusive man . . . if she hadn't struggled with mental illness and alcohol abuse . . . if, if, if, if . . .

But, oh my God, she loves them. And what does it mean for a woman who loves her children to say she is giving them up? The incredible genius of the mediation process—at least as I saw it play out today— is the subtle guidance of a professional who affirms mom's need to believe that the most loving thing she can do is cut them loose.

There was a lot of love to go around today. The grandparents promised that mom can stay in their lives—in her children's lives—come to school events, birthday parties, holidays. I think they have missed her, love her, don't want to be on opposite sides anymore with the kids in the middle. Both girls cried, told their mom they loved her, would always love her, just wanted to live with Grandma and Grandpa so "everyone can be okay" (that's the younger one).

The mom wanted her say. That she had tried her best. Loved her kids. Thought she could do it. Was sorry, sorry, sorry, sorry. Knew this was best. Loved her kids. Then she signed the documents consenting to terminate her parental rights.

I swear Hazel, it was like watching a death and the hope of rebirth all at the same time. I realized I was holding my breath until the last signature went on the forms.

No one cheered or clapped—just sighed—and cried some more. But it's done. Adoption is only a formality now. There's still the older boy to worry about. But for these two . . . maybe, maybe, maybe, maybe . . . a chance . . . a happy ending . . .

Exhausted, happy, sad, love you,

Miri

_____

Miriam Fine
(913) 555-8436

"If I can't dance, I don't want to be part of your revolution." -- Emma Goldman

MISSOURI DEPARTMENT OF SOCIAL SERVICES
CHILDREN'S DIVISION
GENERAL CONSENT TO TERMINATION OF PARENTAL RIGHTS AND ADOPTION
(FOR USE IN CASES FILED PURSUANT TO SECTIONS 211.444 AND 453.030, RSMO)

IN THE ___40th___ DIVISION
OF THE CIRCUIT COURT OF THE CITY/COUNTY OF ___Jackson___
STATE OF MISSOURI

In re the Matter of _Alysha Washington_) ___1416-JU0040988___
Hope Washington) Case No ___1416-JU0040989___
("CHILD")

GENERAL CONSENT TO TERMINATION OF PARENTAL RIGHTS AND ADOPTION

My name is ___Joelle Jean Merritt___
(FULL LEGAL NAME)

I reside at ___4670 Olive St. KC MO 64127___
(ADDRESS)

I am a (☐ male ☒ female) person and my date of birth is ___6/9/82___ . I acknowledge the following statements are completed by me and each statement is true, complete, and correct to the best of my knowledge:

1. ☒ The Child, _Alysha Washington_ was born on __4/7/03__
   (FULL LEGAL NAME)
   in _Hope Washington_ __11/17/04__
   (CITY/COUNTY/STATE)

2. My relationship to the Child is: _Kansas City / Jackson County_
   Missouri

   ☒ (A) I am the (☒ mother ☐ father) of the Child. I OR

   ☐ (B) I have been named as a possible birth father for the Child. I deny I am the birth father of the Child; however, in order to facilitate the location of a stable and secure home for the Child, I am willing to execute this Consent and do so with the full understanding that its terms will apply to me if it turns out I am in fact the birth father of the Child. **I understand if I deny paternity, but consent to adoption, I waive any future interest in the child.**

3. ☒ Because I believe it is in the best interest of the Child and his or her future welfare, **I voluntarily and of my own free will forever consent to the termination of parental rights and obligations and consent to the lawful adoption of the child.**

I UNDERSTAND AND INTEND THAT THIS CONSENT TO TERMINATION OF MY PARENTAL RIGHTS AND CONSENT TO ADOPTION IS FINAL AND IRREVOCABLE ONCE IT IS EXECUTED BY ME UNLESS, PRIOR TO A FINAL DECREE OF ADOPTION, I ALLEGE AND PROVE BY CLEAR AND CONVINCING EVIDENCE THIS CONSENT WAS NOT FREELY AND VOLUNTARILY GIVEN.

---

4. ☒ I understand as the parent of the Child, I may have the primary right to custody of the Child if I so choose, even if I am a minor, and by signing this Consent I am giving up any such right along with all my other parental rights and obligations.

5. I have completed __11__ years of education.

6. ☒ I read and understand the English language; or

   ☐ I understand English and this Consent form was read to me by:

   _____ _____ ; or
   (FULL LEGAL NAME)   (TITLE)

   ☐ this Consent form was read to me in my native language of _____

   by _____
   (NAME OF INTERPRETER)

1

7. Check and complete all that apply:

☐ At the time of the Child's birth, I was married to _____.
(FULL LEGAL NAME)

☐ I was married to _____ within the last 300 days prior to the child's birth.
(FULL LEGAL NAME)

☒ I am not married.

☐ My marriage to _____ was legally dissolved on _____.
(FULL LEGAL NAME)   (DATE)

8. Indian Child Welfare Act:

☒ As far as I know, neither I, nor any member of my family, including the Child, is a member of or eligible for membership in a federally recognized American Indian Tribe or Alaskan Native Village.

OR

☐ Either I, or a member of my family, including the Child, is a member of or eligible for membership in a federally recognized American Indian Tribe or Alaskan Native Village.

9. I understand I have the right to be represented by my own attorney. I understand the court may appoint an attorney to represent me if I request counsel, and if hiring my own attorney would cause a financial hardship. I also understand I may review this document and seek the advice of an attorney before signing this Consent.

☒ I have talked to and am represented by _____Martin Jaylon_____ regarding this Consent.
(NAME OF ATTORNEY)

OR

☐ I HEREBY WAIVE MY RIGHT TO AN ATTORNEY.

10. ☒ The Child is currently under the jurisdiction of the juvenile court/family court in ___Jackson___ County,
___Missouri___, in case number 1416-JU0040988
(STATE)   1416-JU0040989

11. By completing and signing this Consent, I certify to the Court that I am of sound mind and:

☒ i. Hereby submit to the jurisdiction of the Court of the State of Missouri.

☒ ii. Understand this Consent will be filed with the juvenile court/family court in ___Jackson___ County, Missouri and any other court in which proceedings concerning the Child may be pending.

☒ iii. Have had enough time to carefully consider whether or not consent to termination of parental rights and adoption is in my own best interest and the best interest of the Child.

☒ iv. Have given careful thought to my decision to proceed with this Consent.

☒ v. Am not under the influence of any drug, medication, or other substance which might affect my reasoning or judgment.

☒ vi. Have signed this Consent to termination of parental rights and adoption of my own free will and without any duress or undue influence from anyone.

☒ vii. Have not been given any money or gifts, and no one has promised to provide me any money or gifts in exchange for my consent other than payment of expenses allowed by law.

12. I choose to:

☒ waive service of summons and a copy of any petition seeking the termination of my parental rights and/or adoption of the child that may be filed in any court of competent jurisdiction. I hereby waive my right to appear in any such proceedings and consent to a hearing thereof, at any time, without further notice to me;

OR

☐ reserve the right to receive service of summons and a copy of any petition seeking the termination of my parental rights and/or adoption of the child as may hereafter be filed in any court of competent jurisdiction.

13. ☒ I understand the importance of identifying all possible fathers of the child and may provide the names of all such persons:

_____.

2

14. ☒ I am the birth mother, and I have not misrepresented to any man who could be the father of this child that:

_____ i. I was not pregnant;

_____ ii. the pregnancy was terminated;

_____ iii. the child has died; or

_____ iv. the child is not his.

I CERTIFY BY MY SIGNATURE BELOW THAT I HAVE READ, CONSIDERED, AND UNDERSTAND ALL THE ABOVE STATEMENTS.

I, ___Joelle Jean Merritt_____ , hereby acknowledge that the statements provided above.
(FULL LEGAL NAME)

are true, complete and correct.

SIGNATURE OF PARENT	DATE	TIME
Joelle Merritt	9/4/13	4:45 PM
SIGNATURE OF PARENT'S ATTORNEY OR INTERMEDIARY	DATE	TIME
Mark Taylor	9-19-13	4:48 p.m.
SIGNATURE OF PARENT'S GUARDIAN AD LITEM (IF REQUIRED BY § 453.030.9 RSMO OR OTHER APPLICABLE LAW)	DATE	TIME

ACKNOWLEDGMENT OR WITNESSES TO PARENT'S CONSENT
THIS CONSENT MUST BE:
A) EXECUTED IN FRONT OF A JUDGE, OR B) ACKNOWLEDGED BEFORE A NOTARY PUBLIC OR TWO ADULT WITNESSES

JUDGE

On this ___4th___ day of ___September___ , in the year ___2013___ , before me personally
(MONTH)

appeared ___Joelle Jean Merritt___ known to me to be the person who executed this
(FULL LEGAL NAME OF PARENT)

Consent to Termination of Parental Rights and Adoption and acknowledged to me that she/he executed the same for the purposes herein stated, and I have advised the consenting parent of the consequences of the consent.

Hon. Suzanne M. Martell
Judge

NOTARY

STATE OF MISSOURI   )

)

COUNTY OF _____)

On this _____ day of _____ , in the year _____ , before me personally
(MONTH)

appeared _____ known to me to be the person who executed this
(FULL LEGAL NAME OF PARENT)

Consent to Termination of Parental Rights and Adoption and acknowledged to me that she/he executed the same for the purposes herein stated.

_____
Notary Public

My Commission Expires: _____

3

CHECKLIST FOR FILING PETITION FOR ADOPTION

Name of Petitioner(s) _Mabel and Roger Merritt_

Attorney's Name and Bar Number _Ray Johnson 497136_

☒ Adoption in which jurisdiction is pursuant to 211 RSMo

☐ Adoption in which jurisdiction is **not** pursuant to 211 RSMo

☒ Has a Petition for Consent to Adoption/Consent to Termination of Parental Rights been filed?

PETITION FOR ADOPTION WILL NOT BE FILED UNLESS THERE IS A RECEIPT FOR THE FULL FILING FEE OR A MOTION TO PROCEED IN FORMA PAUPERIS/AS A POOR PERSON.

Filing Fee:

☒ $325 Regular (JD) including Recognition of Foreign Adoption

☐ $280 Step-Child (JF)

☐ $215 Adult (JG)

☒ ____ $30 for each additional child _1_ number of additional children

☐ -$30 no amended birth certificate requested

Total _$355_

Documents required to file:

☒ Petition for Adoption

☒ Family Court Information Sheet - Form 17

☒ Certificate of Decree of Adoption for each juvenile

☒ An accounting of any money or anything of value paid, transferred or promised by or on behalf of the Petitioner in connection with the placement or adoption

☒ See Administrative Order Procedures in Adoption Actions

Approved _M. F. Ashby_ _9/6/2013_
Clerk   Date

Welcome **miriam.fine**

Change Password   Log Off

Staff   **Volunteers**   **Volunteers**   **Lookup**   **Cases**   **User**   **Reports**
Dashboard   **Dashboard**   **Tables**   **Administration**

Contact Log

Name	Fine, Miriam
Case Number	594
Activity Date	9/10/2013
Activity Type	Placement Visit
Subject	Child welfare
Location	Gillis School
Contact Type	Face-to-face
Hours	0.75

Notes:

Tyrone seems to be doing quite well at Gillis this time around. He has started classes and he tells me they are going well. I plan to meet with his home room teacher next week to hear more.

I told him that both Jerome and Joelle had consented to give up their parental rights for Alysha and Hope and they would be adopted soon by their grandparents. He said he wasn't surprised, but he did seem genuinely glad to hear the news, as if he could set this burden down after a long time. "They are good girls; they deserve to be really happy."

We talked some more about his decision not to have Mabel and Roger seek to adopt him. I explained we would not ask Joelle to terminate her rights in his case if we are moving in that direction, as there is no need. We just have to wait. I wanted to be sure he understood that means he is deciding to age out of the system and emancipate sometime between 18 and 21. He is very clear on that -- and very clear that is his preference. He continues to say he is too old to be adopted, too old to be someone's child, and just wants to grow up and take care of himself.

He has asked for reassurance several times that he can still see Alysha and Hope, and I have continued to tell him that there is no obstacle, as long as Mabel and Roger agree. They will be the girls' parents going forward. He nods at that.

Activity Status   Approved

Contact Log

Name	Fine, Miriam
Case Number	594
Activity Date	9/29/2013
Activity Type	Placement Visit
Subject	Child welfare
Location	Grandparents' Home
Contact Type	Face-to-face
Hours	1.00

Notes:

I stopped by the Merritts' this afternoon for a final visit with the girls. Everyone was home from church, and the girls were eager to show me the matching outfits Mabel had gotten them for Tuesday's Adoption Hearing -- purple dresses, Alysha's a little more grown up and Hope's a little more "princess" style; black shiny shoes; and white tights. Alysha had a small purple purse, too.

Mabel told me she got a purple blouse for herself and she was even making Roger wear a purple tie. He chimed in: "Anything for this happy day."

We went over the formalities -- the questions the lawyers would ask, and the answers Mabel and Roger were prepared to give. I reminded the girls that the judge might ask them questions, too, but it was all okay -- just tell the truth. I also confirmed the decision to change the girls' last names to Merritt -- which would be entered on the order after the adoption.

I reminded the girls that after the adoption they wouldn't need a CASA Volunteer anymore. So I would just be their friend from now on. Alysha asked: "You're still helping Tyrone, though, right?" I told her, yes, I would be Tyrone's CASA Volunteer as long as he needed one. She seemed satisfied with that.

I told Alysha and Hope Washington I would see them at the Courthouse on October 1 for their Adoption Day. And then I left.

Activity Status   Approved

IN THE CIRCUIT COURT OF JACKSON COUNTY, MISSOURI
FAMILY COURT DIVISION

IN THE INTEREST OF:	**CASE NUMBER:** 1416-JU0040988
ALYSHA WASHINGTON	
	LIFE NUMBER:
SEX: F **BORN**: 07-APRIL-2003	1416-JR57791

IN THE INTEREST OF:	**CASE NUMBER:** 1416-JU0040989
HOPE WASHINGTON	
	LIFE NUMBER:
SEX: F **BORN**: 17-NOV-2004	1416-JR57792

FINDINGS AND RECOMMENDATIONS

Now on October 1, 2013 there being present:

MARLIE VERLET	-	Children's Division
JOELLE MERRITT	-	Mother
ABIGAIL NORRIS	-	Attorney for the Juvenile Officer
HENRIETTA MILLER	-	Guardian ad Litem (CASA)
MIRIAM FINE	-	CASA Volunteer
MARTIN JAYLON	-	Attorney for Mother
ALYSHA WASHINGTON	-	Juvenile
HOPE WASHINGTON	-	Juvenile

The cause comes on for Permanency Hearing.

IT IS HEREBY ORDERED: that the parental rights of Jerome Washington be terminated for the juveniles Alysha Washington and Hope Washington.

IT IS FURTHER ORDERED: that the parental rights of Joelle Merritt be terminated for the juveniles Alysha Washington and Hope Washington.

IT IS FURTHER ORDERED: that Mabel Merritt and Roger Merritt, the juveniles' maternal grandparents, are now the adoptive parents of Alysha Washington and Hope Washington. The adopting parents and the children are now parent and child under the law, with all the rights and duties of the parent-child relationship.

IT IS FURTHER ORDERED: that ALYSHA MARIE WASHINGTON and HOPE SWEET WASHINGTON will now legally be named ALYSHA MARIE MERRITT and HOPE SWEET MERRITT.

IT IS FURTHER ORDERED: that all prior Orders are terminated and the juveniles are released and discharged from the jurisdiction of the Court.

Notice of Findings and Recommendation & Notice of Right to a Rehearing

The parties are notified that the forgoing Findings and Recommendations have been entered this date by a commissioner, and all papers relative to the care or proceeding, together with the Findings and Recommendation have been transferred to a Judge of the Court. The Findings and Recommendations shall become the Judgment of the Court upon adoption by order of the Judge. Unless waived by the parties in writing, at party in the case or proceeding heard by a commissioner, within fifteen days after the mailing of notice of the filing of the Judgment of the Court, may file a motion for rehearing by a Judge of the Court. If the motion for rehearing is not ruled on within forty-five days after the motion is filed, the motion is overruled for all purposes. Rule 130.13

October 3, 2013   *Gerard E. Solomon*
_____
Date   GERARD E. SOLOMON, Commissioner

Order and Judgment Adopting Commissioner's Findings and Recommendation

It is hereby ordered, adjudged and decreed the foregoing Findings and Recommendations entered by the commissioner are adopted and confirmed as a final Judgment of the Court.

October 3, 2013   *Suzanne M. Martell*
_____
Date   Judge

NOTICE OF ENTRY OF JUDGMENT

You are hereby notified that on   OCT 3 2013,   the Family Court, Juvenile Division, of Jackson County, Missouri made and entered the above judgment in this case:

You are further notified that you may have a right of appeal from this judgment under Rule 120.01 and section 211.261, RSMo, which provides that:

1. An appeal shall be allowed to the juvenile from any final judgment made under the Juvenile Code and may be taken on the part of the juvenile by the custodian.

2. An appeal shall be allowed to custodian from any final judgment made under the Juvenile Code that adversely affects the custodian.

3. Notice of appeal shall be filed in accordance with Missouri law.

4. Neither the filing of a notice of appeal nor the filing of any motion subsequne to the judgment shall act to stay the execution of a judgment unless the court enters an order staying execution.

Corrine Adamson
Deputy Court Administrator

Certificate of Service

This is to certify that a copy of the foregoing was hand delivered/faxed/emailed/mailed and/or sent through the eFiling system to the following on OCT 3 2013.

M R Jones

Copies to:

ABIGAIL NORRIS
Attorney for the Juvenile Officer

MARTIN JAYLON
Attorney for the Natural Mother

MARLIE VERLET
CHILDREN'S DIVISION

HENRIETTA MILLER
JACKSON COUNTY CASA

JEROME WASHINGTON
Natural Father

JEREMY VERONA
Attorney for the Natural Father

JOELLE MERRITT
Natural Mother

Care & Custody
Epilogue

IN THE CIRCUIT COURT OF JACKSON COUNTY, MISSOURI
FAMILY COURT DIVISION

IN THE INTEREST OF:

TYRONE MERRITT

SEX: M **BORN:** 19-FEB-1998

CASE NUMBER: 1416-JU0040987

LIFE NUMBER:

1416-JR57790

FINDINGS AND RECOMMENDATIONS

Now on February 19, 2016 there being present:

DUNCAN WALSH	-	Children's Division
ABIGAIL NORRIS	-	Attorney for the Juvenile Officer
HENRIETTA MILLER	-	Guardian ad Litem (CASA)
MIRIAM FINE	-	CASA Volunteer
TYRONE WASHINGTON	-	Juvenile

The cause comes on for Permanency Hearing.

IT IS HEREBY ORDERED: that all prior Orders are terminated and the juvenile is released and discharged from the jurisdiction of the Court.

February 23, 2016

Gerard E. Solomon

Date

GERARD E. SOLOMON, Commissioner

Order and Judgment Adopting Commissioner's Findings and Recommendation

It is hereby ordered, adjudged and decreed the foregoing Findings and Recommendations entered by the commissioner are adopted and confirmed as a final Judgment of the Court.

February 23, 2016

Suzanne M. Martell

Date

Judge

NOTICE OF ENTRY OF JUDGMENT

You are hereby notified that on   FEB 23, 2016,   the Family Court, Juvenile Division, of Jackson County, Missouri made and entered the above judgment in this case:

You are further notified that you may have a right of appeal from this judgment under Rule 120.01 and section 211.261, RSMo, which provides that:

1. An appeal shall be allowed to the juveniles from any final judgment made under the Juvenile Code and may be taken on the part of the juveniles by the custodian.

2. An appeal shall be allowed to custodian from any final judgment made under the Juvenile Code that adversely affects the custodian.

3. Notice of appeal shall be filed in accordance with Missouri law.

4. Neither the filing of a notice of appeal nor the filing of any motion subsequent to the judgment shall act to stay the execution of a judgment unless the court enters an order staying execution.

Corrine Adamson
Deputy Court Administrator

Certificate of Service

This is to certify that a copy of the foregoing was hand delivered/faxed/emailed/mailed and/or sent through the eFiling system to the following on FEB 23 2016,

M R Jones

Copies to:

ABIGAIL NORRIS
Attorney for the Juvenile Officer

MARLIE VERLET
CHILDREN'S DIVISION

HENRIETTA MILLER
JACKSON COUNTY CASA

MARLIN THOMPSON
Putative Father

From: Miriam Fine [mailto:miriamkfine@gmail.com]
Sent: Friday, February 19, 2016 7:03 PM
To: hgoldstein@laramyjones.com
Subject: The End

And . . . just like that . . . it's over. After 4-1/2 years in the system, my CASA kid is "released from juris-diction" and out in the world as an adult. It's what he wants. And it's what he's legally entitled to. But, oh my God, Haze. An 18 year old boy—with no housing, no job, no high school diploma (yet), and no functional parents. How could that be right?

Did you know that 9% of the kids who were released from the system last year were "emancipated"? They call it "aging out." That's code for "we never found you a safe, permanent home." In other words, we failed. Our system fails more than 21,000 kids each year—and mine is one of them.

My kid's luckier than most. He hasn't dropped out of school yet. So maybe, maybe, maybe he'll get his high school diploma. That would be a good thing. And his grandparents haven't written him off. If he wants to reach out to them, they'll give him a meal.

And there's one new benefit for all of these former foster kids. Under the Affordable Care Act, they can stay on Medicaid until they turn 26—just like our kids could stay on our insurance. If my kid's smart enough to sign up and stay signed up, he can get health care. I lectured him a lot about that. Also about condoms. Mostly about condoms.

We know a third of the kids in the system will end up abusing their own children—maybe, maybe, may-be my teen can avoid that sordid statistic. God knows he didn't avoid many others. We took him away from his mother "for his own good." But all we've done since then—best of intentions, of course—is move him around (7 different times); separate him from his sisters; medicate him, un-medicate him (with no withdrawal plan), medicate him again; and generally show him that adults don't have a clue how to get this right. No wonder he wants to be on his own.

It terrifies me, Haze, it really does. I think how often Arielle and Isaac call us for something: There are flies and a bad smell coming from the apartment attic—who do we call? My boss is being a jerk at work—what should I do? A guy dinged my car coming out of the parking lot—what do I do now?

And, to be honest, I still reach for the phone to call Mom at least once a week. She's been dead 2-1/2 years, and I still need her advice.

I've asked my CASA kid a million times where he plans to live, and he remains vague. I think maybe he'll crash at his mom's. My Case Supervisor says a lot of kids who age out do that. Maybe there's a girlfriend. Maybe there's a well-meaning preacher. Maybe there's a pimp. I've made sure he has my cell number in his phone—and made sure he's still got it memorized. I've told him over and over that I'm always in his corner; even though our Court-ordered partnership is ending, he can always count on me.

Do you think he believes it? Would you?

Miri

Miriam Fine
(913) 555-8436

"If I can't dance, I don't want to be part of your revolution." -- Emma Goldman

MARTHA GERSHUN recently retired from Jackson County CASA, where she served as Executive Director for seven years. During her tenure Jackson County CASA grew to become one of the largest CASA agencies in the country, advocating for more than 1,250 children each year. She also served as a board member of the Missouri CASA Association and the National CASA Association in Seattle, Washington.

Gershun earned an A.B. *cum laude* from Harvard University and an M.B.A. from the Harvard Business School. She also holds a graduate diploma in Economics from the University of Stirling, Scotland, where she was a Rotary International Fellow. She lives in Fairway, KS, with her husband Don Goldman.

Her writing has appeared in *The New York Times*, *The New Yorker*, *Kveller*, *The Kansas City Star*, and *The Kansas City Jewish Chronicle*.

Made in the USA
San Bernardino, CA
21 August 2018